# Payback

By the same author

*Billie Jo*
*Born Evil*
*The Betrayer*
*The Feud*
*The Traitor*
*The Victim*
*The Schemer*
*The Trap*

# Payback

Kimberley CHAMBERS

HarperCollins*Publishers*

HarperCollins*Publishers*
77–85 Fulham Palace Road,
Hammersmith, London W6 8JB

www.harpercollins.co.uk

Published by HarperCollins*Publishers* 2013

1



A catalogue record for this book
is available from the British Library



ISBN: 978-0-00-750315-5

Set in Sabon LT Std by Palimpsest Book Production Limited,
Falkirk, Stirlingshire

Printed and bound in Great Britain by
Clays Ltd, St Ives plc

FSC™ is a non-profit international organisation established to promote
the responsible management of the world's forests. Products carrying the
FSC label are independently certified to assure consumers that they come
from forests that are managed to meet the social, economic and
ecological needs of present and future generations,
and other controlled sources.

Find out more about HarperCollins and the environment at
**www.harpercollins.co.uk/green**

In memory of a true gentleman
Richie Mitchell
1932–2009

# Acknowledgments

Firstly, I would like to express my gratitude to the fantastic team at HarperCollins. Some of you I am in contact with on a regular basis, others I only see once or twice a year at parties. But you all have one thing in common: you truly believe in me and my books, and I can't thank you enough for that, and all the hard graft you do to promote them.

Love and best wishes to Sarah Ritherdon, who has now left HC to become a full-time mum. And a huge warm welcome to my new editor, Kimberley Young, who is an absolute joy to work with (or she was until she gave me a shitload of editing). Only joking, Kim! xx

As always, love and appreciation to my agent, Tim Bates, and to typist Sue Cox for all your hard work. Rosie de Courcy for being there from the start, and Lady H.

Before I make this sound like an Academy Award winning speech (just practising in case that day ever comes, lol!), I want to thank everybody who buys, borrows, reads, or recommends my books. Same goes for the shops and supermarkets that stock them. Asda and Morrisons have been especially supportive, which I really appreciate.

*Payback* brought back many special memories while I was writing it. I worked on Whitechapel Market every

Friday for many years. But it was the scenes I set at Kings in Eastbourne that brought a tear to my eye. Reminded me so much of my Mum, Dad, Nan and Granddad who are unfortunately no longer with me. All the star acts you see mentioned in this book actually appeared at Kings, plus hundreds more. It really was the place to be back in the day. Especially the launderette, eh Karen Mitchell? Lol!

One question I often get asked is how much research I put into a book. The answer is not much at all. I tend to stick with subjects that I know quite a bit about. However, *Payback* was far more complex. Lots of police activity, so I needed to see certain parts of the book through the eyes of the law. Luckily for me (although I didn't feel very lucky at the time) I once got my collar felt by Ron Scott, who ended up as Chief Inspector of the Murder Squad. Ron, you've been an absolute diamond answering my endless questions. I can't thank you enough and I definitely owe you and your wife that meal. Who would have thought all those years ago when our paths crossed in such a way, I would end up a bestselling author, you would love my books and we would end up as good friends? You just couldn't make it up, could you? Haha!

If you prick us, do we not bleed?
If you tickle us, do we not laugh?
If you poison us, do we not die?
And if you wrong us, shall we not revenge?

William Shakespeare

# Prologue

Whistling 'Zip-a-Dee-Doo-Dah', Trevor Thomas felt as happy as a pig in shit as he walked the mile-long journey from the pub to his mother's house.

As a lad, Trevor had never truly appreciated the sights, smells, atmosphere, or community spirit of the East End of London. But after years of living in Yorkshire, he sure did now. Had it not been for his good fortune on the football pools, Trevor would probably still be stuck in a loveless marriage in Leeds. Twenty-four thousand pounds was a hell of a lot of money and there was no way that miserable, greedy, nasty bitch he had got saddled with was going to get her mucky paws on his windfall. Leaving his four kids behind was a small price to pay if it meant him keeping all the money to himself. Only his mum knew about it. She had hidden it under her floorboards to keep it away from prying eyes.

What Trevor did not realize as he stopped to chat to an old pal before continuing his journey was that his run of good luck was about to come to a very abrupt and gory end.

Vinny and Michael Butler were sitting in a white Ford Transit van. Michael was in the back, Vinny in the passenger seat as though he were waiting for the driver of the vehicle to return. Both were wearing dark hooded tracksuits to hide their identities, and seeing as they only ever wore the finest designer suits and drove top-of-the-range cars, Vinny doubted even their own mother would recognize them.

'This could be him now, bruv. Nope. Hold your horses, it isn't.'

'I hope he fucking hurries up, Vin, because our alibi will be blown sky high if he doesn't.'

'Stop panicking. We've got stacks of time. Like I told you, you've no need to get your hands dirty at all, Michael. Hold up! Speak of the devil and it appears.'

Still whistling the song he could not get out of his head, Trevor spotted the two tall men in hooded tracksuits leap out of the van. Apart from wondering if they were boxers who had been training at the gym, he thought little of it until they grabbed him from behind.

Before Trevor could shout for help, tape was placed over his mouth and he was chucked into the back of the van like a roll of old carpet. As one man expertly tied him up, the other leapt into the front and drove the van away.

Eyes wide with a mixture of fear and shock, Trevor now wished he had listened to his mother's words of wisdom. 'As much as I love and miss you, it's not safe for you to be living back in the East End, son. That Vinny Butler is a real force to be reckoned with now, and he won't have forgotten what you did to him. He isn't the type of man to let bygones be bygones.'

As the van trundled along, Trevor shuddered as his abductor took his hood down. Vinny had been fifteen, Trevor nineteen, when he had eloped to Leeds with Yvonne. But even at such a young age, Vinny had already carved out a fearsome reputation back then. That was why Yvonne had insisted they left the area. How Trevor now wished he had never clapped eyes on Yvonne Summers.

'Not the greatest choice of song for you to be whistling, was it, Trevor? Because, my oh my, your day is going to be anything but fucking wonderful,' Vinny chuckled as he ripped the tape from his victim's mouth.

It was quite dark inside the back of the van and it wasn't until Vinny switched on a big static torch like the ones workmen used that Trevor could properly see the man whose girlfriend he had stolen all those years ago. With his mop of thick black hair Brylcreemed back, and his menacing eyes that were a piercing shade of bright green, Vinny looked even scarier in the light than the dark.

'What you gonna do to me? Please don't hurt me, Vinny, I beg you. I know what I did was wrong and I am very sorry, but I swear if you let me out of this van, I'll do anything you say. I'll even move away again, if that's what you want. On my mother's life, I will.'

Vinny could not help but grin. He had waited years for this moment, and intended to enjoy every second of it. Trevor had lost all of his hair, had yellow teeth, and reminded Vinny of a fly stuck to one of those sticky tape traps his mum had in her conservatory that was desperately trying to untangle itself. 'If I was a forgiving man, I would let you jump out of this van right now. Unfortunately for you, Trevor, I am not.'

'Please, Vinny, I'm beggin' you not to hurt me. It will be the end of my mum if you do. She has a lot of respect for your mum and aunt, you know. She was gutted over Roy and Lenny's deaths – she's ordered some lovely flowers for their funerals. And I remember your dad well. I used to buy my cigarettes and booze off him once upon a time,' Trevor gabbled.

'So, where is the slag now? Did you marry the manipulative deceitful whore?' Vinny spat. Yvonne Summers had been his first and only true love. Two years older than him she was, but even at fifteen, Vinny had known how to earn a bob or two and had treated that girl like a princess. Jewellery, clothes, hats, shoes – he had lavished Yvonne with expensive gifts. And how had she repaid him? By running off with the skinny little weasel of a man who was currently snivelling while resembling a trussed-up turkey.

Tears of pure fright streaming down his cheeks, Trevor nodded. 'Yeah, we got married and had four kids. Yvonne is still in Leeds, I think. I can give you the address if you want?'

'So, what you doing back here?'

'We split up and I had nowhere else to go. If you want Yvonne back, you can have her, Vinny. I don't mind, honest.'

'Want her back! You having a laugh at my expense, Trevor? Wrong words, mate, wrong words,' Vinny spat. He opened the tool bag next to him and pulled out a pair of pliers.

'No, please God, no,' Trevor screamed, wetting himself with fear as Vinny inserted the pliers into his mouth.

Vinny was no qualified dentist and as Trevor's screams echoed around the van, Michael winced and turned the volume of the radio up.

By the time the Butlers reached their destination, a narrow rural lane that led to nothing but a metal gate in East Hanningfield, Vinny was splashed with blood, and after passing out Trevor was now untied, awake again and rolling about the floor in obvious agony.

'Stop crying, you fucking wuss. Man up,' Vinny ordered, giving his now toothless victim a sharp kick in the head.

Michael parked up next to the Datsun Cherry they'd left there that morning. Even the full volume of the radio had not been able to drown out Trevor's howls.

'Let's just get the job finished, Vinny. The quicker we get away from here and back to Whitechapel, the better.'

Vinny took the small axe out of the tool bag. 'You better go for a walk for five minutes, Michael. I doubt you have the stomach to watch what I am about to do.'

'Don't be insinuating I'm some pussy, Vinny. If I was, I wouldn't be here with you. Just do what you've got to do, and get your skates on.'

Trevor was in too much pain to scream when Vinny dragged him out of the van by the legs. Instead, he whimpered like an injured dog and curled up in a foetal position, covering his head with his hands. He now knew how animals must feel when they were being led inside the slaughterhouse, and he just wanted death to come quickly so the pain would go away.

Vinny Butler had a different plan. In some countries it was classed as normal to chop the hands off thieves. 'Be a good boy now, Trevor. Hold your right hand out for Uncle Vinny.'

Sobbing his heart out, Trevor did as he was told. His mother and his winnings flashed through his mind. He was never going to get the chance to spend that now, was he? And he would never see his kids again.

'Sure you wanna watch this, David?' Vinny joked. Michael bore a strong resemblance to the popstar David Essex. Even had the same cheeky grin. Vinny had thought it hilarious when his brother got chased down Petticoat Lane market by a crowd of screaming tourists the previous Sunday.

Michael did not want to watch what Vinny was about to do, but there was no way he was going to admit that.

'Just fucking hurry up, will you? And if you ever call me David again, I'll be pulling *your* teeth out with pliers.'

Trevor let out a blood-curdling scream as the axe tore into his wrist, then seemed to lose consciousness.

'Those thieving hands of yours had to come off, didn't they, Trevor? Won't be stealing anybody's girlfriend now, will you? Nobody messes with me, and I mean nobody,' Vinny hissed, his face spattered with his victim's blood.

Trying not to throw up, Michael felt a shiver travel down his spine as he heard the rustling of nearby leaves. 'Did you hear that noise, Vin? I heard something coming from the bushes.'

'Probably a hedgehog or a fox. This axe is shit. It's blunt,' Vinny complained, as he continued to hack away at Trevor's flesh.

Averting his eyes from what reminded him of a scene out of a horror film, Michael heard another noise, turned around and nearly shit himself as two pairs of eyes met his. 'Jesus fucking wept! I nearly had a heart attack then. There's cows watching us, Vinny.'

'Well, I doubt they'll be ringing the Old Bill to give a statement,' Vinny replied, laughing at his own wit.

'It ain't funny, Vin. Giving me the heebies, this place is. Let's set fire to the van and get out of here.'

Vinny glanced at Michael, a manic glint in his eyes. 'Not until I've finished chopping the thieving cunt's hands off. He needs to be taught a lesson, taking other people's possessions.'

'But he's already dead by the looks of it. He isn't going to know whether you chop his other hand off, is he? I tell you what, give me the poxy axe and I'll do the honours. You sort out the fire – and whatever you do, don't leave anything lying about.'

Unlike his brother, Michael had never murdered anyone

and the bile rose in his throat as he heard a whimper come out of Trevor's mouth then saw his eyes flicker open. 'Oh Jesus,' he mumbled, dropping the axe in horror. He then took a deep breath, reluctantly picked the axe back up and started to chop at the man's left wrist. Vinny would never let him live it down otherwise.

Flesh and bone was harder to chop through than Michael had thought possible. But by the time Vinny had tidied up after them and doused the van in petrol, both hands had been severed and Trevor looked as dead as a dodo.

'Put them teeth on the front seat, Michael, then clean yourself up and get changed. Just chuck everything in the back of the van,' Vinny ordered.

As strong as an ox, Vinny lifted Trevor's body into the back of the van by himself. He then chucked the hands and tools in, before joining his brother in getting cleaned up. They had come well prepared; the Datsun's boot held soap, water, towels and a change of clothes.

'Trevor's still alive, you know. Amazing how people die from slitting their wrists, yet you can chop their hands off and they don't die immediately,' Vinny said.

'Well, he won't be alive for much longer. I'm gonna throw all this clobber in the back. Where's your gloves? Check all round, bruv, make sure we haven't left anything lying about.'

For the first time in his life, Vinny Butler wondered whether Michael might actually be in the same league as him. He'd always been closer to Roy, who'd been a great sibling and sound business partner, but had never really possessed that killer instinct – until it came to putting a bullet in his own brain. Today, however, Michael had surprised and impressed Vinny immensely.

Before Vinny lit the kingsize match, he gave a little

sermon. 'Bye bye, Trevor. I hope the slag was worth it. May your soul rot in hell, you pilfering worthless wanker.'

The explosion was clearly audible as Michael drove at top speed down the narrow lane. He glanced at his brother in the passenger seat. 'What you gonna do with the teeth?'

Vinny grinned. 'Flick them out the window along the A13. One by one, of course. Be a bit like when we used to flick pebbles at people as kids.'

It was twenty minutes before closing time when Vinny and Michael casually walked into the Blind Beggar. Both men were suited and booted and reeked of expensive aftershave as always.

'Vinny, Michael, let me get you both a drink. Me and the missus were so upset to hear about your Roy and Lenny. Great lads, the pair of them, and they will be sorely missed,' Big Stan said in a sombre tone.

Vinny and Michael rarely ventured into the Blind Beggar. As they had hoped, the pub was fairly busy and already they were the centre of attention with all eyes on their grand entrance. 'I'll get the drinks, Stan. Ask around and see who else wants one,' Vinny said.

'Who shall I ask?'

'Everybody. Just tell 'em I'm buying.'

When Stan toddled off to obey orders, more well-wishers came over to speak to Vinny and Michael, including the landlord. 'Afters isn't a problem, lads. You just say the word if you fancy a late drink.'

'Actually, that is very much appreciated. Been stuck in that club all day, me and Michael have, and after everything that's happened, we're currently sick of the sight of the place.'

It was a good ten minutes or so before Big Stan wandered back to inform Vinny that the round had come to eighty-seven quid. 'It would have been cheaper, but Bobby

Jackson ordered a pint for himself and his pal, plus a large chaser each,' Stan added.

Seeing his brother's eyes glint dangerously as he turned to see where Jackson was, Michael grabbed hold of him. 'Not tonight, Vin. We've had enough drama for one day,' he whispered.

'Big Stan should never have asked him. It's common knowledge that I hate the cunt.'

'But you did say ask everyone, so you can't blame Stan. It's only a poxy drink.'

'I'd like to go over there and ram that glass straight down the back of his throat,' Vinny hissed.

'I'm sure you'll have other opportunities to do that. For the time being, let's just forget about Jackson and chat nicely to the locals. That was the whole point of us coming in here, yeah? We need to act normal, you said. Well, that does not include ramming glasses down the customers' throats, does it?'

'Yeah, you're right,' Vinny replied. He then settled back to watch his brother charm the locals as though he did not have a care in the world.

After leaving East Hanningfield, they had dumped the Datsun not too far from Hackney Marshes, set fire to it, then jogged through Victoria Park in the second set of hooded tracksuits and trainers they had worn that day.

Nobody had seen them sneak into the back entrance of the club, and there was no way they could have been recognized while running through the park. They both had their hoods up the whole time and it was pitch-dark.

Sick of people rambling on about the funerals, Vinny led Michael over to a table. 'I just want you to know that I really appreciate what you did for me today and I won't forget it. You've got a cool head on you, bruv. We are definitely cut from the same cloth.'

Michael shook his head. 'I'm not like you, Vin, and I never will be. You thoroughly enjoyed yourself today – I didn't. If you want the truth, I hated every second of it.'

'So why did you agree to help me then?'

'Because you're my brother, and with Ahmed in hospital, you had nobody else to ask. Nobody you could trust, at any rate. As Mum always drummed into us, once a Butler always a Butler.'

# CHAPTER ONE

Autumn 1976

Queenie Butler opened her front door and cursed the latest downpour. The hottest summer on record was now just a distant memory, but the weather was the least of Queenie's problems.

'Don't put that up in here. You always said it was unlucky to put a brolly up indoors,' Brenda reminded her mother.

Glaring at her daughter, Queenie ignored her wishes. 'As if we could be any more bastard well unlucky, Bren. Our family has had the heart ripped out of it already, so excuse me for not being overly superstitious these days.'

'Where you going?'

'To check on Vivvy again, and while I'm gone I want you to have a bath, young lady. You ain't seen soap or water for three days, you dirty little mare. I expect Roy and Lenny's send-off to be perfect tomorrow – which includes you making an effort to smarten yourself up.'

Umbrella in hand, Queenie made the short journey to her sister's house next-door-but-one. She let herself in with her own key. 'Cooey. Where are you, Viv?' Queenie fully expected her sister to be sitting in the lounge staring aimlessly out of the window as she had been for the past few days since hearing about the car crash that had killed her only son.

'I'm up here.'

Queenie hurried up the stairs and found Vivian in Lenny's room, sorting through his things. 'What you doing?'

'What does it look like I'm doing? I'm clearing Lenny's room out. The dustmen come in the morning.'

Shaking her head in disbelief, Queenie sat down on the edge of Lenny's bed. Her nephew's nickname had been Champ and how very apt that had been. Starved of oxygen at birth, Lenny had overcome his disabilities and grown into a fine young man. His mental age might have been less than his years, but that hadn't stopped Lenny being loved by everybody. He really had been a special lad. 'Viv, please don't chuck his stuff away, love. You're not thinking rationally at the moment and I know you're going to regret what you're doing. Why don't we go downstairs and have a nice cup of tea, eh?'

Ignoring her sister's suggestion, Vivian yanked open a drawer and angrily tipped the contents onto the floor. Mumbling obscenities, she then began to put her son's belongings into a dustbin liner.

Queenie's eyes welled up. 'Viv, I really need you to snap out of this silly behaviour. I've lost a son too, remember.' Queenie had given birth to four children, and her middle son, Roy, was being laid to rest tomorrow after taking his own life. Wheelchair-bound since 1971 after a shooting outside the nightclub he owned, he'd suffered a miserable existence the last five years, finally ending it all by blasting himself in the head with a gun.

'But you've got three other kids, and your grandchildren. Hardly the fucking same, is it?' Vivian spat.

Queenie bowed her weary head. At forty-nine, she was

three years older than Vivian. Both women were thin, had deep facial wrinkles due to their love of cigarettes and the sun, and with their dyed blonde hair and similar features, were often mistaken for twins rather than sisters. This past week, however, Queenie had felt as though she did not know her sister at all. Grief did strange things to people and Vivian was acting stranger than most.

'How can you say such a thing, Vivvy? No matter how many kids or grandchildren I have, nothing takes the pain away of losing my Roy. I'm equally upset about Lenny, he was like a son to me too, but I watched my Roy suffer for years. At least your Lenny led a happy life.'

Her face contorted with anger, Vivian stood up and flew at her sister. 'Get out! Go on, get out of my house.'

Being pushed and prodded was not something Queenie would usually allow, but she knew her sister didn't mean it. It was the grief that was making her doolally. 'Please let's not argue. The funerals are tomorrow and our boys deserve the best send-off ever. If they're looking down at me and you fighting, they'll be devastated.'

'Looking down! Looking fucking down! Don't make me laugh, Queen. There is no bastard heaven. If God existed, why would he have taken my Lenny away from me, eh? It's all a load of old bollocks.'

Desperate to give his brother and cousin the best send-off the East End had ever seen, Vinny Butler had spent the day preparing for the wake. The nightclub he part-owned with Michael had now been transformed into a shrine for their dearly departed.

Satisfied that his mum and aunt would approve of his handiwork, Vinny poured himself a drink and flopped onto one of the leather sofas. It had been three days since he and Michael had disposed of Trevor Thomas and there had not been any mention of a body being found or Trevor's disappearance in the news.

Vinny grinned as his brother appeared. After the car accident that had killed Lenny, relations had been strained between himself and Michael, but thankfully carrying out their plan to kill Trevor seemed to have papered over those cracks. 'You're looking particularly dapper today, bruv. That another new suit?'

'Yep. No flies on you, is there? This is the latest Savile Row addition to my ever-expanding wardrobe.'

Michael was five years Vinny's junior. Both brothers had inherited their father's jet-black hair, piercing green eyes and tall build. But they did not particularly look alike. Michael had a round face with a cheeky smile, whereas Vinny's features were thinner and more chiselled, his lips usually twisted in a sinister smirk. They wore their hair in different styles as well. Michael used far less brylcreem and had what his mum referred to as a 'short back and sides'. With their dark skin tone, both Vinny and Michael were often assumed to be of Italian or Irish descent, but as far as they knew, their ancestors had all been cockneys.

'Well? Notice anything different?' Vinny chuckled, indicating the numerous photos of Roy and Lenny that he'd had blown up to poster-size and displayed on the walls.

'I don't know, Vin. It's a bit much, perhaps? Do Mum and Auntie Viv know you've done all this?'

'No. I wanted it to be a surprise. Why shouldn't we have photos of Roy and Champ on show? It is their special day. The one in the middle – I'm gonna keep that up after the funeral too.'

Michael stared at the photo Vinny was pointing at. It showed the three Butler brothers, and it was the last photo taken before Roy had got shot. They all had dark suits on and were smiling broadly, their arms draped around one another's shoulders. It was a lovely photo, but it made Michael feel very sad. Feeling slightly lost for words, he was relieved when the phone started ringing, giving him an excuse to turn away. 'I'll get that,' he said.

'What's up?' Vinny asked, seconds later. He could tell by Michael's face that something was wrong.

'That was Ahmed. He's out of hospital and wants to see you. He said to meet him at three at his house.'

Vinny felt the colour drain from his cheeks. This was the first time he had heard from Ahmed since the fateful night of the crash. The state Ahmed was in, Vinny thought he'd be burying his best mate as well as his cousin. 'What exactly did he say?'

'Not much. I got the distinct impression he didn't really want to talk over the phone. I did tell him you were here, but he just said to meet him at three. What're you gonna say to him, Vin? I hope he isn't going to cause us grief. I've got Nancy and the boys to think of.'

'I know far too much about Ahmed for him to cause us any grief, Michael. Anyway, he's a mate and I'm sure once I explain things properly, he'll understand why I did what I did,' Vinny replied, sounding far more confident about the awkward situation than he actually felt.

Michael was worried. He was currently trying to win his wife back and another drama just might tip her over the edge. 'But say he don't understand, Vin?'

'Then we'll cross that bridge when we come to it.'

Mary Walker brushed her husband's lapels and gave him one final warning. Donald could be irritatingly cantankerous at times and, for Nancy's sake, Mary was determined that today must go smoothly.

'I have already promised you that I will be polite to the

children, dear. But please do not expect me to welcome their criminal of a father into our home as well, because I just wasn't raised that way.

Sighing, Mary went to check on the buffet she had prepared. Her daughter's choice of husband had caused no end of problems in her relationship with Donald over the years, and it wasn't even poor Michael's fault. It was his brother Vinny's.

Back in 1965, Mary and Donald had fulfilled a lifelong ambition by opening up their own café, set in the heart of Whitechapel. Having spent every penny they had on purchasing and then refurbishing their dream, they worked hard to make a success of it. Business had been booming – until fate struck a terrible blow. Their son Christopher, who was only eight at the time, had witnessed a murder. The killing had been carried out by Vinny Butler, head of a local gangland family, and as soon as he realized that Christopher had witnessed the murder, he had threatened him and forced him to lie to the police.

Petrified for the safety of their children, Mary and Donald had fled Whitechapel one frosty Christmas Day. It had taken time to recover from the trauma of their ordeal, but they had thrown themselves into a new business venture, and moved on with their lives.

The past returned to haunt Mary and Donald in 1971. That was the summer when their beautiful daughter fell in love with Vinny's younger brother, Michael. The lovebirds' relationship had caused Mary nothing but grief ever since. Christopher was now a policeman, and he and Donald were dead against Nancy's choice of husband.

'How do I look, Mum? I feel ever so nervous, but I can't thank you and Dad enough for doing this for me today. I miss my boys so much.'

Mary told her daughter she looked great and held her

close to her chest. Nancy had been ill recently and had ended up in hospital. Being alienated from her father and brother while trying to bring up two kids of her own was bad enough, but when Michael insisted on taking in the son he'd had by a previous girlfriend it had proved too much for her delicate brain to cope with. That was why it had been decided that Daniel and Adam would spend their birthday at Mary and Donald's home, where Nancy was currently recuperating.

'I hope Dad loves the boys as much as you do, Mum,' Nancy said, her voice full of hope.

Mary held her daughter's face in her hands, forcing Nancy to look at her, and she smiled. Whereas she'd had contact with her grandsons since day one, Donald had never met them before. 'Now, dry them eyes. Today is going to be a wonderful day, and if your father doesn't love them boys as much as I do, I'll eat my hat.'

Joanna Preston was feeling rather melancholy. The house that Vinny had bought was lovely, but its lack of furniture made it seem as cold and lonely as she felt. Tomorrow would be Joanna's eighteenth birthday and for the first time since the shit had hit the fan, she realized just how much she missed her family. Her mum always made a big fuss of her on her birthday, but tomorrow Joanna wouldn't be seeing or even speaking to her. Instead, she would be spending the day at a funeral for two men she didn't even know.

Sipping her cup of tea, she allowed her mind to wander back to the summer. She had been working as a cleaner at a holiday park in Eastbourne when Vinny had appeared in her life and literally swept her off her feet. It really had been a case of love at first sight, but what Joanna hadn't realized at the time was the bad blood between her family and Vinny's. Her father was currently serving a fifteen-year prison sentence for shooting Vinny's brother – the same brother who was being buried tomorrow. Jo had only been told the truth recently.

When her mother had learned of her romance, she'd hit the roof. Joanna had then been forced to make a decision. Her family or Vinny? She was so besotted, she'd chosen Vinny, and was now pregnant with their first child. Her mum had been devastated. She'd told Joanna that with her long blonde hair, slender body and beautiful blue eyes, she could get any lad she wanted. But Joanna did not want a lad. She wanted a man, and that man was Vinny.

Moving to Whitechapel had proved to be a bit of an eye-opener for Joanna. She had spent the early part of her life living in South London, but barely remembered that. Tiptree and Eastbourne were the only other two areas she had lived in, and Whitechapel was so very different. The air reeked, the pavements were littered with rubbish, there was graffiti everywhere you looked, and it was very multi-cultural.

'You OK? Hasn't that sofa come yet?' Vinny asked, snapping Joanna out of her daydream.

'No, it hasn't. Vinny, when can I start work at the club?'

Vinny crouched down next to the armchair and began to sweet-talk Joanna. When she had been working at the holiday camp, he had promised her a job as his secretary. That offer had merely been intended to entice her to London. He didn't love her; neither did he want her working for him. Their whole relationship was based on revenge. Vinny hated Joanna's father with a passion and would do anything to get even for what he'd done to Roy. Absolutely anything.

Michael Butler felt as if he had the weight of the world on his shoulders as he drove towards Nancy's parents' house. Being the only one, bar Ahmed, who knew that Vinny was responsible for Lenny's death was preying on his mind. On top of that, his wife had temporarily left him, and he was currently trying to bring up his three sons alone. Trevor Thomas was another worry. Say he and Vinny had left some kind of evidence at the scene? A long prison sentence did not bear thinking about.

Thankfully, Lee was at school today. It was him moving into their family home that had tipped Nancy over the edge. Lee's mum and gran had died in a car crash a few months ago, so the poor little sod had had nowhere else to go.

'Dad, we want you to come to our birthday party with us, don't we, Adam?' Daniel said.

Michael bumped the car up on the kerb and switched the engine off. As fate would have it, both his sons were born on the very same day. Daniel was four today, Adam two, but there was no way Michael could join in the celebrations. Although they were yet to be properly introduced, Nancy's father hated him.

Michael locked the car door, grabbed his sons by their tiny hands, and led them up the pathway. It was Mary who answered the door, as he guessed it would be. 'Any chance I can have a quick word with Nance, Mary? I miss her so much.'

Mary squeezed her son-in-law's hand. She liked Michael, she really did, but it had taken all her strength to force Donald to allow their grandsons into the house. She couldn't push the issue any further by extending the invitation to Michael. 'Not today, love, but Nancy is on the mend. I can promise you that she'll be ready to see you again soon.'

Closing the door on Michael she led the boys through to the living room. Donald looked awkward as he came face to face with his grandsons for the very first time. Both were dressed in matching beige suits, had jet black hair, bright green eyes, and looked nothing like anybody in his family.

'Are you our granddad? We've been wanting to meet you for ages. My name is Daniel and this is my brother Adam,' Daniel said politely.

Donald Walker was not usually a man of emotion, but when his youngest grandson held his arm out in hope that his hand would be shook, Donald could not help but smile. He had always been a fan of impeccable manners. 'Yes, I'm your granddad, and I've been looking forward to meeting you too.'

Watching the bonding session unfold before her, Mary shared a smug smile with her daughter. Daniel and Adam already had Donald eating out of the palms of their hands. Gone was her miserable-looking bolshy husband. In his place was a happy, loving grandfather.

Vinny Butler walked into the room and for the first time since the accident locked eyes with the best pal he had left for dead. Ahmed looked awful, wearing only pyjama bottoms his face and body was covered in cuts and bruises.

Ahmed glanced at Vinny, his face devoid of emotion, and then turned to his wife. 'Make yourself scarce, Anna. Vinny and I have business to discuss.'

When Anna left the room, Vinny's eyes welled up with pure guilt as he tried to explain his actions on that fateful night. 'I am so fucking sorry, mate. No way would I have left you if I had thought you were still alive. I really thought you were a goner.'

'Pour us both a Scotch, then I want you to tell me exactly what happened. I don't remember anything about that evening at all,' Ahmed lied. He could sense that Vinny was nervous and so the bastard should be. Making it awkward without being too nasty was exactly how Ahmed had planned this conversation.

Vinny took a large gulp of his drink. 'Do you remember going to the whorehouse in Dalston?'

'Nope.'

'Well, me and you were three sheets to the wind when we got there. We'd been boozing all night at the club. Champ overheard us saying where we were going and begged to come with us. Anyway, we had a great time and I offered to drive your car home. I'd sobered up a bit by then. But as I was driving, some van came towards me with its full beam on. I was momentarily blinded, which is why I lost control. We smashed into a building, but it was the left-hand side of the car that took all the impact. That's where you and Champ were both sitting.'

'Carry on,' Ahmed urged.

Reliving the awful experience was something Vinny would rather not be put through, but what choice did he have? A thorough explanation was the very least he owed Ahmed. 'Well, I hit my head against the steering wheel and it dazed me for a minute or so. When I came to and looked at you, there was a big piece of metal sticking out of your chest and a small piece in your head. There was blood everywhere. I checked for a pulse and couldn't find one, then I got out the car to see if Champ was OK. The crash had almost fucking beheaded him. It was awful, the worst thing I have ever seen in my life. I checked you over once more before I left the scene, but I was positive you were dead. I would never have left you to die, you have to believe that, mate.'

Ahmed took a sip of his drink. He had nearly died and had only got out of hospital the previous day. 'So, was you thinking straight when you legged it?'

'My mind was all over the place. I was devastated, Ahmed, about you and Champ. It was like a bad fucking dream.'

'What I cannot understand is how a devastated man

would move his best pal's body into the driver's seat to avoid taking the rap himself. That is a callous, cowardly act in my eyes.'

'I just panicked. It weren't the Old Bill I was bothered about, it was my mum and aunt finding out I'd been driving the motor. If they thought it was me who'd killed Champ, they would both disown me. What did you say to the filth? I wouldn't blame you if you dobbed me in it. It's no more than I deserve.'

Ahmed chuckled. 'I am not a grass, Vinny. It was my car that was written off and I was found behind the steering wheel, so you wasn't even a suspect.'

'Have you been charged with anything?'

'No. I had internal bleeding, therefore needed an emergency operation. I was questioned, but there was no proof I had been drinking because my blood test ended up on the missing list.'

'Well, I'll buy you a new car obviously, and thanks for not saying anything. My mum and aunt are absolutely broken-hearted as it is. Roy's dead as well. Shot himself in the head right in front of me. This past week has been the worst of my life.'

'It's not exactly been my best, Vinny.'

'I know it hasn't, mate. So, what happens now? I'll understand if you don't want to be my business partner any more,' Vinny said. Michael was his partner in the legit business, the nightclub, but Ahmed had been his partner in the drug trade. Thanks to their astute business brains the two of them had built up quite an empire over the past few years, and the bulk of heroin and cocaine currently available on the streets of London was their merchandise.

Ahmed forced a smile at the man he now hated so very much. 'I was not happy that you left me for dead but now you have explained yourself, I can understand why you did what you did. I am willing to let bygones be bygones.'

Relieved, Vinny hugged his pal. 'I will make it up to you, I swear.'

'I know you will. Now, if you don't mind, I'm very tired and could do with some sleep. When is Champ's funeral, by the way? Such a shame, he was a good kid.'

Vinny nodded, his face etched with grief. 'The funeral is tomorrow. We're having a joint one, burying Champ and Roy together.'

'What time and where?'

'The service is at St Leonard's at two. You can't come though, mate. You don't look well enough and my mum and aunt will go apeshit if they see you there. They think you were driving, remember?'

'And what about Michael?'

'He knows the truth. I told him it was me.'

'Well, that's OK then. I loved Champ, Vinny, and I am determined to pay my respects to him. I don't care if your mum and aunt hate my guts. I and God know that Lenny's death had sod all to do with me, remember?'

Aware that Ahmed was being sarcastic, Vinny shrugged. 'OK, but try and stay out of my mum and aunt's way. I'll smooth things over in time, but it's all too raw at the moment.'

When Vinny said goodbye and shut the door, Ahmed smirked. He had no intention of staying away from Queenie and Vivian. He intended to make life as difficult for Vinny as he possibly could from now on. As for the Judas cunt thinking he had been forgiven, there was more chance of hell freezing over than that ever happening.

Thanks to Vinny, he had endured internal bleeding, three broken ribs and forty-two stitches in his face and stomach. Scars would heal, but Vinny's betrayal wouldn't. Every time he looked at those scars, Ahmed would be reminded of what his so-called best friend and business partner had done to him.

When Ahmed had first woken up and learned what had happened, his head and heart felt weighed down with feelings of shock and disappointment. Not any more though. Over the past few days, those feelings had been replaced by fury and an urge to get even.

Vinny Butler had disrespected him in the worst possible way. Moving his body into the driver's seat, then leaving him for dead was an act of evil that Ahmed could never forgive or forget.

Ahmed grinned as he laid his head back on the pillow. The five most important things in Vinny's life were money, his liberty, reputation, mother and son. Now, what should Ahmed take away from him first? Decisions, decisions . . .

# CHAPTER TWO

On the morning of her son and nephew's funerals, Queenie was woken up by the sound of torrential rain pounding against her window. 'Poxy bastard weather,' she mumbled as she pulled back the curtain. Funerals were miserable enough occasions at the best of times, but there was nothing worse than standing at a graveside in the rain.

Queenie Butler marched into her daughter's bedroom and yanked the blankets from over her head. It was nine days since Brenda's husband had left her. Dean had gone out for a newspaper one morning and had not come back. It had since come to light that he had cleaned out his bank account that very day. Unable to face life as a one-parent family, Brenda had moved into Queenie's with her four-year-old daughter Tara. Both were high maintenance and loved a tantrum, and Queenie just wished they would sod off home.

'Out of that pit and get yourself ready – and don't forget to wear your cross,' Queenie ordered. She and Vivian loved their gold, and always wore their big gold crosses supported by thick belcher chains for funerals, weddings and christenings in hope of impressing the vicar.

'I don't feel well, Mum. I feel sick again. Can't I stay here and look after Tara?'

Brenda had only had her pregnancy confirmed by the doctor the previous day. Dean had really left her in the lurch and if Queenie ever got her hands on her son-in-law, she would wring his scrawny neck.

'Don't give me all that old flannel. You get your arse out that bed now, and make yourself look tidy. Not attend your own brother and cousin's funerals? Never heard such cobblers in my life. Selfish little mare you are, Brenda. Well, today isn't about you, it's about Roy and Lenny, and if you don't do me proud, I shall disown you.'

About to run a bath, Queenie heard a noise outside and looked out of the window again. 'What the bleedin' hell's she doing now?' she muttered. Vivian was dragging what looked like Lenny's bedside cabinet up the garden path, and making quite a racket as she did so.

Putting on her shoes and coat, Queenie ran downstairs and out the front door. 'Whatever are you doing? It's not even six o'clock yet. You'll wake the neighbours up, and you'll catch pneumonia in this weather.'

'I'm putting Lenny's stuff out for the dustmen. Not going to be needing it any more, is he?'

Queenie stared at her sister. When they had first learned about Lenny's death, Vivian had cried and wailed like an injured animal, but since then she had shown hardly any emotion. She had barely mentioned the funeral and Queenie found it very odd that she wanted to chuck all the poor little sod's belongings away. There was no way she could part with anything of her Roy's. 'Viv, there'll be flowers arriving soon. Leave sorting out Lenny's belongings until after the funeral. If you still want to get rid of them, I'll get one of the boys to take the stuff to the dump for you.'

'I wish you'd stop telling me what to fucking do, Queen,' Vivian spat, dumping two cardboard boxes full of toys next to her sister's feet.

Queenie looked down and immediately felt a lump in her throat. Zippy the monkey had been Lenny's favourite toy. He had carried it everywhere with him as a kid, and had always slept with it in his bed until the day he died. Queenie picked the toy up. No way was she going to allow her sister to throw that away. It should be buried with Lenny.

Michael was shocked to receive an early morning phone call from his wife. It was the first time they had spoken since Nancy had been taken into hospital. She had wandered out one evening in her nightdress and slippers and had been found by a man in an alleyway the following morning. The doctors had suggested that Nancy's odd behaviour could be down to post-natal depression, but seeing as Adam was now two, Michael found that hard to understand.

'Nance, I've really missed you, babe. The boys had a great time yesterday and were full of it when they came home. They didn't stop talking about their granddad, so I take it it all went well?'

'Yes, it went very well. My dad adored them, and I'm ever so pleased. It feels like a weight has been lifted off my shoulders. How are you? I was so sorry to hear about your brother and Lenny. When are their funerals?'

'Today. Will you come with me, Nance? My mum and aunt are both in a dreadful way and I could really do with your support.'

Nancy sighed. She had only just started to feel like her old self again, and didn't fancy spending time with Michael's family yet. Vinny had a way of making her feel anxious, and Brenda would be bound to kick off with her over Dean going away. 'I'm sorry, Michael, but I don't feel up to attending funerals. I will look after the boys for you though. Mum said you were taking them with you and I'd rather you didn't. They're far too young to be surrounded by death.'

Michael was cross. He had cared for his sons almost single-handed these past couple of months. It also hurt him that Nancy had only called because she had wanted to have Daniel and Adam for the day. Did she not love him any more? Was their marriage over? Well, there was only one way to find out. An ultimatum should do the trick. 'Nance, I cannot believe what you just said. "I will look after the boys for you" – have you forgotten you're their mother? Look, I know you've been ill and I sympathize with that, but now you're feeling better, you need to have a think about us. I'll give you a week to get your arse back home, and if you don't, I shall start divorce proceedings. Our sons are unsettled enough as it is at the moment and I won't allow you to keep fucking them about. They miss you, I miss you, and you should be back at home where you belong. You can't hide behind your parents for ever. As for the funeral, the boys are coming with me, end of. It's not fair on Lee if they don't.'

'I'm sorry I've been a bad mum and wife, but I have been really ill,' Nancy replied, her voice full of emotion.

'No, you haven't been ill, Nance, you've been depressed. Two different things, so my mum reckons. Don't you think I get depressed too? My cousin has just been beheaded in a car crash, Roy has blown his brains out, and I'm currently trying to run a business and bring up three kids on my own. Do you wanna swap fucking places? Listen, I've got to go now. I need to get round my mum's and the boys haven't had any breakfast yet. I meant what I said though, Nance. You've got a week to make up your mind, or we're finished.'

Joanna Preston held Vinny's arm as they strode towards Queenie's house. It had been her boyfriend's idea that she ring her mum this morning. He had said that her eighteenth birthday was as good a time as any to try and patch things up. He'd also insisted she tell her mum that she was pregnant.

'You OK? Shame your mum went off on one, but she will come round in time you know,' Vinny said. He had been dying for Johnny Preston to find out that he had got his daughter up the spout. Deborah was bound to tell him the news, and Vinny only wished he could be there to see the look on the bastard's face.

'Are all these people here for the funeral, Vinny?' Joanna asked, as they turned the corner. There was a crowd of about a hundred or so.

'Yeah, must be. Bit early they are, though. I hope they haven't knocked on my mum's door. I told them to leave her be,' Vinny replied. His mother had insisted that, apart from family, she wanted nobody inside the house.

The flowers spread across his mum and aunt's front gardens brought a lump to Vinny's throat. The wreath he had chosen, with 'Champ' spelled out, was that big it literally shone out like a beacon.

Little Vinny was ten years old and with his black hair and piercing green eyes it was like looking at his father at the same age. Unfortunately for Queenie, her grandson had picked up many of Vinny's traits. He was obstinate, had a temper on him, and once he got a bee in his bonnet, there was very little reasoning with the child.

'I'll say this once more, Vinny. Get upstairs and put your suit on before I brain ya. I really don't need you performing today, boy. I've got enough on my plate as it is.'

When Little Vinny didn't move out of the armchair, Queenie was moving in to give him a good clout round the earhole when she heard the front door open and close. 'About bloody time too. I've had all them nosy bastards out there knocking on the door, and now your son reckons he isn't coming to the funeral,' Queenie told Vinny.

Ordering Joanna to keep his mum company in the kitchen, Vinny walked into the lounge and shut the door. 'What's the matter, boy?'

'Don't like funerals. They remind me of my mum dying.'

Vinny crouched next to his son. Little Vinny had barely known his mother. Karen had been a stripper at the club when she'd fallen pregnant by Vinny. He'd paid her off and brought his son up with the help of his mum. When Little Vinny was five, Karen had turned up on his doorstep like a bad penny. He'd had her done away with, ordering that her murder be made to look like a heroin overdose. 'Look, boy, I know you aren't happy about me being with Joanna and her being pregnant, but I bet once your brother or sister is born, you'll be in your element.'

'No, I won't. I hate babies,' Little Vinny replied, his lip protruding sulkily.

'But it won't stay a baby for long. It will soon be old enough for you to talk to and take out. I remember sulking when your nan fell pregnant with Roy. I wanted to be the only kid. When Roy was born, I soon grew to love him – and you'll be the same when Jo's baby is born. You're my first-born, Vinny, and you're always going to be more special to me than any other kid.'

'Really?'

'Yes, really. I've always been closer to Nanny than Roy, Michael or Brenda were, and that's because I was her first-born. Number one son you are, boy. Very special that is.'

When Little Vinny grinned, Vinny ruffled his hair. 'Now, go and put your suit on.'

*

Vivian Harris took one last look inside Lenny's old bedroom and shut the door. It looked bare and cold now, just like her heart felt. The dustmen must have taken away his stuff because she'd looked out of the window an hour ago and it was gone. A mass of flowers had replaced her son's belongings.

Hearing voices outside, Vivian peeked through the curtain again. 'Nosy fucking bastards. Go away and leave me alone,' she muttered. She had only ever been interested in her family. In her eyes, nobody else mattered.

Aware that somebody was staring up at her, Viv jumped away from the curtain. She poured herself another brandy and lay down on her bed. As soon as her pest of a sister left for the funeral, she planned to fall asleep and never wake up. Lenny needed her, he always had, and she was determined to be there in heaven for him. That's if the bastard place existed, of course.

When Michael arrived, Queenie Butler battled her way through the well-wishing mourners to get to her sister's house. Vivian had insisted on being left alone earlier and had promised she would knock at Queenie's as soon as the coffins arrived. She hadn't. Queenie put her key in the door, but the chain was on. 'Viv, it's me. Let me in.'

When she still received no reply, Queenie started to get angry. 'Vivvy, open this bastard door now,' she yelled.

Aware of Nosy Hilda and Mouthy Maureen staring at her, Queenie pushed past the gawping mourners and marched back to her own house. 'Vinny, you're going to have to do something. Viv's locked herself in and she won't answer the door. It's all your fault for fitting that poxy chain lock, so best you sort it. What with your sister and son, I've had enough drama for one day.'

Vinny snatched the key off his mum, then darted next

door. 'Auntie Viv, come and take this lock off please. We have to leave soon, the cars are here.'

After five minutes of begging his aunt to answer the door and receiving no reply, Vinny took a couple of steps back and booted the door open. He looked in the lounge first, then ran up the stairs.

'Go away and leave me alone,' Vivian screamed when her bedroom door flew open.

'What you doing, still in bed? We have to leave in a minute. Why aren't you dressed?' Vinny asked.

'Because I ain't coming. Nothing is going to bring my Lenny back. Why would I want all them nosy cunts out there gawping at me, revelling in my misfortune?'

Clocking the bottle of brandy on Vivian's bedside cabinet, Vinny sighed. Only his mother could sort this one out and she was going to go apeshit when she found out Viv was sloshed. He ran back to his mum's, drew her aside and told her, 'Viv reckons she isn't coming to the funeral. She's still in bed and she's slurring. I think she's pissed.'

Queenie Butler was out the door like a bat out of hell. Her black hat flew off in a gust of wind as she ran down the path, but she did not stop to retrieve it. First Brenda playing up, then her grandson and now Vivvy. Did the selfish bastards not realize that she was grieving too?

'Is everything all right, Queenie?' asked Nosy Hilda.

'Mind your own fucking business for once,' Queenie snapped, barging past her open-mouthed neighbour. She ran up her sister's stairs and into the bedroom. 'You are going to the funeral even if I have to drag you there. Now, get your arse out of bed and get a grip woman.'

'I can't face it, Queen. My Lenny knew I loved him, so did Roy. I don't have to go to no funeral to prove that to anyone.'

Queenie ripped the blankets off her sister just as she had

with her daughter earlier. 'Now, you listen to me, Vivian Harris. Get out of that bed and get yourself dressed. It's unheard of in our neck of the woods for a woman to miss her own child's funeral – and may God be my judge, you ain't gonna be the first. We're the talk of the town as it is, what with Vinny having to kick your front door in. I will not have our boys' funerals become a laughing stock, not on your nelly. Now, up you bloody well get.'

Albie Butler could feel his heart beating like a drum as he approached St Leonard's church. He hadn't spoken to Vinny since his son had threatened to kill him and he was also on bad terms with Queenie and Viv. Even his daughter and eldest grandson hated his guts.

'What's up, Albie?' Bert asked, when his brother stopped in his tracks.

'Let's wait here. Big Stan is standing outside the church and I know he'll kick off if he sees me. I told him I had cancer that time and he bought me drinks and bunged me money,' Albie explained, truly regretting his terrible lie. He had only told his family and neighbours he had cancer so he could have contact with his children again. His deceit had backfired though. Vinny had found out and tried to blackmail him, and when Albie refused to get involved in his son's evil plan to ruin Roy's engagement, Vinny had outed his lie in front of half of Whitechapel.

'The funeral cars have arrived by the looks of it, Albie. Let's go and find your Michael. He won't allow anybody to have a go at you.'

Albie still had a good relationship with his youngest son. When Vinny had forced him to leave the East End, it was Michael who had driven him down to Ipswich to start his new life. Moving in with Bert had been a blessing. Albie had cut down his drinking and really sorted his life out. He had even met a lovely lady. Dorothy now lived with him and Bert and she was an absolute diamond. She treated him with far more respect than Queenie ever had. His marriage to Queenie had been doomed as soon as she had fallen pregnant. From the moment Vinny was born, Vivian had taken over his husbandly duties and he had been pushed out of the family circle like an unwanted bag of old rubbish.

'Dad, I've spoken to Mum and Vinny and they've agreed that it's only right you sit in the front pew with us,' Michael said, hugging his worried-looking father.

'Thank you, Michael.' Albie's eyes filled up with tears and he was too choked to say more. He had loved Roy and was so glad his son had taken the trouble to phone him before ending his life. Their conversation had been relatively short, but bridges had been built, truths had been told, and that meant the world to Albie.

The actual service was a far cry from the typical East End funeral. Both Queenie and Vivian regularly visited their mother's grave and spoke to her as though she were still alive, but neither was particularly religious. Their lives and luck had taken far too much of a bashing for them to truly believe in God. When the vicar had visited her at home to make arrangements, Queenie had insisted that the pianist play songs rather than hymns.

'Bye Bye Blackbird' was the song she had sung to all her children to get them to sleep when they were babies, so seeing as her Roy was now asleep for ever, it seemed an appropriate choice. Lenny was a big Elvis fan, so Queenie had chosen 'The Wonder of You' especially for her nephew. Vivian had been in no fit state to have any input into the playlist, but Queenie was sure her sister would have opted for the same song, as it had been Lenny's all-time favourite. 'On Mother Kelly's Doorstep' was Queenie's final request.

Both she and Vivian loved that song and had taught it to their offspring, so Queenie saw it as a fitting family tribute.

Vinny locked eyes with his father as he sat down in the pew and gave him a polite nod. Michael had agreed to cover up that it was Vinny who had been driving the night Lenny was killed on condition that he promised to make things right with their dad. Roy had requested the same thing in his suicide note, and Vinny knew he owed it to his brothers to abide by their wishes.

'Today we are here to remember the lives of Roy Butler and Leonard William Harris,' the vicar's voice boomed.

Squeezing Vivian's hand, Queenie glanced down the pew. Albie, Vinny, Michael and Little Vinny all had tears rolling down their cheeks. Roy's ex-fiancée and her parents were seated in the opposite pew. Colleen was sobbing, but Queenie was annoyed with her. Roy's only child, Emily-Mae, was four now and she had wanted the girl to attend her father's funeral but Colleen had rebuffed the request. Queenie hadn't seen her granddaughter since Colleen had returned to her native Ireland, and she had been desperate to tell the child what a wonderful man her daddy was.

'God! What fucking God?' Vivian muttered as the vicar began sermonizing about the afterlife.

'Shush, Viv. Your voice carries and people can hear you,' Queenie whispered.

'Couldn't give a toss what people think. No God would have taken my boy from me. That's how I know he don't fucking exist.'

When the pianist played 'The Wonder of You', Vivian's anger turned to anguish. 'My baby. My beautiful boy. Mummy loved you so much, Lenny. You were my world.'

Vinny bowed his head when the vicar recited the Lord's Prayer. He had begged his brother to give a eulogy on behalf of the family, but Michael had flatly refused.

'Accidental or not, both Roy and Champ would still be alive if it wasn't for your mistakes, Vin. The least you owe them is to stand up, be a man, and say a few words,' had been Michael's blunt reply.

After the prayer, the vicar called Vinny up to speak. Feeling physically sick, he took the piece of paper out of his pocket and glanced at the sea of faces all staring his way. The church was packed to the brim. 'My brother Roy and cousin Champ were two of the nicest people you could ever wish to meet. Both had a wicked sense of humour, especially Champ, who would have me in hysterics every day with his off-the-cuff one-liners and jokes.'

Knowing he was about to mug himself off by crying, Vinny paused. As he took a deep breath to try and compose himself, he locked eyes with Ahmed and knew he could not continue. Guilt would not allow him to do so. 'I can't do this. I'm sorry,' Vinny said, handing the piece of paper to the vicar.

When her tearful son sat back down, Queenie bravely stood up. 'I would like to say a few words and I don't need no piece of paper.'

She turned to face the mourners. 'Roy and Lenny's passing has left a huge gap in all our lives, but instead of being morbid, I want to share with you some of the good times. Roy was a finicky little sod as a kid, would never eat his vegetables. I tried the old clout-round-the-earhole routine and, when that didn't work, I threatened to put him in the orphanage. Soon ate his greens after that, he did.'

Queenie paused as the mourners chuckled. She then went on to tell other funny stories about her son, before reverting to a serious tone of voice. 'The happiest I had ever seen my Roy was when he met Colleen. Loved the bones of her, he did, and I am so glad they had a beautiful daughter together. In Emily-Mae, part of my Roy will always live on, and that is a great comfort to me. Due to his injuries, my son was not happy in the latter part of his life and I like to think he is in a better place now, God rest his soul.'

'And I hope he's looking after my Lenny for me,' a sobbing Vivian shouted out.

'Of course he is, Vivvy. You can be assured of that. Which brings me to Lenny. Such a wonderful boy, whose smile could light up a room. Never stopped laughing, that lad. I bet he's looking down on me now, begging me to tell some funny stories about him. Well, Champ – as my boys liked to call him – was a brilliant little DJ, but he would drive me and his mother mad at home by continuously playing rock 'n' roll. Thought he was Mr Presley himself, the little toerag did, and I bet as soon as God opens those pearly gates, Lenny's first question to the big man above will be, "Where's Elvis?"'

Aware that all her family were crying yet laughing at the same time, Queenie continued: 'Another of Lenny's bad habits was he used to flop his dingle-dangle out in public. Vivvy used to get so embarrassed and Lenny would look at me with a twinkle in his eye and I knew he only did it to wind his mother up. Used to flash at people he did not like, so if anybody here today had the misfortune of coming face to face with Lenny's dingle-dangle, sorry, but you obviously was not one of my nephew's favourite people.'

Queenie told two more funny stories, then wrapped her speech up by saying, 'Rest in peace, Roy and Lenny. Your family loved you both very much.'

The service came to a close with 'On Mother Kelly's Doorstep' and it was then that Queenie finally broke down. She had tried to be so strong for the sake of her sister and family, but the tears she had been storing seemed to all flow out at once.

Vinny held his mother close to his chest. Her shoulders

were hunched like those of a much older woman, and it was as though she had aged ten years in the past ten days. All he could do was stroke her hair and tell her, 'I know it's terribly sad, Mum, but Roy will be happier in heaven, I know he will.'

Michael was the first to notice the criminal element amongst the mourners. As he left the church, he tapped Vinny on the shoulder. 'Lots of faces here, bruv. I've just spotted the Mitchells, and I'm sure I saw David Fraser as well.'

The Mitchell firm, led by Harry Mitchell, were out of Canning Town. Harry's three sons, Paulie, Ronny and Eddie worked alongside him in the pub protection racket, and over the years they had built up a fearsome reputation in the East End.

David Fraser was not a man to be messed with either. Son of Mad Frankie, who was currently banged up at Her Majesty's pleasure, David came from south of the water. 'That's Sid the Snake who David is talking to. I know him quite well. You go and find the Mitchells, Michael, thank them for coming and invite them to the wake. I'll do the same with David and Sid,' Vinny ordered.

'Vinny, why you faffing about here? We don't want to keep the vicar waiting at the graveside,' Queenie scolded. She had been bowled over by the wonderful flower arrangements Roy and Lenny had received. There had been hundreds of people standing in front of her house and a big crowd outside the club as the undertaker had walked in front of her dearly departed on their final journey.

'You go ahead with Auntie Viv, Mum. Michael and I just need to speak to a few people, then we'll follow.'

'Well, don't be too long. As I told you this morning, I expect this to be the perfect send-off.'

*

The moment the congregation reached the cemetery, Queenie's wish for the perfect funeral was ruined.

It had been decided that Roy and Lenny would be buried side by side in Plaistow – Bow Cemetery having stopped burials a while back, thus scuppering Queenie and Vivian's wish to have their sons buried close to their beloved mother. Among the mourners waiting for the cortege to arrive was Ahmed.

When Vivian spotted him, she stopped dead in her tracks. Ahmed was chatting to a couple of men, casually smoking a cigarette as if he didn't have a care in the world. 'Who invited that murdering bastard? I'll kill him! I will bastard-well kill him,' she screamed as she ran towards him.

'Ruined our lives, you have. Broken our hearts!' Queenie shouted, joining Vivian in throwing punches at the man they blamed for Lenny's death.

Humiliated because the Mitchells were standing nearby, Vinny grabbed hold of his mother and ordered Michael to restrain Vivian. 'Ahmed loved Lenny, and he wanted to say farewell to him. What happened was an accident, Mum.'

'Accident! An accident! I'll give you fucking accident, sticking up for that murdering Turkish cunt,' Queenie yelled, slapping her son repeatedly around his stupid head.

'Ahmed, I think it's best you leave now. This is meant to be a funeral and it's turning into a circus,' Michael said, aware that everybody including the vicar was gawping.

'Let me at him! Let me at the evil murdering shitbag!' Vivian shrieked, desperately trying to shrug off her nephew's grip.

Ahmed held his hands up in surrender. 'I wanted to pay my respects, but I shall leave now. I am sorry if I have upset anybody.'

With Vivian and Queenie still shouting obscenities in the background, Ahmed turned up the collar of his black Crombie coat and slowly walked away, smirking to himself.

Things went from bad to worse as the vicar said a few words after both coffins had been lowered into the ground.

'What's that? What you just thrown in my boy's grave?' Vivian hissed, prodding her sister's arm.

'Zippy the monkey. He loved that toy and you put it out for the dustmen. I thought it should be buried with him, Viv. It was always his comfort thingy.'

'Noooo! You can't bury Zippy! I want him. I want to keep him,' Vivian shrieked. Shoving the vicar out of the way, she literally threw herself on top of her son's coffin.

As every single mourner present stood frozen, open-mouthed, Queenie was the first to react. 'Do something, Vinny. Get her out of that hole,' she screamed.

Dutifully obeying his mother's orders, Vinny wished the hole could be filled with earth with him in it. His brother and nephew's expensive farewell had turned into a joke. One that the East End and criminal fraternity would dine out on for years.

# CHAPTER THREE

Desperate to save face after such a public display in front of the vicar, Queenie made a point of putting on her poshest voice and personally inviting all of the neighbours back to the wake.

'You can count me out, Queen. I'm in no mood to socialize. I just want to be on my own,' Vivian told her sister, clutching Zippy the monkey tightly to her chest.

'Hold that monkey normally please, Viv. People are staring at you. You are coming back to the club. Our neighbours must already reckon you've lost your marbles after the way you threw yourself on top of Lenny's coffin, and if you don't show your face at the wake, they'll think you've lost the plot completely. Mouthy Maureen and Nosy Hilda will be the first to spread such rumours, you mark my words.'

'Like I give a shit what any of the bastards think,' Viv snarled.

'Yes, you do. You're just not thinking straight at the moment. We haven't got to stay at the club long. But we do need to show our faces, especially after today's little fiasco. That's the least we can do for our sons' memory,' insisted Queenie in a tone that brooked no argument.

*

Not wanting the wake to be a sombre affair, Vinny had hired a band for the occasion. Max Bennett was an old timer when it came to the East End pub circuit, and he always encouraged punters – or in today's case, mourners – to stand up and belt out a song or two.

The professional caterers had put on a nice display. As well as the usual buffet food, there was every type of seafood you could imagine, including a dozen big tubs of jellied eels.

'Good idea of yours, getting Max in to sing, Vinny. I can't believe the amount of people that turned up. I expected a big crowd, but not quite this big. The Davisons from Charlton are here, and Freddie the Fox,' Michael informed his brother.

The Davisons were a very big crime family who ran a scrap-metal business in South London as a front for their illegal activities. Freddie the Fox was an ex-bank robber who originated from Whitechapel but had moved to the Costa del Sol after his latest prison sentence had ended. 'I've already spoken to Freddie. Bowled over that he travelled all the way from Spain just for the funeral. I feel such a mug though that I couldn't go through with the speech. And what with Mum and Auntie Viv's performance at the graveside . . .'

Michael put a comforting arm around his brother's shoulders. 'You should be proud of yourself today. I have never seen such a well-organized funeral in my life, and you arranged it all.'

'Did you invite the Mitchells to the wake?'

'Yeah, but they had some important business to attend to, so couldn't make it. Nice of them to attend the funeral, though, eh? Proper respectful people.'

'Old school, Michael. Eddie's the one to look out for in the future. Very charismatic and has a good head on his shoulders, by all accounts. Much more feared than his brothers are, and his reputation is growing by the day.'

'Did they know Roy personally?'

'Only to say hello to. Roy and I bumped into Eddie, Paulie and Ronny in a bar once when you were just a kid. It was around the time we bought this gaff and they wished us good luck with it. Haven't crossed paths with them much since then, but I did see Eddie in a restaurant once when I was with Karen. We exchanged pleasantries and that was it.'

'Well, given the number of faces that turned up today, it just goes to show how highly regarded we are. Nobody is going to give a toss that you didn't give a eulogy, nor will they care what happened at the graveside. Perfect families do not exist, especially in our world, Vinny. Just hold your head high and give yourself a pat on the back for giving Roy and Champ such a great send-off.'

Not for the first time that week, Vinny looked at his brother with renewed admiration. Michael was so much more of a man without that lunatic of a wife around him.

Determined to restore her family's credibility, Queenie Butler plastered on a false smile as she chatted jovially to the neighbours and locals. Truth be known, she did not want to be at the wake any more than Vivian did, but she was determined to act her way through it.

Spotting old Mr Arthur heading her way with his medals pinned proudly on his suit jacket, Queenie ducked out of sight. Listening to that silly old bastard rambling on about the war was the last thing she needed today of all days. Using the well-wishers for cover, she darted back to the table where Vivian was sitting with Joanna.

'Brenda is the bane of my life, honestly. Only caught her necking alcohol! Silly little mare is pregnant again, and if she harms that baby, I will kill her stone dead. Sent her back to mine with the kids. Little Vinny was playing up, and Michael's three were bored.'

When neither Vivian nor Joanna replied, Queenie could not help but lose her cool. 'Say something then, the pair of you, even if it's only "arseholes". Never seen two faces look so much like a wet weekend. Best you snap out of your little sulk, Joanna, else Vinny won't be amused. I know you've got the ike because he told you to sit here while he chats to the men, but men of importance like Vinny always stand with the blokes, love. When they're talking business, they don't want their birds stood by their side, do they? It isn't the done thing.'

'Can somebody get me another sherry? I'm not walking up the bar myself,' Vivian said.

When Joanna leapt up to get it for her, Queenie turned to Vivian. 'Did you see the way Daniel, Adam and Lee greeted Albie at the church?'

'No.'

'All over him like a rash, they were. That is definitely not the first time they have met that old bastard. Michael must have taken them to visit him behind my back. I asked Michael outright, but he reckons the boys were just excited because he'd told them Albie was their granddad. I told him not to insult my intelligence. Do I look like I just got off the banana boat?'

'Is Albie here?'

'No. Went straight home after the funeral with that drippy brother of his. Wouldn't have had the guts to come here after the terrible lie he told. I'm surprised the arsehole even had the front to turn up at the funeral.'

'This is all we fucking need,' Vivian mumbled, as Mr Arthur sat down in Joanna's chair.

'Sorry to bother you, ladies, but I just wanted to pay my

respects to you in person and say how very sorry I am for your loss. I also wanted to tell you—'

Before Mr Arthur had a chance to finish the sentence, Queenie cut him dead. After excelling herself being polite to people who got on her nerves all day, she'd reached the point where she'd had enough. 'If it's about your war escapades, Viv and I really aren't in the mood to listen to such cobblers today.'

Mr Arthur looked hurt. 'I just wanted to tell you about Jeanie Thomas, Queenie. I know you chat to her on her stall sometimes.'

Jeanie Thomas was the mother of Trevor who had run off with Vinny's first love, Yvonne. At the time, Queenie had been that annoyed she had vowed never to speak to the woman again. But Jeanie was such a nice lady, Queenie hadn't been able to stay angry with her for long. What had happened was hardly her fault.

'I've not been down the market lately. Not dead, is she?'

'Jeanie's in a terrible state, Queenie. Her son moved back to the area recently and he's disappeared off the face of the earth. Been missing days now he has, and Jeanie thinks that something terrible has happened to him.'

Vivian, who had kept quiet until now, suddenly piped up: 'Whatever has happened to Jeanie's son cannot be any worse than what happened to mine and Queenie's, can it? Now sod off and leave us alone.'

When Mr Arthur scuttled off like a naughty schoolboy, Queenie turned to Viv. 'I bet Trevor's disappearance has something to do with Vinny. Both he and Michael went on the missing list earlier this week and I had to look after Michael's kids, didn't I? I had no idea Trevor had moved back to the area. Jeanie never mentioned it.'

When Joanna reappeared with two glasses of sherry, Vivian knocked hers back and then stood up. 'It's breaking my heart looking at Lenny's photos on that wall. I need to get out of here.'

'Wait ten minutes and I'll come with you,' Queenie said.

'No. I did what you asked and came back here, now I want you to do as I ask and leave me in peace for the night. I need to be alone to collect my thoughts. I'll see you in the morning.'

Clutching Zippy the monkey in her hand, Vivian left the club. Once outside, she held the toy to her nose. She had always begged Lenny to let her wash it, even scolded him and told him he would catch diseases if he didn't do as she asked, but she was glad now that Lenny had refused, throwing a tantrum every time she asked. The monkey had her son's scent all over it. Closing her eyes, she whispered, 'Not long now, boy, and Mummy will be there to take care of you. You just behave yourself until I arrive.'

Vinny Butler was having a chat with David Fraser when his mother rudely poked him in the arm. 'Me and you need to have a little chat, now!'

Annoyed that she had shown him up yet again, Vinny gave his mother his coldest stare. 'Mum, this is David Fraser. Mad Frankie's son.'

Putting on a completely different tone to the one she had just used, Queenie smiled at the handsome dark-haired chap and held out her right hand. 'Lovely to meet you, David. How is your father?'

'He's doing OK, thanks. Giving the screws the runaround as always. I'll be visiting him again next week.'

'Well, do give him our regards – not just from me but from all of my family.'

'Will do. I have to make a move now, Vinny. I've got to be somewhere. Look after yourself, and tell your brother I said goodbye.'

Vinny shook David's hand, then waited until he walked away before tearing into his mother. 'Do you get off on embarrassing me or something? The Mitchells were stood by the graveside when you and Auntie Viv made a show of me earlier, now you've just spoken to me like I'm a ten-year-old child in front of David Fraser. Cheers for that, Mum. He must think I'm some right mug.'

'I didn't know it was Mad Frankie's son, did I? I didn't even know you knew the Frasers.'

'There's lots of things you don't know about me, Mother. Just try not to make me look a fool in front of people in future, eh? And drop the silly posh voice, it really doesn't suit you.'

Queenie was not one to be told off. 'And would one of those things I don't know about be Trevor Thomas, by any chance? Don't you even think about lying to me, because I knew you and Michael were up to something earlier this week. Never going to be able to look poor Jeanie in the eye again, am I?'

'I have no idea what you're on about, Mum. I haven't seen Trevor since he ran off with that slag, Yvonne.'

'Swear on my life,' Queenie demanded.

Before he could speak, Michael ended the conversation by grabbing Vinny's arm. 'Bobby Jackson's only had the nerve to show up. Shall I throw the cheeky bastard out, or do you want to do the honours?'

Vinny's lip curled into a snarl. He hated Bobby almost as much as he had despised his father. 'Where is he?'

'Stood at the corner of the bar. Christ knows how long he's been here. I reckon some idiot left the main door open and he just wandered in.'

Usually, whenever the club was open Pete and Paul were on the door, but because they were lifelong friends of Roy and extremely fond of Lenny too, Vinny had given them the day off to enjoy a good drink at the wake like everybody else. 'He's overstepped the mark this time, bruv. We can't let this go, we'll be a laughing stock.'

Michael nodded. The whole of Whitechapel was aware of the bad blood between Vinny and Bobby, therefore he'd have to be taught a lesson for taking such a liberty.

'What's going on?' Queenie demanded. She could barely hear herself think over Big Stan's rendition of Johnnie Ray's 'Cry'. Talk about murdering a great song.

'It's nothing to worry about, Mum. Just an uninvited guest, that's all. Go and sit back down with Joanna and keep her company for me. I'll be over with some more drinks in a minute,' Vinny ordered.

Bobby Jackson had been out on one of his little benders. He had celebrated his thirty-fifth birthday the previous day and ended up pulling some bird in the Ilford Palais, so he was still in yesterday's clothes. He'd been on his way home when he had spotted the door of the club open, and unable to resist the lure of free alcohol, Bobby had decided to sneak in. The worst Vinny would do was chuck him out, surely?

A sucker for a pretty face, Bobby was busy chatting up one of the barmaids and did not see Vinny creep up behind him. 'You're not the first to say I look like Les McKeown. I get it all the time, I do,' Bobby chuckled.

'Well, you won't be looking like Les by the time I finish with you – you'll be looking more like a fucking corpse,' Vinny hissed, grabbing Bobby by his long brown hair and dragging him backwards towards the exit.

Having gone to a lot of trouble to model his look on the lead singer of the Bay City Rollers, Bobby was more worried about his appearance than anything else. 'Mind me barnet, will ya? The door was wide open. I didn't gatecrash, honest I didn't.'

Max was singing 'New York, New York', and lots of the mourners were in a circle on the dancefloor doing that stupid dance where you put your arms around one another's shoulders and kick your legs from side to side.

Vinny smiled at Nosy Hilda as he dragged Bobby past her feet. 'Nothing worse than a pisshead who turns up at the wake in jeans, is there? Didn't even have the nous to wear black. I don't know what the world is coming to these days, Hilda. No respect for the dead any more.'

Not one person said a word as Vinny dragged Bobby outside. Nobody followed either. It was none of their business and anybody with even half a brain knew not to interfere.

Joanna Preston was worried. Following Queenie's stare, she had just seen Vinny drag a man out of the club backwards. 'Should we go outside and make sure Vinny is all right, do you think?'

Queenie glared at Joanna. 'Are you tuppence short of a shilling or something? I told you earlier that men like Vinny do not want or appreciate their birds sticking their oar in. How old are you again?'

Joanna's eyes welled up. She was having her worst birthday ever. 'I'm eighteen today, and I was only trying to help.'

Feeling a bit guilty, Queenie softened her tone. She'd had no idea that it was Joanna's eighteenth birthday. Vinny had failed to mention it. 'Sorry if I was a bit abrupt with you, love, but it's only for your own good. Did you notice how all these people inside the club, including myself, ignored Vinny dragging that man outside?'

Joanna nodded.

'Well, that's what you've got to learn to do. Hear no evil, see no evil – you get what I'm saying?'

If there was ever a moment when Joanna wondered if she had bitten off more than she could chew, then that moment was now. Did she actually know Vinny Butler at all?

Down the side of the club was a small alleyway where the bins were kept. 'What you gonna do to me? I've already said I'm sorry, Vinny. I didn't do anything wrong in the club. Please just let me go home.'

'You did do something wrong, Bobby. You disrespected my brother and cousin by turning up at their wake smelling like a brewery and dressed like a cunt. You also disrespected Michael and myself by entering our club,' Vinny said, grabbing an empty vodka bottle out of a nearby bin.

Flinching, Bobby put his hands over his head to protect himself. He already lost a clump of hair, he'd felt it rip out as Vinny dragged him along the floor. The next thing he knew, Vinny smashed the bottle against the wall, yanked Bobby's head upwards by his fringe, then stabbed the jagged edge deep into the left side of his face.

'You bastard! What you done to me?' Bobby yelled as blood began to spurt out of his face at a rapid pace.

'Think yourself fucking lucky I've only scarred you, because I am telling you now, you ever cross my path again, Jackson, I will kill you stone dead.'

# CHAPTER FOUR

Queenie put her coat on over her nightdress. It was the middle of the night, but she had to check on Vivvy. Sleep was out of the question until she'd put her mind at rest.

Vinny had organized a locksmith to mend the lock and remove the chain from Vivian's door, so Queenie was able to let herself in with her own key. She poked her head around Viv's bedroom door and was alarmed to see the bed empty. 'Vivvy, where are you?'

The answer to Queenie's question came when she opened Lenny's bedroom door. Her sister was laid out like a starfish, face down, on the centre of his bed.

'Vivvy? Wake up, sweetheart.'

After a couple of minutes of prodding and poking, Queenie tried to move her sister. It was then she saw the empty tablet container. Panic-stricken, she let out a deafening scream.

Vinny Butler woke up at midday with the headache from hell. The phone had been ringing all morning, but he had felt incapable of lifting his bonce off the pillow.

Picking up an empty glass, he filled it with water and downed it in one. Since Lenny and Roy's death, he had kept his promise to Michael and stayed off the coke. Trouble was, before he had snorted the shit he had been able to hold his drink, but now he couldn't. After cutting Bobby Jackson last night, he had got well and truly hammered.

When the phone rang again, Vinny staggered into the lounge to answer it. 'Slow down, Mum. I can't understand you. What's happened?'

'It's Vivian. She's tried to kill herself.'

Ahmed Zane sat down opposite his cousin in the small restaurant situated just off Tottenham High Road. The establishment had been funded by Ahmed. Burak ran it, and the two men split any profits straight down the middle. 'How's business?' Ahmed asked.

'Good. It's been busy lately. How's that loyal friend of yours? You seen him yet?'

Ahmed told him about Vinny visiting him at home, then filled him in on what had occurred at yesterday's funeral.

'So, what happens now? I am still on good terms with the Finsbury Park lads. Do you want me to sort something?' Burak asked. He was livid at the way Vinny had treated his cousin, especially after the loyalty he and Ahmed had shown him. Burak had got himself involved in three murders on Vinny's behalf in the past: Karen, the mother of his son, Kenny Jackson and Terry Smart had all had their lives ended prematurely thanks to Burak and his Finsbury Park pals helping Vinny out in return for a substantial amount of cash.

Ahmed took a sip of his Scotch and swilled the drink around in his mouth before swallowing it. 'Killing Vinny does not satisfy my lust for revenge. I want to ruin him, take away everything of importance in his life, then watch him suffer.'

'You mean his son? His mother? I can sort that for you.'

Ahmed shook his head. 'We'll let the family live for now. Money, his reputation and his freedom are the other most important things in Vinny's life, and those are the things, if taken away, that will hurt him the most. I plan to strip him of all three.'

'How?'

'Not sure yet, but I will find a way. First though, I must be patient. If things start to go wrong now, Vinny will become suspicious. I need him to relax, assure him that I hold no grudges before I strike. Vinny Butler is a clever man, but he is not as clever as me. He who laughs last, laughs the longest, Burak, and that shall be us.'

Nancy Butler was sitting in silence at the dinner table. Her brother was rambling on about his job again, and even though Nancy was pleased that being a policeman obviously suited Christopher, she found the daily conversation ever so repetitive and tedious.

When Christopher began bragging about receiving praise from his boss yet again, before he could actually recite the conversation word for word, Nancy butted in: 'Isn't it about time you found yourself a girlfriend, Christopher? I think it would be good for you to have something else in your life other than work.'

Mary stopped chewing her food. Nancy and Christopher had always been so close as children, but not any more.

'You've got more front than British Home Stores, Nancy. How dare you comment on my life when you've made such a mess of your own? You should think yourself lucky you have a roof over your head, after the way you've treated us in the past, eh, Dad?'

'Your brother is right, Nancy. He'll have plenty of time to charm the ladies once his probation period has finished. His career should come before anything else, and if he stays focused, he will climb that ladder to the very top,' agreed Donald.

'And when I get to the top, I shall arrest all the scumbags in this world, like your husband and his family,' Christopher added.

Nancy stood up.

'Where are you going, love? Sit back down and eat your dinner,' Mary urged.

'I'm going to ring Michael. We had a heart-to-heart the other day and he told me a few home truths. He said the boys were unsettled and I should be back at home taking care of them. He's right, Mum. My sons need me and I can't stay here for ever.'

'But I thought you'd left Michael for good?' Donald queried.

'I never said that, Dad. All I said was I wanted a break from him to sort my own head and problems out. It isn't Michael's fault that I've suffered from depression. He has always been a good husband. I shall make sure I bring the boys to visit you regularly, if that's OK?'

Donald would have been more inclined to argue with Nancy's decision had it not been for his grandsons. Since meeting Daniel and Adam, Donald had felt so much happier in himself, and he couldn't wait to spend more time with them.

'Once a gangster's moll, always a gangster's moll,' Christopher said cockily.

'Shut up, you,' Mary ordered her son. She then turned to Nancy. 'Go and ring him then, love. You owe it to them boys to make your marriage work, and I'm sure now you're feeling better, it will.'

Queenie Butler sat down next to her sister's bed and squeezed her hand. The quick reaction by medical staff, plus the help of a stomach pump had saved Vivian's life.

'Why isn't she talking to us, Mum?' Brenda asked.

'Because she's ill, that's why. Now, I reckon you should take Tara home, Bren. She's obviously bored and I don't need her whinging around me. I doubt Viv does either. Go on, off you go.'

As Brenda left the small ward, Dr Baker walked in. 'I got here as soon as I could. Sorry to hear about what happened. How is our lovely patient?'

Vinny led the family GP outside and gave him a rundown of his aunt's recent behaviour. He then begged the doctor to prescribe some stronger drugs.

'I'll be honest with you, Vinny, nothing I can prescribe is going to work. Your aunt has suffered a mental breakdown due to grief. She needs professional help of the twenty-four-hour kind.'

'What you trying to say? I ain't having her put in no loony bin, if that's what you mean.'

'A "loony bin", as you so politely put it, is the only place where your aunt is going to get the correct help for her condition. If she returns home in her current mental state, what's to say that she won't make another attempt to take her own life?'

'Me and Mum will look after her.'

'Oh, don't be daft, Vinny. You have a club to run, and if your mother takes on the burden of watching over Viv day and night, then she might end up suffering a breakdown herself. She's grieving too, the poor woman. I'm sorry to be brutal with you, but I insist your aunt be hospitalized. I am very fond of Vivian and I would never forgive myself if I sanctioned her as well enough to go home, then disaster struck. My conscience won't allow it.'

Reluctantly, Vinny agreed with the doctor. His mum wasn't going to be happy, but he would break the news to her gently. Vivian's welfare must come first.

*

Michael put the phone down and walked into the lounge. All three of his sons were giggling away at the *Muppet Show*.

'Look, Daddy, look,' Adam urged, pointing at the TV.

Michael grinned. Lee had settled in exceptionally well and he was thrilled by how close the three boys had become. 'Guess who's coming home tomorrow?'

Daniel shrugged.

'Well, come on, guess,' Michael urged.

'Mummy?' Daniel asked.

'Yep. Are you looking forward to Mummy living with us again?'

When neither Adam nor Lee replied, Daniel thought that it was his duty to do so. He had missed his mum when she had first gone away, but that feeling had now worn off. His mum always seemed to be screaming or crying and he'd come to prefer the house without her. 'Suppose so, Dad.'

Queenie cried when Vinny broke the news to her on the way home. 'I can't have her going to one of them awful places, Vinny. You'll have to step in and stop it. Give you electric shock treatments and all sorts in them shitholes.'

'Mum, I can't stop it. Dr Baker knows what is best, we don't. I know you want to care for Auntie Viv, but she really does need professional help. We have to do whatever it takes to get her better, and if that means her going away for a bit, then so be it. I promise you faithfully, wherever she goes, I will take you to visit her regularly.'

'But what about the neighbours? Them nosy load of bastards will have a field day discussing Viv being carted off to the funny farm. No, Vinny. I'm not letting her go. She'll never live the shame down.'

'Fuck the neighbours! Surely Auntie Viv's health is more important than what they think? Anyway, we don't have to tell them. We can say that she's gone to stay with a friend in the country to recuperate.'

Queenie looked at her son as if he had gone mad. 'But she ain't got no friends. And you know how rumours spread, we'll never be able to keep it quiet . . . unless we just keep it between me, you and Michael. Bren can't be trusted. Got a mouth as big as a shark when she has a drink. The kids can't be told either. Little Vinny is bound to tell Ben Bloggs, and I don't want him telling his whore of a mother or thieving old gran.'

'Calm down, Mum. Nobody will know bar me, you and Michael, I promise.'

Queenie didn't answer. She was too busy staring at the object on her front lawn. 'What's that, Vinny? Is it more flowers?'

Vinny could see better in the dark than his mother and he saw that the flowers were shaped in what looked like a gun. 'Yeah, it's flowers. Somebody must have got the day wrong. You go inside and put the kettle on, Mum. I'll bring these in.'

He went to the arrangement and crouched down, his heart beating faster than its usual pace. The flowers were a mixture of red and white, which his mum hated. She always said it was the sign of blood and bandages and swore it was unlucky. The flowers were made up in the shape of a pistol and Vinny looked at the attached card with trepidation. He was right to be wary. The words read 'YOU ARE NEXT'.

'What you doing out there, Vinny?' Queenie shouted from the house.

Vinny hurriedly stuffed the flowers in the boot of his car, then darted inside the house. 'The flowers aren't for us, Mum. They were delivered to the wrong street. I'm going to drop them off at the right address on the way home.'

'Thank Christ for that! They looked red and white. That's all we need – more bad luck.'

He tried not to let on, but Vinny was feeling physically

sick. Because the flowers had been left on his mother's front lawn it was hard to say whether the message was meant for her or for him. Ahmed popped into his mind, but Vinny quickly dismissed the thought. Even though Ahmed had forgiven him a bit too easily for his liking, he was sure that a stunt like this was not his pal's style. If Ahmed planned to harm him, he certainly wouldn't be issuing any warnings. Perhaps Bobby Jackson had sent them? But Vinny doubted it, given the damage he'd done to Bobby's face and his threat to kill him. Jackson was a mouthy, gutless piece of shit just like his father had been. The only other suspect Vinny could think of offhand was Johnny Preston. The fact he was in prison wouldn't have stopped him asking somebody to send the flowers, especially once he'd found out Joanna was pregnant. Well tomorrow Vinny would visit every florist in the vicinity to try and find out who the culprit was.

'What's the matter with you? Been struck dumb?'

Vinny recovered himself and fished in his pocket. 'No. I have something for you, Mum. You've had so much on your plate, I thought I'd wait until after the funeral to give it to you.' He produced a white envelope and handed it to her.

'Who's it from?'

'It's from Roy, Mum.'

Unaware that he was currently on Vinny Butler's mind, Johnny Preston sat down opposite his ex-wife in the visiting room. Deborah hadn't changed her name after their divorce, which was just as well as Johnny had recently proposed again, and she had accepted. 'How's things, love? Did you hear from Jo?'

Deborah felt sick with worry. Johnny had been adamant that Joanna would ring home on her eighteenth birthday, and he had been right. Now all she had to do was break the awful news to him.

'Well?' Johnny asked, his voice overloaded with impatience.

'Yes, Jo rang me, Johnny. She said she missed us both and wanted to build bridges.'

Johnny grinned. 'Well, that's a start, ain't it? Before you know it, she'll see that no good prick for what he really is, Deb.'

Deborah squeezed the hands of the man she loved so very much. Johnny had once been a South London gangster, was in the know, so would hear the news anyway. Surely, it was kinder and better coming from her? 'John, love . . . Jo's pregnant.'

The breakfast in the Scrubs wasn't the best and Johnny immediately felt his rise to the back of his throat. Moments later, he was violently sick.

Michael Butler was doing his best to tidy up in preparation for Nancy's homecoming when the doorbell rang.

'Dad, it's Uncle Vinny,' Lee shouted out.

'What's up?' Michael asked. It was unusual for Vinny to turn up at his house without prior warning.

Vinny gesticulated for Michael to follow him outside. 'I didn't want to speak on the phone for obvious reasons. But I thought you should know that the van's been found.'

'How do you know?'

'I caught the back end of a news bulletin. We picked a good spot there as the farmer only discovered it yesterday morning. Try not to worry because even if Trevor has been reported missing, no way will the Old Bill be able to confirm it's him after my dentistry work. I used gallons of petrol and all that will be left of the cunt is his ashes and some fragments of bone,' Vinny chuckled.

'It ain't no laughing matter, Vin. Say the Old Bill do come sniffing around?'

'And why would they do that? Nobody bar me or you

knows that we were watching Trevor's movements and there's sod all to link us to East Hanningfield. Stop panicking, for Christ's sake, Michael. As I've said all along, the filth will not be able to identify Trevor, you mark my words.'

When Bobby Jackson strolled into the Blind Beggar, the pub immediately fell silent. Most of the customers had gone to Roy and Lenny's funeral, then the wake afterwards, and the few that had not were well aware of Bobby being dragged out of the club by Vinny. News tended to spread like wildfire in Whitechapel, especially when the Butlers were involved.

'What you lot staring at? Haven't you ever seen stitches before?' Bobby shouted out, before marching over to the corner of the bar where his pal Micky was.

'Jesus, Bob. That's gonna be some scar you're left with there. I heard what happened. Whatever possessed you to set foot inside the Butlers' club?'

'I was pissed and the door was open. Unlike you and most of the mugs round here, I ain't frightened of the Butlers. Fronted Vinny outside, I did. Called him every name under the sun and I told him I knew he'd done my old man in,' Bobby exaggerated.

'How many stitches you had?' Micky shook his head. 'I'm sure you've got a death wish at times, mate.'

'Thirty-odd – and don't you be worrying about me, Mick. I'll strike one day and when I do that cunt Vinny won't know what's hit him. He'll get his comeuppance, you wait and see.'

Queenie waited until Brenda, Tara and Little Vinny had gone to bed before she sat down and opened Roy's letter. She had honestly thought her son had left this world without saying a proper goodbye to her and was so chuffed to discover that he hadn't. Taking a sip of her sherry and a deep breath, Queenie rested her eyes on the page.

Dear Mum

I know if you are reading this letter then my plan and wish to die have been successful. I must explain why I did what I did, and I pray that you will understand.

I could never cope with being confined to a wheelchair from day one, and being paralysed down one side of my body was so awful. Even my face looked terrible where my mouth had dropped and I felt like a freak.

It made me bitter and I know I was nasty to people. Often in the night, I would dream of working at the club and being the man I used to be, then I would wake up and remember that I would never be that man again . . .

Queenie put the letter on the arm of the sofa. Her tears were dripping onto it, and she didn't want it ruined. She wanted to treasure it for ever.

Five minutes and another sherry later, she found the strength to continue reading.

You were so lovely and kind every time you came to see me, Mum, and so was Auntie Viv. You deserved so much better than spending the rest of your lives worrying about and visiting some miserable bastard like me. Colleen and Emily-Mae both deserved more too, which is why I set them free.

I have forgiven Vinny, Mum, as not only do I want to rest in peace, I also know it is what you would have wanted. It was down to his past mistakes that I got shot, but he never pulled the trigger on the gun, so I could never truly hate him. It just used to make me angry when I saw him casually walking towards me in those smart suits, as I so craved to be able to do the same again myself.

Before I end this letter I want to ask a few favours from you. Firstly, I want you to be nice to my dad from now on. I know he was a bastard to you years ago, but he isn't a bad man. I think he just felt very left out because Auntie Viv was always at the house, which is probably why he turned into a drinker and a womanizer.

Secondly, I want you to make sure Emily-Mae gets her inheritance. I still have quite a sum of money in my bank account and I want every penny to go to her when she is sixteen. I know Colleen has a new man now, but that does not alter my wishes. Emily-Mae is my daughter and I want to be the one to support her when she leaves school.

And last but not least, I want you to promise me that after reading this letter you won't be sad any more. You have always been the strong one of the family and they all need you – Vinny, Michael, Brenda, Auntie Viv, and especially Champ and Little Vinny. You must be happy, Mum, please don't cry any more.

Until we meet again,

Your loving son,

Roy xxx

Queenie put the letter down beside her and cried more than she had ever cried before.

# CHAPTER FIVE

## Spring 1977

Hearing the wonderful voice of Barbra Streisand enhance the radio airwaves, Queenie Butler turned up the volume. Chart music had been wonderful back in the fifties and sixties, but apart from the likes of Barbra, Queenie hated it now. The charts were full of disco music, and as for that punk rubbish, she could not even understand what those vagrant-looking creatures were singing.

Queenie sat down on the armchair and sipped her tea. 'Morning, boys,' she said to the photo that now took pride of place on her lounge wall. She didn't have many photos with just Roy and Lenny in them, but this one was a beauty and she'd had it blown up.

The farewell letter Roy had written her had helped Queenie cope with his death. She had always known how unhappy he'd been after the shooting, though she'd never wanted to admit it. The letter had helped her face facts, and if she were honest it was a relief knowing her son wasn't suffering any more. Lenny's death, however, was a different kettle of fish. That boy had died way before his time and, unlike Roy, he had been a happy little soul.

Queenie was amazed Vinny hadn't yet sorted that Turkish bastard out, but her son assured her he planned to and was just biding his time. Queenie would never be able to rest until that day came. An eye for an eye and a tooth for a tooth had always been her motto.

When the phone rang, she answered it and smiled as she heard the sound of her sister's cheery voice. Vivian's recovery had been a long and winding road, but she was more than on the mend now. For the past seven months she'd been residing at Goodmayes Hospital – or West Ham Borough Asylum as it used to be known, which Queenie could never understand as it wasn't even situated in West Ham.

'Not long now, Vivvy. Five days and you'll be back in your own bed,' Queenie reminded her sister. Vivian had her three-monthly review this coming Wednesday, and the doctor had already told Queenie and Vinny that Viv was ready to return home.

'Oh, I can't bloody wait, Queen. Nutty Nora's been at it again. Yesterday she was a bestselling author and today she's a famous film star. Been flouncing around in her nightie this morning quoting lines from *Sunset Boulevard*.'

Queenie chuckled. Now that Viv's humour had returned, the pair of them could share a right old giggle at the expense of some of the other patients.

'How's Bren and the baby doing, Queen? No news on Vinny's little 'un yet, I take it?'

'No, no news. Jo is long overdue now. She has another hospital appointment on Monday and I reckon they'll keep her in and start her off. She can barely move and feels ever so uncomfortable, the poor little cow. Vinny said she's been having trouble sleeping as well. Bren's OK. She came out of hospital yesterday and is going to stay here for a week or two before she goes home. Tommy's a gorgeous baby,

Viv. Big fat cheeks, arms and legs. You wait until you see him. Happy little soul he is, too. Rarely ever cries. Shame the same can't be said about the other one,' Queenie said, referring to her sulky granddaughter.

'Has Bren mentioned Dean lately?' Vivian asked. It had been over seven months now since her niece's husband went out for a newspaper and never returned.

'Not since the birth, but I can tell she's missing him. That's why I suggested she stay here for a while. Not going to be easy for her, bringing two up on her own. If I ever find out where that Dean Smart is, I swear I will pay him a visit and string him up by the bollocks. How a man can walk away and leave his kids is beyond me.'

'Well, my Bill did,' Viv reminded her. 'What time you coming up to see me today? Will you be on your own?'

'Yes. Michael's going to drop me off and Vinny said he'll pick me up. I'll stop at Mum's grave and put some fresh flowers down, then I'll come straight to you. About two-ish, I reckon. I've written out a list of ideas for the street party. We'll go over it together and you can add to it. I want our contribution to be better than anybody else's, Viv. Vinny suggested setting up a music system in the front garden so we can play all the old wartime songs.'

Vivian smiled. She loved a sing-song and a royal celebration. The Queen's Silver Jubilee was just what the doctor had ordered for her imminent homecoming.

Little Vinny Butler was currently in the doghouse. A fortnight ago, he and Ben Bloggs had broken into the general store run by the Indians along the High Street. The robbery had not been successful. An alarm had gone off and, even though the lads had scarpered quickly, the police had caught them hiding in an alleyway shortly afterwards with their hoard of stolen cigarettes.

Queenie Butler had gone apeshit when the police had knocked on her door in the middle of the night. Not only had her grandson lied to her about his whereabouts, he had also robbed a store that she used regularly.

The following morning, Queenie had rung her son to inform him Little Vinny would not be living with her any more. She had also marched the boy round to the Patels' shop to make him apologize in person and offer his services to do any odd jobs on a Saturday for the next year.

'Dad, please can I go out and play? I won't go far and I'll behave myself, I promise,' Little Vinny begged.

'No, son. I have to pop out in a bit and I need you to stay here and look after Jo for me. The baby might come anytime now, and Jo can't be left alone.'

'But I don't want to stay 'ere with Jo, and I'm sick of hearing about the baby. I don't like living here. I want to live with Nan again.'

'Well, you should have thought of that before you robbed Mr Patel's shop. Your nan won't have you back, so best you get used to living here and start treating Jo with a bit more respect. Fucking rude you were earlier when she made you that sandwich. I want you to apologize to her.'

Unable to control his temper, Little Vinny punched the wall. He and his dad used to be so close once upon a time. Not any more though, and Little Vinny rued the day his dad had met Joanna Preston. In fact, he wished she would die.

Ahmed Zane met his cousin at their restaurant in Tottenham. Being Sunday lunchtime, the gaff was packed, so Ahmed followed Burak into the small office.

'What's that?' Ahmed asked, clocking an unlabelled bottle.

'Raki. I found us a new cheap supplier. Taste it.' Burak

poured a glass and handed it to him. 'So, how's it going with Vinny?'

'OK. Since I started making more of an effort to spend time with him, he's more like his old self. He still won't touch any cocaine though, which is a damn shame. He was a lunatic on that stuff and would have had a really bad habit by now. It would have been so much easier to pull the wool over his eyes if he was permanently high like in the old days.'

'Why don't you try snorting in front of him?' Burak suggested. 'Lay a big mound out so he can't help but be tempted. Once an addict, always an addict.'

'I've already tried that. Reckons he won't touch it because he promised his dead brother he wouldn't. He's acting all saintly at the moment and doesn't even want to visit the whorehouses. He says it isn't right because he has a new baby due any day.'

'And what about his surprise gifts? Has he received any more of those?'

Ahmed shook his head. Vinny had not told him about the pistol-shaped flower arrangement until two weeks after the event. That was how Ahmed knew that his pal was wary of him now. Had the incident happened before the car crash, Vinny would have told him immediately.

The flowers had sod all to do with Ahmed, which meant somebody other than himself obviously had it in for Vinny. His car had recently been vandalized too, and the front of his club daubed with threatening and obscene graffiti. 'I think it is time to put our real plan into action. As soon as the baby is born, I will make a fuss of the child. Then, we will start stitching its cunt of a father up good and proper. Those who sin must pay for their wrongdoings, Burak.'

*

'Get away from us. Go on, go away,' Vivian ordered. Mad Malcolm had a habit of staring at her and Queenie while trying to listen in on their conversations.

'Gives me the fucking willies, he does,' Queenie said when Malcolm slunk away like a scolded puppy.

Vivian laughed. She still missed her Lenny like mad, always would, but it was so nice to be able to smile and feel normal again. Some parts of the past seven months were a complete blank to Viv, especially around the time she tried to kill herself and first arrived at Goodmayes. There was no point crying over spilt milk, but Viv could never forgive herself for certain things. How could she have put Queenie through her attempted suicide and chucked all Lenny's things away? She must have been really ill to do either.

'I've been thinking, Queen. Can we go down to Kings on the first weekend I'm out? I would love a game of bingo and an hour or two in the amusements. I wonder if that handsome Mike is still running the arcade?'

Queenie squeezed her sister's hands. Vinny had been trying to entice her down to Eastbourne ever since the holiday park reopened in April, but Queenie hadn't been able to face it. She and Vivvy had loved that place and, without her sister by her side, it just didn't feel right. 'Oh, Viv, of course we can. I am so glad to have you back. My life was empty when you were ill.'

Vivian's eyes filled up with tears. 'And I'm sorry for what I put you through. I love you, Queen, and once I get out of this funny farm I intend to live the rest of my life to the full. I know we've both lost sons, but your Roy and my Lenny wouldn't want us moping around.'

Queenie smiled. 'You bet they wouldn't.'

Michael Butler picked up the newspaper and immediately threw it back on the kitchen top. 'BURNED ALIVE' was the front-page headline and Michael could not stomach such stories any more.

Trevor Thomas's death still played on Michael's mind. Three days after his remains were found, the police had turned up at the club asking questions. Trevor had been identified by breaks he'd suffered in his collarbone and left leg in the past. He'd also had a plate and screws put in his knee, which made him even more identifiable.

Vinny had been as cool as a cucumber when the Old Bill showed up, insisting that he had not seen Trevor since he ran off with Yvonne. 'No disrespect, officer, but I was no more than a child when Trevor ran off with my bird. I am now a man in a stable relationship with my second kid on the way. Do you honestly think I would still be bothered about some teenage love affair that happened all those years ago?'

Michael had been anything but cool, but had backed up the alibi that he and Vinny had concocted. Forensics had managed to narrow down the day the fire had been started on, and the guvnor of the Blind Beggar had verified that Vinny and Michael had been in the pub that particular evening.

Thankfully, the police hadn't returned. Michael had asked Vinny not to talk about Trevor's death any more. He did not admit to his brother that he kept having reoccurring nightmares about it. What would be the point? Vinny would only have taken the piss out of him.

Daniel and Adam running into the kitchen snapped Michael out of his daydream. 'We're going now, Dad,' Daniel said, hugging his father's leg.

Michael Butler ruffled his sons' hair and kissed his wife goodbye. Nancy was spending the night at her parents' house with Daniel and Adam, which she now did a couple of times a month. Michael was quite happy with the set-up, as it gave him and Nancy a break from one another.

Life had been OK since Nancy came back home, but it hadn't exactly been a bed of roses. His wife was very needy and it grated on Michael that when he wasn't around to give her a helping hand she struggled with the basics of motherhood. She also treated Lee differently to her own sons, and that pissed Michael off immensely. In his eyes, if Nancy was a decent human being she would include Lee in the trips to her parents and the days out they had. She knew Lee had no grandparents on his mother's side.

'I'm looking forward to seeing the dog, Dad, but I am gonna miss my brothers,' Lee told his father on the journey to his aunt's house.

'I know you will, boy.' Lee had an aunt in Bow whom he stayed with whenever Daniel and Adam went to their grandparents, and he adored her old bull terrier, Spike.

After Michael had dropped Lee off, he got back in the car and grinned. His best pal Kevin was usually under the thumb but his wife was away visiting relatives, so today he and Kev were going out on a good old-fashioned pub crawl. Letting his hair down was just what Michael needed.

Vinny Butler was feeling anxious. He had never found out who had sent those flowers, and knowing somebody had it in for you, but not knowing who that person was, was driving him insane. He had always been paranoid when it came to his safety and that of his family, and now he felt as though he was constantly looking over his shoulder. He had even purchased two guns recently. One was hidden at the club and the other at home, just to be on the safe side.

Vinny had completely ruled Ahmed out of his list of suspects now. Things had been a bit stilted between the two of them for a month or so after the accident, but they had since got their friendship back on track. The drug business was becoming more and more profitable by the day, and Vinny knew Ahmed well enough to know vandalizing cars and daubing graffiti was not his pal's style. Like himself, Ahmed had class, and would never resort to something so petty.

Vinny stared at the photo of himself, Roy and Michael that sat proudly on his office wall. It had been taken years ago, long before Roy's accident. 'If I were a betting man, Roy, my money would be on either Bobby Jackson or Johnny Preston pulling these stunts. What do you reckon, eh, bruv?'

Averting his focus from his unknown stalker, Vinny thought about Joanna. He had only got her up the spout to piss her father off and pay him back for shooting Roy, yet he was now really looking forward to the birth of his second child. He had dreaded the birth of Little Vinny when Karen was pregnant, but he loved being a dad and was hoping for a daughter this time around. Girls were more of a worry, but far less trouble than boys, he imagined.

Michael Butler was having a whale of a time. He was in the Carpenter's Arms, and it had been a long time since he had really let his hair down.

'Slow down a bit, mate. You're drinking for England,' Kevin said.

'You've been sinking 'em like there's no tomorrow as well. Talk about pot calling kettle,' Michael retorted.

'Are you insinuating I is black?' Kevin joked.

Michael burst out laughing. Kev was mixed race and they went back years. When they were in their early teens there had been far fewer black faces in the East End, and whenever the pair of them came across some bigot, Kev would always lay on a thick Jamaican accent just for fun. His mum's family were white and he barely knew his father, so Michael could never work out how he managed to do the accent so well.

'What's up? Who you looking at?' Kevin asked.

Unable to tear his eyes away from the girl, Michael continued to stare at her. She was tall, dark-skinned, with long glossy hair and the sexiest body that Michael had ever seen. She was wearing high-heeled boots, a black leather jacket that had tassels swinging from the sleeves, and faded jeans.

Kevin changed seats and chuckled. 'Put your tongue away, mate, you're a married man now, remember?'

With his handsome face, cheeky grin and legendary chat-up lines, Michael had been a real player in his heyday. He had slept with so many girls his mum and aunt nick-named him Alfie after the womanizing rogue played by Michael Caine in the film. Meeting Nancy had changed all that, but when the girl locked eyes with him, Michael could only think of one thing.

Fucking her senseless.

Vinny Butler was dumbfounded as he listened to what Paul had to say. 'You sure it was her?'

When the doorman said he was positive, Vinny thanked him for the information, replaced the receiver, then grabbed his car keys. Seeing was believing and he needed to see the slag with his own eyes.

Joanna Preston clutched hold of the sink for support as the searing pain shot through her body again. Where was Vinny? He should have been home ages ago.

Feeling a strange sensation, she started to panic. There was water gushing out of her and it had created a puddle by her feet. Overcome by another jolt of pain, Joanna sank to her knees. 'Vinny, Vinny. I need you to ring the club, and find out where your dad is. I think the baby's coming,' she screamed out.

Little Vinny was sitting on his bed listening to this week's chart countdown. Debating whether to respond to Joanna's desperate cries for help, he quickly decided against it. Instead, he turned the volume up on his radio and sang along with Joe Tex. 'Ain't Gonna Bump No More (With No Big Fat Woman)' was such a catchy tune.

Vinny Butler's heart was beating like a drum when he pulled up outside the Three Travellers pub in Dagenham. He hated the bitch with a passion, but felt anxious and sick to the stomach at the thought of seeing her again.

With her lithe body, long flowing hair, infectious laugh and perfect white teeth, Vinny Butler had fallen in love with Yvonne Summers on sight as a lad. She was the most beautiful girl he had ever seen, yet the slut had used him and then tortured his mind.

His mouth bone-dry, Vinny approached the pub window. He peered through and could barely believe his eyes. 'No longer petite' had been Paul's assessment of her. Well, that was the understatement of the century. Yvonne Summers was that fat she resembled a whale that had been washed up on the beach.

In complete shock, Vinny stood rooted to the spot. He could not believe this was the same woman whose memory had taunted him for so long, but it was. The fat cow looked like she had fallen out the ugly tree and hit every fucking branch on the way down.

Hearing voices behind him, Vinny turned around. There were two teenage girls staring at him and giggling. 'You looking for someone?' one asked.

'Yeah, my mate. I don't think he is in there though,' Vinny replied.

'Well, we'll keep you company, won't we, Barb?' the blonde one said, nudging her pal.

'Not 'arf! We don't often get talent like you in the Travellers, do we, Wendy?' the ginger girl replied, smiling at Vinny.

Vinny grinned falsely, and handed the girls a tenner just to get rid of them. 'Go in the pub and order yourselves a drink, ladies. Get me half of lager – any kind will do. I'll be in in a couple of minutes.'

When the girls disappeared, Vinny looked through the window once again. Seeing Yvonne laughing and joking with a customer, Vinny felt the urge to stroll inside and wipe the smile off the whore's face by smashing her big fat head against the bar, but he managed to resist. No way was that monster worth getting nicked over, not on your nelly.

# CHAPTER SIX

Joanna Preston forgot all about the fright and pain she had endured when her baby was placed in her arms for the first time. 'Hello, I'm your mummy,' she said, crying tears of pure joy while grinning broadly.

Outside in the corridor, Vinny was experiencing a mixture of fury, guilt and panic. He was furious with Little Vinny for not keeping an eye on Joanna like he'd asked him to, and felt as guilty as hell because instead of heading straight home as promised he'd chosen to track down Yvonne Summers. And he was panicking because Joanna had been screaming blue murder and now it had all gone quiet. If something was wrong with his kid, he would never forgive himself, he knew that much.

When the door of the delivery room opened, he felt his heart race even more. 'What's going on? Everything's OK, isn't it?'

The old Jamaican midwife chuckled. 'Listen for yourself. Got better lungs than me, that child. You can go in and say hello now.'

Vinny had never been a man to show much emotion but the moment he laid eyes on his daughter, the tears poured down his cheeks. With her mop of curly blonde hair, she looked nothing like him. And she wasn't ugly, the way Little Vinny had been when he was born. She was absolutely perfect.

'Do you want to hold her? She's gorgeous, isn't she?' Joanna gushed. She had already forgiven Vinny for not being at home when she went into labour. At the time, she'd been petrified, but somehow she managed to crawl to the phone, ring the emergency services herself and open the front door for them. Vinny had arrived home amidst the mayhem, and she knew from his face he was genuinely sorry.

Vinny kissed Joanna on the forehead, then lifted the baby out of her arms and cradled her in his. 'I am so sorry I wasn't there when your mum needed me earlier, but I promise you this, baby girl, I will never let you down again, not ever.'

Queenie and Vivian had had a wonderful afternoon together. It had been just like old times. They had shed a few tears over their wonderful sons, but then they'd cried with laughter as they relived some of their antics.

'Do you remember the time Lenny started undoing his trousers when he saw Mad Freda coming and she ran off screaming blue murder? She was threatening to tell the police he was a flasher, if I remember rightly.'

Queenie chuckled. 'He was only a nipper at the time. I'm sure he only did it because he knew we couldn't stand her. Proper little character that boy was.'

Seeing her sister close to tears again, Queenie hugged her. 'Now let's not get down in the dumps. We've had a great day and we've got the Jubilee to look forward to. We'll show them neighbours of ours how to party, Viv. And don't forget, this time next weekend we'll be down at Kings. You don't want to start getting upset now in case they keep you in this funny farm. Who will I play bingo with then, eh?'

'I'm fine, Queen. I just have my moments and I dare say I always will.'

Pleased her sister was OK, Queenie glanced at her watch. 'My Vinny was meant to pick me up over an hour ago. I hope everything's all right. It's not like him to be this late, Viv.'

'Perhaps Jo's gone into labour. Ring him at home, Queen.'

Before Queenie had a chance to move, a nurse approached her. 'Your Vinny is on the phone, Queenie. He wants to speak to you.'

Queenie's heart leapt in her chest as she followed the nurse. Since losing Roy and Lenny, she dreaded her own phone ringing in case it was more bad news, let alone being summoned to the one in Goodmayes Hospital. Breathlessly she took the receiver and asked, 'What's up, boy?'

When her son began to gabble excitedly about the baby and how beautiful she was, Queenie couldn't wipe the grin off her face. After all the trauma and bad luck her family had suffered, life was looking decidedly rosy for them again.

Albie Butler rarely ventured out to restaurants. It seemed pointless, seeing as his Dorothy was such a good cook. But today he was sitting in a carvery in Ipswich town centre with Bert and Dorothy, celebrating Bert's birthday.

'Nice bit of lamb, eh, Dorothy? What's the beef like?' Bert asked his brother.

'Very tender,' Albie replied, before ramming another forkful in his mouth. A moment later he froze at the sound of a familiar voice coming from behind him, then spat his beef back onto his plate.

'You OK? Did it go down the wrong hole?' Bert asked, slapping Albie on the back to stop him from choking.

Trying desperately to stop his coughing fit as the last thing he wanted was to draw attention to himself, Albie hissed at Bert to leave him alone and act normal. Hearing her distinctive squeaky voice again, Albie sank his pint. The last time he had seen Judy Preston was in 1965 when she had turned up to visit him in hospital at the same time as Queenie. All hell had broken loose when Queenie had realized that Judy was his pregnant bit on the side, and his indiscretion had ended his marriage and seen him kicked out of his own home.

Vinny and Roy had paid Judy a threatening visit and ordered her to abort his child, then shortly afterwards Judy had done a runner. Albie had been told by somebody a few years back that Judy now lived in Ipswich, but he hadn't quite believed it until this moment.

'What's the matter, Albie? You look ever so pale,' Dorothy remarked.

When he heard a child refer to Judy as Mum, Albie knew he had to get out of the restaurant. She might not recognize the back of him, but if she went to the toilet, she would be bound to spot him. The thought of coming face to face with her or a child he didn't know had existed was making Albie feel nauseous. 'I need some fresh air, Dorothy. Please don't say my name out loud or make a scene as there is somebody on the table behind who I really don't want to see. You and Bert finish your meals and I'll wait for you in the car park.'

'Whatever is the matter?' Bert asked.

'Shush,' Albie hissed. He then darted out of the restaurant as fast as his trembling legs would carry him.

Michael and Kevin had planned to have a curry in Brick Lane after their drinking session, but those plans were scuppered when Michael returned from talking to the mystery dark-haired woman and informed Kev that he had invited her and her friend to join them.

Kevin was extremely happily married. His wife and son meant the world to him and no way was he sitting in some restaurant with two birds. 'Sorry, mate, but you can count me out. My Jemima would chop my bollocks off if I was spotted somewhere with those two. I doubt your Nancy would be too happy either.'

'Where's the harm in going for a meal? And if someone clocks us, I'll just say it's two of the barmaids from the club, or an old family friend.'

Seeing Michael and the dark-haired girl share an intimate glance, Kevin gave his pal a talking to. 'If you go for that meal with her, you'll end up fucking her, mate – then how you gonna face Nancy in the cold light of day? Think of them sons of yours. Is it worth losing them because you fancy some fresh pussy?'

'You and Jemima might still be love's young dream, but Nancy and I haven't been that for a while, Kev. You don't know what I've had to put up with, what with her mood swings and depression. I can't even remember the last time we had sex. Weeks ago it must have been. Every time I try it on with her she reckons she's too tired or she's worried about the boys getting wind that we're at it. I'm only twenty-seven, not seventy, and I still have fucking needs.'

Not wanting to get into an argument, Kevin asked Michael what he had said to the girls.

'I just asked the usual and offered them a drink. The dark one's name is Bella, the blonde one's Sam. They live in Chelsea and are both models, so they say. Bella's twenty-one and from Italy. Sam is nineteen and from Liverpool. Please, just come for the meal, Kev? We'll share a cab home afterwards, just me and you, I promise.'

Kev downed the rest of his lager and stood up. 'I'm

shooting off, mate. Enjoy your meal, and don't do anything you might regret tomorrow. If I was you, I'd concentrate on getting your marriage back on track rather than shagging young birds. Ever heard of the frying pan and the fire?'

Following Vinny's instructions, Queenie got a cab from Goodmayes, picked Little Vinny up on the way, then headed straight to the hospital. 'My oh my, she's an absolute angel. Isn't she big! How much did she weigh?' Queenie asked, as she peered inside the cot.

'She was ten pound. No wonder I had a struggle getting her out,' Joanna replied.

'Well, you did a brilliant job, darling. Reminds me of Emily-Mae with those blonde curls. I can't wait for Vivvy to see her. We'll babysit whenever yous two fancy a day or night out,' Queenie volunteered.

'Don't you want to see your little sister then?' Vinny asked his sullen-faced son, who was loitering at the end of the bed. Vinny was absolutely mesmerized by his new addition, could not believe she already had the power to melt his heart like never before.

'There ain't no room, is there?' Little Vinny snapped. His dad was sitting next to the cot, and his nan was standing in front of it, blocking his view.

Vinny locked eyes with his offspring. 'Oh, and don't forget to apologize to Jo for sodding off upstairs and leaving her in the lurch earlier. Bang out of order you was, boy.'

'What happened?' Queenie asked, unable to tear her eyes away from her beautiful granddaughter.

Joanna knew that Little Vinny didn't like her and although she would never admit it to Vinny, the feeling was mutual. However, now Little Vinny had moved in with them, she had no option but to try to get along with him, so did her best to smooth over the situation. 'It was nothing, Queenie, honest. Anyway, Little Vinny was only in his bedroom playing music. I was in that much pain, I couldn't scream as loud as usual, so it's not his fault,' she lied. She had in fact screamed blue murder and was sure Little Vinny had turned his music up to blank out her cries for help on purpose.

Little Vinny smirked. 'See? It weren't my fault. If anyone's to blame, it's you. You shouldn't have gone out, Dad.'

As Vinny leapt up to clout his belligerent son, Queenie grabbed his arm. 'Don't hit him. He's bound to be a bit green, after all he's been the only child for years. You were the same when I had Roy.'

'I'll give him fucking green, he'll be black and blue if he carries on,' Vinny mumbled. He had no idea what was wrong with his son lately, but he was becoming a real pain in the arse. He wasn't even eleven yet, but the little bastard already had the attitude and lip of a cocky eighteen-year-old.

'Ooh, she's waking up. What you gonna call her? Best you think of a name soon,' Queenie remarked.

Vinny smiled at Joanna. They had been discussing names earlier and he was so pleased that she had finally given in to his wish. He knew how much this would mean to his beloved mother.

'We've chosen Molly, Mum.'

Queenie's eyes filled up with tears. Her wonderful mum had been called Molly. 'Sod you, you've started me off now. What a lovely gesture. Wait till I tell Vivvy, she'll be made up.'

Little Vinny giggled. 'Molly is an old pensioner's name.'

It was Queenie's turn to glare at the child. Looks-wise, Little Vinny might be the spitting image of his dad at that age, but her boy had been a saint in comparison to this bolshy little so-and-so. 'No, it's not. It's a lovely name and my mum was called Molly. Now shut that trap of yours and come and meet your little sister.'

When his nan lifted Molly out of the cot, Little Vinny

decided to play along with the happy family theme. He was sick of being grounded and desperate to change that. 'Hello, I'm your big bruvver,' he said, grinning at the baby and allowing her to clasp one of his fingers in her chubby hand.

'Aw, look, they've bonded already,' Queenie remarked.

Vinny smiled at the touching scene. As her big brother, it would be Little Vinny's duty to protect Molly through life and look out for her like he had with Brenda. 'Sit on the chair and you can hold her properly.'

Little Vinny did as he was told, then inwardly squirmed as the baby was placed in his arms. Apart from wishing she had never been conceived, he felt nothing for his sister whatsoever.

Albie Butler had been honest about his past from day one with Dorothy, so she had known about his affair with Judy Preston and why he had felt the need to leave the restaurant. He had also told Bert all about Judy when he had first moved to Ipswich. 'I'm so sorry I spoilt the day. I really am,' Albie slurred yet again.

Dorothy hated seeing Albie drunk. He had a tendency to repeat himself constantly, but she could understand his need for a good drink today. He'd had a nasty shock. 'I'm going to leave you boys to it. I want to finish my book. Don't drink too much more tonight, Albie. You fell down the stairs last time you got very drunk and you know how I worry about you.'

'I won't, darling. Night night, love you.'

When Dorothy left the room, Bert turned to his brother. 'I didn't want to say anything in front of Dorothy, but I guessed who it was and swapped seats after you left the restaurant so I could do a bit of detective work. I take it Judy was the one with the squeaky voice?'

Albie nodded.

'Well, she had two kids with her. A boy about sixteen and a girl about seven. How old would your kid be now if she'd had it?'

Counting the years with his fingers, Albie felt relief wash over him. 'Would have been about eleven now. I reckon the boy you saw was her son Mark. He was about three when I was with her, and the girl sounds far too young to be mine. You sure she weren't older than seven?'

'Eight tops, but she certainly weren't bleedin' eleven, Albie. I reckon you're in the clear, mate. Perhaps she did a runner, aborted your kid and made a fresh start?'

Albie grinned and cracked open another can. It suited him to believe that Judy had aborted his child. It made his thoughts far less complicated. Most men in his position would have turned around and confronted Judy. Not Albie though. He'd had enough drama in the past to last him a lifetime, and was happy to just let sleeping dogs lie.

Michael Butler followed Bella into her Chelsea apartment and was immediately taken aback by its opulence. He had thought she was joking when she pointed at the brand-new Porsche in the car park and said it was hers. 'Jesus, babe, this is some gaff. How long you lived here?'

'Two years. What would you prefer – red or white wine?'

'Whatever you're having,' Michael replied, looking around in awe. The kitchen and bathroom were both state-of-the-art and knocked spots off his own. The lounge was absolutely striking. It had a multi-coloured carpet, beige being the base colour, with red, blue and green circles all over. The sofas were bright red leather, and in two corners of the room stood life-size carved wooden figurines of a Romany-looking naked man and woman.

Michael opened the sliding glass door and walked out onto the balcony. The view of London was incredible this time of night. The lights of the greatest city on earth literally lit up the sky.

'Do you want to drink your wine out there?' Bella asked.

'No, I'm coming in now,' Michael replied, shutting the glass door. He sat down on the sofa. 'So, how comes if you were brought up in Italy you speak such good English? Do your parents both speak English?'

'Yes, but not in the home. My dad hired a private tutor to teach me from very young. He said it was important I learn the language. I can speak Spanish too. I must tell you something, Michael.'

'What?'

'Even though your eyes are green and your hair is darker, you really remind me of David Essex.'

Michael laughed. 'But he's got a bird's hairstyle.'

'You look like he did in *That'll Be the Day* and *Stardust*, when his hair was shorter. I loved him in those films.'

Michael took a sip of his wine and stared at Bella. He wasn't just mesmerized by her beauty; it was so much more than that. She was unlike any girl he had ever met in his life and he couldn't help but be impressed by her and her obvious wealth and lifestyle. 'So, what type of modelling do you do then?'

'I get asked to do all sorts of shoots. I've done catwalk too. I might get into acting soon. I've just hired myself a new agent.'

'Do you have to strip off and all that?'

Bella chuckled. 'I do glamour shots, but never nude. My dad is well-respected back in Italy and he would kill me if I ever went overboard. I show plenty of cleavage, but won't go topless. My dad is a proud man and I respect his wishes.'

'Well, you must be doing something right to be renting a gaff like this,' Michael replied.

'I do not rent this apartment, Michael. I own it.'

Apart from when he had lost his virginity at a very young age, Michael couldn't remember feeling so nervous around a female before. Bella was having a strange effect on him and he wanted to fuck her more than he had ever wanted to fuck Nancy or any other bird he'd known. He could tell she wanted him, but he had to be straight with her first. 'Look, there's something I need to tell you. I'm married, Bella.'

'So? I wasn't intending on proposing to you, Michael. I just want to make love with you. Let's fuck, shall we?'

Feeling his body shake with pure lust, Michael stood up and grabbed Bella by the hand. 'Where's the bedroom?'

Ignoring the question, Bella sank to her knees and undid the zip on his trousers.

Michael thought he had died and gone to heaven when she began expertly sucking his penis. No bird had ever been this forward with him in the past and it was such a turn-on, he was sure his erection was bigger than usual and his cock about to burst.

Grabbing Bella's head to stop himself from coming too soon, Michael stared at her as she let go of his manhood. Her eyes were a mesmerizingly pale blue. 'Take your clothes off,' he ordered, his voice husky with lust.

Bella stood up, pouted seductively and took her clothes off in a slow, tantalizing manner.

Transfixed by her naked beauty, Michael forgot all about his wife and kids as he ripped his own clothes off then rammed himself inside Bella as hard as he could. What followed was the most mind-blowing sexual experience of Michael Butler's entire life.

# CHAPTER SEVEN

Michael Butler poured himself a large Scotch and settled into one of the new sofas. The club had recently been refurbished. Gone was the old burgundy leather furniture that Vinny and Roy had originally bought in 1965. That had now been replaced with opulent green leather sofas and chairs. The walls were now covered in new orange-based patterned wallpaper, and Lenny's old DJ console had made way for a performance area to accommodate the live bands and singers they hired these days. The DJ equipment had just been a constant reminder to both Michael and Vinny that Champ was no longer with them, so they had made a joint decision to get rid of it.

Rubbing his tired eyes, Michael leaned back and stared at the ceiling. Guilt was eating away at him and he could barely look Nancy in the eye any more. As for Bella, he could not stop thinking about her. He had resisted the urge to contact her again, but that did not stop him yearning for her.

'Whatever is wrong with you? You look like a tramp and you've had a face like a slapped arse for days. You ain't still fretting we're gonna get banged up for Trevor's murder, are you? Only that's chip-wrapping now, that is,'

Vinny said. This was his first full day back at the club since Molly had been born and it had been a real wrench for him to leave her.

Michael sat up and put his unshaven face in his hands. Knowing his pal would disapprove, he had not felt able to confide in Kevin and he needed to tell somebody. 'I've done something stupid, bruv.'

'What?'

'I stayed round some bird's house last Sunday and I can't get her out of my mind.'

Vinny grabbed a chair and sat on it the wrong way round so he could face his brother. He had always hated Nancy, so this was welcome news to him. 'Well, well, well. Alfie strikes again! Don't feel guilty, bruv, not after the shit you've had to put up with. Been a crap mother and wife, has Nancy, and I just don't fall for all that depression bollocks. Auntie Viv's been mentally ill, the real deal – Nancy's only playing you. So, who is this bird then? Where did you meet her?'

Michael explained about his day out with Kev and where he'd met Bella. 'She's really beautiful, Vin, and stinking rich. I've never met a bird that could mesmerize me like she did. I stayed the night at hers and, even though I felt as guilty as hell in the morning, I had to have her again. The sex was incredible, it really was.'

'Well, if I was you I'd get straight on that blower and call her. Birds like that don't come along too often. I'll always cover for you here if you want to get your nuts in.'

'But what about Nancy?'

'What about her?' Vinny shrugged. 'This is the same Nancy that can't be bothered with or accept your eldest son, isn't it? I rest my case.'

Johnny Preston was sitting in the visiting room opposite his ex-wife, who was now his fiancée again. She had just informed him that Joanna had given birth to a baby girl and instead of going ballistic, as he would have done in the past, Johnny was calm and deep in thought.

'Well, say something then, Johnny. You're making me feel uneasy,' Deborah urged. She couldn't shake off the memory of what had happened when he found out Joanna and Vinny were a couple. Such was his pain, Johnny had tried heroin for the very first time, taking an overdose which had very nearly resulted in Deborah losing the man she loved.

'How did Joanna sound on the phone? Did you speak to her for long?' Johnny asked.

'We chatted for about five minutes. She seemed happy enough in herself and spoke constantly about the baby. She's called her Molly and said she weighed ten pound. Obviously, Jo asked about you. She also said she'd love me to meet the baby. I refused, of course. My loyalties will always lie with you, Johnny, and I want nothing to do with that bastard Vinny whatsoever.'

Squeezing Deborah's hands, Johnny forced a smile. He had done a lot of thinking while waiting to be told his grandchild had arrived and now he had come to a decision. The thought of Vinny Butler being anywhere near his beautiful daughter still made Johnny feel physically sick, but there was sod all he could do about it so long as he was stuck inside. He didn't have that many links to the underworld and there were only two guys he'd have trusted enough to ask for help, but both were unfortunately dead now. 'I want you to do something for me, Deb. I want you to make things right with Jo and visit her regularly.'

'What! Are you mad? I can't sit there playing happy families, Johnny. He makes my skin crawl.'

'He makes mine crawl too, but this isn't about Vinny, it's about making sure our daughter is OK. It will drive me bonkers trying to get through the rest of my sentence not knowing how Jo is coping with that bastard and a kiddie. I'm just relieved she had a girl and not a boy. At least it won't turn out like him. Please say you'll do this for me, Deb. That girl will need you, you can bet your life on that.'

Deborah reluctantly nodded. She was still angry with Joanna, but all the same she missed her, and if it put Johnny's mind at rest, it was the least she could do.

Johnny grinned. 'That's my girl.'

Ahmed Zane sat down opposite his cousin in their restaurant. He had a severe stiff neck today, a regular occurrence since the accident, but he knew he had been lucky over all.

'Is your neck playing you up again?' Burak asked.

'Yes, but it's nothing that tucking up Vinny won't cure, which is the reason for my visit today. I have set the ball rolling already. Hakan and Bora Koç are coming to London to play our two Mr Bigs. They are perfect for the role, especially Hakan. I have agreed to pay them ten grand each for their trouble, and they will also get a two-week holiday, no expense spared. What do you think?'

Burak grinned. Hakan and Bora were old associates of his and Ahmed's from Istanbul and were more than capable of pulling the wool over Vinny Butler's eyes. 'When will they arrive?'

'I haven't booked their flights yet. We need to make sure Vinny falls for my lies first. I'm sure he will though. And seeing as he hasn't any contacts himself, he has no option but to trust me,' Ahmed replied. Vinny had never met his supplier. The guy was Turkish and would only ever deal with his own kind. He didn't trust the English.

'When will you tell Vinny?'

'This afternoon. I have a carload of presents for his baby and I am meeting him at his house at four.'

Chuckling, Burak poured them both a drink. He chinked glasses with his cousin. 'Let payback begin.'

Nancy Butler eyed her husband suspiciously. He had been acting strange all week and had just handed her a big bouquet of flowers. 'What you done wrong, Michael?'

Michael felt himself blush. 'What you talking about? I ain't done nothing wrong. Jesus, is it a crime to buy my wife flowers?'

Chuckling at his annoyance, Nancy put her arms around Michael's neck and kissed him. He had been ever so patient with her and now Daniel was at school with Lee, and her mum looked after Adam a couple of mornings a week to give her a break, she felt much better in herself.

'What you doing?' Michael asked.

'I think it's about time we made some special time for ourselves, don't you?' Nancy replied, taking her husband's hand and leading him up the stairs.

Michael felt a mixture of emotions as he stripped off and slipped into the bed beside her. He hadn't used a condom when he'd slept with Bella, and even though he'd had the sense to withdraw in time so he didn't get her pregnant, what if he'd caught a dose off her? There'd be hell to pay if he passed it on to his wife.

'What's up?' Nancy asked when he tried to insert himself inside her but struggled to do so.

Michael had never suffered with impotence in his life and he knew it must be guilt that was stopping him from getting an erection. 'I'm so sorry, Nance. I haven't been sleeping well and I think I'm just tired.'

When he went to put his finger inside her vagina, Nancy pushed his hand away. If he couldn't make love to her, then what was the point in staying in bed? Feeling as though she wanted to cry, she sat up and got dressed in silence.

Unlike the trendy café they had once owned in Whitechapel, the one that Mary and Donald ran now was just a clean, plainly furnished café. Donald had forbidden Mary to make it showy like their previous one. He insisted that they should learn by past mistakes and not bring any unwanted attention to themselves.

Donald was wiping the tables down and humming along to a song on the radio when there was a knock on the door. 'We're closed,' he shouted out. On the two days a week that Mary looked after Adam, Donald couldn't wait to tidy up and dash home to see the boy. Nancy would pick Daniel up from school and bring him to the house too. The café was deemed unsuitable by Donald for two young boys – there were far too many dangerous utensils lying around to have the grandchildren running in and out of the kitchen.

'It's me – Freda,' Donald heard a voice shout out.

He opened the door. When they had first moved to Whitechapel, Freda was the woman who had warned them that the Butler family were bad news. At the time Donald had thought she was the local scaremonger, but he knew now she was far from it.

'Hello, Freda. How are you? Recovered from your operation now, I hope?' Donald asked politely. Freda had been in hospital when Nancy was admitted for depression the previous autumn. She had been very kind to Nancy, and Donald was grateful for that.

'I'm doing fine, thank you. Take more than a bit of cancer to kill me off. How's your Nancy now? It's her I've come to see actually.'

'She's doing well, thanks, Freda. Back with Michael unfortunately, but Mary and I see our grandsons now. Wonderful lads they are. Very polite and loving.'

'Well, they won't stay that way. If they were girls they might have stood half a chance, but those boys will be forced into the same lifestyle as their father soon as they're old enough, you mark my words. Vinny's brat of a son is at it already. Robbed the Patels' shop recently. Smokes like a chimney as well and he's only ten. You wanna tell your Nancy all this, make her see sense before it's too late.'

Feeling dizzy at the thought of his grandsons robbing shops at the age of ten, Donald sat down on a chair. Everything Freda had said about the Butlers thus far had been proved right, so he was not about to argue with her. Nancy insisted that Michael was a legit club owner, but Donald guessed there was more to his business than met the eye. You certainly did not get a reputation like that family had by being law-abiding citizens. 'So is that what you come to tell Nancy?'

'No. I came to give her a message from my Dean. Got himself sorted now with a job and a flat, and he asked me to give Nancy his phone number. Thinks the world of her, he does. Such a shame he got with that Brenda. I'd have loved to see him settle down with a decent girl like your Nancy. I'm not allowed to see Tara any more. I'm sure that old cow Queenie put the block on it. Just had a son as well, Brenda has. Fat Beryl said she's called him Tommy. I'll never be allowed to get to know him either – my own flesh and blood. Not right, is it, Donald?'

Seeing the tears in Freda's eyes, Donald felt incredibly sorry for her. Her son Terry's body had never been found, but he had supposedly been murdered by Vinny. Dean was her only grandchild and he had been forced to flee the area. Now the poor old dear had no family left whatsoever.

'Look, I know nothing will make up for not being able to see your family, but why don't you pop round our house for tea, seeing as you've travelled here from Whitechapel? Mary's cooking, and Nancy will be there with Daniel and Adam. You can give Nancy your message personally then, and I'm sure she will be thrilled to see you.'

Freda smiled. Because of her blunt independent nature, she had no close friends and the only creatures that were nice to her were her cats Moggers and Midge. 'Thank you, Donald. I would like that very much.'

Ahmed smiled as Vinny placed his daughter in his arms. He had never seen a newborn baby with such a mop of blonde curly hair. 'I can't believe how big she is. She really is a beautiful baby.'

'Wow, look at this, Vinny,' Joanna exclaimed as she unwrapped the last of Ahmed's gifts. It was a gold baby bangle engraved with flowers and hearts.

'Aw, thanks, pal. You needn't have bought so much stuff, but we really do appreciate it, don't we, Jo?' Vinny said.

'You haven't opened the card yet,' Ahmed reminded Joanna.

Having already unwrapped a massive teddy bear, two pretty dresses, a rattle and the bracelet, Joanna was gobsmacked when she opened the large card and saw it was full of twenty-pound notes. 'We can't take money from you too, Ahmed. You've bought Molly plenty already.'

'It's to open a building society account for her. It is the custom in my country to give money to babies. Although I think Molly might have just thanked me by having a little dump in my arms,' Ahmed chuckled.

'Take Molly upstairs to change her, Jo. Ahmed and I need to talk business, so make yourself scarce for a bit and I'll give you a shout when we're done,' Vinny ordered.

When Joanna left the room, Vinny shut the lounge door and poured himself and Ahmed a Scotch.

'So, how's it going with you and Jo? You seem to be getting along OK,' Ahmed pried.

Vinny sat opposite his pal in his favourite armchair. 'All right, I suppose. She don't seem to grate on me as much as some birds do, and she's gonna be a good little mum. Her old man must know she's had Molly now 'cause Jo rang her mother the other day. I wonder how he's handling the news?' Vinny said, smirking sadistically.

'Have you fallen in love with Jo?'

'Don't be daft! I can't even be arsed giving her one any more. But she's the mother of my kid and I need someone to look after Molly and Little Vinny. As long as she does as she's told and don't get in my face, then we'll get along just fine. This was all your fucking idea, me moving her in in the first place,' Vinny reminded his pal.

'So, when are we going to the whorehouse again? It's been months,' Ahmed asked. He wanted to act as normal as possible in case Vinny smelt a rat.

'Soon, pal, soon. How's business? Did the last drop-off go OK?'

'Yes, it went fine, but we do have a slight problem now.'

'What?' Vinny asked, alarmed. He had always been happy to be the silent partner and let Ahmed be the active one. His mother and Auntie Viv would disown him if they knew what he was up to, so he'd kept his involvement in the drug trade under wraps, though he was sure Michael had a hunch.

Secretly enjoying the look of panic on his so-called friend's face, Ahmed took a couple of sips of his drink before explaining. 'You know Emre, my main man? Well, he has a court case coming up in Turkey for tax evasion charges. His brief reckons he is looking at a two-year sentence, and his trial starts the end of June.'

'So what we going to do? Surely Emre will leave somebody in charge while he's away?'

All their heroin and cocaine came from Emre, and they bought in such bulk now that they only needed to place an order every few months.

Ahmed shook his head. 'Emre will not trust anybody to run his empire. He would rather take a break.'

'Well, you must know somebody else we can buy from.'

'Not that I can trust like Emre. Look, how long have we been buying off him? Never had any problems with him or the Old Bill, have we? Why change something that works, eh? What I suggest we do is stock up before he goes inside. Buy enough to last us for the two years.'

Vinny immediately shook his head. 'Fuck off, Ahmed. You pay Emre up front and I've never met the bloke. How do we know his court case story is true? He might rip us off for a fortune.'

'Of course he won't! Emre is my friend. I have known him since I was three years old. He hasn't suggested we buy two years' supply up front. He doesn't even know about it yet and for all I know he might not even be able to supply us that amount. I've spoken to you about it first. We know the gear off Emre is good. If we buy it elsewhere it will probably be cut to fuck and if we take a break while he is in prison, then you know full well that somebody will step in our shoes. We have the money to buy it, Vinny, the perfect place to hide it, so why not take the plunge? In the years we have been dealing with Emre, at least fifty times we must have given him money up front and he has never conned us out of a penny. The man is like my brother, I swear,' Ahmed said, holding his hand on his heart.

Vinny knocked his drink back and put his hands on top

of his head. He and Ahmed usually parted with three hundred grand between them every three months. The gear was the proper uncut stuff, so it could be turned into millions in street value once it was mixed with other substances. It did involve a big outlay though. Vinny and Ahmed never got their own hands dirty, which meant a long line of people on the payroll, from the boys who cut the stuff right down to the two-bob merchants who punted it out in wraps on the street.

'I'm gonna need to think about this one. Is there no way you can bypass Emre and go straight to his suppliers while he's inside?'

'Are you fucking kidding me, Vinny? I know for a fact the drugs come from Nicaragua. Do you fancy a trip out there? Because I sure don't.'

Vinny shook his head, then put it in his hands. 'I've had a hectic week, mate, and I'm not thinking straight at the moment. No way I can give you a decision right now. This is something I need to sleep on.'

Little Vinny was sitting with Ben Bloggs in their den. It was a remote spot they had found about a year ago and it was what they referred to as their special place. Little Vinny had only had his going-out ban lifted the day before and even though he had promised his dad he would be good from now on, today he and Ben had stolen two bottles of cider from the off-licence along with six packets of crisps.

'I don't like the taste of this. I wish we'd nicked lemonade instead,' Ben said, screwing up his face and passing the bottle to Vinny.

Vinny didn't like the taste either. Neither he nor Ben were used to alcohol, but seeing as they had taken the trouble to steal it, he was determined it wouldn't be wasted.

'I don't want to go home. Let's kip here tonight, Ben. It will be exciting and we'll have a laugh.'

Ben shook his head. His mother wouldn't care if he didn't come home for a week, but he knew Vinny's dad would go mad. 'You got to go home, Vin, else your old man will kick off and blame me. Then, he won't let you out again.'

'My dad don't care about me no more. All he cares about now is Molly. You should see how he is around her. He don't leave her alone. I never remember him being like that with me. He loves her more, I know he does.'

Seeing his best pal near to tears, Ben Bloggs put a comforting arm around his shoulder. 'It's only 'cause Molly's a baby, Vin. You ain't used to having brothers and sisters, but I am. I've got six of the buggers, and you get used to it. My mum barely notices me; neither does my nan, but I just go out to play to get away from them all.'

Little Vinny took another mouthful of cider. 'I wish my mum was still alive. Her name was Karen and she was lovely.'

'How did your mum die?'

'My dad said she was a drug addict, and killed herself.'

'My mum takes drugs too, Vin. I've seen her, she smokes them, injects them – it's horrible. I don't really like her much. I wish I had a dad like yours. At least he buys you nice things and cares about what you do.'

Little Vinny glared at his pal, then pushed him in the chest. 'No, he don't. Since he met that slag Jo, he's changed. All he cares about is her and Molly now. I fucking hate him and I hope Jo and Molly die in a car crash like Lenny did.'

# CHAPTER EIGHT

On the day of Vivian's homecoming, Queenie Butler was all of a fluster. A few months ago, Vinny had treated her to a posh new kitchen. It had gold Formica counters, an electric double oven, harvest gold vinyl flooring and dark wooden-looking Spanish-style cabinets. It even had something called a dishwasher, but Queenie couldn't get on with that. No machine could clean her plates and cutlery as well as she could.

It was Vinny's idea that Vivian would like a similar kitchen, but now Queenie wished she had said no. Vinny had said it would be good for Viv if she came home to a nice surprise, but Queenie knew what an old stick-in-the-mud her sister could be at times and she was dreading her arriving home and hating it.

Going over Viv's house once more with the duster and polish, Queenie put the vase of fresh flowers in the centre of the coffee table. She had popped in every day to check on things while Vivian was in hospital and had put air fresheners in all the rooms and opened the windows regularly to keep it smelling sweet.

Remembering she had not yet dusted Viv's old grandfather clock that sat in the corner of the hallway, Queenie smiled. Another couple of hours and her wonderful sister would be out of that nuthouse and back where she belonged.

Another person in a fluster was Joanna Preston. Her mother had rung her out of the blue and said she wanted to visit. She was travelling to London today with her friend Sandy and even though Joanna was looking forward to her mum meeting Molly, she was also very nervous. Little Vinny had been treating her like shit lately whenever Vinny wasn't about, and Joanna knew if he did it in front of her mother, Deborah would say something back and that might cause an argument with Vinny. Her mum's sudden change of heart was bothering her a bit too. Only last week Deborah had flatly refused to come and see Molly, and Joanna couldn't help wondering what had happened to change her mind.

'You OK, babe? Don't be worrying about your mum's visit. It'll be fine, I promise,' Vinny said, cupping his hands around Joanna's cheeks and kissing her on the forehead.

When Joanna tried to put her arms around his neck and kiss him properly, Vinny grabbed her wrists and chuckled. 'I've got to go out, Jo, so don't start getting me all excited.'

It was a lame excuse. They hadn't made love or even had a proper kiss in months. 'You do still fancy me don't you, Vinny? I will lose this bit of baby weight soon, I promise.'

Feeling guilty, Vinny took Jo in his arms and squeezed her tightly to his chest. When they had first hooked up he had enjoyed the sex immensely, but that was only because he was getting one over on her father. Vinny had always hated kissing, he found it too intimate, and the only sex he ever enjoyed was the really rough kind. 'I'll tell you what, how about we get the Jubilee out the way then shoot down to Kings at the weekend? My mum and Auntie Viv will come, so they can look after Molly and we can have some us time. What do you say?'

Desperate to feel loved and wanted again, Joanna grinned. 'That sounds like a great idea.'

Nancy Butler looked at Michael in total disbelief. Not only had he tried to make love to her again this morning and failed miserably, he had just had the cheek to inform her that Daniel and Adam would not be going to her parents' street party, they would instead be going to Queenie's.

'But I've already told my mum and dad that I'm bringing the boys to theirs.'

'Well, best you untell them. You don't think I'm gonna leave Lee to spend the day with just us adults, do you? The Silver Jubilee is a once-in-a-lifetime experience and, seeing as they're so close, the boys should spend it together. I don't mind you going to your mum's party, but only if you take Lee as well.'

'And why would I want to do that? He isn't even my bloody kid, Michael. It's bad enough I have to suffer him day in, day out, without forcing my parents to suffer him too,' Nancy screamed, unaware that her sons and Lee were all ear-wigging outside.

Furious that his mother's nasty comments had made Lee cry, Daniel opened the back door. 'Me and Adam don't want to come to your party, Mum. We want to go to Nanny Queenie's party with Daddy and Lee.'

Aware that Lee had tears streaming down his face, a guilty Nancy bent down to comfort the child.

'Get away from him. You've already said enough for one day,' Michael spat, before ordering all three of his boys to play in the bedroom upstairs. Michael then turned back to his wife. 'You are one selfish cunt, Nancy. No wonder I can't get a fucking hard-on when I try to make love to you.

How do you think that little boy feels, now he's heard you slate him, eh?'

Nancy burst into tears. She'd had no idea the boys were listening to her and Michael's conversation and she now felt dreadful. 'I'm sorry, Michael, I really am. I'll speak to Lee and apologize to him. It was said in the heat of the moment, I didn't mean it. Where are you going?'

Snatching his arm away from his wife's grasp, Michael stormed out of the house, slamming the front door behind him.

Vinny was quiet on the journey to Goodmayes. Shelling out a hundred and fifty grand up front to a complete stranger was one thing, but shelling out over a million was a gamble he was not sure he could take. He knew he owed it to Ahmed to trust him on this, especially after the accident, but if a million pound plus went astray it really could mean financial ruin. The club earned him and Michael a decent living, but the takings were nowhere near what they'd been raking in at their old club down the Commercial Road. It had taken Vinny a long time to become as wealthy as he was, and there was no way he was gambling his daughter's future away.

'What's up with you? And don't say nothing, because I know you like the back of my hand,' Queenie said.

Vinny smiled. 'I've had a business proposition put to me. I don't want to go into detail, but I think it's too much of a gamble.'

Queenie had never been one to pry too much. She knew Vinny had business interests other than the club and it would only worry the life out of her if she knew what they were. 'Go with your head and not your heart, Vinny. You inherited that brain of yours off me – it certainly never came from your father's genes – so use it wisely.'

Vinny pulled up in the hospital car park, switched the engine off and gave his mum a hug. 'I know I don't say it as often as I should, but I really do love you, Mum.'

'And I love you too, boy, much more than you'll ever know. Right, let's go and get your Auntie Viv and pray to God she likes that fucking kitchen.'

Hoping to break the ice quickly, Joanna opened the door to her mum and Sandy with the baby in her arms. It was a bank holiday, Little Vinny had gone out to play and Joanna was praying the little sod wouldn't come back while her mum was here.

'Aw, Jo, isn't she beautiful!' Sandy gushed.

Deborah stared at the child. She had expected it to be dark-haired and olive-skinned like Vinny and had been prepared to dislike it on sight, but Molly was nothing like her father. She was blonde, chubby and the bonniest baby that Deborah had ever laid eyes on. 'Can I hold her?' she asked, her eyes brimming with tears.

'Of course you can, Mum.'

The next hour or so passed pleasantly. Both Sandy and Deborah complimented Joanna on her house, Vinny wasn't mentioned at all unless Jo said his name, and baby Molly had them all eating out of the palm of her chubby hand.

When the front door opened, Joanna's heart lurched. Vinny had gone to pick up his Auntie Viv and said he was going to make himself scarce for the rest of the day, so Jo knew it had to be Little Vinny. It was, and he was accompanied by Ben Bloggs.

'Where's me dad?' Little Vinny asked.

'He's gone to pick your Auntie Viv up from hospital. Mum, Sandy, this is Vinny's son, Vinny, and his friend Ben.'

'Pleased to meet you both,' Little Vinny replied politely.

'Pleased to meet you too,' Ben Bloggs added.

'Jo, did Dad leave me any money? Only me and Ben are bored and we want to go to the pictures.'

'No, he didn't, but let me get my purse and I can give you some.' Jo was so relieved the child hadn't showed her up in front of her mother that she would happily have given him the contents, but instead she handed him a five-pound note.

'Cheers, Jo. Bye, ladies and Molly,' Little Vinny shouted, as he and Ben marched out of the door.

As they ran off down the road, Little Vinny waved the five-pound note in Ben's face. 'Told you I would get money off the silly slag, didn't I? Now who can we ask to get us some fags?'

Vivian stood open-mouthed as she stared at her kitchen.

'I knew it, she don't like it,' Queenie mumbled, punching her son in the arm.

'It's even got a dishwasher, Auntie Viv, look,' Vinny said, pointing out the appliance.

All of a sudden, Vivian clapped her hands together in glee. 'It's the bollocks! I love it!'

'Thank goodness for that,' Queenie muttered.

'And we've got another surprise for you, haven't we, Mum?'

Queenie nodded. She had been worried how Viv would react on walking into the house, having to face how empty it was without Lenny, but so far she had been fine. However, Viv hadn't seen her second surprise yet and even though Queenie thought she would be thrilled, she was nervous in case it had the opposite effect and send her sister back into a depression.

Vivian followed Vinny and Queenie up the stairs and gasped as they opened Lenny's bedroom door. All his toys, clothes and other belongings that she had thrown out for the dustmen were now back in the room, including Zippy the monkey, who was perched in his usual place on the bed.

Vivian burst into tears, but they weren't sad tears, they were ones of happiness. Out of all the things she had done when she was ill, chucking her beloved son's belongings out was the thing she had regretted the most. 'Oh dear God. This is wonderful! How did you get the stuff back from the dustmen?'

Crying happy tears too, Queenie hugged her sister. 'The dustmen never took it – I did. I knew how much you would regret throwing Lenny's belongings away once you felt better, Viv, so I rang Vinny and he collected it from mine and stored it at the club.'

'I am so relieved. This has to be the nicest thing that anyone has ever done for me. I feel like a part of Lenny is back here with me now. Thank you both so much.'

Vinny took his aunt in his arms, rocked her side to side and kissed her on top of her head. 'No need to thank us. We're your family. Welcome home, Auntie Viv.'

Nancy Butler poured herself a glass of wine and dejectedly flopped onto the armchair. She had just been upstairs to apologize to Lee and entice the boys downstairs. Lee had been understanding, but Daniel had looked at her with hatred and refused to come out of his bedroom until his father came home, which had upset Nancy immensely. As for Adam, he was far too young to understand what was going on.

Desperate to speak to somebody, Nancy debated who to phone. Her friend Rhonda had gone to stay with family and Nancy knew her mother wouldn't be very sympathetic, as she always sided with Michael when it came to Lee.

Picking up her handbag, Nancy opened her purse and

stared at the phone number that Freda had given her the day before. She'd had no intention of contacting Dean, didn't think it was right now she was back with Michael, but she was desperate for a friendly ear to tell her troubles to. Freda had told her under no circumstances should she ever call Dean from her home phone, so Nancy folded the number up and put it back in her purse. She then ran up the stairs. 'Come on, boys, get your coats on. I'm taking you out for a burger.'

Vinny walked into the club and was surprised to see Michael sitting alone with a bottle of Scotch. 'What's up with you? You had another row with Nancy?'

When Michael explained what had happened earlier, Vinny tutted and shook his head in disgust. 'You need to get rid of her, bruv, she's a wrong 'un. What about that other bird? Have you got back in touch with her yet?'

Michael shook his head dismally. He was still constantly thinking about Bella and was sure she was the reason why he couldn't get an erection with Nancy. 'If I tell you something, you won't take the piss, will you?'

Vinny shook his head, but when Michael admitted he had erectile dysfunction, Vinny couldn't help but burst out laughing. 'Alfie can't get it up! Who would ever have thought it, eh?'

'You ain't fucking funny. I wish I'd never told you. If you tell anybody else, I swear to you, Vinny, me and you are finished.'

'Calm down, you tart. I'm just messing with you. The only reason you can't get it up with Nancy is because you've met someone else. Go on, ring the other bird – what you waiting for?' Vinny asked, pouring himself a large Scotch and downing it in one.

'What you doing here so early? You got problems as well? I thought you were picking Auntie Viv up.'

'I did pick Auntie Viv up. She's back at home, loved the kitchen, and you should have seen her face when she saw Champ's room, Michael. Bowled over, she was. As for problems, I have my fair share, trust me on that one.'

'You not getting on with Jo?' Michael asked. He had been gobsmacked when he found out Jo was Johnny Preston's daughter, and guessed that Vinny had only got with her out of some sadistic lust for revenge.

Vinny shook his head. He then admitted that Little Vinny had started to spiral out of control, and told Michael that he had found Yvonne Summers. 'You should have seen the state of the fat slag, bruv. Made me feel ill to look at her. Reminded me of a sow on a fucking pig farm.'

Michael felt his blood run cold. He knew his brother had a tendency to wipe out people who had upset him and he only hoped Vinny wasn't going to ask him to help. 'If you want my opinion, you'd be mad to bother with Yvonne now. You could lose everything if you get banged up, Vin. Is she worth it?'

Vinny took a sip of his drink. 'No. She ain't worth a wank, Michael. However, I would still like to set the fat cunt on fire and watch her go up in flames.'

Queenie and Vivian were both hard at it in Queenie's new kitchen. All the neighbours were bringing food for tomorrow's street party, but being the type of women they were, both sisters were determined that their input into the occasion would beat any other.

'Well? What do you think? Ain't lost me touch, have I?' Vivian asked, as she showed Queenie her tray of homemade Cornish pasties.

'Oh, Vivvy, they look handsome, girl. Look at the gloss

on that pastry. Do you know what, I'm amazed they didn't let you help out with the cooking in that loony bin. You could have taught that mob a thing or two.'

Vivian chuckled. The pair of them had been sipping sherry while they worked, and with Mrs Mills on in the background it was just like old times. 'I offered once, but the nurse looked at me in horror. I think she thought I was going to shove my head in the oven and gas meself.'

'Well, don't forget I told all the neighbours you've been recuperating in the country. Them nosy load of bastards will be prying tomorrow, you can bet your life,' Queenie warned her sister.

Vivian smiled. It had hit her like a ton of bricks, walking into her own home without her Lenny being there to greet her, but she hadn't wanted to show it. She might cry a few tears when she climbed into bed tonight, but she was determined not to wallow in grief again. Her Lenny had gone for good, and however many tears she cried he wasn't coming back. If being institutionalized had taught her one thing, it was that. 'Sod the neighbours, Queen. I couldn't give a shit what they think. Now, turn Mrs Mills up and let's have a singalong.'

Vinny and Michael were still having a brotherly heart-to-heart when the phone rang. 'I'll get it. You can bet your life it's Nancy,' Michael stated.

'If it's Ahmed, I ain't here, bruv,' Vinny said.

'What's going on, Vin? That's the third time in the last two days you've made me tell Ahmed that you ain't around. I'm not stupid, so please don't lie to me. Have you got yourself involved in the drug game with him?' Michael asked, when he sat back down. He knew Vinny wasn't snorting any more. He could see it in his eyes and hear it in his speech, but he wouldn't put it past his brother to deal in the stuff. Vinny was a greedy git when it came to money. Always had been, and always would be.

Knowing he'd have to come clean to a certain extent, Vinny told him, 'It's not drugs, Michael. There's a business deal he wants to involve me in and I'm not sure about it.'

'What sort of deal?'

'Don't worry, it's nothing too serious, just a bit of a gamble. And there is a lot of dosh involved.'

'Do you want my honest opinion?'

Vinny nodded.

'If you think Ahmed has forgiven you for that accident, then you must be mad. I can see the truth in his eyes. I reckon he's trying to rip you off, and if I was you I wouldn't trust the Turkish cunt as far as I could throw him.'

Vinny took a swig of his drink. Before the accident, he had trusted Ahmed like a brother, but intuition told him that Michael might be right. Scraping together over a million in cash was a difficult enough task, but parting with it was even harder.

'Where you going?' Michael asked when Vinny stood up.

'I'm going to ring Ahmed. If he thinks he can get one over on me, then he's picked on the wrong fucking person.'

The two figures put the hoods up on their matching Adidas jackets and giggled as they approached Vinny Butler's house. Both were in high spirits, thanks to the bottle of cider they had just polished off.

Seeing a woman in a hairnet walking towards them pulling a shopping trolley behind her, the boy grabbed his older accomplice's arm and gesticulated for him to sit on the kerb alongside him.

When the woman passed without even glancing in their direction, the boy stood up. Satisfied that the coast was now clear, he held out his right hand. 'Give it to me. I want to do it.'

The boy's accomplice shook his head. 'No. This was my idea and I can throw further than you.'

'No, you can't.'

'Yes, I can.'

'Give it to me.'

Ignoring the boy's wishes, the older lad ran towards Vinny's house and hurled the brick straight through the downstairs window.

At the sound of the blood-curdling scream from inside the house, both boys then ran for their lives.

Queenie and Vivian were both cooing over baby Tommy when the doorbell rang.

'I'll get it,' Brenda said. Having moved back home two days ago, she already hated living in the house without Dean. She was hoping that, if she made herself useful, her mother would let her and the kids stay at her place for a while.

'I am so sorry for bothering you, but I didn't know where else to go. Somebody threw a brick through the lounge window and it nearly hit Molly,' Joanna gabbled when the door was flung open. She'd been in such a rush to leave the house, she'd carried her daughter in her arms.

Overhearing the conversation, Queenie darted into the hallway. Lots of women would never have forgiven their son for taking up with the daughter of a man who had virtually ended the life of one of their other sons, but Queenie was different to those shallow people. She trusted her first-born implicitly and if Joanna made him happy, then it made her happy too. 'Whatever's the matter, sweetheart?'

Joanna explained once again. 'I tried to get hold of Vinny, but he's not at the club,' she wept.

Queenie led Joanna into the lounge. 'Now you sit down, with Molly, my angel. Brenda will make you a nice sweet cup of tea and I'll ring around and see if I can track Vinny down.'

Vinny Butler rammed his rather large penis up the blonde bird's backside and grinned as Ahmed did the same to the black girl. He and Ahmed had often joked in the past that they had bonded as friends because they shared the same sadistic nature and warped sense of humour, and Vinny was pleased that their friendship seemed to be on track once again.

When Molly had been born and he had first held her in his arms, Vinny had made a mental pact with himself to give up the whorehouses for good. Abusing females in the sometimes violent manner that he had become accustomed to did not seem morally right now he had a daughter himself. However, after Ahmed had so gracefully accepted his decision and his reluctance to part with such a massive amount of money, Vinny had felt unable to say no to his suggestion that they have a night out, like old times.

'Please do not squeeze my throat. You are hurting me,' the blonde croaked.

'Shut the fuck up,' Vinny hissed, squeezing the girl's throat even harder. He got off on inflicting pain and terror; had done since the day he beat a lad senseless in the school playground at the tender age of eight.

Vinny shut his eyes and thought of how Yvonne Summers used to look, upping the speed of his thrusts as he did so. When his orgasm arrived, it was a belter. But as soon as it was over, Vinny thought of his daughter, leapt off the bed and got dressed. 'I'll wait for you outside. It's stuffy in here,' he told Ahmed.

When Ahmed emerged minutes later, he asked Vinny why he had left so swiftly.

Not wanting to sound like a numpty by admitting that having a daughter had put him off whores, Vinny shrugged. 'I was just hot. Come on, I need a drink.'

The two of them stepped into a nearby pub and found a quiet spot in the corner. Ahmed had known from the way Vinny had been avoiding his phone calls the last couple of days that he wasn't going to part with the dosh, so Plan B was already well under way.

'So, what happens now? Are you still going to go ahead with the deal?' Vinny asked anxiously.

'No. We are partners and in this together, which is why I have already spoken to another supplier. I think we might be able to set up a deal with them, but they have insisted on meeting you also. They are in London at the moment and have suggested we meet tomorrow evening.'

'That's fine by me. Thanks for being so understanding about the other deal, pal.'

Inwardly seething, as he had been desperate to rip Vinny off for over a million, Ahmed forced a smile. 'No need to thank me. That's what friends are for.'

In a far more upmarket part of London, Michael Butler was feeling like some stupid lovesick schoolboy as he stepped into the posh lift. Unlike the lifts in his neck of the woods, this one didn't stink of sick and piss, and the walls weren't covered in graffiti. In fact this one was so clean you could eat your dinner off the floor.

When the lift stopped, Michael could feel his heart pounding in his chest. He had tried his hardest not to ring her, he really had. But here he was in Chelsea, like a lamb being led to the slaughter.

Bella opened the door in a red see-through negligee. Being

the red-blooded male that he was, Michael immediately felt his penis jump to attention.

'Do come in, Michael. Would you like a glass of wine?' Bella asked.

Michael nodded and followed her into the kitchen. Her voice was just as sexy as the rest of her. Husky, with an Italian lilt to it.

Making sure she was showing plenty of cleavage, Bella sat at the table opposite him. 'So, what can I do for you? You said on the phone you had something to tell me.'

'I do, but now I feel like an idiot saying it.'

'Don't be shy, Michael. You weren't shy on the evening we met,' Bella said with a smirk.

Michael stared at her. Her lipstick matched her negligee and all he could think of was fucking her senseless. 'OK, I'll be honest. I can't stop thinking about you. You are on my mind every minute of every day.'

Bella took a sip of her wine. She was secretly thrilled by Michael's confession, but didn't want to show it. 'You took your time getting in touch with me.'

'I know and I'm sorry. I was just trying to fight it, I suppose.'

Bella stood up, undid her negligee and let it fall to the floor. 'I think we need to make up for lost time then, don't you?'

Michael did not need asking twice. He positioned Bella against the kitchen table and entered her like a rat up a drainpipe.

# CHAPTER NINE

Vinny Butler woke up with the most excruciating headache. He hadn't taken cocaine since Roy had killed himself, but last night after they had left the whorehouse, Ahmed had insisted that they must try the sample that his new contact had supplied.

Hearing the phone ring yet again, Vinny staggered into the lounge to answer it. He and Ahmed had ended up in some Soho nightclub and he hadn't got back to the club until six a.m.

'Where you been? Worried sick about you, I was. I never slept a wink last night.'

'I'm sorry, Mum. I had a business meeting and didn't get back until late, which is why I crashed here. I'd had a few bevvies, so didn't want to wake Jo and the baby.'

'Wake them! They were already bastard well awake, Vinny, which probably had something to do with the brick that flew through the window and nearly wiped out poor little Molly's life.'

Vinny felt his blood run cold. 'You what? Is Molly OK? What happened, Mum? If anyone has hurt her, I swear I will fucking kill 'em.'

'Molly's fine. Her and Jo stayed here the night. Best you

get round yours and see if Little Vinny's there. Poor sod's been on his own all night, and I couldn't go round there – not with Jo in a state and Vivvy just getting out of hospital. You want to take a good look at your life, son. You're not a teenager any more, you're a grown man with responsibilities. Those kids of yours should be top of your list of priorities, not your dodgy business dealings.'

'I'm really sorry, Mum. Can I talk to Jo?'

'No, she's feeding Molly. Just get your arse home, then round here – and bring Jo and Molly a change of clothes and the pram. I just pray, with that window smashed, you haven't been burgled as well.'

Vinny felt as guilty as sin when his mother ended the call. No way would he take cocaine again or visit whorehouses, ever! Molly deserved far better than that. Not knowing who had it in for him was driving him insane, but somebody obviously did, and when he found out who that individual was, he would personally chop their fucking head off.

Michael Butler groaned in ecstasy as Bella brought him to a shuddering orgasm. Nancy wasn't a lover of blow-jobs and on the rare occasion she did give him one, it was with a very half-hearted attitude. Bella was the opposite. She couldn't get enough of his cock and gave the best head that Michael had ever received in his life.

'Babe, I've got to go now. My sons will be waiting for me to take them to my mum's street party.'

'Will we be seeing one another again? Only I'm not the type to sit at home staring at the phone hoping you might call, Michael.'

'How about I take you out on Sunday? We'll go up the West End if you like?'

Bella smiled. 'I like that idea very much.'

*

Vinny Butler felt as guilty as hell when he walked into his mother's lounge. He picked his baby up, held her close to his chest and turned to Joanna. 'I'm so sorry you couldn't get hold of me last night. You must have been terrified. Did you clock who did it?'

Joanna shook her head. 'The brick only missed Molly by an inch or so. It could have killed her, Vinny. I looked out of the window, but whoever did it must have already run off. I was too scared to go outside. Where was you? I thought you were working at the club?'

'I was, but I then had to go out on business. I didn't get back until late.'

'Well, you should let Michael run the club for the next few nights and stay at home with Jo and the baby, Vinny. It was probably kids, but you can never be too careful,' Queenie warned her son.

Vinny sighed. Michael had mentioned he had seen two little herberts hanging around outside the club earlier this week, so perhaps they were the culprits? But why would two kids have it in for him? It just didn't add up.

'I need to shoot out tonight, so best Jo stays here until I get back. I shouldn't be too late.'

'Where's Little Vinny? Did you find him?' Vivian asked.

'Yeah, he's round at Ben Bloggs'. They're both coming to the party later and somebody is fixing the window as we speak.'

When Joanna left the room to get changed, Queenie stared at her son. 'Has somebody got it in for you, boy? Best you tell us the truth in case we're all in bloody danger.'

Not wanting to worry his mum or aunt, Vinny chuckled. 'Don't be daft. As you said, it was probably just kids.'

Nancy Butler had tears streaming down her face as she drove towards Queenie's house. Michael hadn't come home last night, hadn't even contacted her, and Nancy knew their relationship was in trouble. Dean hadn't been much help. Their conversation had been cut short as the kids were playing up outside the phonebox, but he had urged her to leave Michael. 'Just get away from that family before it's too late, Nance. You'll regret it if you don't,' were Dean's exact words.

'Why you crying, Mummy?' Adam asked innocently.

'Because she was nasty to Lee, now Daddy hates her,' Daniel replied.

Feeling panicky as a lorry overtook her, Nancy bumped the car up a nearby kerb. She had only passed her driving test a couple of months ago and Michael had bought her a Mini, but she rarely drove alone as she wasn't confident enough. Feeling dreadfully sorry for herself, Nancy took a tissue out of her bag and blew her nose. No wonder Michael hated her right now. She was a crap driver, mother and wife.

Having helped decorate the street and tables with Union Jacks and bunting, Queenie and Vivian set about getting themselves glammed up. Most of their neighbours were as scruffy as arseholes, but Queenie and Vivian enjoyed standing out from the crowd. It was what they were all about.

'Does this look OK, Queen? I lost weight in that hospital. Don't look too big, does it?' Vivian asked. She was wearing a pale blue sleeveless dress, navy shoes and a big straw hat.

'You look a million dollars, Viv. But don't forget to put your gold on. I'm wearing my sovereign today, and you should wear yours. What about my outfit? Not too over the top, is it?' Queenie replied. She'd chosen a white sleeveless dress which she'd matched with a big red hat and red shoes. Both women had thought they were the bees knees since they were teenagers.

'You look fabulous. When's Vinny setting the disco system up in the front garden, Queen?'

'He's sorting it now. Right, shall we start taking the food out? I wonder what Stinky Susan has made?'

Vivian chuckled. Stinky Susan had moved into the house next door while she was in hospital. An unkempt-looking woman with permanently greasy hair, she had knocked on Viv's door this morning and Viv had been greeted with a distinct whiff of unadulterated piss. 'Christ knows, but I'm not eating anything she or anybody else brings. None of their homes are that wholesome, so we'll just stick with our own grub.'

Queenie agreed, then linked arms with Viv. Usually, they avoided the neighbours like the plague, but there had been rumours flying about that Viv had been carted off to the nuthouse, and Queenie was determined to restore family pride. 'Come on, let's go and knock the nosy bastards dead.'

Having never driven to the East End before, Nancy panicked when she found many of the roads, including Queenie's, were blocked off for street parties. Instead she headed for Michael's club and was fortunate to find a parking space nearby.

'Look, there's Daddy! Dad, wait for us,' Daniel screamed, as he and Lee chased after their father.

Picking Adam up, Nancy walked towards Michael. He had obviously stayed at the club as he was wearing different clothes to the ones he'd left home in the previous day. Nancy was relieved about that, as when she had rung the club late last night and again this morning she had been informed that her husband was not there.

'I'll take the boys from here, so you can go to your mum's party,' Michael said, avoiding direct eye contact with his wife. He could tell she had been crying and he knew if he looked at her, he would feel guilty.

'I'm not going to my mum's party. I want us to spend the day together as a family. Michael, I'm so sorry Lee heard what I said. He is a good kid and I swear, from now on I shall treat him the same as my own. Please forgive me. I love you and we owe it to our sons to make our marriage work, don't we? Can you imagine how upset they would be if we split up? It would break their little hearts. Daniel and Adam would miss Lee so much if he went to live with you, and I could never give our boys up, Michael.'

'And neither could I,' Michael spat.

When Nancy broke down in tears, Michael held her close to his chest. His heart felt torn in two. He still loved her, but was that just because she had given him two wonderful sons? Bella made his pulse race every time he thought about her. But was it lust that he felt for her or true love?

The one thing Michael did know was that he thought too much of both women and his kids to lead a double life. He would have to make a decision, and he would have to make it fast.

Queenie and Vivian's food outclassed everybody else's. Two cooked chickens, ham knuckles, ribs of beef, a pot of dripping, pork pies, pasties, sausage rolls, and a massive bowl of salad, pickles, crusty French sticks and a block of thick butter had the rest of the neighbours drooling, and they hadn't even brought their cakes and desserts out yet. 'If that obese fucker tries to take one more thing off this table, I'm gonna chop her big fat hand off with this knife,' Vivian informed her sister.

Guessing that Viv was referring to Big Stan's greedy wife, Queenie laughed.

'Urgh, this is disgusting. Did you make this, Nan?' Little Vinny asked, handing Queenie a half-eaten sandwich.

'No, I bloody well didn't! It's fish paste. Put it down or you'll get poisoned. Stinky Susan made it,' Queenie whispered.

'What did you bring to the party, Nancy? Didn't see you turn up with bags of food,' Brenda asked, smirking.

Queenie kicked her daughter under the table. Brenda had been knocking back the booze like it was going out of style. 'Shut it, you. Michael and Vinny have gone to pick up the seafood, so that's Nancy and Jo's contribution sorted. Besides, you cooked sod all yourself, Bren. Me and Viv did extra for you.'

'Well, perhaps that's because I'm a single mother with two kids. Not my fault my husband turned out to be a wanker, is it? You heard from him, Nancy? He always lusted after you,' Brenda said, glaring at her sister-in-law.

Wishing Michael would reappear, Nancy stared at her plate of food. 'No, I haven't heard a word,' she lied. Dean had only mentioned Brenda once on the phone, said he didn't miss her at all. He sounded tearful when he spoke about Tara though, and he had asked after Tommy.

'You're lying. That's why you won't look me in the eye,' Brenda spat.

Seeing Nosy Hilda looking their way, Queenie grabbed her daughter by the arm and yanked her off the chair. 'Time to put some Mrs Mills on. Come and help me choose a record, Bren,' she said, pasting on a false smile.

Having hauled Brenda up the garden path, Queenie waited until they were inside the house before giving her what for. 'Look in that mirror, Bren, go on, then tell me what you see.'

'Well, me of course. What you going on about?'

'Now, I'll tell you what I see, shall I? I see a fat, drunken lush who looks like she needs a decent haircut and a good scrub in the bath.'

Brenda burst into tears. 'How can you be so nasty, Mum? You know I'm not feeling good about myself since Dean left.'

Queenie pointed at the mirror. 'And that's the reason why he left, love, not because of Nancy. You've let yourself go so much so, I'm embarrassed to call you my daughter. You don't see me and your Auntie Viv walking about like tramps, do you? Now, I know you think I'm being unkind, but you'll thank me for it one day. If I can't tell you, who can, eh? Come on, dry them eyes and we'll put some records on and enjoy the rest of the party. Then tomorrow, I'll take you out shopping and we'll get that bastard hair cut and you'll start a diet, OK?'

Not knowing how else to react to her mother's stern words, Brenda merely nodded miserably.

Because of the Jubilee celebrations, the East End was buzzing. Everybody had massive smiles on their faces and the area was flooded with street traders selling their wares. Plastic Union Jacks and hats, tea towels, china mugs and plates, key rings and even plastic crowns were being sold by the dozen. Unfortunately for Vinny, he had too much on his mind to get into the festive spirit. As did Michael, which was why both brothers were now strolling along in silence. 'You OK, bruv? You seem preoccupied,' Vinny said.

'I could say the same about you, Vin.'

In an effort to lift their spirits, Vinny gave Michael a light punch in the arm and grinned. 'Do you know what I think of every time we go to Tubby's stall?'

'No. Enlighten me.'

'You, as a kid. Whenever Mum used to take us to the eel stalls in Brick Lane or Roman Road, you used to cry your eyes out when they took the eels out of the tank and chopped them up. I remember you begging Mum to let you take them home and keep them as pets.'

Michael laughed. 'And I remember you getting great pleasure out of watching the poor little fuckers being chopped up alive. Once a sadistic bastard, always a sadistic bastard – that's you all over.'

Vinny grabbed his brother in a playful headlock. 'Moooooo,' he shouted in his ear.

Still laughing, Michael pushed Vinny away. His brother had kept to his promise and not mentioned Trevor's death any more, but Vinny had never let him forget that the cows had scared the living daylights out of him that evening in East Hanningfield.

'Shall we have a beer in the Beggar before we head back to Mum's?' Vinny suggested.

'Yeah, why not.'

There was a real party atmosphere inside the pub. Men had left their women at home to prepare for the street parties and the pub was packed. Laughter filled the air and Vinny only wished he felt as happy as every other bastard.

As usual, whenever Vinny and Michael set foot inside a local pub they were treated like royalty. Men fell over themselves to chat to them and buy them drinks, but Vinny knew that it wasn't because he and Michael were overly popular. It was because they were feared.

Vinny handed Big Stan a wad of notes. 'The drinks are on me. Shout one up for yourself and whoever else wants one. Get me and Michael a pint of lager and a whisky chaser each. We're gonna sit at that table in the corner 'cause we've got some business to discuss.'

'What's up?' Michael asked as they sat down at the only free table in the pub.

Vinny was about to reply when a group of men at the next table broke into an out-of-tune rendition of 'Land of Hope and Glory'.

'Oh, for Christ's sake! Tell 'em to shut the fuck up, Michael,' Vinny ordered.

Michael turned around and smiled at the war veteran, Mr Arthur. He was singing at the top of his voice and had his medals pinned proudly on his suit jacket. Nobody knew the old boy's first name; rumour had it that he'd been christened Arthur Arthur, which would explain why he kept quiet about it.

Turning back to Vinny, Michael said, 'Look, I know you've got a lot on your plate at the moment. Believe me, so have I. I am in no fucking frame of mind to celebrate and party today, but we can't stop other people enjoying themselves. In fact, we should make an effort to forget our troubles just for today for the sake of our family. Mum and Auntie Viv won't be happy if we turn up at the party with faces like smacked arses.'

'Yeah, you're right. So, what's bugging you?'

'You go first.'

Vinny admitted to Michael how worried he was about the safety of his children. 'If someone has got it in for me that badly they could be capable of anything, bruv. Jo said her mum hadn't long left when that brick was chucked through the window, and it's made me wonder if someone was watching the house. At first I thought it might be Bobby Jackson, but he's banged up now so it can't be. And surely Preston wouldn't organize for somebody to frighten and potentially hurt his daughter and grandkid just because he hates me?'

'Well, apart from those flowers being sent in the shape

of a gun, everything else that has happened is the sort of stuff kids would do. The graffiti, your car being done and the window being smashed – that isn't the work of some big boy. I told you I saw two little herberts sat opposite the club the other day. Perhaps it was them? You ain't upset any kids lately, have you?'

'No, only me own son.'

Michael raised his eyebrows. 'Well, perhaps you should look a bit closer to home then. I mean, if Little Vinny is jealous of Molly, who knows what strokes he might pull.'

Vinny felt sick. Surely he wasn't being terrorized by his own flesh and blood? Desperate for a change of subject, he enquired about his brother's problems.

Michael admitted he had spent the previous night with Bella and told him the sex was the best he had ever had. 'I don't know what I'm gonna do. I think I'm falling head over heels for her. If it weren't for the boys, I'd walk away from Nancy tomorrow, but I can't care for them on my own and do my job, and I know Nance would fight me tooth and nail for them.'

'Nancy's a registered nutjob, Michael. Get yourself a good brief. If you move in with Bella, she can look after the boys while you work.'

Michael shook his head. 'Bella's not like that, Vin. She's a model, a good-time girl. Her gaff is like a palace and I just know she wouldn't be very child friendly. Anyway, she's often away for a week or two at a time. She's off to Italy next week to do a shoot and visit her parents.'

'Get a live-in nanny then,' Vinny suggested.

'It's not that easy, Vin. Nancy said something to me earlier that made me think. She said how heartbroken Daniel and Adam would be if we split up and they couldn't live with Lee any more. Nancy is right. The boys would all be devastated.

Vinny tutted. 'The crafty bitch is playing mind games with you. Ignore the fucking psycho.'

Michael sighed. 'I know Nancy isn't the best mother in the world, but she does love them boys. I couldn't take them away from her, even if the court gave me custody – which they wouldn't. Her mother would go apeshit too, and I'm very fond of Mary.'

'So, what you gonna do then?'

'I suppose I'll have to finish with Bella before I get in any deeper. I can't see that I've got much choice.'

Back at the party, Queenie and Vivian were having a whale of a time. There had been a few tears this morning when they had spoken about their sons who were no longer with them, but they had then made a pact not to mention them during the party so they could enjoy themselves.

Mrs Mills had certainly livened up the day. 'My Old Man's a Dustman', 'Any Old Iron', 'Underneath the Arches' and 'Maybe It's Because I'm a Londoner' had already been sung loud and proud, but when 'I've Got a Lovely Bunch of Coconuts' blasted out of the speakers, Queenie and Viv both stood up to do their little party piece.

'Is Nan and Auntie Viv drunk, Mum? They're dancing funny,' Tara asked her mother.

'Yes, and she has the cheek to talk about me,' Brenda hissed.

Nancy and Joanna were getting along as if they had known one another for years. Neither had properly met before and both girls were so pleased that the other was at the party as their men seemed to have done a disappearing act. They had mainly chatted about their kids, but Joanna had just told Nancy about the brick flying through her window.

'Oh my God! That must have been awful. Thank goodness

it missed Molly and you. I can't believe how gorgeous she is, Jo. She's made me want a little girl.'

'You'll have to get Michael into a baby-making mood.'

'Chance would be a fine thing. We rarely get any us time now. It's all about the boys.'

'I know that feeling and I've only got the one child.'

Brenda glared at Nancy and Joanna. Both were pretty and slim and neither would ever have to worry about money, having got their claws into her brothers. 'You want to think yourself lucky, yous two, instead of moaning. You should be in my shoes, bringing up two nippers with no man and no money. You'd have every right to whinge then.'

'We was only joking, Brenda,' Joanna said apologetically.

'Don't be worrying about her. She's had a face like it's been smacked with a wet fish all day,' Vivian said as she sat back down at the table.

Spotting Michael and Vinny walking along with the seafood, Queenie shouted, 'Where you two been? Get them eels in the fridge. All the bloody jelly will be melted, the time you took, and you know how I love me jelly.'

'Dad, can me and Ben have a lager shandy? Billy Malcolm's dad said he can have one, but Nan said I had to ask you first.'

Vinny stared his son in the eyes. He so hoped what Michael had said wasn't true, but the more he thought about it, the more he reckoned it was a strong possibility. There was no way the flowers were anything to do with the boy, but the other three incidents could well be his and Ben Bloggs' handiwork. And Little Vinny certainly had a motive. He was as jealous as hell of Jo and the baby, that much was obvious to a blind man.

'Well, can I, Dad?'

'No,' snapped Vinny. 'You fucking well can't.'

*

After the party ended, Queenie and Vivian both sat glued to the telly, watching the highlights of the Jubilee. 'Dead smart in that turquoise, the Queen, ain't she, Viv?'

'Looks lovely. Weren't it a good day? Shame we don't have street parties more often. I even quite liked the neighbours today. Reminded me of the war. It was that type of British bulldog spirit, wasn't it?'

'I loved the singalong. Took me back to the old days, when every pub had a piano in it. Not that me and you ever got taken out that often, mind. Our fault for marrying arseholes, I suppose.'

'Speaking of the singalong, I ain't 'arf missed me *Wheeltappers and Shunters*. Has it been as good? I never saw it when I was in hospital. The miserable bastards wouldn't let me watch it.'

'It's the last in the series this week. Mouthy Maureen said they ain't making no more. How the hell she knows is anyone's guess. Perhaps Bernard Manning rang her up personally? Good job she went to her daughter's today, eh? Party wouldn't have been the same with her sticking her oar in. I'm sure she was the one who spread the rumour that you were in a nuthouse. I pulled her on it, but she denied all knowledge. Did anyone say anything to you?'

Vivian giggled. 'Nosy Hilda and Big Stan asked me. I told them that I went to stay with our distant cousin in the Cotswolds and I spent months there because I met a rich man.'

Queenie was open-mouthed. 'Viv, you didn't say that.'

'Yeah, I did, but the best part was when Nosy Hilda pulled me aside just after we all sang "Daisy Daisy". She wanted to know if my fancy man would be visiting me in Whitechapel.'

'What did you say to her?'

'I told her I split up with him because his dingle-dangle

didn't work properly. Oh, Queen, it was hysterical. I don't know how I didn't laugh. Her face was an absolute picture.'

Queenie burst out laughing. Any worries she might have had about Viv sinking back into depression had now well and truly vanished. 'That story will be round the whole of Whitechapel by tomorrow.'

Such was her laughter, Vivian had a stitch and was holding her sides. 'Good! At least while the nosy bastards are talking about me, they're leaving some other poor unsuspecting sod alone.'

Vinny Butler pulled up outside the restaurant in Stratford he part owned with Ahmed and Nick and got out of the car. He had an uneasy feeling in the pit of his stomach and he wasn't sure if it was down to his son or his distrust of most Turks.

Ahmed was inside the restaurant already. Probably because of the Jubilee, the place was nigh-on empty. 'Vinny, my friend. It is a pleasure for me to introduce Hakan and Bora to you.'

The first thing that struck Vinny was how well dressed both men were. Hakan was in a black pin-striped suit, Bora in a plain charcoal-grey one, but Vinny knew his suits and could tell the expensive from the cheap.

Hakan was the main man, Vinny knew that immediately. He spoke the better English, was extremely charismatic and self-assured, and it was he who did most of the talking. 'Could we have bottle of your finest champagne please, sir?' he said, clicking his fingers at a waiter. He turned back to Vinny. 'Ahmed has told Bora and I all about you. He says all good things. Is there any questions you want to ask about us?'

Vinny asked where the two men lived, how long they had known Ahmed, and enquired about their families. He wanted to make the meeting as informal as possible before they got to the nitty-gritty. There was something about Bora that Vinny couldn't quite take to. He had beady eyes, looked a bit shifty, and said very little, but Vinny guessed the lack of conversation was because Hakan ran the show and perhaps there was a slight language problem.

The conversation flowed nicely during the meal and Vinny knew he felt comfortable enough to do business with Hakan. 'So, what's the score then? How much we looking at and for what amount?'

Vinny's ears pricked up when he heard the price and he glanced at Ahmed. They would be getting slightly more for their dosh than they had with their previous supplier, but the cocaine was nowhere near as pure. 'I take it the gear is the same as the sample we had?'

Hakan nodded. 'We only deal in best.'

When Nick came out of the kitchen, Vinny put his fingers to his lips. Even though he had rung Nick earlier to tell him they were meeting pals of Ahmed's there to discuss importing leather goods from Turkey, Vinny still did not want to say too much in front of the guy. Nick's brother-in-law was East End Old Bill, and you could never be too careful.

After a quick chat, Nick walked away and left them to it. As soon as he was out of earshot, Vinny turned back to Hakan. 'How's the cash part going to work? And where do we collect the goods from? Is it a straight handover?'

Hakan shook his head and spoke to Bora in Turkish. He then told Vinny that Bora would explain.

'My brother-in-law. He work with us and fly plane. You wait for plane. We want half money up front and other half when you receive goods.'

'I don't fancy meeting no plane, Ahmed, and I take it it don't land in Whitechapel? You up for meeting it?'

Ahmed chuckled. 'I can do the pick-up, if you prefer?'

'Nobody, and I mean nobody must ever pick up apart from one of you. Our location top secret, you understand?' Hakan said sternly.

Vinny and Ahmed both nodded their heads in unison. 'Excuse me while I use the toilet,' Vinny said. There were parts of this deal he was not at all happy with, and if Hakan and Bora thought they were going to get one over on him, they could fucking think again.

When Vinny left the table, Hakan asked Ahmed in Turkish if he thought Vinny had fallen for their deception.

Ahmed lifted his glass aloft, clinked it against Hakan and Bora's and replied in Turkish. 'The silly English fool has fallen hook, line and sinker into our trap. Well done, my friends. Well done.'

# CHAPTER TEN

Vivian clasped her hand over her mouth as she stared at her son's grave. She had been too ill at the time to have any input into the inscription or choice of headstone, but her family had done her proud.

In Loving Memory of a True Legend
Leonard William Harris
1956–1976

A much-loved son, nephew and cousin,
you are in your family's hearts and thoughts
every minute of every day
Sleep Tight Champ

Love Mum, Auntie Queenie, Vinny, Roy, Michael, Brenda,
Little Vinny, Tara, Daniel, Lee and Adam

Lenny and Roy's graves stood out from all the others around them. The headstones were posh marble and they were surrounded by fresh flowers.

'You do like it, don't you, Viv? Vinny said he'll change the headstone if you don't. He can't visit here, it upsets him too much, but Michael brings me over regularly to make sure the graves are kept nice. I haven't been able to come over here on my own yet though.'

'It's lovely, Queen. A real tribute to my wonderful boy. Roy's headstone is special too. I'm sorry I'm crying, but I can't help it. I'll be all right in a minute.'

Queenie hugged her sister, then said a few words to both Roy and Lenny. She was weeping too. It couldn't be helped.

Vivian bent down next to her son's grave and laid the flowers she had brought with her. She had wanted to tie Zippy the monkey on the grave somehow, but Queenie had urged her not to, insisting some bastard would steal it.

Putting her right hand to her lips, Vivian planted a kiss on it and held it against her son's headstone. 'Mummy misses you so much, Lenny. I loved the bones of you, I really did,' she wept.

Queenie bent down and coaxed her sister to stand up. 'Come on, darling, we've had enough for one day. Let's go home and pack our stuff for Kings.'

In a West End hotel, Vinny was with Ahmed, Hakan and Bora, discussing their business transaction in finer detail. He'd had a rethink of the situation and, after a sleepless night, had decided to go ahead with the deal for the sake of his daughter's future.

Whitechapel was and would always be close to Vinny's heart, but he did not want Molly to grow up there. His daughter had exposed a soft side to him, a vulnerability he hadn't realized existed until now. He only had to look at that little girl and his heart melted, and he wanted her to be brought up in a posh area and send her to the best possible schools.

It had just been agreed by all that Ahmed would wire £125,000 to an account in Turkey. Once the money was received, the drugs would be delivered by plane and picked up by Ahmed in a remote field in Essex. Then, providing Vinny and Ahmed were happy with their investment, they would immediately wire the outstanding £125,000. The dates of the first exchange had been agreed and a few other small details clarified.

'Have you any more questions?' Hakan asked, directing his smile towards Vinny.

'Actually, I have, as I mentioned to Ahmed on the way here. The brown I haven't sampled, but Ahmed said a pal of his has and it was good, so I'm happy with that. I have a slight concern over the cocaine though. The gear we was getting before was something like ninety-seven per cent pure. Obviously, with stuff that strong we can cut it to fuck and make a fortune out of it. No disrespect, but that sample you gave us was nowhere near the same quality.'

'Vin, I've already told you that the other stuff came straight from Nicaragua, hence the quality. We can search high and low, but we aren't going to find that again,' Ahmed replied, sharing an awkward glance with Hakan and Bora. In the restaurant the other evening Vinny had seemed happy enough to proceed with the deal, and it was only on the way to the hotel today that he'd dropped this little bombshell. Obviously, that had given Ahmed no time to warn his pals.

'Vinny, my cocaine is best money can buy in Turkey, and I do you very cheap deal. Do you know what mine and Bora's names mean in our country?'

Vinny shook his head. He wasn't really bothered what their names meant, but he couldn't be rude in case it left himself and Ahmed without a supplier.

'Bora means violent storm, and my name, the emperor. That is what we are in our country. I rule and Bora not so quiet as he seem. He have very violent temper when he upset.'

Vinny didn't take threats from anyone, and realizing

what Hakan had just said sounded like one, Ahmed pushed his pal out of the room and told Hakan they needed to have a private chat.

'Was that cunt threatening me?' Vinny asked as they took the lift down to the bar.

'No, of course not. He tells that story wherever he goes. It wasn't aimed at you.'

'It better fucking not have been.'

'Vinny, chill out. You've got the wrong end of the stick. Now, what do you want to drink?'

Two large Scotches later, Vinny had to make a decision. Ahmed had explained that he could still put together the deal with their previous supplier, but Vinny wasn't about to chance that. Aside from Ahmed, he didn't like or trust Turks.

Ahmed also insisted that they could still cut Hakan's cocaine and earn the same profit as before. 'The mugs who buy from us probably won't even notice the difference,' he assured Vinny.

'OK, I've made my choice. Let's go with your pal Hakan, but I'm telling you now, I don't fucking like him and I like his shifty-eyed sidekick even less.'

Ahmed allowed himself a smirk as he led Vinny back to the lift. The cocaine being weaker than the stuff from their previous supplier was all part of the plan. What Vinny did not know, was that the cocaine he'd snorted was actually from their previous supplier. Ahmed should know, he'd cut it himself.

Michael Butler was sitting in a restaurant just off Oxford Street. With Vinny going away for the weekend, there was no way he could take Bella out on Sunday now, so he had arranged to meet her today instead.

When she walked into the restaurant, Michael noticed most men's heads turning. She was wearing a short red leather jacket, black shiny leggings and high-heeled red leather boots. 'This is a pleasant surprise, I must say. I didn't think I'd get to see you until Sunday.'

'Well, I knew you had a photo shoot up here today, and I had a business meeting nearby, so I thought I'd give you a bell,' Michael lied. There was no business meeting; he'd come because he knew the longer he put off finishing with Bella, the worse he was going to feel.

When she leaned forward and squeezed Michael's hands she immediately knew something was amiss. He seemed edgy and wouldn't look her in the eye. 'What's the matter? Is something wrong?'

'Let's order some food, shall we?' Michael suggested.

'No, tell me what's wrong first.'

Michael poured Bella some wine and topped his own glass up. He could not afford to bottle this. He had come here to end their affair, and end it he must.

'I'm sorry, Bell, but I can't do this any more. My feelings for you are too strong, and if we continue seeing one another my marriage will be over. If I didn't have kids I'd leave Nancy tomorrow, but I can't be parted from my sons . . .'

Bella stood up. 'I understand, Michael. It was good while it lasted.'

'Don't go yet. Let's at least have some lunch and a proper chat,' Michael said.

She picked up her handbag and smiled. Michael Butler had the handsomest face she had ever seen in her life and she would never forget him. 'There's nothing left to chat about. Look after yourself, Michael.'

When Bella walked out of the restaurant, part of Michael wanted to chase after her, tell her he loved her and had made a big mistake. The thought of never seeing her again just didn't bear thinking of and as he sipped his drink, Michael felt like crying.

*

Queenie and Vivian had both cheered up by the time they got to Eastbourne. Vinny had bought a bungalow on Kings Holiday Park and both women loved it there. Kings wasn't just any old holiday park. It had a massive clubhouse that attracted lots of star acts and there were even plans to build an upstairs to it.

'What shall we do first, Viv? We're bound to need some bits from the little shop, so shall we pop to the amusements, then get some shopping on the way back?'

'Ooh yeah. The prize bingo should start soon,' Viv replied.

'Can I go and see if Gary and Steve are here, Dad?' Little Vinny asked. There hadn't been any room in the car for him to bring Ben Bloggs, and Little Vinny was already sick of being surrounded by adults and a screaming baby.

'No, not yet. You're coming out with me somewhere first.'

'Where?'

Vinny took no notice of his son's question and turned to Joanna. 'You'll be all right on your own with the baby for a bit, won't you?'

Joanna nodded, then grinned. She'd had butterflies in her stomach all day. Life at home was hectic, what with Molly to look after and Vinny working nights, but life in Eastbourne was different. Queenie and Viv were bound to go over to the clubhouse this evening, and Little Vinny would be out playing with his pals, which meant her and Vinny would have the bungalow to themselves. It had been a long time since Joanna had been ravished by her man and she couldn't bloody wait.

Michael Butler rarely got drunk, but today he was steaming. After leaving the restaurant he couldn't face going home, so had driven straight to the club instead.

The knock on the door had been a welcome surprise. Matthew Palmer had been Michael's pal as a young child, and they hadn't seen one another for years due to Matthew's parents moving to Australia. Michael hadn't needed much persuasion to go on a pub crawl, but now he could barely stand up.

'Matt, it's been great seeing you, pal, but I'm gonna have to shoot off. I'm lagging,' Michael slurred.

Matthew put his arm around Michael's shoulders. His accent had a slight Australian lilt to it now, and he had done well in life, just like Michael had. He was the lead singer with a rock band, hence his trip to London. 'You can't go home. I haven't seen you for years. Have a livener,' Matthew urged, pressing something into Michael's hand.

Apart from taking some blues when he was a Mod, Michael had never touched a drug in his life. 'What is it?'

'Cocaine. It's cool, man. You won't get addicted to it. It just sobers you up and makes you feel damn good.'

After the day he'd had, Michael would have done anything to feel good, so when Matt suggested they go to the toilet and take some cocaine together, Michael eagerly followed his pal.

Back in Eastbourne, Vinny Butler drove towards the Moorings pub in silence. He hadn't had the best of days and he was not looking forward to what he had to do next.

'You got the hump with me, Dad? I ain't done nothing wrong,' Little Vinny said when his dad slammed his foot on the brake.

'Get out of the car. We're gonna have a little chat on the beach,' Vinny spat.

Little Vinny followed his father, then sat down opposite him on the sand. It was getting dark now and, apart from a couple of dog walkers, the beach was empty. 'What's wrong, Dad?'

Vinny grabbed his son by the shoulders and stared him straight in the eyes. 'I'm gonna ask you something and I need you to tell me the truth. If you do that, I won't be angry with you whatever your answer is. But if you lie to me and I find out, I will be fucking fuming. Now, do we understand one another?'

Little Vinny nodded.

'Did you throw or get Ben to throw that brick through our window the other night?'

'No! 'Course not, Dad.'

Vinny knew he had to keep calm to extract the truth, so did his utmost to keep his notorious temper in check. 'Look, Vin, I've had my car done over, my club door sprayed with graffiti, and now my window put through. As you well know, boy, I ain't silly. All that stuff is the work of a kid. Please tell me the truth and I promise I won't shout at you. I realize it's been difficult for you with me and Jo getting together and Molly arriving in your life, so in a way I will understand why you did it. You're a growing lad and I had many temper tantrums like that when I was your age.'

'But I ain't done nothing, Dad. I swear on your life I ain't.'

Unable to stop himself because he was positive his son was lying, Vinny put his hand around his son's throat and squeezed it gently. 'Unfortunately for you, I don't fucking believe you, boy, and I'm warning you, if you ever put Molly's life in danger again, I will break your fucking neck, comprende?'

Little Vinny burst into tears. If he had ever needed proof that his dad loved Molly more than him, then this was the moment.

Over in the East End, Michael had now forgotten his woes, sobered up, and wanted to carry on partying. 'Let's go back to my club, Matt. We've got a good singer on tonight. She doesn't sing rock, but does plenty of other stuff, and she's a babe.'

Matt chuckled to himself as they walked back towards the club. Michael had taken to cocaine like a duck does to water. He only hoped his pal didn't ask for any more as he had virtually run out. 'Hey, man, look at that smoke.'

The cocaine had made Michael more alert than usual, and he immediately sensed that the smoke was rising from a location very near to his club. 'Come on, let's jog.'

When they reached the club there were three fire engines, two ambulances, and a police car parked outside. The building was on fire. Not at the front, but at the back. 'Paul, what the fuck has happened?' Michael asked his doorman.

'Some kid got in the back and set fire to it. Pete just spoke to the ambulance man and they reckon the kid's in a bad way. Loads of people have been injured, Michael. They tried to save the boy.'

Michael looked around at the mayhem. There were shocked women, dumbstruck men and quite a few people were being given oxygen, probably for smoke inhalation. 'My brother is gonna fucking kill me, Matt.'

'Why man? You wasn't here. This isn't your fault.'

Vinny had a rule that when the club was open on a Friday and Saturday night, at least one of them had to be there. The fact Michael had been on the gear was making him more paranoid than ever. He knew there was no way he could speak to the police in his current state. He felt good, but out of his nut. 'Matt, let's go. I need to get away from here.'

'You can't, man. Your club's on fire.'

Feeling like he was about to have a heart attack, Michael turned on his heel and ran.

# CHAPTER ELEVEN

Vinny Butler had driven back to London as soon as Pete had rung him. Thank God he'd had the brains to have a phone installed in the bungalow, else he would still be none the wiser.

Joanna had pleaded to travel back with him, but she was the last person Vinny wanted around him in a crisis. He'd insisted she stay in Eastbourne for the time being, saying he would call her in the morning.

When he arrived at the club, the police and fire brigade were still milling around. Spotting one of his trusted doormen, Vinny led him away from listening ears. 'What exactly happened, Paul? And where's Pete?'

'Pete's at the hospital being treated for burns. I think he's feeling a bit guilty.'

'Why? He never started the fire, did he?'

'No, course not. He ran out the back when the smoke started billowing through the club. He ain't told the Old Bill this, but the kid who must have started it was climbing out of the window. Pete grabbed his legs and pulled him back in, then the ceiling collapsed on top of the kid. The whole storeroom was on fire by this time, so Pete had to leave the kid in there.'

'Good! And I hope the little fucker is burnt to cinders. Was the kid alone?'

'No. Pete said he had a mate outside. He heard him shout something out. A few of the customers tried to help the kid, but they couldn't get to him either.'

'More fool them. They should have just left the little cunt to die. Did you catch a glimpse of him?'

'No, he was covered over when they put him in the ambulance. I could smell the burnt flesh though. Horrible, it was. A few of the customers had to be treated for burns as well. I don't think any of them are critical though. I got your thingy out the safe, by the way. It's well hidden. The police wouldn't let Pete out of their sight, so he gave me the code and I sneaked in the office.'

Vinny breathed a huge sigh of relief. He knew how much the Old Bill hated him and had been frightened the fire would give them an excuse to have a good old root around. Obviously, they wouldn't have known the code to his safe, but Vinny wouldn't put it past them to bring an expert in to open it. A firearms charge was the last thing he fucking needed.

'How bad is the damage? I told the Old Bill that I needed to collect some personal belongings from upstairs, but they said it was too dangerous for me to go in there.'

'It's pretty bad. The fire spread from the store room into the club itself. It never got as far as the stage or the bar, but some of the furniture went up in flames. The firemen said that it's not structurally safe any more.'

'Oh, for fuck's sake. I bet we're gonna be closed for months. If that kid ain't dead, he will be when I get my hands on him, and so will fucking Michael be for going out on the lash. I wonder who the kid is. Did Pete say how old he looked?'

'He reckoned he was about sixteen.'

Vinny racked his brains, trying to remember if any of

his enemies had sons or grandsons of that age. He couldn't think of any off the top of his head. 'Right, you wait here while I go to the phonebox. I'll only be five minutes and then we'll shoot up the hospital and see Pete.'

'Who you gonna ring this time of the morning?'

'Geary. I wanna know that kid's name and find out if he's alive or dead.'

George Geary was anything but happy when he was woken by the phone at five a.m.

'What the fuck, Vinny! You have just woken my wife up. This had better be important.'

Vinny went back years with Geary. Before he retired, Chief Inspector Geary had pocketed thousands in backhanders. He still had pals in the force and would happily exploit those connections in exchange for a bung, which was why Vinny had rung him.

'This is extremely important, George. Some kid burned my club down tonight. He was taken to hospital in a bad way. I want to know who the cunt is and if he's still alive. I'll ring you back in an hour.' Without waiting for a reply, Vinny ended the call.

After visiting Pete and urging him to keep his trap shut about grabbing the boy's legs as he tried to escape, Vinny dropped Paul off, then headed home himself. The club was insured for fire and contents, so he was well covered, but that didn't include wages and he would still have to see Pete and Paul all right, plus a few of his other more important staff. He wasn't too bothered about most of the barmaids as they were easily replaced.

Relieved that he hadn't flown into a rage and ballsed the drug deal up the previous day, Vinny let himself indoors and poured a large Scotch. At least while the club was shut he would have plenty of money coming in. Knocking his drink back in one large gulp, he picked up the phone. 'Well?' he asked Geary.

'You might want to sit down, Vinny.'

'Why?'

'Well, the boy was dead before they even got him to hospital. His name is Mark Preston. He's Johnny's sister's boy.'

Thanking George for the information, a shell-shocked Vinny ended the call. To say he was stunned was putting it mildly. He'd only ever seen Mark Preston once, when he had visited Judy at home to instruct her to abort his father's child. Mark had been a fresh-faced toddler then and Vinny could barely believe that, all these years later, the kid had come back to haunt him.

Pouring himself another drink, he collapsed onto the sofa. The flowers, the graffiti, his car being done over, the window being smashed, must all have been Mark Preston's handiwork. And no doubt Johnny had been the one who'd put him up to it.

Wondering how Joanna would react to the news, Vinny tried to look on the bright side. At least now his mystery stalker had been identified, he could stop worrying about the safety of his family and looking nervously over his shoulder the whole time. And the little shit was dead, that was another bonus. Good riddance to bad rubbish, as they say.

Annoyed with himself for accusing his own flesh and blood of such terrible crimes, Vinny silently vowed never to disbelieve his son again. He also vowed that one day he would torture and kill Johnny Preston in the most excruciating way possible. Perhaps he should pull Johnny's teeth out, chop his hands off, then set fire to him like he had Trevor? Or was there a more painful way to kill someone? Vinny smirked. He would have to do some research.

# CHAPTER TWELVE

Summer 1980

Queenie Butler made herself a cup of tea and sat on the step of the bungalow. Vivian was still fast asleep in the bedroom and Queenie was glad of some peace and quiet for once. Since Michael had bought the bungalow opposite it was usually like Casey's bloody Court with the grandkids running in and out.

Kings Holiday Park had changed for the better since Vinny had first purchased the bungalow in 1976. The clubhouse now had a posh upstairs to it, and Queenie and Viv loved nothing more than getting glammed up, then rushing over to the club early to ensure they got the best seats.

Coachloads of visitors would arrive from far and wide at weekends to watch the fabulous entertainment. The Drifters, Boney M, Les Dawson, Des O'Connor and Jimmy Jones were just some of the wonderful acts that Queenie and Vivian had seen, but being staunch royalists, nothing beat the evening a couple of years ago when Prince Charles and the Three Degrees appeared there. It was a royal charity event and Queenie and Viv had been so keen to meet

Charles and have a photo taken with him that they had nearly pushed the poor prince over.

Seeing the next-door-but-one neighbour walking along whistling with his newspaper, Queenie darted inside. Her and Viv had nicknamed him and his wife 'the notrights' and both were sure that he was a pervert. He had a habit of standing in front of them while they were sitting in deckchairs with Speedo trunks on and his bulge on show. Viv had sworn she had once seen his helmet poking out of the top and vowed if she ever saw it again, she would chop the fucking thing off.

Queenie put the TV on, then turned the volume down. The news was all about strikes and unemployment lately and she found it bloody depressing. So much seemed to have changed over the past few years. Elvis Presley had died, Margaret Thatcher had become the first ever female prime minister, there was sod all worth watching on TV, and today's fashion left a lot to be desired. Skinheads were the current craze and Queenie thought they looked vulgar. If her Vinny, Roy, or Michael had ever come home with shaved heads, Doctor Marten boots, tattoos or rings dangling from their earlobes, Queenie would have given them such a good hiding they wouldn't have been able to sit down for a month of Sundays. Much to her disgust, Little Vinny was now a skinhead. He'd recently had his hair cut without his father's permission and Vinny had gone ballistic when he had seen it. He had punished his son by smashing up his record collection and burning every single item of skinhead clothing he owned – quite right too, in Queenie's opinion.

'Morning, Queen. Nice day, isn't it? How long you been up?' Vivian asked.

'I didn't sleep well again, Viv. I got up at five. I was just sitting here thinking, ain't times changed? I wish we could go back to the sixties sometimes. Apart from being married to Albie, life was good back then. Like a load of sheep youngsters are these days. They have to be part of a flock.'

'Don't you remember when your Michael was a Mod back in the sixties? Kids go through these phases. First time my Lenny saw a punk, he wanted to be one. It's what youngsters do. Anyway, this isn't the real reason why you're miserable. You're worrying about those boys of yours again, aren't you? I know it's difficult, Queen, but they're adults now, and if you don't stop fretting and start sleeping, you'll end up in that funny farm where I was.'

Queenie sighed. Brenda had always been her biggest worry in the past, especially after Dean disappeared, but since losing three stone in weight and having her hair cut and dyed blonde, her daughter was much happier in herself.

'I'm determined to get the truth out of my Vinny and Michael, Viv. They are definitely hiding something from me, and seeing as I gave birth to the bastards, I have every right to know what the bloody hell is going on.'

Vinny Butler sat stony-faced as he counted up the week's takings. Once again, they were poor and even though bringing in strippers on a Sunday lunchtime had worked a treat, ever since Denny McCann, another known villain, had opened up a similar type of club in Shoreditch, Vinny and Michael's earnings had dipped dramatically.

Vinny blamed a mixture of things for his and Michael's misfortune. Their run of bad luck had begun with the fire, which had closed the club for four months. Unbeknown to Vinny, the insurance had run out so he'd had to pay for all the damage out of his own pocket. Michael had offered to chip in, but Vinny refused. It had been his job to renew the insurance, therefore his mistake. It was during that terrible time that Denny's club had opened. Then, last year, there'd been a shooting inside the club. Mitchell Moran had not been the most popular of men, but when a gang of masked gunmen ran in firing shots galore and blasted Mitchell's brains out in front of a club full of terrified punters, business had taken an almighty dive.

Checking out his appearance in the full-length mirror, Vinny put some Brylcreem into the palm of his hands and ran it through his jet-black hair. He still had that mafia look off to a tee.

'Morning, bruv. Has Nancy rung?'

Staring at his dishevelled brother, Vinny shook his head. Michael was currently bedding one of the strippers and was spending more nights at the club than he was at home. He was also more than partial to a line or two of cocaine these days and although he never usually took it during working hours, Vinny knew he had last night. His pupils had looked enormous and he had been talking utter shit.

'You look fucking dreadful, Michael. Have a butcher's in the mirror, go on. Snorting charlie isn't the answer to your problems – I should know, I've been there, bruv.'

Michael sat down and put his messed-up head in his hands. He had never got over losing Bella and had regretted his rash decision to end their short, but passionate affair every day since. He had tried to contact her a couple of months after ditching her, but her phone had been disconnected and, according to the new tenants in her apartment, she had sold up and moved to New York.

Nancy was still in love with him, Michael knew that, but even though she had now overcome her depression, no matter how much he tried, he could not make himself fall back in love with her. He adored his sons though. They were his pride and joy.

Vinny handed his brother a mug of black coffee. 'You've got to sort yourself out for your boys' sake. I know you see them during the day, but Lee and Daniel are now old enough to know that there must be something wrong if you're staying out at night. Mum's worried sick about you, ya know. She's always grilling me and I can't keep making excuses for you. Mum isn't silly.'

Michael glared at his brother. Anybody would think Vinny was a saint, the way he carried on. 'OK, I'll come clean to Mum then, shall I? I'll explain to her that one of the reasons why I'm so unhappy in my life is carrying the burden on my shoulders of how Champ really died. Wonder what her reaction to that will be?'

'You nasty bastard! It was after you split up with Bella you started snorting, so don't be blaming me.'

Michael stood up and glared at his brother. 'It was a mixture of everything, Vin. Roy dying, Nancy's illness, you burdening me with the truth about Champ's death, the fire, and Bella. Because I'm not as vocal as you, you think I'm daft, bruv, but I'm not. I've known for ages that you are dealing in the shit you keep lecturing me about, so next time you fancy getting all sanctimonious on me, think again.'

When Michael stormed out of the office, Vinny slammed his fist against the desk in frustration. Everything seemed to be falling apart lately, including his once-lucrative business partnership with Ahmed. These days it was paying peanuts compared to what it used to, and Vinny knew it was due to the poor quality of drugs they were buying. He hadn't trusted Hakan and Bora on sight, so should have gone with his instincts. Ahmed had even admitted recently that the strength of the cocaine and heroin they were purchasing had deteriorated badly over the years.

Picking up the photo of Molly that took pride of place on his desk, Vinny felt his anger lessen. Molly had turned three in May and had the face, smile and nature of an angel. The photo had been taken on her birthday and she was sitting on her favourite present, a rocking horse. Apart from having inherited his piercing green eyes, she looked nothing like Vinny. She had fair skin and a mop of curly blonde hair. She was such a pretty child that whenever he or Jo took her out, people would stop in their tracks just to comment on her beauty.

Vinny put the photo back on his desk and debated what to say to Ahmed. He was sick of being ripped off by Hakan and Bora and he was even more sick of his ever-decreasing bank balance. Vinny was a man of style and taste, always had been. He liked to eat, drink and wear only the very best. He also loved to splash the cash and made sure his family never wanted for anything. From the age of eighteen, he had supported his mum and aunt pretty much single-handedly. It wasn't Michael who had paid for their new kitchens and bathrooms, it was him. And he'd been the one that handed over the two hundred grand it took to get the club up and running again after the fire.

Vinny picked up the phone. He was determined to buy his dream house in Essex before Molly started school, so the quicker circumstances changed, the better.

'Ahmed, it's me. Can you pop over to the club later? We need to talk, urgently.'

Little Vinny was standing outside his old school. They had expelled him last year for punching a male teacher and he now attended a new school, which he despised.

Walking up to a nearby car, he checked his reflection out in the wing mirror. He was a massive fan of Madness and the Specials and he liked to model his appearance on Suggs or Terry Hall.

When his dad had set fire to all his beloved clothes and boots in the incinerator in the back garden, Little Vinny had been devastated. What his old man hadn't realized though, was how easy it was to steal money out of his pockets and shoplift these days. Many a time, he and Ben had paid a visit to Mintz & Davis in Romford. They would wear baggy outfits, take a dozen items into the changing rooms, then walk out with a pair of Sta-Prest and a Ben Sherman shirt under their own clothing. They would then celebrate their cleverness by drinking cider and sniffing glue.

Unlike himself, Ben Bloggs had had a tough upbringing. He had no idea who his dad was, his mum was a druggie and a prostitute, and his nan was forever in court for thieving. The eldest of seven children, Ben had never been bought nice clothes or given nice things like he had and Little Vinny felt sorry for his pal and partner in crime. Poor Ben hadn't even been taught about cleanliness or allowed regular baths, which was why he was now being picked on at school. Without Little Vinny around to protect him, Ben was an easy target for the likes of Stephen Daniels and his cronies.

Seeing Daniels emerge from the school, Little Vinny hid behind the car and then followed him. He knew the route Daniels walked home and he knew by the time he reached the end of the alleyway, he would have bumped into Ben.

The plan worked like a dream, and Little Vinny waited until he saw Daniels grab Ben by the scruff of his neck before he ran towards him. He pulled the gun from the waistband of his trousers and prodded it in the side of Daniel's head.

When the two lads who were with Daniels tried to flee, Little Vinny screamed at them to stop by threatening to shoot them too.

'I'm sorry. Please don't shoot me,' Stephen Daniels begged.

Enjoying the fear in Daniel's and his pals' eyes, Little

Vinny lined them up against the fence. 'Go and check that end of the alley, make sure no one is coming,' he ordered Ben. The other direction had a clear view.

Ben did as he was told, then ran back. 'Coast is clear.'

'Good. Now get on your fucking knees,' Little Vinny ordered his victims. He had seen his dad in action, so knew exactly how to frighten people.

'Look, we're sorry for having a dig at Ben. It won't happen again. I promise, Vinny. Please don't kill us. We was only messing,' Daniel stammered. He was petrified that he was going to die and could tell his pals were too.

'I want all three of yous cunts to beg forgiveness and apologize to Ben.'

All three lads immediately did as they were told. Noticing a wet patch around Stephen Daniel's crotch area, Little Vinny had great pleasure in poking the gun into the side of his head again. 'I swear on my baby sister's life, if you upset my mate Ben ever again, I will blow your fucking brains out.'

Ahmed Zane chuckled as he counted up the week's takings. Unbeknown to Vinny, he had never changed supplier. He still brought all his drugs from Emre, and was absolutely raking it in.

When he had first moved to England, Ahmed had not had the financial clout to buy the amount of drugs he needed at the right price. That was why he had gone into partnership with Vinny in the first place. They had made a good team, so Ahmed had thought, until the Judas shitbag had left him for dead.

He could have forgiven Vinny for panicking on the night in question and even doing a runner. What he could not forgive was Vinny moving his body into the driver's seat. That was a cold, calculating, despicable deed.

Vinny was paying the price now though. Ahmed had robbed him of hundreds of thousands of pounds over the past few years and had enjoyed every moment of it.

Ahmed grinned as he put the takings in the safe, then picked up his car keys. He knew exactly what Vinny wanted to speak to him about, which is why he had planned ahead. Vinny Butler would have a very nasty surprise coming his way soon. A very nasty one indeed.

Joanna Preston and Nancy Butler were sitting in Barking Park with a picnic which included a bottle of wine. They used to meet up in a local pub that was child friendly, until Vinny found out and blew a fuse. Apparently, by going to a pub, Jo was not only putting Molly's life in danger, she was also acting like a single woman and a whore. According to Vinny, only old slappers sat in boozers without being accompanied by a man.

Joanna's relationship with Vinny was a strange one, to say the least. He was an amazing father to Molly and incredibly generous to both her and her daughter. But his possessiveness drove Joanna bonkers at times. He hated her close friendship with Nancy, and always questioned where they had gone and what they had spoken about, and if any man ever dared to look her way or speak to her while they were out together, Vinny would fly into a terrible rage. Joanna could have understood Vinny's unusual behaviour if they were Whitechapel's answer to Romeo and Juliet, but the truth was, their sex life was virtually non-existent. She could count on one hand the times they had made love over the past year.

'So, how's things your end?' Jo asked Nancy.

'Crap. Michael didn't come home again last night. That's three times in the past week he has supposedly stayed at the club. I want to confront him, say I know he's having an affair, but I wish I had some proof. Can't you pump Vinny in a roundabout way? I will never let on that you said anything, Jo.'

Joanna sighed and comfortingly squeezed her pal's hand. How she would have coped with the ups and downs of her relationship with Vinny over the past few years without having Nancy as a shoulder to cry on, she did not know. However, she was very reluctant to start asking awkward questions indoors, because if Michael was having an affair there was no way Vinny would tell her. He never spoke about business or discussed members of his family with her.

'Nance, there's no point me asking Vin. You know what he's like: he tells me sod all, and if he thought I was sniffing around for information, you can bet your life on it that he would warn Michael you was on to him. Anyway, I don't reckon he is having an affair. My Vinny has been acting weird too. He went mad when Brenda asked him for some money last week and that is so not like him. He would give every penny he had to his family, so my guess would be perhaps our men have some financial difficulties. I know the club isn't anywhere near as busy as it once was, because I overheard Queenie and Vivian talking about it last weekend at Kings.'

'Well, I hope you're right, Jo. Obviously, I don't want the boys' business to be in trouble, but Michael is as cold as ice to me lately and I would rather it was down to money troubles than another woman. I wonder what's wrong with me sometimes. I know I'm probably half a stone or so heavier since I first met Michael, but I do try to keep myself looking nice. March was the last time he came anywhere near me and now we're in July. He makes me feel so ugly,' Nancy admitted, close to tears.

Joanna knew what it was like to feel sexually unwanted.

She still fancied Vinny like mad, and many a night had cried herself to sleep when he had turned his back on her in bed yet again. She often wondered if her cousin Mark burning down his club was the cause of Vinny's lack of intimacy towards her, but she had a feeling it wasn't. Vinny didn't even like kissing, and apart from the odd peck on the lips, had not kissed her properly in years.

The awkward conversation was brought to an end by Molly running over to her mum and aunt. 'Can I have an ice lolly please, Mummy?'

Joanna picked her daughter up and swung her in the air. For all Vinny's faults and possessiveness, he had given her the most beautiful child in the world and for that Joanna would always be grateful. Molly was such a happy child. She loved dancing and singing and was obsessed with *Sesame Street* and *Tom and Jerry*. 'You, my little cherub, can have anything you want, and do you know why?'

Molly giggled and shook her head.

'Because you are good and you are beautiful and your mummy loves you so very much.'

Albie Butler could barely contain his excitement as he showed his brother the ring. 'Michael helped me out with it, so I could get a real diamond. Isn't it pretty? Do you think Dorothy will like it and say yes?'

Bert grinned. Albie was a changed man since Dorothy had arrived on the scene. Tomorrow was her birthday, and he and Albie were taking her out to lunch to celebrate. Albie planned to propose at the restaurant and Bert was as excited as if it were him about to get wed. 'She won't just like it, she'll love it, Albie. As for her saying yes, you have no worries there. That woman adores the bones of you.'

'I know, but I can't help feeling nervous. Never thought

I would want to marry again after bloody Queenie. Thought that old witch had put me off getting hitched for life.'

Bert wrapped an arm around his brother's shoulder. When Albie had first moved to Ipswich he was skin and bone and his clothes had hung on his tall frame. Now, he looked the picture of health and even had the cheeky twinkle back in his eye. 'Dorothy is a lovely lady, Albie, nothing like Queenie. If you want to get your own place once wed, I will understand you know.'

'Don't be daft! Dorothy loves living here and so do I. Why would we want to move? We're one big happy family.'

Johnny Preston sat down opposite his soon-to-be wife. He had some fantastic news that he'd been itching to tell her and he couldn't wait to see the look on her face.

'Come on then. Spill the beans,' Deborah urged. Johnny had said he had something important to tell her when they had spoken on the phone last night.

'My brief paid me a visit. He's asked for parole and reckons I'll get it. I might even be home in time for my birthday, so best you start planning the wedding. Don't book an actual date yet though, as I don't want to jinx it, but you can start looking for a dress and somewhere for us to live. I don't want to move back to Tiptree, babe. I want to be nearer to Jo and Molly.'

Even though Deborah was absolutely ecstatic that Johnny might be home soon, she thought moving near Joanna and Molly was a terrible idea. According to Jo, Vinny had been furious when Mark had burned his club down and even though Johnny swore that he'd had no idea what Mark was planning, Deborah guessed that Vinny would think differently. 'I really don't think we should move to London, Johnny. There's too many bad memories there, and I would miss Sandy dreadfully if we upped sticks.'

'And there's plenty of bad memories in Tiptree too, Deb. I hated working in that fucking slaughterhouse, and we split up there. My fault, I know, but I would never have given that tart a second glance had I not felt so useless and unhappy in myself. I can't live there again. Nice area if you like strawberry-picking, but it isn't for me.'

'But how are we going to afford to move? I've been managing week to week, Johnny, but we've no savings.'

Johnny leaned forward and cupped Deborah's face in his hands. 'Billy One Ear has a job waiting for me on the outside, babe. And before you start shouting and screaming, I swear it's all above board. He's a second-hand car dealer and wants me to run one of the garages. The dosh is far more than I will ever earn in Tiptree, so I have to take it, Deb. It will be a new start for us and seeing as both of our kids now live in London, it will give us the opportunity to become a proper family again.'

Deborah looked in Johnny's handsome face. Even though he was forty-two now and had lines and wrinkles, his hair was still strawberry blond and he was as handsome as ever. 'Are you sure the job is legal, Johnny?'

'Positive! Being on parole means I'll be banged up as soon as I put a foot wrong, Deb. No way would I ever chance that. I just want to move on with my life, work hard and build a relationship with my children again. But most of all, I want to marry you.'

Deborah smiled. Johnny could have had his pick of women, and even though they had had their ups and downs over the years, Deborah still felt like the luckiest woman on earth to have snared him. 'OK. Let's move back to London then.'

When Ahmed left his office, Vinny Butler breathed a sigh of relief. He thought his insistence to end their business deal with Hakan and Bora would prove far more difficult, but Ahmed had not only agreed his concerns were valid, he had also admitted business was that bad, he wanted out too.

Vinny felt as though he'd been treading on eggshells with Ahmed ever since the accident. They remained close, but their relationship had never been quite the same. Nevertheless, business was business and Ahmed had told him he had already sounded out a promising new contact. Nothing could be worse than the shit they were buying off Hakan and Bora, so Vinny had told Ahmed to arrange a meet as soon as possible.

He was reaching for the bottle to pour himself a drink when the phone rang. He immediately heard the panic in Joanna's voice. 'Slow down. I can't understand what you're saying, Jo.'

'I said the police just knocked at the door. Little Vinny has been arrested for threatening some lad with a gun. You need to come home, quickly.'

An hour later, Ahmed Zane was sitting in a pub in Wembley. Carl Thompson sat opposite him and they had just shaken hands on a deal. 'So, your name is Richie Simpson. You come from Barking and you are a pal of my cousin's, OK? Just remember everything I have told you to say and whatever you do, do not slip up – he's a clever cunt. If you think you might have made a mistake, you need to talk your way straight out of it. I really do not want this to go wrong.'

Carl grinned. 'It won't. For the fifty grand you're paying me, I'll learn and recite the whole fuckin' bible if you want me to.'

Ahmed chuckled. 'That's the spirit.'

*

Vinny Butler sat down opposite his son's headmaster. The police were thankfully not pressing charges. Under questioning, Little Vinny had claimed that the gun was a realistic-looking toy one. After he had led them to the spot where he had hidden it, they had accepted his story and let him off with a caution.

When the headmaster explained he had no option but to expel his son, Vinny begged him to reconsider. 'Look, I know what my boy did was wrong, and so does he. He's sitting outside this office as we speak, full of remorse. He has promised me nothing like this will ever happen again and I believe him. All he was doing was sticking up for a pal who was being bullied. I really don't see why you have to expel him, seeing as the incident didn't even happen at your school.'

'I am very sorry, Mr Butler, but no matter where the incident happened, I have to put the safety of my pupils above all else. Threatening another pupil with a gun, whether it was a replica or not, is totally unforgivable.'

'How about if I make a generous donation to school funds? Will that help change your mind?'

The headmaster looked at Vinny in disgust. He knew who the man was and what he represented. He also knew that his horrid son was destined to follow in his footsteps. 'I am very sorry, Mr Butler, but I shall not be blackmailed. Now, if you would kindly leave these premises and take your son with you, I would be most grateful.'

Somehow restraining the urge to knock the pompous prick's teeth out, Vinny stormed out of the office. He then vented his anger on his son, prodding and punching him all the way along the corridor.

Little Vinny was shocked by his dad's hissy fit. He knew he had done wrong by borrowing his father's gun, but thought his dad would be pleased that he'd had the brains to stash a toy one in case the Old Bill came knocking. 'What did the headmaster say, Dad?'

Vinny ignored his son's question until they got outside. He then picked Little Vinny up by the throat and slammed him against a nearby wall. 'He said you're fucking expelled – what d'you think he said? And you'd best hope that my gun is still where you've hidden it, 'cause if it's not, I shall chop those thieving hands of yours off.'

Little Vinny had never seen his dad so angry. 'Please put me down. You're strangling me.'

Eyes bulging, Vinny loosened his grip so his son's feet made contact with the pavement. He then grabbed him by the chin and stared him straight in the eyes. 'Things are gonna change from now on, boy. You won't be going back to school; neither will you be knocking about with that fucking div Ben Bloggs any more. You'll be coming to work for me.'

'How much will I get paid?' Little Vinny brazenly asked.

'Zilch! For years you've been a disappointment to me and your reward for your hard work will be me turning you into a man. Molly is worth ten of you. I really fucking mean that, boy.'

# CHAPTER THIRTEEN

Albie Butler sat bolt upright in bed. He'd had that awful nightmare again where Queenie and Vivian had locked him in a cupboard with no food or water and left him there to die.

Relieved that it was not true, Albie smiled as he leaned towards Dorothy. 'Happy birthday, my darling. I'll go down and make us a cuppa, shall I?'

When Dorothy did not stir, Albie decided to let her lie in for a bit while he made her some tea and toast. Dorothy was not a regular drinker of alcohol, only ever indulged on special occasions, but she'd gone out for a birthday meal with her old work colleagues from the library yesterday evening and drank a couple of snowballs. She had talked the hind legs off a donkey when she had arrived home, which had amused Albie and Bert immensely.

'Morning, Albie. Is the old lush not awake yet?'

Albie chuckled. 'No. I reckon she's nursing a hangover. You going to the allotment this morning?'

'Yes, as soon as I've read my paper. You stay here with the birthday girl. I'll water your patch for you.'

Putting the tea and toast on the tray, Albie walked slowly

up the stairs. 'Wakey, wakey, darling. I've made you some breakfast.'

Receiving no reply, Albie put the tray on the dressing table. He then knelt on the bed and gently shook the love of his life. His smile was replaced by a grimace of panic and disbelief as his fingers made contact with her skin. It was cold as ice, and no matter how he pleaded, his beloved Dorothy was unable to respond. The poor woman was as dead as dead could be.

'Nanna, Nanna,' young Molly Butler shouted as her mum answered the front door.

Deborah Preston picked her beautiful granddaughter up and gave her a big hug. Molly was nothing like her father, thankfully, and she had an adorable nature. Deborah had taken many photos of the child to send to Johnny in prison and even he admitted she resembled a little angel. He had joked that Jo must have been knocking off some other bloke on that holiday camp as there was no way Vinny's sperm could produce such a gorgeous child.

'I was surprised when you rang me earlier, Mum. I wasn't expecting you to visit until next week.'

'Is Vinny here?' Deborah whispered. She had thoroughly enjoyed spending time with her daughter and Molly when Johnny had first suggested she keep an eye on them. But over the past couple of years, apart from two occasions, Vinny had always been hanging around whenever she visited.

Deborah hated Vinny even more now than the first time she had laid eyes on him. He obviously adored Molly, was polite to her in front of Joanna, but Deborah could see through the bastard. And how she had held her temper when he'd smirked at her, then asked her how Johnny was doing on her last visit, Deborah did not know.

'Vinny went out early this morning, Mum. He isn't due back for ages.'

'Good, because we need to talk.'

When her mum explained that it was highly likely her dad would get parole soon and they were planning on moving to London, Joanna felt the colour drain from her face. Since the fire at the club, Vinny had banned her from having any contact with her father ever again.

'Please don't move to London, Mum. If you do it will really cause me trouble. I love Dad, you know I do, but there is no way I can see him or introduce him to Molly. Vinny swears blind that it was Dad who put Mark up to starting that fire. If I disobey him, he won't let you see Molly either.'

'But you've been writing to your father behind Vinny's back. We'll just have to be careful. Your dad loves and misses you terribly, Jo, and not being able to meet his granddaughter will break his heart. He swears to me he had no idea that Mark had planned that fire, and I know he's telling the truth. Believe me, I know your father well enough to know when he is lying.'

'Shame you didn't know about his affairs then, Mum. You can't be that psychic when it comes to Dad, seeing as it was me who caught him out.'

Deborah gave her daughter a look of distaste. Johnny messing about with one of Joanna's school friend's mums was the reason their marriage had ended, but she saw no reason to bring it up now. 'I know what you're trying to do, Jo. You're trying to turn the tables and make me look like a door mat, just because you're too scared to put your foot down with that bastard who rules you. I am not stupid, love. I gave birth to you and I know deep down you aren't happy with him.'

'Yes, I am. Vinny loves me and Molly,' Joanna replied defensively.

'And me and your dad love you and Molly too. Look, Jo, I know your dad hasn't met Molly yet, but even though she is part of Vinny, he loves her to death. You cannot ban him from seeing her. You must speak to Vinny and come to some arrangement. Even if your dad gets to see you and her once a month, I'm sure he will be happy.'

'What Nanny say, Mummy?' Molly asked innocently, holding her chubby arms out for a cuddle. Raised voices had given the child an inkling that all was not well.

'Nothing important, darling. Why don't you pop upstairs and get your new dolly. I'm sure Nanny would love to meet Molly Dolly.'

Giggling because she knew the doll had been named after her by her daddy, Molly toddled happily up the stairs.

Joanna moved over to the sofa and gave her mum a hug. 'I'm sorry for bringing up Dad's affair, and I promise I will try to talk to Vinny. But I doubt he will ever allow Dad to be part of Molly's life, Mum. It's not just the fire. You have to remember, Dad shot his brother Roy.'

Deborah held Joanna to her chest as she had done when she was a child. 'Don't get upset, angel. Everything will work out in the end, I just know it will.'

About to tell her mother that there was more chance of hell freezing over than things working out, Molly's re-appearance made Joanna reconsider. Her mum was only trying to be positive, so what was the point of ruining her visit?

When Vinny Butler walked into The Bull in Hornchurch, Splodgenessabounds' 'Two Pints of Lager and a Packet of Crisps Please' was playing on the jukebox and the pub was full of bikers.

'Well, this wasn't a very good choice. How we meant to have a business meeting in here? I can't even hear myself fucking think.'

Ignoring his protests, Ahmed led his business partner over to a dark-haired bloke who was stood at the bar. He was wearing light trousers, a brown short-sleeved Gabicci shirt, and looked about thirty.

'Richie, this is Vinny. Vinny this is Richie.'

Vinny shook hands and was about to speak when AC/DC's 'Whole Lotta Rosie' started blasting out of the jukebox. 'I ain't staying in this dive. I cannot abide bikers or their shit taste in music,' Vinny yelled in Ahmed's ear.

Richie knocked back the short he was drinking and gestured for Ahmed and Vinny to follow him. Once outside the pub, he grinned. 'I only live down the road. I don't usually invite strangers back to my gaff, but I've heard lots of good things about you via Ahmed, so I trust you are sound,' Richie said, directing the comment at Vinny.

Richie's gaff was a two-bedroomed flat in Emerson Park. Vinny immediately clocked that Richie had class. The flat was immaculate. It had a smart oxblood-coloured Chesterfield sofa, a stunning triangular-shaped glass table that sat in the centre of the lounge, and even though Vinny knew little about art, he could tell that the big painting on the wall was an expensive one. 'That your kids?' Vinny asked, pointing at a photo of Richie with two babies on his lap.

'Yeah. Twin boys. Six now, they are. I miss seeing them wake up every morning since I split up with their mum, but I get to see them every weekend. They only live in Barking, which is where I come from.'

'Sorry to hear that, pal. Must be tough for you. I've got a boy and a girl myself and I would hate to live apart from them,' Vinny replied. He had warmed to Richie already.

Richie poured out three large brandies and handed a tumbler each to Ahmed and Vinny. 'Taste that. Thirty years old that is.'

'Beautiful, Richie. Now, let's talk business, shall we?' Ahmed suggested.

Richie walked over to his bookcase, pulled out an autobiography, opened the cover, and threw two see-through bags towards Ahmed and Vinny. One contained white powder, the other brown.

Vinny opened one bag. The cocaine was rock hard and looked completely uncut. 'You got something I can bash this up with?'

As soon as Vinny snorted a small line, he turned to Ahmed and grinned. 'Jesus! That's knocked my block off. Try it. It's proper.'

Ahmed did as Vinny asked, then smirked at Richie. 'How much of this can you get your hands on?'

'I've got ten kilo around me at the moment, and can get more in a fortnight. It's not cheap though. I don't know what you were paying your previous supplier, but this stuff is forty grand per kilo. With its purity, as you well know, you can turn it into hundreds of thousands of pounds. Charlie is becoming more popular by the day. A pal of mine has been selling tons of it at eighty quid per gram.'

'Do you mind if me and Ahmed have a moment alone to chat, Richie?' Vinny asked.

'No, not at all. I'll leave you to it.'

When Richie left the room, Vinny turned to Ahmed. 'That's fucking well steep, mate. We have to try and knock him down on the price a bit. Don't get me wrong, the gear is top drawer, but it's a hell of a lot more than we've been paying.'

'In this world you get what you pay for, Vinny. I know it's expensive, but such is the purity we can turn that ten kilo into twenty before we sell it on. I feel completely out my nut on that small line. It's like the old stuff we used to get from Emre and I don't want to mess this deal up by bartering. The heroin is even dearer, I think. I'm sure he told me that was fifty grand per kilo, but that's meant to be top-drawer stuff too. Obviously, we will need to get a guinea pig to test that for us, but you can just see and smell the quality of it,' Ahmed said, handing the bag to Vinny.

'I don't care what quality it is. Fifty grand a kilo is daylight robbery. That's virtually double what Hakan was charging us for the brown. Why don't we forget about the heroin and just concentrate on the coke, eh? That's where the big profit for the future lies.'

'I think you are right. The demand for cocaine is getting bigger by the day.'

'Let's tell Richie our decision then.'

When Richie re-entered the room, he listened to what Ahmed had to say, then nodded. 'Before we shake on this, I need to stipulate my rules. Obviously, you're to tell nobody that you are dealing with me. The deals will take place at this flat and only one of you comes to collect and exchange money. I'll be honest – and I don't mean any disrespect to you, Ahmed – but I would rather Vinny be the one who comes here. With you being Turkish, he looks far less conspicuous if he bumps into any of my neighbours.'

Vinny held his hands up, palms facing outwards. 'I won't be picking it up. Ahmed sorts out that side of our business. That's the deal we have.'

'Yes, but this is different, Vinny. We are not picking up from a remote airfield any more. We are coming to Hornchurch, to Richie's flat,' Ahmed stated.

'I'm sorry, Ahmed, but the agreement we had when I first came into this business with you was that I am the silent partner. No way am I driving about with ten kilo in my car.'

'Well, I don't exactly want to drive about with ten kilo in my car either, Vinny, but some mug has to do it.'

'Look, lads, I'm not being funny, but this is something you need to thrash out in private. If you don't want to go ahead with the deal, there'll be no hard feelings. I've got to pop out in a bit, so get back to me in a day or two, once you've had a chance to discuss things your end. I'm sure between the three of us we can still come to some arrangement.'

Ahmed winked as he and Richie shook hands. Carl Thompson had more than earned the first instalment of wedge that was heading his way. The geezer had played a blinder.

Donald and Mary Walker were in exceedingly good spirits. They had spent a lovely day with their grandsons, and this evening they would be meeting their son Christopher's girlfriend for the very first time.

'Auntie Mary, can we play in the swimming pool again, please?' Young Lee asked politely.

At first Donald had been totally opposed to the idea of Lee visiting them with Daniel and Adam. He had said Lee was Michael's flesh and blood, and not their responsibility. However, when Nancy had begged her father to reconsider, saying the situation was causing problems in her marriage and Michael had insisted that, if Lee wasn't included, then Daniel and Adam would not be allowed to visit as often, Donald had reluctantly agreed.

Lee was a lovely, polite little boy. He called Donald and Mary Uncle and Auntie and both of them had become very fond of him. Mary hugged the child. 'No more swimming pool today, darling. Nancy is picking you up soon and she will be annoyed if you get in her car all wet, won't she?'

Donald chuckled. The children had just broken up from school for the six-week summer holidays and it had been his idea to purchase a large-sized paddling pool to keep them entertained. Today was the first time the boys had seen the pool and his gift had been a great success. 'Are you looking forward to your holiday at Kings, Lee?'

'Yeah, but Daddy never comes to Kings with us any more and we miss him, don't we, Daniel?'

'And Daddy doesn't come home at night,' Adam blurted out.

Mary and Donald shared a worried glance. 'What do you mean, Daddy doesn't come home at night? He's there when you wake up in the morning, isn't he?' Mary asked.

'Only sometimes. Nan, are you and Granddad coming to stay with us at Kings? Mum said you might,' Daniel asked.

'I'm not sure yet, love,' Mary replied. Nancy had invited her and Donald to spend some time at Kings with her and the boys during the school holiday. Nancy had promised Michael wouldn't be there, but Donald was still set against the idea as he knew Vinny owned the bungalow opposite. 'The thought of bumping into those two old witches Queenie and Vivian or that monster Vinny makes my skin crawl, Mary,' were her husband's exact words.

Mary had suggested that they book their own bungalow or chalet so they would not have to bump into their in-laws, but even though Donald had thawed slightly, he had yet to agree.

When Adam climbed onto his grandfather's lap and begged him to come to Kings, Donald sighed, then winked at Mary. 'I suppose me and your nan are long overdue a holiday, so perhaps we will come to Kings after all.'

Back in Ipswich, Albie Butler was necking the brandy like water. His heart was broken and unrepairable. 'Thank you for coming to see me, boy. I loved my Dorothy so much. What am I going to do without her? It's so cruel that she died today of all days. I will never have the chance to tell her how much she meant to me and ask her to be my wife now, will I?'

When his dad staggered towards him, then fell into his arms, Michael held him tightly. 'I drove here as fast as I could, Dad. I am so sorry for your loss. Dorothy was a lovely lady.'

'I'm going to pop out for a walk. I need to clear my head. Will yous two be OK for a bit?' Bert asked.

Michael nodded, then led his dad over to the sofa. 'What happened, Dad?'

Albie tearfully explained how he had made Dorothy breakfast, then realized she was dead. 'It was awful, Michael. The doctor came, then the police turned up, and then the undertakers took her body away. I can't believe I'm never going to see her again. It's like a bad dream. I don't think I want to live without her. I want to die as well.'

'Don't talk like that, Dad. You taught me how to be strong, and Dorothy would want you to be strong too. Me and Bert will help you through this, and Daniel, Lee and Adam love you dearly. What will they do without their favourite granddad, eh?' After years of the boys calling Albie 'uncle', Michael had recently come clean and told them that Albie was their grandfather.

'Good job your mother, aunt and Vinny didn't know about my Dorothy. Be laughing their socks off, wouldn't they?'

Michael said nothing. Unbeknown to his father, the family did know about Dorothy. He hadn't said anything, but the boys had spoken fondly of her, and his mum and aunt had put two and two together.

'Pass me that bottle of brandy, Dad. I'm staying here tonight, so I might as well get pissed with you.'

Taking a breather from his own grief, Albie studied his son. Not only had Michael lost weight over the past year or so, a father's intuition told Albie that he wasn't happy. 'What's wrong, boy?'

'What you on about?'

'Michael, I know you better than you think, and I can tell something is wrong.'

'Now isn't the time or place, Dad. Have you thought about Dorothy's funeral yet? I'll pay for a decent send-off for her.'

'Thank you. You have always been a wonderful son to me. The best a dad could wish for, but can we talk about the funeral tomorrow? I really can't handle it tonight. Everything's too raw,' Albie said, bursting into tears.

Michael hated to see his father so upset, so decided to change the subject. 'I met a woman, Dad, a few years back now. She could have been to me what Dorothy was to you. I only knew her for a short while, but I loved her in a way I have never loved any woman before. Her name was Bella and I just can't get over her. I try not to think about her, but when I close my eyes I can still see her face.'

Albie took a slurp of brandy. His Michael had always had an eye for a bit of skirt, just like he had. 'Does Nancy know about the affair?'

'No. I ended it with Bella for the sake of my marriage.'

'Well, you did the honourable thing, son.'

'But why doesn't it seem like that? I don't love Nancy any more, Dad. I respect her because she is the mother of my boys, but I still yearn for Bella. A couple of months after I ended it, I realized I'd made a big mistake and tried to find her, but it was too late. She had moved to New York. Anyway, I'm now shagging one of the strippers at the club and drinking too much,' Michael admitted. There was no way he was going to burden his father with the knowledge that he liked to indulge in a gram of cocaine after work. His old man would be so disappointed in him, and he had enough on his plate as it was.

Albie sighed. 'What am I gonna do with you, eh? You

are so much like me, Michael, and I have always known that. Your brothers and sister always took after your mother's side of the family, but not you, thankfully. I remember you first getting pissed. You were only about eleven and I managed to sneak you indoors and put you to bed without your mother ever knowing.'

Michael forced a smile. 'I remember that, Dad. I was sick in the night and you told Mum that I had a bout of gastroenteritis.'

'And do you remember when your mother caught you having a fumble with that blonde girl that used to live opposite us? I can't remember her name, but she was a good few years older than you,' Albie reminded his son.

Michael chuckled. 'Lucy Parker that was, I had my first-ever French kiss with her and I remember showing her my willy.'

Albie put a supportive arm around his son's shoulders. 'Listen, Michael, I'm bound to hit the booze again now my beloved Dorothy has left me. But before I die, I need to see you settled and happy. I only ever got bladdered and had affairs because I was so unhappy with your mum. I know you love her, but you remember how nasty she was to me over the years. Nancy isn't like her, boy. That girl has a good heart and she loves you very much. Forget about Bella, she's history and might be married to some Yank by now for all you know. Try to get your marriage back on track, and lay off that bloody booze, else you'll end up looking like me by the time you're forty, and you don't want that, do you?'

With tears streaming down his face, Michael hugged the most unselfish man he had ever known. Even in his own hour of need, his dad was more concerned about him. That's what being a father was all about. 'I love you, Dad.'

Albie kissed Michael on the forehead. 'And I love you too, son.'

Unaware that their daughter's future was currently being discussed, Mary and Donald were standing by the window in eager anticipation. Christopher had never had a girlfriend in the past, and even though he had only met Olivia just over a month ago, both Mary and Donald could sense that the relationship was already very serious.

'I feel ever so nervous, Donald, don't you? I do hope we like Olivia and she likes us. I never thought we would see the day when our Christopher found love.'

'Whyever not?' Donald exclaimed.

'Because he's twenty-three and has never had a girlfriend before.'

'And good for him, biding his time! Unlike our daughter, Christopher has his head screwed on, my dear. He was never going to search for his wife-to-be until he had gained promotion first. How wonderful that Olivia's father is a detective inspector. I cannot wait to welcome her into our family.'

'For goodness' sake, Donald, please don't refer to the poor girl as his wife-to-be this evening. You'll have her running a mile!'

'Don't be daft, Mary. Now our son is a detective sergeant, he shall be able to marry any young lady he chooses.'

Vinny Butler was at the club and his mood was not good. In an effort to win some custom back from Denny McCann, he had organized a comedy night.

Billy Smith was a funny geezer, in the same mould as Jimmy Jones. Trouble was, the club was only a quarter full and to say Vinny was disappointed with the poor turnout was an understatement. No matter what he tried to do to boost business lately, apart from the strippers, nothing seemed to work.

Vinny stared at his décor. He had the best leather sofas, multi-coloured stage lighting and big silver disco balls that hung over the dancefloor. He only ever sold quality spirits these days, yet still that bastard McCann was pulling in the custom. Denny's club was a shithole in comparison, with its shabby furniture and watered-down booze, so Vinny could only put his lack of punters down to last year's unfortunate shooting. A lot of people had got caught in the crossfire that night, and if that tosser Mitchell Moran hadn't died, Vinny would have finished the bastard off himself for the damage he'd done to the club.

'You OK, pal? I couldn't leave things as we left them earlier.' Vinny was shocked to see Ahmed. They'd had strong words on the journey home from Richie's flat, which had resulted in Ahmed reminding Vinny that he had taken the rap for Lenny's death to save him from the shame.

Gesturing to Ahmed to follow him into the office, Vinny poured them both a good measure of Scotch.

Ahmed threw the bag of cocaine onto Vinny's desk. It was the sample from earlier. 'Be a shame to waste this, eh?'

Vinny held his hands up. Once upon a time, he would have snorted the whole bag to himself, but his daughter had changed all that. He adored his little girl more than life itself, and apart from testing cocaine for business purposes, no way was he ever going to take it for fun again. It didn't seem right somehow. Not when he had an angel like Molly indoors.

'Not for me, mate, but you go ahead. As you said, be a shame to waste it.'

Ahmed put the small plastic bag back into his pocket. 'No, you're right. Let's speak sensibly.'

Vinny took a sip of his drink. 'I liked Richie, but how well do you know him?'

'Not that well, to be honest. But my cousin has done business with him, and there has never been a problem. Besides, the guy seemed sound enough to me. He took us to his home, and he didn't ask for the money up front. We can't go wrong with that kind of set-up, surely?'

Vinny shrugged. 'It all seems above board, but there is no way I am driving anywhere with gear in my motor, Ahmed. It's too much of a risk.'

'I agree. When I used to do the pickups from Essex, I made sure the stuff never came near my car. My cousin's friend Mohammed has a van with a false bottom – we'd load the drugs in there and for two grand he'd drive it back to Burak's place. Of course, I always followed the van, just to make sure it arrived at its destination. Mohammed's a good guy, but that's a lot of temptation to put in anyone's way. We could use the same set-up, that way you and I won't have to get our hands dirty.'

'I can't imagine Richie being too happy with you, me and Mohammed all turning up at his flat. He wanted to keep things low key.'

'If he wants our business, he'll have no choice but to do things our way. We shall speak to him tomorrow, see if we can arrange a more secluded meeting place.'

Vinny felt his stomach churn. Being a silent partner had suited him just fine, but since the crash Ahmed had been less accommodating. Any sign of reluctance from Vinny was met with a shrug and a none-too-subtle reminder that Burak would be only too happy to step in and take over the responsibility – as well as Vinny's share of the business.

'So, do you want in or out?' Ahmed asked bluntly.

Vinny held out his right hand. 'Count me in.'

# CHAPTER FOURTEEN

Little Vinny felt like death warmed up as he gingerly got dressed. Every muscle in his body ached from the long hours and hard graft his dad was forcing him to do at the club. And to top it all, he now had a stinking cold.

'You up yet, boy?' Little Vinny heard his father bellow.

'Yes, Dad . . .' As soon as he heard his father's footsteps fade away, Little Vinny added the word 'cunt'.

When he had led his dad to where he had hidden the gun and they had retrieved it without any problem, Little Vinny had thought his father would mellow towards him. He hadn't though. Apart from going to work, Little Vinny was not allowed outside the door, and he felt like a prisoner in his own home.

He trudged dejectedly down the stairs. 'Dad, I feel really ill. I can't stop sneezing and I ache all over. I think I've got the flu, so can I have the day off, please?'

'No, you bloody well can't! I want you to scrub the cellar today and I expect it to be that clean, we could eat our lunch off the floor.'

'Vinny, say hello to Molly Dolly,' Molly ordered, toddling towards her brother with her doll in her hand.

Little Vinny picked his sister up and was immediately

ordered to put her back down. 'She doesn't want to catch your cold, does she, you div? Take this and get yourself some breakfast in the café,' Vinny said, handing his son a five-pound note.

'Aren't we going to work together?'

'No. I've promised Jo I'll take her out to lunch, so I'll be in later this afternoon. Oh, and while I remember, your granny Maureen rang me at the club yesterday. She was asking after you and said she hasn't spoken to you in ages. What have I told you about ringing her every couple of weeks, eh? Anyway, I said me and you will drive down to Hornchurch on Friday and take her out to lunch. That'll give your aching bones a rest.'

Little Vinny nodded, then stomped out of the front door. His Grandma Maureen was his mum's mum and even though he had quite liked visiting her when he was younger, she now bored him rigid. She treated him as if he were about ten, and had even bought him some stupid toy car on his last visit.

Hating his father more than ever, Little Vinny kicked a nearby dustbin in frustration. There had already been one fire at his dad's club in the past and if the tosser didn't lighten up towards him soon, there might just be another.

Nancy Butler was not in the best of moods. Michael had stayed out again last night, the boys had been little bastards this morning, and to top it all, Joanna had just cancelled their picnic in the park because Vinny wanted to take her out.

Having purposely avoided speaking to her mother on the phone earlier, Nancy could have screamed when she heard the key go in the front door, followed by Mary calling, 'Cooey.'

After giving her grandsons and Lee a hug, Mary handed them a bag of penny sweets each, and ordered them to go play in the garden. 'What's going on, Nance? And what's all this about Michael not coming home at night? Where is he now?'

'Who told you he hasn't been coming home?'

'The boys slipped up. They aren't babies any more, love, and can sense when something isn't right. They even mentioned that their dad never goes to Kings these days. So what's up? Have you and Michael been arguing?'

Nancy's eyes welled up as she opened her heart to her mother. She admitted everything that had been upsetting her, apart from Michael turning his back on her in bed. She really didn't feel comfortable discussing her sex life with anybody other than Joanna. 'Be honest with me, Mum. Do you think he is having an affair?'

'Probably. Why would he be staying out all night if he wasn't? I'm bloody fuming with him, Nance. Always stuck up for Michael, I have. Even rowed with your father and brother over him. How dare he treat you like this? You wait until I see him. I'll give what for, all right.'

'Noooo. You can't say anything, Mum. This is why I didn't want to tell you in the first place. Promise me you won't get involved,' Nancy said, panic in her voice.

'Well, best you start standing up for yourself then, Nance. I never brought you up to be treated like a door mat. Do you think I'd have put up with your father staying out all night? I'd have chopped his penis off, love. I know me and your dad have had our ups and downs over the years, but don't you remember what I used to do when he made me really angry? I left him. Worked every time, it did. Men soon learn which side their bread is buttered when you walk out the door. You are such a pretty girl, you could still have your pick of men.'

'Mum, no man is going to want me with two young boys as baggage, especially not when they find out who the boys' father is.'

'The right man wouldn't be put off, love. I bet that Dean Smart would still walk across hot coals for you. Have you spoken to him lately? Last time me and your dad saw Freda was the day your brother got promoted.'

'No, I haven't spoken to him. Last time I saw Freda, she said Dean had a new girlfriend, so I stopped all contact after that. Anyway, I wouldn't want Brenda's leftovers, thank you very much. I can't deny I'm pissed off with Michael at the moment, but I still love him, Mum.'

'Well, I can't live your life for you, Nancy, but if I were you I would give that husband of yours such a kick up the arse he won't sit down for a week.'

Joanna Preston waved at her daughter. Molly was playing in the sandpit with two other little girls and was giggling away. Joanna smiled at the two ladies on the next table. 'Are those your daughters playing with mine?'

'Yes, the one in the yellow is my Sarah and Kayleigh is my friend's daughter. Your little girl is ever so pretty. What's her name?'

'Molly. She loves other children and they seem to love her too.'

'She really looks like you. Is that Molly's dad who you are with?' the other woman asked.

Joanna could not help but smirk. She had seen the two women staring at Vinny earlier and instead of feeling jealous, she was proud. Vinny looked really handsome today in his dark suit and black sunglasses. 'Speak of the devil, he's coming back from the bar now. Yes, Vinny is Molly's dad and my other half. I'm Joanna, by the way.'

The auburn-haired woman introduced herself as Diana and her blonde pal as Lucy.

Vinny handed Joanna a menu and smiled at the women. 'Can I get you a drink, ladies?'

'No thanks. But thank you for asking,' Diana replied. She and Lucy had been commenting how hot Vinny was; it hadn't occurred to either of them that he and Joanna were a couple. The pair of them did not look at all suited to one another.

'I'm just going to ask Molly what she wants to eat, babe. I won't be long,' Vinny informed Joanna.

'Are you married?' Joanna asked Lucy and Diana.

'I'm divorced and Di has recently split up from her bloke. Both our men were useless fathers, weren't they, Di?'

'Yep! The lazy gits were best friends, always in the pub and didn't even get off their backsides to work. What does your Vinny do?' Diana asked nosily. Judging by his smart clothes and expensive aftershave, the man had serious money.

Joanna felt as proud as a peacock as she explained that Vinny was a nightclub owner in Whitechapel.

'Yous ladies talking about me?' Vinny grinned, walking towards Joanna with Molly in his arms.

'Yes, I was just telling Diana and Lucy about your nightclub. They asked what you did for a living.'

Molly had one hand around her father's neck and giggled as she took his sunglasses off with the other. 'Oi, what you doing, you cheeky little monkey? Give us them back.'

When Molly shook her head, Vinny swung her around in the air. 'Stop it, Daddy,' Molly chuckled.

Laughing himself, Vinny laid Molly on the grass and tickled her until she begged for mercy.

Diana and Lucy glanced at one another. The love between father and daughter was clear to see and both women were thinking the same. Why had they had the misfortune of meeting such arseholes? 'Shall we go now, mate?' Diana suggested.

Lucy nodded. Seeing such a happy family was making her

feel depressed. Some girls had all the luck, they really did. She would give her right arm for a rich handsome man like Vinny.

Joanna said goodbye to Lucy and Diana, then took a large gulp of wine. Vinny was in an especially good mood today, so surely now was the best time to ask him?

'You picked what you want to eat yet? Molly wants fish fingers and chips,' Vinny said.

'And tomato sauce, Daddy. Can I go and play with that little boy, please?'

Vinny glanced around. Even though Molly was only young, he had to check out any boys she wanted to play with. He dreaded to think what he would be like when she was older. She was his little princess and the thought of her ever dating a lad made him feel sick to the stomach. 'Go on then, I'll call you when your lunch is ready.'

'Vin, can we have a quick chat before we order lunch? There's something important we need to discuss,' Joanna said.

Vinny smiled. He had only suggested taking Joanna out for lunch to stop her spending the day with Nancy. It really grated on him when Jo and his sister-in-law got together, as he was always paranoid they were discussing him. 'Fire away, babe.'

'It's my dad. He's up for parole and my mum says he might be free soon. He wants to see me and Molly. Vin, I know you and my dad hate one another, but you must understand how awkward this situation is for me.'

'So, what you trying to say, Jo? Are you asking for permission so you and Molly can spend time with your old man?'

Not noticing the dangerous glint in Vinny's eyes, Joanna nodded. 'Obviously, it would only be minimal contact, Vinny. My loyalties lie with you, you know that. But I was thinking perhaps Molly and I could have lunch or something with my mum and dad once a month? What do you think?'

Vinny smirked, grabbed Joanna's right hand and twisted

it so violently, her wrist very nearly snapped in two. 'I'll tell you what I think, shall I? If you ever take my daughter within one hundred yards of that shitcunt of a father of yours, I swear I will kill you.'

Queenie Butler was lounging outside the bungalow at Kings. For the past half an hour, herself and Vivian had amused themselves by ripping the piss out of the notrights next-door-but-one. As per usual, the pervert had his Speedos on, and he and his fat wife were playing some silly game. It was like tennis, but the ball was attached to a pole. 'Her fucking lils look like they're going to bounce out that swimming costume. Do you reckon they're swingers?' Queenie asked Vivian.

'What's a swinger?'

'Those perverts who try to entice other people into having sex with them. My Vinny told me about them. Said there are some clubs in London now where they all run around showing their meat and two veg and their snatches.'

Vivian burst out laughing. Her and Queenie had only learnt what a snatch was recently, thanks to Little Vinny using the expression. 'Well, I wouldn't fancy seeing her snatch, would you?'

Queenie was about to reply when she heard the voices of her grandchildren. Tara was eight now and Tommy three, and Brenda rarely visited them at Kings. 'Where's Mummy, love? Who brought you down here?' Queenie asked. Brenda could not drive, and as far as she was aware Michael and Vinny weren't due to arrive in Eastbourne any time soon.

'Mummy's coming now, and her new boyfriend Scott drove us here. He has a really posh car, Nan. We had the roof down,' Tara explained.

Queenie looked at Vivian in amazement. She had last spoken to Brenda a few days ago and even though her daughter had sounded full of the joys of spring, there had been no mention of a new man in her life.

Vivian nudged her sister as she spotted Brenda walking towards them with a tall handsome blond chap. 'Well, I'll be blowed.'

Michael didn't exactly expect Peters and Lee to be crooning 'Welcome Home' as he strolled through the front door, but neither did he expect his wife to fly at him like a bull in a china shop. 'What the fuck are you doing? Where are the boys?' Michael asked, protecting his head from his wife's punches.

'The boys are at my mum's, and I want to know who the slut is, Michael. I know you're having an affair, so don't fucking lie to me.'

Michael grabbed his wife's wrists. He could smell the alcohol on her breath, but could not tell how drunk she was. 'Look, I'm sorry I got Paul to ring you. I should have called you myself, but I swear I've been with my dad. Dorothy is dead, Nance. She died in her sleep.'

'You're lying to me, Michael Butler,' Nancy screamed.

'No, I'm not, babe. Ring my dad if you don't believe me. And what do you think I am? As if I would make up a lie as awful as that. Dorothy died on her bloody birthday. The day my dad was due to propose to her. He's in bits, bless his heart.'

Nancy collapsed to her knees. 'Oh, that is so sad. Poor Albie. But what about all the other nights you've stayed out? I need to know the truth, Michael. I can't carry on like this.'

Michael sank to his haunches and held his sobbing wife in his arms. His dad's little speech had given him food for thought. Bella might well be hitched or have children by now. As he had driven back from Ipswich, he had vowed never to let thoughts of Bella torture his mind again.

'Babe, I'm so sorry I haven't given you the love and attention I should have just lately. The business has been going down the drain, if you want the truth, and that's why I've been dossing at the club. I've been drinking far too much as well, what with the worry of it all, and the last thing I wanted was to come home pissed and burden you with all my problems. I thought it might make you depressed again.'

'Swear on the boys' lives there is no other woman,' Nancy ordered.

Having already decided he was going to end his meaningless affair with the stripper and give his marriage another go, Michael gave his solemn oath. 'Seeing as the boys are at your mum's. Let's go to bed,' he suggested.

Feeling a mixture of relief and desire, Nancy grabbed her husband by the hand and led him up the stairs.

To say Joanna Preston was in a state of shock was putting it mildly. After nearly breaking her wrist, Vinny had refused to have lunch, dragged their daughter out of the sandpit, then driven her and Molly home in complete silence. He had then driven off like a bat out of hell.

Desperate to share her woes with somebody, Joanna rang Nancy. There was no answer.

When the phone rang seconds later, Joanna thought it was Nancy ringing her back. It wasn't. It was her mother. 'Brilliant news, Jo. Dad's parole hearing is on Wednesday week. His brief rang me today and he said he was ninety-five per cent sure your dad will get parole. I'm so excited. I can't wait to have him home with me again. Will you and Molly be bridesmaids at the wedding? Have you had a chance to speak to Vinny yet?'

Not wanting to burst her mother's bubble, Joanna felt she had no option but to lie. If she told her mum that her right wrist was currently double its usual size, that would cause mayhem. 'I've not had the chance to speak to Vinny yet, Mum. He's got problems at the club, so I'm waiting for the right moment. Sorry to cut you short, but I have to go. Molly's in the bath, and last time I left her alone there I had loads of mopping up to do. I'm really pleased for Dad though. Give him my love.'

Slamming the phone down, Joanna put her head in her hands. Her dad's homecoming was going to cause so much aggravation and she didn't know which way to turn. Vinny was the man she loved, but blood was thicker than water . . . wasn't it?

Queenie and Vivian were sitting in the club at Kings. Tara and Tommy were having a ball with the children's entertainer Charlie Case, so it gave Queenie the chance to study Scott, or Scotty as he preferred to be called.

'So, what exactly do you do for a living, Scotty?' Queenie asked politely.

'I'm a bit of an entrepreneur, Mrs B. I see an opportunity and I take it. Stocks and shares are my current thing. Made a lot of money out of those recently, I have.'

'Where do you live? Do you own your own property?' Vivian asked bluntly.

'Mum, Auntie Viv, will you stop interrogating Scotty. You've only just met him. Let's go up the bar, babe,' Brenda said, grabbing her boyfriend's arm.

When Scott and Brenda walked away from the table, Queenie turned to Vivian. Since Brenda had lost weight, had her hair cut short and dyed blonde, she did look good again. However, she did not look good enough to bag a rich, handsome man like Scott. 'Well, what do you think?'

'Wouldn't trust the bastard as far as I could throw him. He won't look you properly in the eyes,' Vivian replied.

'I'm not overly struck either. Bit of a flash Harry, ain't

he? No point saying anything to Silly Lily though. She's already smitten, I can tell. She ain't known him five bastard minutes and she's already staring at him with those sickly puppy-dog eyes. It'll be left to me to pick up the pieces when she gets her heart broken again. And she will. You mark my words.'

Little Vinny Butler thought he was about to drop from exhaustion when his hard task master of a father entered the cellar. Even though Little Vinny had felt as rough as a badger's arse, he had still worked like a Trojan.

Vinny had a quick inspection, then turned to his son. 'You've done a good job, boy. Carry on as hard as you have been working, then after your month's trial, we'll have a chat about wages.'

'Thanks, Dad. Do you forgive me now for taking your gun? I am sorry and I'll never touch it again, I promise.'

'Too right you won't. You'd never fucking find it again to touch it. I've made sure of that.'

'So, am I forgiven?'

Vinny studied his prodigy. All he had ever wanted was to turn his son into a man like himself. Judging by the way the lad had behaved since being expelled from school, Vinny reckoned he'd done the right thing by forcing his son to work at the club.

'I wouldn't say you're forgiven just yet, but you keep out of trouble, and carry on grafting as you have been, I'm sure my mood will soon soften.'

'Am I allowed out again now? It's really boring being stuck indoors every night.'

'Don't push your luck, boy. You gotta earn your stripes first. Once I'm sure you've learnt your lesson, then you can go out. I meant what I said about Ben Bloggs, though. The kid's a div and I don't want you knocking about with him no more. Find yourself some new pals, ones that have brains preferably, and who aren't fucking skinheads.'

'OK.'

Realizing his son looked rather crestfallen, Vinny put an arm around his shoulders. 'Look, I've spent far too much time with Jo and Molly recently, so how about I take you out tonight for a bit of grub? You can choose where we eat and you can even have a couple of halves of lager now you're a working man.'

'Will it be just the two of us?'

'Yep.'

Little Vinny grinned. 'I'd like that, Dad. I really would.'

Christopher Walker had had a big smile on his face all day. Olivia and his parents had got on really well, and for the first time in his life, Christopher knew what it was like to be in love. It was a wonderful feeling and reminded him of the buzz he had felt when he had first gained promotion to detective sergeant.

The drug squad was the path that Christopher had chosen in his career, and that was how he had met Olivia. Her father was his old boss and he'd introduced them to one another at a party. Like himself, Olivia had never been in a serious relationship before and her dad was over the moon that they were now dating.

When his phone rang, Christopher half expected it to be his mother. He had called her earlier to ask privately what she and Dad had thought of his girlfriend, but she had cut him short. She was waiting for a phonecall from a holiday park to confirm some reservation, and had promised to ring him back.

'There's some weird-sounding bloke on the phone, boss. He asked for you in person, says he has some information for you. Shall I put him through?'

Christopher waited for the caller to be connected, then said, 'DS Walker. How may I help you?'

'I think it is I who can help you, Christopher.' Surprised that the caller knew his christian name, Christopher sat bolt upright. 'Who are you? And what is this about?'

'I'm an acquaintance of a man I am sure you would very much like to arrest. He is evil, deserves to be behind bars and I have devised a little plan where I aim to hand him to you on a plate. This particular arrest will be a biggie, and you should be able to lock him up for a large part of his sorry life. It will do wonders for your career, trust me on that.'

Instinct told Christopher that this was no crank call, but something about it made him feel extremely edgy. 'Who is this man you are referring to?'

'I will not discuss names over the phone. It is more than my life is worth and yours. I will meet you, but you must come alone. You are the only officer I am willing to deal with.'

Deciding to call the anonymous informant's bluff, Christopher did his utmost to sound cool. 'I can assure you that nobody bar me is listening to this conversation. And I can also assure you that I will not be travelling alone to meet you unless you give me a name.'

The caller chuckled. 'Let's just say it's a chap who you could have put behind bars when you was a kid. It's a shame you lied on his behalf, because you could have saved the pair of us all this grief now, couldn't you? I take it you know who I'm talking about?'

Feeling the hairs on the back of his neck stand up, Christopher dropped the phone in shock.

# CHAPTER FIFTEEN

'I don't believe you, Ahmed! I know you want to see that scumbag get his comeuppance – as do I – but not at the risk of our own liberty. You think that policeman of yours is going to be satisfied with arresting Vinny? Once you mention drugs, he's going to be watching us like a hawk, waiting for a chance to put us away too.'

Seething with anger, Ahmed forced himself to remain calm in the face of his cousin's insolence. 'I am disappointed by your lack of faith in me, Burak. Do you seriously think I would be so stupid as to put our necks on the line? The police can watch all they want – once this is done, I won't be making any more drug deals.'

'But the drugs are our biggest earner, Ahmed. You think we can live like we do on what the restaurant business brings in?'

'Money makes money, Burak. I fancy investing some of my millions in building the most upmarket hotel Turkey has ever seen. Have you any idea how much money can be made out of tourism these days? Especially if the clientele are wealthy.'

'How do you know you can trust the copper that you spoke to? Say he double-crosses you?' Burak warned.

Ahmed chuckled. Five days had passed since he had rung the police station and he had every intention of making Christopher sweat some more before calling back again. 'I have the upper hand over our friend DS Walker, and if he tries to double-cross me, he will wish he had never been born.'

Michael Butler put a supportive arm around his father's hunched shoulders. Dorothy's funeral had been a small affair with no more than thirty people in attendance, but she'd had a pleasant send-off and Michael had given a lovely speech on his father's behalf.

'Come on, Dad. The car's waiting for us. Dorothy wouldn't want you hanging about here. She'd want you to go back to the house and toast her memory with a few brandies.'

'I hate that house now, boy. Everywhere I look I picture her there. I see her in the kitchen, cooking, sitting in her favourite armchair doing her knitting. All her clothes are still in the wardrobe and it breaks my bloody heart,' Albie wept.

'Look, I'll tell you what. We'll go back to the house and finish giving Dorothy the send-off she deserves, then when I drive back to Barking tomorrow, I want you to come with me. A change of environment will do you good, and it will only be me and you there. Nancy's going to Kings with the boys at the weekend.'

'OK, son. And thank you for making the speech and paying for the funeral. You did my wonderful Dorothy proud.'

Queenie and Vivian were in deep discussion as they sat waiting for their washing to finish in the launderette. Almost a week had passed since Brenda had turned up at Kings with her mystery boyfriend and the kids in tow, and there was no sign of them sodding off home.

Like every normal nan, Queenie adored each and every one of her grandchildren. But eight-year-old Tara and three-year-old Tommy were a handful, to say the least. Tara was a child who had tantrums on a regular basis, especially if she didn't get her own way, and Tommy was as boisterous as Little Vinny had been as a child. The little bastard had even broken her new plant pot yesterday, which had cost her twenty quid. Queenie had been fuming ever since.

'Gonna say something as soon as I get back, Viv, I am. I mean, it's bad enough being lumbered with Bren and the kids without warning, without her bringing Billy Big Bollocks with her an' all. We don't even know the geezer, and I can't empty my bowels knowing he's sitting outside the khazi listening. Four times I've had to walk over to that public toilet just to have a crap.'

'I agree, it ain't on, Queen. I had to have a dump in the clubhouse yesterday and you know how I hate having to do number twos in public places. What you gonna say?'

'Well, Vinny's bringing Joanna and Molly down at the weekend, so I shall tell 'em we're short of space and insist they piss off home. What you looking at?'

'Ray's outside in his roller. Give us me bag so I can put some lippy on, quick!' Vivian said impatiently.

Ray King was the owner of the holiday park, and was often seen driving around in his smart Rolls-Royce. A pleasant-natured chap, Ray often stopped to chat to owners and holidaymakers, but cursed his luck when he saw Queenie and Vivian marching towards him. Whenever they accosted him, he could never get away.

'Cooey, Mr King. Beautiful day, isn't it? How have you been keeping?' Vivian asked, in her posh voice.

'I'm fine thank you, ladies. How about yourselves?'

Now it was Queenie's turn to put on a posh voice. Some people fondly referred to Ray as Mr Eastbourne, and Queenie wished she had married a man with such a profile instead of that useless drunken tosspot Albie. Queenie would never admit how she felt about the handsome Mr King to anyone, not even to Vivian, but her heart skipped a beat whenever she saw the man.

'I wanted to ask you something, Mr King. You know you have your initials on your number plates, well I would like my Vinny and Michael to have their initials on theirs. What shop did you buy them in? Was it Halfords?'

When Mr King chuckled as he explained to her that you could not just walk into a shop and buy personalized number plates, Queenie felt such a fool that she wanted the ground to open up and swallow her. Her cheeks glowing as red as her lipstick, she grabbed her sister by the arm and started to drag her away. 'Thank you for your time, Mr King. Come on, Vivian, our washing's ready.'

Nancy Butler was sitting in her usual spot in Barking Park. She wasn't due to meet Joanna until two, but had decided to get there early as the boys seemed to play her up indoors.

Checking the boys were still playing nicely, Nancy laid back on the grass and smiled. She and Michael had made love twice in the past week and it felt so nice to feel loved and wanted once again.

'You're pulling funny faces, Nancy. You haven't swallowed a wasp, have you?'

'Auntie Nancy. Say hello to Molly Dolly.'

Nancy leapt up and hugged Joanna and her niece. 'You're early. I came over here because the boys were driving me mad indoors, so what's your excuse?'

When Molly ran over to her cousins, Joanna flopped down on the grass. Even though she had spoken to Nancy since Vinny had nearly broken her wrist, she had felt too embarrassed to tell her what had happened. However, she had to get her problems off her chest and if she couldn't trust Nancy with her dilemma, who could she trust?

Nancy sat with her mouth open as Joanna told her what had happened. 'Vinny's still not talking to me properly, Nance, and I've got my mother ringing up every five minutes asking if I've had a chance to talk to him yet. What am I meant to do? I love my dad and I love Vinny. I feel like I'm torn between the Devil and the deep blue sea.'

Knowing she had to choose her words carefully, Nancy thought about her answer. She had always hated Vinny with a passion. He had been the man who had forced her parents into leaving their beloved café in Whitechapel by blackmailing her brother Christopher to lie for him as a child. He was also the man who had broken both of his own father's legs and tried to break things off between his brother Roy and his fiancée.

'Well, say something then?' Joanna urged.

Nancy squeezed Joanna's hand. She had never admitted her true feelings about Vinny, or anything Michael had told her in confidence, so there was little point in worrying her pal now. 'You will just have to tell your mum the truth, Jo. Tell her you had a word with Vinny about your dad seeing Molly and he went ballistic. Don't tell her he was violent towards you though. That will only worry her. Can I ask you something?'

'Yeah.'

'Are you afraid he might attack you again?'

'Vinny didn't attack me, Nance. All he did was twist my wrist, and he hasn't touched me since. He's not some lunatic you know. He just got angry. Anyway, it's not him I'm worried about, it's my dad. He's desperate to be part of Molly's life and mine, and if Vinny stops that from happening, I'm worried my dad might do something stupid.'

'Like what?'

'I'm not sure, but I do know my dad has a streak of madness in him. If he shot Roy, who's to say he won't go mental again and shoot Vinny? You have to remember, that bullet was meant for Vinny in the first place. What am I gonna do, Nance?'

'I don't know, Jo. It's such a bloody awkward situation, but I will give you a piece of advice: if Vinny ever hurts you again, you should leave him. Michael's no angel, but even though we've been through our fair share of strife, I know in my heart he would never lay a finger on me. If a man hits or hurts you once, you can be sure they will do it again.'

Vinny Butler met Ahmed at the Ship and Shovel pub in Barking. 'Where's Richie?' he asked his pal.

'Busy. One of his kids has been taken ill. Richie gave me the keys and I've already checked it out, Vin. It's well out the way and the perfect place to do business such as ours.'

'It had better be,' Vinny replied warily. He still was not happy being actively involved in the drug trade and had even been thinking about pulling out. The only thing that was stopping him from doing so was Molly. She would be starting school soon and Vinny was determined that his daughter would be brought up and attend school in a much better area than Whitechapel.

Aware that Vinny was quiet, Ahmed decided to call his bluff. 'If your heart isn't in this, Vin, then it isn't too late to pull out.'

'I have no intention of calling it a day, Ahmed. But as you well know I was much more comfortable being a silent partner. This gives me the heebies, if you want to know the truth.'

'You'll soon get used to it. I did.' He nodded at a fence up ahead. 'We've arrived.'

Vinny got out of the car and followed his business partner into the yard. It appeared to be full to the brim of used tyres. 'So who owns this gaff? I thought you said Richie had rented it.'

Ahmed had actually rented the yard off a pal, but he was not about to admit that to Vinny. 'That's right. Richie's renting it off a guy who's just been given a two-year stretch for fraud. He didn't want to lose his business while he was away, so he's letting Richie have it for fifty quid a week. This is perfect for us. There's a salvage yard next door, so this place is crawling with vans and trucks in the daytime. I've told Richie that we'll pay half towards the rent, and I've insisted we only do our pick-ups late afternoon, early evening. Vans and trucks are much more liable to get a tug late at night, and even though we'll only be following our investment in a car, we don't want any slip-ups, do we?'

Vinny had a nose around the yard, then a look around outside. 'I feel much more at ease doing business here than at Richie's flat.'

Ahmed grinned. 'So, shall I call the first deal on? I was thinking Friday, if that's OK with you?'

'Yep, bring it on.'

Joanna Preston read Molly a bedtime story, kissed her daughter goodnight, then crept down the stairs. She'd decided that Nancy was right, and the quicker she broke the news to her mother, the better.

Dreading the conversation she was about to have, Joanna could feel her hands shaking as she picked up the phone.

'Hello, love. How are you? Just this second put the phone down to your dad, I have. So excited about the prospect of coming home, he is. You had a chance to speak to Vinny yet?'

With her heart feeling like a lump of lead, Joanna explained the situation as gently as she could. 'Mum, I'm really sorry, but there is no way Vinny will allow Dad to be part of Molly's life at present. I'm hoping in time he might change his tune, but please don't have a go at me. I feel like piggy in the middle as it is.'

'The evil bastard! I knew it! If there was one person who was going to piss on your father's homecoming parade, it was always going to be Vinny. I bet he's told you that you're not allowed to see your dad either, hasn't he?'

Rather than admit her mother was right, Joanna turned the tables: 'Mum, I know you hate Vinny, but you can hardly blame him for not wanting us all playing happy families. Have you forgotten the reason Dad got banged up in the first place? He tried to kill Vinny and ended up shooting his brother Roy instead. You expect Vinny to overlook that?'

'Don't be trying to twist this conversation around, young lady. I know, and deep down you know, that Vinny only made a play for you in the first place because of who your father was. I can see in your eyes that you're not truly happy with him, and I bet now Vinny has what he wants, revenge and a beautiful daughter, he doesn't come anywhere near you in the bedroom. Am I right? Or am I wrong?'

Unable to listen to any more home truths, a tearful Joanna slammed the phone down.

As soon as Mary left for her weekly game of bingo, Donald tapped on his son's bedroom door. Christopher had been acting oddly for a while now, and Donald knew there was more to his son's change of behaviour than Christopher was letting on.

Though still only twenty-three, Christopher considered himself to be more mature than most men his age. However, when his father started asking questions, he felt an overwhelming urge to throw himself into his arms, just like he had when he was a small child.

'Whatever is it, son? Is it Olivia? Have you split up with her?'

Christopher shook his head. Ever since he had received the anonymous phone call, he had felt as jumpy as a cat on a hot tin roof. It was affecting his work, his relationship with Olivia, everything. Unable to confide in his colleagues and desperate to relieve himself of some of the burden, Christopher blurted it all out to his father in three long sentences.

Donald felt his face drain of colour. He was so proud of his son's career and recent promotion, and he had honestly thought that what had happened all those years ago in Whitechapel would never rear its ugly head again.

'What should I do, Dad? Whoever it is knows everything. I know it can't be proved that I lied on Vinny's behalf as a kid, but any investigation could ruin my career. Mud sticks, doesn't it?'

As a child, Donald had had a habit of chewing on his lip when he was nervous, and even though he could not remember doing so for years, he was chewing away with a vengeance now. His son joining the police force had filled him with pride, but Christopher becoming a detective sergeant just days after his twenty-third birthday had left Donald in a state of euphoria. The thought that his entire future could be in jeopardy filled him with horror. 'You can't tell anybody at work about this, son. You must meet this mystery caller on your own if he rings back.'

'But that's against police policy. We're supposed to inform our superiors of such situations, and it's official policy that we meet informants in pairs, never alone. Don't get me wrong, a lot of officers do bend the rules and don't record these meetings, but I take after you, Dad. I have morals and I play by the book.'

Donald put his hands on his son's shoulders and stared him directly in the eyes. 'I know you do, son, and I'm proud of you for that. But in this instance, you need to take a different approach. As you said, whoever contacted you with information obviously wants to see Vinny Butler put behind bars just as much as we and the police probably do. Imagine what being involved in such a high-profile arrest would do for your career, eh? You could be a detective inspector before you know it.'

Christopher forced a smile. His dad had always been his hero. He had never given him wrong advice in his lifetime, so why should he distrust his wise words now? 'OK. As soon as I get the phone call, I'll meet this informant alone. But you mustn't tell anybody about this conversation, and there is no way you can go on holiday to Eastbourne now, Dad. Vinny could be there for all we know. It's far too dangerous.'

'What am I meant to say to your mother, Christopher? The holiday's booked and our chalet is nowhere near the Butlers. I only agreed to go for Daniel and Adam's sake. I know you refuse to have anything to do with them, but even though they're Michael's sons, they are fine boys.'

'I don't give a damn how fine they are, Dad. I do not want you going to Eastbourne and that's final. I need you here with me.'

# CHAPTER SIXTEEN

Donald waited until the Friday before he feigned a bad stomach bug. 'I can't travel at the moment, love, not while I'm like this. I need to be near a lavatory for obvious reasons. You go down to Kings with Nancy and the boys, and I'll follow as soon as I'm feeling up to it.'

'Aw, but you might feel better by tomorrow, Donald. Most sickness-type bugs only last twenty-four to forty-eight hours, you know.'

'Mary, I would never forgive myself if I passed this on to you or the boys and spoilt everyone's holiday.'

'OK, but I want you to promise me you'll drive down as soon as you feel better. I know what you're like for not being able to tear yourself away from the café. Don't you let me and the boys down.'

Rather than make his wife a promise he knew he could not keep, Donald put his hand over his mouth and bolted towards the bathroom again. Christopher's career and his needs were far more important than a week's bloody holiday.

Little Vinny finished stocking up the mixers, then without being prompted, made his father a cup of tea.

'Good lad. Take your lunch break now. What do ya fancy? I could murder a lump of cod and chips.'

'I'll go down the chippy, Dad. I fancy a saveloy and a sausage in batter.'

Vinny handed his son a tenner, then allowed himself a rare moment to remember the departed. Little Vinny had all but taken Lenny's job over now, and even though he enjoyed having his son work with him, watching him do all the jobs his cousin used to do brought back painful memories.

Reminiscing about Roy was a different kettle of fish. Vinny could think about his brother all day long without getting upset. He was glad they'd had one final chat and he treasured the letter Roy had left him. He had even abided by most of his brother's wishes, and he was sure if Roy was looking down he'd be pleased that he had now stopped taking cocaine. He wouldn't be so chuffed with Michael though, which is why Vinny had rung his father for a chat the other day. Dorothy's death had given him the perfect opportunity to do so.

Feeling his stomach churn, Vinny shuddered. The first deal with Richie had been arranged for seven o'clock this evening and even though Vinny was looking forward to earning decent money again, he was also shitting his pants. Killing people had never bothered Vinny, but there was something about participating in a big drug deal that put the fear of God in him.

Little Vinny checked out his reflection in the chip-shop window. He looked a right numpty in the old tracksuit he had on. All the skinhead clobber he'd recently thieved was hidden at Ben Bloggs' house, and Little Vinny hated not being able to dress in the style he had become so accustomed to. His hair was growing rapidly as well. He'd asked the barber for a number one when he'd first had it cut, but it had grown into at least a number three now. Give it another month and he wouldn't even resemble a skinhead at all.

Running back to the club to ensure lunch would still be piping hot, Little Vinny plastered a false smile on his face as he handed his dad his food and change. There was a method in his madness. His old man had driven Jo and Molly down to Eastbourne first thing this morning and Little Vinny was sure if he played his cards right, he would be allowed to go out again this weekend. His dad would be working, so surely he wasn't expected to sit at home alone?

Michael Butler opened the front door and carried his father's small suitcase over the threshold. Vinny had given Nancy and the boys a lift down to Eastbourne with Jo and Molly earlier and Michael was glad. He felt his dad needed a bit of quiet father-and-son time, rather than the chaos that came with having three young boys running around the house.

'Nice gaff, Michael. Beautiful leather suite. Is it new?'

Michael poured two large brandies. 'Yeah. We had a beige one, but Adam drew all over it with a felt-tip pen, so we decided to get a black one instead.'

Watching his father sip his drink, Michael's heart went out to him. He had really loved Dorothy and he looked a broken man. 'You can stay here as long as you like, Dad. There's two or three pubs in walking distance and I'll give you some money so you can go for a pint whenever you want. Nancy and the boys will probably stay down at Kings for the rest of the school holidays, so when I'm at work you'll have the house to yourself. A change is as good as a rest, they say.'

'Thanks, Michael. Shame the boys aren't here though. I think their constant chit-chat might have been the best medicine for me.'

'Well, I did promise Nancy that I'd try and have a week down at Kings with her and the boys myself. You can come too. It's a wonderful holiday park and I'm sure you'd love it. You'll probably bump into Mum and Auntie Viv though. Can you handle that?'

Albie winked. 'I can handle anything as long as my favourite son and grandchildren are by my side. I've never been to a holiday park before. Is there lots to do there?'

When Michael explained how fabulous the clubhouse was and what famous acts appeared there, Albie's eyes opened wide. 'Vinny might be there an' all though, Dad. I know you and him ain't exactly the Waltons.'

'I'm no fan of your brother, but I'll be polite if I see him, Michael. Actually, he rung me to say he was sorry to hear about Dorothy.'

'Did he? When?'

'Last Monday, I think it was. He was on the phone for about ten minutes. He spoke about the club and other stuff too. I must admit, I was surprised to hear from him.'

Michael immediately smelt a rat. Not only had Vinny failed to mention he had spoken to their father, his brother had never met Dorothy and was the most unsympathetic bastard God had ever put breath in. 'Did he mention me at all, Dad? I know he did, so don't lie to me.'

Wishing he hadn't opened his big mouth, Albie nodded sheepishly. 'Vinny didn't slag you off, boy. He's just a bit worried about you, that's all.'

'Worried! What do you mean worried?'

'He knows you've had problems with Nancy and he seemed a bit concerned your drinking and that was getting out of hand.'

Michael chuckled sarcastically. 'I get it – "and that" says it all, Dad. He told you about the drugs, didn't he?'

Feeling awkward, Albie stared at his hands. 'Vinny wanted me to have a chat with you, make you see sense. Please don't let on I've told you though. He wanted me to pretend I'd heard it through the grapevine. Promise me you won't say anything, Michael. You know how handy your brother can be with his fists.'

Remembering the time his dad had been laid up in hospital with two broken legs and three broken ribs thanks to Vinny, Michael shook his head. 'I would never dob you in the shit, but I am fucking livid! Vinny's got some brass neck, ringing you to talk about me. He was bang on the gear himself before Molly was born, and he's dealing in it now. I overheard a conversation between him and Ahmed not that long ago. They're both at it.'

'Doesn't surprise me at all, boy. I wouldn't put anything past your brother. But it's not him I care about, it's you. You're a wonderful son and a fantastic father, so please don't throw your life away. I know I can talk, seeing as I spent most of your childhood drunk, but I've never touched a drug in my life. Worried sick about you I am, boy, which is one of the reasons why I wanted to come and stay with you. I might be too old to put you over my knee, but I'm not too old to keep an eye on you. I've already buried one son and I'm damned if I'm gonna bury another.'

Seldom one to lose his temper, Michael smashed his fist against the wall. He might look like some pop star or pretty boy, but he was anything but. He was Michael fucking Butler and he was sick of being treated like some soft prick. How could Vinny betray him after everything he had done for him? Had Vinny forgotten who had helped him kill Trevor Thomas? Yet ever since Ahmed had been back on the scene, Vinny seemed to treat him with a lack of respect.

'Sit down, son. I didn't mean to upset you. I'm just worried because I love you, that's all,' Albie said. The look in Michael's eyes reminded him of Vinny and he did not care for that one bit.

Michael knocked back his brandy, sat down and slammed the glass against the coffee table. 'I'm sorry, Dad. I'm not angry with you and I am glad you told me what Vinny said, because I swear to you, hand on heart, I will never touch a drug again. It's him I'm pissed off with, that wonderful loyal brother of mine. He still thinks I'm some wet-behind-the-ears kid who lives in his shadow, but I'm not. Does he honestly look in the mirror and see Saint Fucking Vinny staring back? Because I don't and neither do you. He's a cunt and he ain't mugging me off no more.'

Queenie Butler put the tray of drinks on the table and waved at her grandchildren. Kings had a marvellous children's entertainer called Charlie Case, and he organized different games, activities and competitions on a daily basis. Of an evening, Charlie would act as bingo caller and compere in the clubhouse. 'Poxy weather today for August, but it don't matter to the little 'uns, does it?'

'No. They're having a whale of a time. Look at Adam dancing. He's so cute,' Nancy replied.

Joanna chuckled. 'Molly's wiggling her hips now as well, look.'

'Aw, bless their little hearts,' Queenie said, her face beaming with pride. She loved nothing more than when Jo and Nancy brought the kids down to Kings. It was just a shame Vinny and Michael didn't accompany them more often to make her happiness complete.

'Where's Viv?' Nancy asked.

'Gone in them bleedin' amusements again. Got the hots for that Mike, and she's addicted to them two-and-ten-pence fall machines. She stands there watching until the kids run out of money, then she pushes the poor little sods out the way when the coins look ready to drop.'

When Joanna and Nancy both laughed, Queenie decided they looked relaxed enough to be able to answer a few questions. She'd had no joy when she had quizzed Vinny and Michael on the phone. Getting information out of those two was like trying to get blood out of a stone. 'So lovely to see yous two looking happy and enjoying yourselves, 'cause I know things ain't been great back at home. What's going on, girls? You can trust me to keep me trap shut. I won't tell the boys, I promise.'

Joanna glanced at Nancy. 'I don't know what you're talking about, Queenie. Do you, Nance?'

Queenie preferred a thief to a liar and there was no way she was being fobbed off that easily. 'Look, you might as well tell me because I shall find out anyway. Gave birth to them men of yours, I did, and I know when something's bleedin' well wrong.'

'Look, I'll be honest, Queenie, Michael and I did go through a bit of a rough patch, but we're back on track now,' Nancy admitted.

'Well, I'm glad to hear that. All marriages have their ups and downs. I should know, I married Albie,' Queenie chuckled.

Joanna stood up. 'Who wants another drink?'

'Sit back down. We haven't finished this conversation yet,' Queenie ordered.

Joanna did as she was told and when Queenie started interrogating her, chose her words carefully. 'Vinny and I have been going through a rough patch too. My dad's up for parole and it has caused some friction.'

Having just taken a sip of her lager and lime, Queenie spat it back in the glass. Nine bastard years was all Johnny

Preston had done in nick. Was that all her Roy's life was worth?

Noticing that her mother-in-law's complexion had turned a whiter shade of pale, Nancy asked Queenie if she was OK.

'No. I'm having one of me funny turns. I'm going outside to get some fresh air.'

Vinny handed the money over to Richie and silently thanked whoever had invented Scotch for his hands not shaking.

Ahmed counted the kilo packages, weighed them, then tested one by piercing it with a penknife then tasting it. 'This all looks in order. You want to check it, Vin?'

'Nope. If you say it's all right, it's all right.'

Richie gave the money a swift count, then nodded. 'OK, let's part waves. Give us a bell if there's any problems your end, and I'll count this properly when I get home. I'll bell you tomorrow if it's not correct.'

When Ahmed shook Richie's hand, Vinny did the same, then watched as Ahmed put the drugs inside the false bottom of the van. Richie had been insistent that the van driver wasn't to know where his yard was, so Mohammed was sitting down the bottom of River Road in Ahmed's car.

As soon as they'd swapped vehicles and hit the A13, Vinny felt a mixture of adrenalin and relief seep through his body.

'You OK?' Ahmed asked, as he swerved into the slow lane to stick close to the van.

Vinny laughed. 'Yeah, I'm more than OK. In fact, once we've conducted our business duties for the day, how do you fancy going out and getting bladdered?'

Ahmed did not particularly feel like a wild night out, but the more normal he kept it, the less suspicious his business partner would be when he got arrested. 'Let's go up the West End for a change. I know a great club that's just opened.'

Vinny grinned. 'Yeah, why not.'

Alison Bloggs opened the front door and treated Little Vinny to a toothless grin. 'Come in, boy. What you got in your bag? I'll swap you a joint for some booze, if you want?'

Little Vinny took a bottle of strong cider out of the carrier bag and handed it to his pal's mum. His dad had obviously been in a good mood earlier. Not only had he granted him permission to go out, he had also given him forty quid wages. 'Is Ben upstairs?'

'No. He's popped to the quacks to pick up my methadone prescription. I lost the last one, if you know what I mean?' Alison chuckled.

Little Vinny knew exactly what she meant. Alison was on more prescription drugs than anybody he knew and she was forever swapping or flogging her medicine to acquire her next hit of heroin. Ben told him everything.

When Alison grabbed him by the arm and dragged him into the lounge, Little Vinny screwed his nose up. Unlike his own home that smelled of fresh flowers and air fresheners, Alison's stank of piss, sick and cannabis. She ponged as well. An unwashed, musty smell, like she hadn't bathed in weeks.

'Go upstairs and play, you little fuckers,' Alison screamed at her brood.

Little Vinny stared at Ben's youngest sister. She was about Molly's age, but instead of being dressed immaculately and having her hair in bunches like his spoilt little sister, poor Kylie was filthy dirty, running about naked, with bruises all over her body.

When the last of her children left the room, Alison slammed the lounge door shut, opened the bottle of cider, then sat down next to Little Vinny on the sofa. 'Ben said you're working at the club now. Is your old man paying you well?'

'Me dad ain't paid me sod all yet,' Little Vinny lied. He knew what a ponce Alison was and if he admitted he had over thirty quid left in his pocket, she would probably barricade him in a cupboard until he agreed to hand it over.

Alison sparked up a joint, then gave it to Little Vinny. 'Got yourself a bird yet, have ya?'

'Er, no. Not yet.'

'Nice-looking boy like you should have the girls queuing up,' Alison replied, putting her grubby hand on Little Vinny's leg.

Frozen through fear, Little Vinny could not move as Alison's hand travelled towards his penis. As much as she repulsed him, he could feel himself becoming erect. When the front door slammed, Little Vinny felt relief wash over him as he leapt off the sofa.

'Hello, Vin,' Ben shrieked, chucking the prescription at his mother before giving his pal a boy-hug.

'I bought us some cider. Let's go to your room, Ben. I want to put my clobber on, then we'll go out,' Little Vinny gabbled. There was no way he would tell his friend what had just happened. Ben would be mortified.

Alison Bloggs chuckled as Little Vinny darted out of the lounge. If he was old enough to work at the club, then he was old enough to pay her for her services. Next time he visited and Ben wasn't present, she would suck him off in exchange for a tenner.

Having recovered from her earlier state of shock, Queenie Butler was now on her soapbox. 'Fuming I am, Viv. This government has got it all wrong, you know. The justice system in this country is a fucking joke. An eye for an eye like it was in the old days, that's how it should be. Makes my blood boil to think that bastard Preston will soon be free to enjoy his life, and it's only because of him my Roy is pushing up daisies.'

'I know what you mean, Queen. I feel the same about that Turkish piece of shit. Killed my Lenny, yet he's still walking about without a care in the world. I've got to be honest with you, I am very surprised and disappointed with Vinny. I really thought he would have sought revenge for Lenny's death, but he ain't done sod all about it.'

'Well, don't you be worrying, Vivvy, because I shall be having strong words with Vinny when I see him next. I will demand he sorts out Ahmed and Johnny Preston. Nobody messes with our family without getting their come-uppance, and I mean nobody.'

It had been Little Vinny's idea that he and Ben spend their Friday evening travelling up and down the District Line on a train. When his dad had given him forty quid earlier, his parting words had been 'Enjoy yourself, son, but I'm telling you now, if I find out you are hanging about with that div Ben Bloggs again, I will break your fucking neck.'

Now he was dressed in a blue Fred Perry short-sleeved shirt, beige three-quarter-length Sta-Prest trousers and his beloved Doc Martens, Little Vinny felt the personality his father had tried so hard to suppress rise to the surface once again. The only thing that pissed him off was that his hair was too long, which was why he had invested in a pork-pie hat.

'Can I have another snout, Vin?'

Little Vinny chucked the packet of Benson and Hedges at his pal. Ben had no money, which is why he had already spent twenty-five quid of his hard-earned wages on booze, fags, puff and glue.

Seeing the woman in the grey jacket glare at him, Little Vinny stood on the seat and wrote 'SKINS 4 EVER' on the ceiling of the carriage with his permanent marker pen.

Ben giggled when the train stopped at Dagenham East and the appalled woman tutted before stomping onto the platform.

When the train didn't move for five minutes, Little Vinny put some Evo Stik in an empty crisp bag, sniffed it, then handed it to his pal. Apart from two old boys sat at the end, the carriage was empty.

'Too much too young,' Ben yelled, when he recognized the sound of Terry Hall's vocals.

Little Vinny poked his head out the door and saw two skinheads strolling down the platform with a stereo system. 'Oi, in here, lads,' he yelled.

By the time the train had reached Elm Park, not only had Little Vinny and Ben made new friends and learned that Madness wasn't the first band to record 'One Step Beyond' it was actually Prince Buster, they'd also been invited to a party the following evening.

# CHAPTER SEVENTEEN

Vinny Butler was not a man with your average sexual appetite. He liked it rough, bordering on violent, which is why rather than be intimate with Jo, he preferred to satisfy his cravings elsewhere.

Last night, Vinny had experienced the most explosive sex he'd had in ages. He and Ahmed had met two birds in a nightclub, then ended up in some West End hotel. Vinny had got it on with the stunning dark-haired one and the sex had blown him away. He would have liked to have seen her again, but when he had woken up this morning, the bird had already gone.

Letting himself indoors, Vinny was pleased to see his son at the kitchen table eating a bowl of cornflakes. 'You all right, boy? Sorry that you've been on your own all night. I had a few bevvies so stayed at the club,' Vinny lied.

'That's OK, Dad. I came home before eleven like you told me to. Can I go out again tonight? I took your advice and met some new friends.'

'Not skinheads, are they?'

'No. They're Mods,' Little Vinny lied.

'Yeah, you can go out again tonight. So, they local lads? What's their names?'

'Danno and Tim, and they live in Dagenham. I met them near the train station. They were visiting someone round here and asked me for directions. They've invited me to a party tonight in Dagenham, so I wondered would it be all right if I stayed out a bit later? I'm gonna look a right dickhead if I have to be home by eleven.'

Vinny sighed. His son was tall for his age, but he'd only turned fourteen this summer, and Vinny couldn't help but worry about him. 'I tell you what, I'll give you a score to get a cab, but I want you home by midnight. I shall be ringing here at twelve on the dot and if you ain't back, there'll be big trouble. Understand?'

'Yes, Dad. I understand.'

Mary Walker was in her element as she sipped her Guinness and watched Daniel, Adam and Lee splash about in the swimming pool. She could not swim herself, was petrified of deep water, but her grandsons were fabulous and swam like little fishes.

'Shame about Dad, isn't it, Mum? Do you reckon he's really ill or do you think he had a change of heart?' Nancy asked.

'Oh, he is ill. We had to stop at least four times on the journey here this morning because he had the trots. You know what an old stick-in-the-mud he is though. I bet you a pound to a pinch of salt that he don't bother driving down when he feels better. He'd rather work in that café than enjoy a holiday.'

'Never mind. We'll still have a good time, Mum. They have so many activities on for the kids here, and the adults.'

'Like what?'

'Well, the boys' favourites are the donkey derby, It's a Knockout and the trip to Treasure Island. And you are just going to love going to the club of a night. They have bingo on before the entertainment kicks off, then they have a resident band. There's different competitions on every night: ballroom dancing, Knobbly Knees, Mr and Mrs – and you must enter the glamorous granny competition. The boys would love that.'

'Oh, I don't fancy standing on stage, Nance. Shame your father isn't here, he'd have won the Knobbly Knees contest hands down.'

Nancy chuckled. 'The American horse racing night is great fun. They put a big screen up on the stage and I let the boys have a little bet. They get so excited. It's hilarious watching them.'

'Good job your father isn't here. I'm sure he'd have something to say about the boys gambling. So, do Queenie and Vivian go to the club every evening?'

'They always come over for the bingo, but they don't usually stay that late. They will be in the upstairs club tonight. Freddie Starr is appearing and they both love him.'

'Oh well, if I bump into them at all, I will just ignore them,' Mary said.

'Mum, please don't make things awkward for me. Queenie and Vivian have always treated me and the boys well.'

'Yes, I know, and I'm grateful for that, even if I don't like the women. Last time I saw them, they were scrapping like two fishmongers' wives in our old café. Hitting your father and all sorts they were. Rough old malts, the pair of them.'

Nancy suddenly felt anxious. It had been her suggestion in the first place that her mum visited Kings and she only hoped her idea wasn't about to backfire on her.

As the afternoon wore on, Vinny Butler became more and more annoyed with himself. The bird from last night had been a real stunner. Dark-skinned and dark-haired like himself, she'd had long legs, an ample-sized arse, big firm tits, luscious full lips and a voice as sexy as any he could recall.

Her name was Izzy, but other than that, Vinny knew sod all about her other than she enjoyed being raped.

Vinny tilted back his reclining chair, put his hand behind his head, shut his eyes and visualized the scene once again. When Izzy had asked him to pretend to be a rapist and take her by force, Vinny thought he had died and gone to heaven. He had immediately granted Izzy's wish by grabbing her from behind, overpowering her then pinning her to the bed.

Izzy had fought back hard. She had bitten, kicked and even punched him, which had turned Vinny on to a point of no return. He had then tied Izzy's arms and legs to the bedposts, shoved his big throbbing cock in her mouth, then fucked her senseless.

Tempted to return to the club where he had met Izzy to see if he could spot her or find out more about her, Vinny sat up, stared at the photo of Molly on his desk and immediately felt guilty. Shagging the odd prostitute to satisfy his warped sexual appetite was one thing, but to start up a full-blown affair was another.

Vinny knew just by the way he was feeling that Izzy had the potential to mess his head up. So perhaps it was for the best that she had sneaked out of the hotel room before he'd had the chance to exchange details with her? His brother had never been the same man since that Bella had ripped his heart to shreds, and no way was Vinny going to allow the same to happen to him.

The thought of Michael made him reach for the phone. 'All right, bruv? You OK taking charge of the club for a couple of nights? Only I'm missing Molly and Mum and I fancy a couple of nights down at Kings.'

When Michael agreed to the idea, Vinny ended the call, then grabbed his car keys. He had been a proper bastard towards Joanna ever since she had mentioned her father was up for parole, and for the sake of their daughter if nothing else, he should try and make things right between them.

The Kings Holiday Park shop was extremely handy between visits to the nearest supermarket. It sold everything from eggs and bacon to postcards and lilos.

'Right, I've got the cheese, ham, bread and butter. What else do we need?' Vivian asked her sister.

Feeling a bit lost for words, Queenie pointed down the aisle. 'What are they doing back here?'

Vivian was just as shocked as her sister to see Brenda and her new boyfriend strolling towards them with a basket full of groceries. 'Well, I hope they don't think they are staying with us again,' Vivian hissed.

Quickly regaining her composure, Queenie smiled. 'Hello, love. What you doing here? Where's Tara and Tommy?'

Brenda pursed her lips. 'Got nothing to do with you where the kids are. Last time you saw them you chucked them out of your bungalow, along with me and Scotty. Hardly grandmother of the year, are you? Oh, wait a minute – you are when it comes to Vinny and Michael's kids. It's just mine you can't be arsed playing the doting nanny with.'

'What you on about? Not been drinking again, have you, Bren? I only asked you to leave because Jo and Molly were on their way down here. It is Vinny's bungalow, not mine, and there wasn't enough room for us all. I love Tara and Tommy just as much as I love all my grandchildren, so there's no call for you to go on the turn.'

'I'm just stating facts, Mum. Anyway, Scotty has paid for our own chalet for the week, so you can stick Vinny's bungalow up your arse.'

Queenie was immediately alarmed that Scott had paid for a chalet. There was something fishy about him that she had sensed from the very start. Was he undercover Old Bill, only hooking up with Bren because he knew who her brothers were? With his blond hair, tall frame, twinkling eyes and good looks he could do a damn sight better than her sullen, drunken, drama queen of a daughter. And Scott had no kids himself, so he said. So why on earth would he want to saddle himself with Brenda's two?

'Are you OK, Mrs B? Brenda didn't mean what she said, did you, Bren? You only get one mum, darling.'

Queenie's lips curled into a snarl. 'It's got fuck all to do with you, and if you call me Mrs B again I shall kick you right in the goolies. I've got your card marked, Sonny Jim. My daughter might be as thick as two short planks, but I bloody well ain't. Come on, Viv. We're leaving.'

Screaming abuse at her mother, Brenda went to chase after her, but Scott held her back. 'Leave it, babe. We're on holiday, so let's just enjoy ourselves.'

'She is so bloody rude, my mother. I hate her! No wonder Dean walked out on me. What was she on about? What did she mean, she's got your card marked?'

Scott Mason had always been an opportunist. After meeting Brenda in a boozer he'd initially planned on having a one-night stand and then dumping her. However, as soon as he found out who her brothers were he had decided it would be worth his while to form a relationship with Brenda. What better way to see off all the people who were chasing him for the money he'd swindled them out of with his timeshare scam? They'd soon back down once they found out he was part of the Butler family. With a bit of luck he could smarm his way in with Vinny and Michael and land himself a job at their club. Brenda had told him they'd employed her ex, so why shouldn't they do the same for him? Scott still had his fingers in a few pies, but none of them were paying too well at the moment and he was sick of looking over his shoulder for enemies and creditors. If he worked at the club with Vinny and Michael, then all his worries would be over. A regular income and serious back-up was exactly what he needed right now.

'I have no idea what your mum was on about, Bren. Perhaps she was just in a bad mood, eh?'

'But she had no right to talk to you like shit. I tell you, Scott, I'm fuming, I really am.'

'Don't worry about it – I'm not. Perhaps your mum is worried because of who your brothers are? She might think I'm undercover Old Bill or something? I think we should arrange a meet with your brothers, Bren, to put everyone's minds at rest. What do you reckon?'

'Can't do any harm, I suppose.'

Christopher Walker was sitting at his desk filling in some forms when his phone rang. A chill ran down his spine as his colleague explained there was a man on the phone who insisted on being put through to him, yet refused to give his name. 'He says he's an old friend of yours, Chris.'

'DS Walker. How can I help you?' Christopher asked, desperately trying to keep the anxiety out of his voice.

'I think it is me who will be helping you, Chris. Now, when we going to have this little meet?'

Feeling his stomach churn, Christopher knew the sooner he got this meeting out of the way, the better he would feel. Not knowing who the mystery caller was was doing his head in. 'Do you know Hainault Country Park?'

'Yep.'

'Well, as you drive in, there are two car parks. I'll meet you at the one furthest away from the entrance at eleven a.m. tomorrow. I'll be in an unmarked car, a brown Ford

Cortina. What will you be driving? Just so I know who I'm looking for.'

'Don't be concerning yourself about looking for me, Chris. I shall find you, but a word of warning, if you tell anybody else about our little meet and I learn of your betrayal, I won't be a happy man. Please remember, I'm holding all the cards.'

When the mystery caller cut him off, Christopher put his head in his hands. He hated breaking the rules, but he could hardly risk confiding in a colleague. Lying to protect Vinny Butler had already cost him his childhood and there was no way he would allow it to cost him his career as well. No way, José.

After spending an hour in the amusement arcade, Queenie and Vivian took a slow walk back to the bungalow. Lots of the bungalows, chalets and caravans were privately owned, but the site always had its fair share of holiday-makers too. There was even an area over the back for touring caravans, and Queenie and Viv loved to have a nose around. 'State of them curtains in that one, Viv. Look, they're black. Dirty bastards, people are. Wouldn't take ten minutes to take them down and wash them, would it?'

'People have low standards in this day and age, Queen. Got no pride like us old school. 'Ere, is that your Vinny's motor?'

Vinny had always been a fan of Jaguars and the previous year he'd bought himself a brand-new XJ6 in black. 'Yep, that's his number plate. Really glad he's popped down. Still fuming about that Johnny Preston getting parole, I am. He needs to have a serious chat with Joanna. Over my dead body will Molly ever be in his company, let me tell you. All but killed my Roy, that bastard did. Took away his spirit, pride and personality. I'll never rest until Preston gets his comeuppance, Viv. What goes around should come around.'

Albie Butler sipped his brandy and had a good old look around. It had been years since he had paid a visit to his son's club and with the fluorescent spotlights in the ceiling, expensive-looking carpet and furniture, and gold wallpaper with a red velvet pattern, it looked top notch. 'What's them big silver things, boy?'

'Disco balls, Dad. All the rage now, they are. We don't have discos as such, but they still set the gaff off when people are dancing. Do you like the new décor?'

Albie nodded. The only thing that he didn't like was the blown-up framed photo of Roy and Champ that was hung in the reception. He had welled up when he had seen it and still felt upset now. 'Looks lovely, boy. What sort of entertainment do you have then?'

'We've got a singer on tonight. Good he is, and lots of our punters get up and give a song. You should sing Al Martino, Dad. Got a great voice you have and I love you singing "Spanish Eyes".'

Albie immediately shook his head. It felt strange being back in Whitechapel after so long, and too many local people knew about his cancer lie for him to get on stage. He could just imagine being pelted with eggs and rotten tomatoes.

Guessing what his father was worried about, Michael did his best to reassure him. 'No one will say anything to you, Dad, and if they do, they'll have me to fucking answer to. That cancer story is old news now, so hold your head high. If anybody says one bad word to you, I want you to tell me, OK? Because if they disrespect you, they're disrespecting me as well, and no fucker mugs me off in my own club.'

Pretending he had cancer years ago had been a stupid thing to do, and Albie had rarely set foot in Whitechapel since. 'I'm not sure I'm ready for a night out, boy. I'd rather just go back to the house.'

Michael squeezed his father's hand. 'Look, I'll make a deal with you. You spend tonight and tomorrow night at the club with me, then next weekend we'll shoot down to Kings and spend some time with the boys, eh? What do ya say?'

Albie forced a smile. 'I would like to spend some time with the boys.'

'Right, now that's sorted, I'm gonna pour us another drink.'

When his son walked up to the bar, Albie thought of Dorothy. *Hi-de-Hi!*, *Family Fortunes* and *Play Your Cards Right* had been Dorothy's favourite TV programmes, and even though Albie used to joke with her that she only watched old crap, he would give anything to be sitting at home holding her hand and watching any of those programmes with her now, absolutely anything.

'Daddy, can you sing me the rabbit song again please?' Molly asked, as she took another lick of her ice cream.

Joanna chuckled. Queenie and Vivian had taught Molly the words to the old war song 'Run Rabbit Run' yesterday and Molly would not stop singing it. 'Stop driving Daddy mad, Molly. He's only just arrived.'

Vinny grinned, sung the words to 'Run Rabbit Run' once again, then as soon as Molly had finished her ice cream, lifted her up above his head.

'Mind she's not sick, Vinny,' Joanna warned. She loved family moments like this, and had been thrilled when Vinny surprised her by turning up unannounced earlier.

'Run rabbit, run rabbit, run run run,' Vinny sang.

Molly loved her father. He always brought her lovely presents and made her giggle. 'Can you buy me a rabbit, Daddy?'

'Rabbits are naff pets. All they do is sit in a hutch all day and eat lettuce. Dogs are much better. One day when you're older, I'll buy you a little puppy.'

'Don't be putting ideas into her head, Vinny,' Joanna warned. She knew what Molly was like. Very intelligent for her age and once she got a bee in her bonnet she would keep on about it.

'Can I call the puppy Fred, Dad?'

Vinny grinned at Joanna. 'She's old before her time this one. Loves a war song and where did she get the name Fred from?'

Joanna laughed. 'I have no idea, Vin. She doesn't even know anybody called Fred. It might be because she overheard Queenie and Viv mentioning Freddie Starr. He's in the upstairs club tonight.'

'I want to go swimming now,' Molly announced.

'I'll take her, Jo. You stay here with the stuff.'

Joanna smiled as Vinny gently lifted Molly into the children's pool. She looked so cute with her pink swimsuit and armbands. Her blonde curly hair was even lighter than usual due to the sun and she really did look like a little princess.

'You all right, Jo?' young Billy asked, sitting down on Vinny's sunbed.

Joanna immediately felt panicky. 'You better not sit there, Bill. That's my fella's sunbed and he gets a bit funny.'

Billy was only eighteen and was on his first ever lad's holiday. He and his pals were staying in a caravan and having a whale of a time. 'I'll move as soon as your bloke comes back – and remind me to give you my phone number before I go home in case you ever want to leave him,' Billy joked.

'Where are your friends?' Joanna asked, nervously glancing around to see if Vinny had clocked her and Billy talking.

'Playing pool in the club, the boring gits. Where's your mate, Nancy? My pal Ian, the tall blond-haired one, proper fancies her. I don't, I fancy you,' Billy chuckled.

Realizing that Billy sounded tipsy and had more than likely been on the lager all day, Jo stood up to get away from him, but as she saw Vinny marching towards her with a tearful Molly in his arms and a face like thunder, she knew she should have moved sooner. 'I was just coming over to the swimming pool, Vin.'

'Who is that cunt? And what's he doing on my sunbed?' Vinny asked, none too quietly.

Aware that people on nearby sunbeds were now looking their way, Jo did her best to try to defuse the situation. 'Billy's on holiday with his friends, Vinny. He has a girlfriend back home and was telling me and Nancy only yesterday how much he missed her, wasn't you, Bill?' Jo said, praying that Billy wasn't too drunk to sense the danger he was in.

Unfortunately for Jo, Billy was too drunk. He grinned at Vinny. 'Yeah, I have a bird back home in South London. She ain't as hot as your missus though, so if you ever wanna do a swap, let me know.'

To say Vinny was furious was putting it mildly. He wanted to smash the living daylights out of the cocky little bastard there and then, but knew he could do no such thing in front of his daughter and tons of sunbathers in broad daylight. He would find out where the little shit was staying though, and when he did, he'd give him the hiding of a lifetime. 'Pick your stuff up now. We're going,' he spat at Jo.

When Vinny stomped off with their sobbing daughter in his arms, Joanna quickly shoved her towel, book and suntan lotion into her bag and chased after him. 'Billy's just a kid, Vinny. He was only joking, he didn't mean no harm.'

Vinny looked at his partner with pure hatred on his face. 'So this is what you and that slut Nancy get up to when me and Michael aren't about, is it? Do you lounge around chatting up young fucking geezers all day while we're working our bollocks off to pay for the privilege?'

'Don't be daft, Vinny. You're over-reacting. Nancy and myself would never act in such a way, and deep down you know it.'

'It's that fucking blonde hair of yours that attracts these cunts, I'm telling ya. How many rows have we had in the past over geezers chatting you up, eh? And how many times have I asked you to become a brunette? Why can't you just play ball with me and do something I ask, eh? I treat you well enough, don't I?'

'Stop it, Mummy. Stop it, Daddy,' Molly begged.

Desperate to pacify Vinny and prevent him upsetting their daughter any more, Joanna decided to agree with him. Vinny had often told her that her hair was a similar style and colour to his first love Yvonne Summers, and Joanna had privately wondered if that was the reason for their lack of intimacy. 'I think you are right, Vin. It is my blonde hair that attracts these chancers. I actually fancy a change now, so how about I book an appointment with that good Italian hairdresser as soon as I get back to London?'

Vinny Butler was a man who liked to get his own way and Joanna's willingness to comply with his rules immediately took the sting out of his temper. 'OK, babe. I'd like that.'

Little Vinny and Ben Bloggs got off the train at Dagenham East, then followed the directions that Danno and Tim had given them. They found Ibscott Close easily, and hearing

Bad Manners' 'Lip Up Fatty' blaring out, they followed the music.

An hour later, Little Vinny was pissed, stoned and jumping up and down to the Specials' 'A Message to You, Rudy' when his pork-pie hat flew off.

'You need a haircut, Vin,' Danno said, rubbing his hand over Little Vinny's overgrown skinhead.

'I've been so busy working, I've not had time to get to the barbers,' Little Vinny lied. He could hardly say that his arsehole of a father had forbidden him to get it cut again. That would make him look like a right wally.

'I'll do it for you. I cut me own and I've got clippers upstairs.'

Little Vinny glanced around. Even the girls at the party had shorter hair than him, apart from their long fringes. 'OK, then. Cut it for me now.'

Desperate to get a good view of Freddie Starr, Queenie and Vivian decided to skip bingo, get glammed up to the nines, and go straight to the upstairs club to grab a good table. 'I love that green dress on you, Viv. Is that the one you bought down the Roman?'

'Yeah. Fits nice, don't it? Couldn't wear me gold with it though as it would have clashed with the silver neck. Bought this necklace and bracelet when I popped down there to get our pie and mash last week. I'll only wear it with this though, I feel lost without me gold.'

Queenie nodded in agreement. Over the years, both she and Vivian had accumulated quite a collection of gold jewellery. They had everything from sovereign earrings and necklaces to ingots and gate bracelets. Every birthday and Christmas the boys would buy them more, and Queenie knew they were the envy of all their neighbours.

'Ooh, my Vinny's just walked in,' Queenie said, standing up to wave at her son. 'Viv, don't say nothing yet about Scotty. If we mention he might be Old Bill, Vinny will kill him and I don't want a creation down here. I'll have a word with Vinny on the quiet.'

Vinny bought his mum and aunt a sherry each, and himself a large Scotch. 'Don't mind me joining yous tonight, do you? Nancy's mother is on holiday here apparently, and I didn't fancy sitting downstairs with her. Jo and Nancy seemed to be joined at the hip lately, don't they?'

'Aw, it's nice they get along, Vin. Can't believe Nancy's mother is here though. Not seen that old cow since she had that café near us. Is she staying in Michael's bungalow?' Vivian asked.

'No. She's got her own chalet.'

'Bet she was too frightened to stop opposite us. Last time I saw her was when I was battering that sour-faced husband of hers over the head with my umbrella. We must have a drink downstairs after we've seen Freddie, Queen. I want to see the look on Mary from the dairy's face when she spots us. Bet she won't look us in the eye,' Vivian said, chuckling at her own wit. 'Mary from the Dairy' was an old Max Miller song.

'We will be nosy, but we can't be too nasty, Viv. It is Nancy's mother,' Queenie said.

'Changed, this family has, over the years. Time was, we always stood our ground – and look at us now,' Vivian replied bitterly.

'What you going on about?' Vinny asked his aunt.

'Your sister is down 'ere too with her new fella, Billy Big Bollocks. Spoke to me and your mother like a piece of shit earlier, didn't she, Queen?'

'I didn't even know Bren had a new bloke. I wish she would fucking let me know these things. The geezer could be undercover Old Bill for all we know,' Vinny said, his temper rising to the surface once more.

Queenie glared at her sister. It was a silent warning for her to shut the fuck up. 'It's not your sister your aunt's upset about, love. We had a chat earlier this week and we're both very disappointed that that Turkish bastard is still breathing. He killed your cousin, Vin – surely that means something in our world? Ahmed needs to be dealt with, as soon as possible. And while we're on the subject, Joanna let slip that her scumbag of a father was up for parole. I expect him to be dealt with as well, Vinny. We can't have him walking the streets, enjoying life after what he did to Roy, can we now?'

Suddenly wishing he was back in bed with the bird from last night rather than in Eastbourne, Vinny nodded his head. Ahmed had done sod all wrong, but Johnny Preston would have to be dealt with at some point.

'All will be sorted, Mum, when the time is right. I can't do anything rash though, because of Molly. Little Vinny can look after himself, but my daughter needs me. No way am I chancing getting banged up for murder and leaving her.'

Little Vinny had never been very popular with boys or girls. Apart from Ben, he had no friends, and apart from Ben's mother, no female had ever made a move on him. Tonight though, his luck seemed to have changed. Not only had he integrated well with Danno, Tim and his pals, he now had a nice-looking bird staring at him.

'She well fancies you, Vin. Go and talk to her and see if you can fix me up with her mate,' Ben urged.

Little Vinny stared back at the girl. She had her head shaved, but the back and fringe were long. She wore lots of earrings, had a big tattoo on her forearm and was dressed in the style of a proper skinhead bird. When she smiled at him, Vinny quickly looked away. She had a really pretty face, a cute slightly turned up button nose, and was making his stomach feel funny. 'She's beautiful, Ben, but I can't talk to her. I dunno what to say.'

Ben nudged his pal. 'Well, you better think of something quick. Her and her mate are walking towards us.'

When the record changed to Janet Kay's 'Silly Games', not knowing what else to say, Vinny asked the obvious. 'Wanna dance?'

Still unable to stop thinking about the bird he had met the previous evening, Vinny had been knocking back the Scotch far quicker than he usually did, and by the time Freddie Starr walked off stage, he was merry to say the least. 'Best I go downstairs in a bit and check on Molly. Caught her mother flirting with some young lad around the swimming pool today. Thought yous two were meant to be keeping an eye on Jo while I weren't here?'

'Oh, don't talk bollocks, Vinny. Jo's not like that, she's a good girl. I think we'll come downstairs too,' Queenie said, nudging her sister. She knew her son better than anyone, and was very aware of the dangerous glint in his eyes.

'Let's see if we can get backstage and meet Freddie first, Queen. Bleedin' handsome, he is.'

'No, Viv! You made a right show of me when you tried to get hold of Des O'Connor and snog him when you were pissed, and you ain't embarrassing me again. We're going downstairs, now!'

Mary Walker had had a wonderful evening. The Mr and Mrs competition had been hysterical, the resident band had played some wonderful catchy songs from the seventies, such as Tony Orlando and Dawn's 'Knock Three Times' and Sylvia's 'Viva España', and her grandsons, daughter, Joanna and Molly had been wonderful company.

'Would you like another drink, Mary? It's been such a nice evening, I think we should all have one for the road,' Joanna suggested.

Mary nodded, then smiled. How that awful Vinny Butler had ever attracted such a lovely girl as Joanna she would never know. And how his sperm had ever produced such a beautiful child as Molly was even more of a mystery.

When Joanna went up to the bar, both Mary and Nancy were stunned to see a drunken-looking Brenda plonk herself on Jo's chair. 'Not good enough for you, are we, me and my family? Meet my new man, Scotty. Been sitting four tables behind you all night, we have, and I can tell you've been blanking us.'

Apart from when they had first met at school, Nancy had never really liked Brenda. However, she was Michael's sister and for that reason alone, Nancy had always done her best to be polite. 'I would never blank you, Brenda. Where are Tara and Tommy? Jo and I had no idea you were here, I swear we didn't,' Nancy said honestly.

Sensing trouble on the horizon, Mary nudged her daughter. 'The boys are tired now, love. Shall I take them back to my chalet? It's only a spit's throw away and I'm yawning myself.'

'Yeah, OK, Mum. They hate that long walk back to our bungalow at night. Michael couldn't have chosen one further away from the club.'

'Hello, Brenda. I never knew you were here,' Joanna said, as she put the tray of drinks on the table.

Desperate not to be in Brenda's company for one minute longer, Mary stood up and told Joanna she could have her chair.

'So, what do you think of my Scotty? Far more handsome than that lanky streak of piss I married, isn't he?'

Knowing how jealous and possessive Brenda could be

over her men, rather than reply to her sister-in-law's question, Nancy grabbed Joanna's hand. Chris Gentry the DJ had just kicked off with Odyssey's latest chart hit 'Use It Up and Wear It Out'. 'Let's have a dance, I love this song. You coming, Bren?'

'I am, Auntie Nancy,' Molly said excitedly. She loved to dance and always got lots of attention when she did so.

When the record changed to Tom Browne's 'Funkin' for Jamaica' Joanna leaned towards Nancy. 'Not only are we lumbered with Brenda, that bloody Billy and his mates have just walked in. I hope they don't start pestering us again. Vinny will go mad if he sees them talking to us. I thought he was going to punch Billy's lights out earlier.'

'Shit, they've spotted us,' Nancy informed Jo.

'All right, ladies? Best-looking birds we've seen at Kings, yous two are,' Billy slurred, grinning at Joanna while trying to pull off some John Travolta moves.

'Let's go and sit back at the table,' Joanna said to Nancy. Billy and his pals were very drunk and could barely stand up, and she was petrified that Vinny would walk in and it would all kick off.

'Put her down, Billy,' Nancy ordered, when Billy picked up Molly and started swinging her around in the air.

The timing could not have been worse for Billy to lose his footing. Vinny walked in just in time to see his daughter hit the floor. 'Don't hit him in here, Vinny. You'll get us barred,' Queenie yelled, chasing after her son.

Vinny's first concern was for his daughter. He ran onto the dancefloor and scooped Molly into his arms. 'You OK, sweetheart? Daddy's here now to look after you.'

Molly stared at him in a state of shock, then burst into tears. 'My head feels sore, Daddy.'

'Where does it hurt, princess?'

'At the back.'

When Vinny spotted a slight trace of blood in his daughter's blonde hair, he saw redder than the fucking blood. 'Hold Molly for me, Mum,' he demanded.

Holidaymakers screamed in terror when Vinny started kicking Billy around the dancefloor as though he was kicking a football. 'Stop it! Stop it! You'll get us slung off the camp,' Vivian shrieked.

'Leave him alone, Vinny. You'll get arrested,' Joanna screamed.

When Billy's mates waded into the brawl, a terrified Nancy dragged Joanna away. Scott turned to Brenda. This was his big chance to impress the Butler family. The chance he had been waiting for. 'I'm gonna get your brother out of here. There's five of them and one of him. I'll sort it.'

'Don't get involved, Scotty. Vinny won't thank you for it,' Brenda begged her boyfriend.

Desperate to show his worth to Brenda's family, Scott ran over to the dancefloor and grabbed hold of Vinny from behind. 'Come on, pal. Let's get you out of here before you get yourself hurt, nicked, or both.'

Not knowing Scott from Adam, his interference and dumb words were like a red rag to a bull. 'Me, get hurt? Who do you think you're talking to, you muggy cunt?' Vinny yelled. He then treated Scott to one of his infamous headbutts.

When Scott landed on the dancefloor with a sickening thud, Brenda became hysterical. 'You bastard, Vinny! You're bang out of order. Scotty's my boyfriend and he was only trying to help.' Kneeling down next to her new love, Brenda began to sob. 'I don't think he's breathing. I think he's dead,' she screamed, much to the horror of the open-mouthed onlookers.

Kings Holiday Park was known as a family-friendly place, where there was never any trouble. Unused to the sort of fracas taking place, terrified holidaymakers were fleeing the club in droves.

'Vinny, don't argue,' Queenie ordered as the doormen waded in. Apart from a tiny cut on the back of her head, Molly seemed fine and Joanna was now taking care of her.

'I have every right to argue. This ain't our fucking fault. Some prick nearly killed my daughter. What would any decent dad do?'

All the doormen knew who Vinny Butler was and were accordingly very wary of him. 'Can you please leave and take your family with you, Vinny? We will have to involve the police otherwise,' one bouncer said.

Queenie grabbed hold of her son's arm. 'We're going now, and don't you dare argue with me. Me and Viv don't have a lot to look forward to in life and if we can't play our bingo and enjoy our nights out over here any more, we might as well both be dead. I swear to you, Vinny, if you get us chucked out of this holiday park, I will never ever forgive you.'

'Where's Molly?'

'Jo took her outside.'

Vinny glanced around. He had seen Silly Billy being scraped off the dancefloor by his muggy little pals, but Scott still seemed to be out for the count, judging by the crowd surrounding his prone body and trying to revive him. 'I'm going now, but bring Brenda outside, Mum. I need to speak to her.'

'And how am I meant to do that? Look at her. She's in Bette Davis mode.'

'Just drag her out by her fucking hair, will ya. This is important.'

Vinny allowed the doormen to escort him from the club. He guessed they had to save face by showing holiday-makers and staff alike that they were not frightened of him. Once outside, he spotted Joanna immediately. She had Molly in her arms, was crying, and busybody Nancy was comforting her.

Not caring one iota about Jo or Nancy, Vinny marched over to them and snatched Molly out of her mother's arms. 'How is she? Has she shown any signs of concussion?'

'No. She seems OK, Vinny. She saw you fighting though and keeps mentioning it. It's really upset her.'

Vinny smothered his daughter's face with kisses. 'Daddy's so sorry if he upset you, princess. But he got angry when that nasty man dropped you. Do you remember him dropping you?'

Lip pouting, Molly nodded. 'Yes, Daddy.'

'Well, dads are meant to stick up for their daughters, and because the nasty man had hurt you, I had to hurt him. I'm sorry if I upset you, Molly. I will never upset you again, I promise,' Vinny said, putting his daughter's head on his shoulder.

'Will you sing "Run Rabbit Run" to me, Daddy?'

Joanna and Nancy glanced at one another as Vinny sang and Molly started to giggle. They had tried everything to cheer her up and neither were comforted by the fact she seemed to be such a daddy's girl.

Seeing his mother dragging Brenda towards him, Vinny handed Molly back to Joanna. 'Wait here,' he ordered.

'You bastard! I hate you! You ruin every relationship I have,' Brenda shouted, pummelling Vinny in the chest.

Vinny grabbed hold of Brenda's arms. 'Is lover boy awake yet?'

'Sort of. But he isn't talking properly and he has to go to hospital.'

Dragging Brenda away from Joanna and Nancy's evil stare, Vinny told her exactly what was expected of her. 'You go to the hospital with your bloke and you tell him if he grasses me up, I'll do more than knock him out next time, Bren. Do you understand me?'

Brenda's bottom lip wobbled. She despised her family at times. All she had ever wanted was to lead a normal life, but being a Butler made that impossible. 'Yes, Vinny. I understand.'

# CHAPTER EIGHTEEN

Vinny paced up and down the corridor like a man desperately trying to wear the soles of his shoes out. Molly had seemed fine, just a little sleepy, but Vinny was worried she might have concussion. He would never forgive himself if he did not get her checked out properly and as a result something bad happened to his little angel.

'For Chrissake, Vinny, sit your arse down. Making me feel dizzy, you are,' Queenie complained.

'And he's making me feel edgy. What's the betting that old Nan sticks her oar in and tries to get us all barred? She ain't never liked me and you, Queen,' Vivian said, referring to the woman who sat at reception in the clubhouse. Nobody knew the woman's real name. She was just known to all as Nan and had a reputation of being a tyrant. Even the kids were scared of her, and she reminded Viv of the Queen Mother to look at.

Vinny glared at Joanna as he sat down. Their daughter getting dropped on the floor was all her fault as far as he was concerned. If she hadn't been chatting up young geezers in the first place, then none of this would have happened. 'Go and get us some hot drinks,' Vinny demanded, throwing a fiver at Jo.

'Don't blame her, Vin. Me and Vivvy have always kept an eye on Jo and Nancy down here and not once have we seen them flirting with other blokes. They're just not the type, love,' Queenie said, when Joanna walked away.

'Well, it certainly ain't my fucking fault, is it? Nor yours or Auntie Viv's. Perhaps it's Freddie Starr's fault. Let's all blame him, shall we?'

Queenie tutted. 'Sarcasm doesn't wash with me, son.'

'Look, I'm sorry. I just hate hospitals. It brings it all back to me what happened to Roy.'

'Well, don't you think it brings it back to us too? You nigh-on disappeared for the first week your brother was in a coma. It was me who sat by his side day and night. You was out on the lash with that murdering Turkish bastard.'

'And me. I sat there too,' Vivian reminded her nephew.

Desperate to change the subject, Vinny repeated some of the conversation he'd had with the bouncer. 'It's all gonna be cool. I know that Ron quite well. He told us to lay low for the next couple of weeks, then said we'll be all right to go back in the club again. I suppose he just wants to wait until this batch of holidaymakers have sodded off home.'

'What? Me and Queen an' all?' Vivian asked horrified. Two weeks without her bingo was like asking an alcoholic to go two weeks without their booze.

'They can't stop me and Viv going to the club. We haven't done sod all wrong. I want you to go and speak to Ray King personally, Vinny. He likes me and Viv, he does. You tell him that somebody nearly killed your daughter and he will understand. Apologize for fighting, but tell him that Viv and I were in no way involved in anything that happened. That clear?'

Vinny sighed. 'Crystal, Mother.'

*

Little Vinny woke up with a mouth as dry as a bone. He stumbled into the bathroom, shoved his mouth under the cold tap, and swallowed the water greedily.

'You all right, Vin? Didn't we have a good night? I feel a bit sick this morning though, and I got a headache.'

Staring at his reflection in the mirror, Little Vinny felt sick too. His dad was going to murder him when he saw his hair cut. 'You better go home, Ben. My dad was gonna ring me at twelve last night and we didn't get home until three. I reckon he might drive back from Eastbourne and if he sees you here, I'm dead meat.'

Ben chuckled. 'I bet you're dead meat when he sees your number one. What you gonna do? Do you reckon he'll ban you from going out again?'

'Well, there ain't a lot I can do, is there? I'm sure if I say abrafuckingcadabra, me hair ain't gonna grow back, is it? I might just wear me hat for a while and hope me dad don't notice. No way is he stopping me from going out. I can't wait to see Shazza again tonight. She's beautiful and I'm gonna ask her to be my girlfriend.'

'Can't you get Shazza to bring her mate and we go out in a foursome, Vin?'

Not wanting to upset Ben by informing him that Shazza's mate wasn't interested in him, Little Vinny patted his pal on the back. 'That Pauline bird has already got a boyfriend, Ben. But I'll have a word with Shazza tonight and see if she can fix you up with one of her other mates. Now, get going, in case my old man walks in.'

When Ben left, Little Vinny laid on his bed, thought of Shazza and fondled his penis. She had let him touch her titties last night and later he would be going round her house to sit in her bedroom and play records. Imagining what her naked body would look like, Little Vinny sped up his hand movement.

*

Molly had not been given the all-clear by the doctor until the early hours of the morning, so Joanna was very surprised when just three hours later, Vinny woke her up. 'What's the time?' she asked sleepily.

'Time for you to go to the hairdressers. I've booked you an appointment at one in Eastbourne town centre.'

'If I'm having my hair dyed, Vinny, then I would rather use that Italian hairdresser back in London,' Jo answered bravely.

'OK, get dressed then and you can travel back to London with me.'

'Can't I have it dyed after my holiday? Nancy and I have arranged to go to Treasure Island later with her mum and the kids.'

'Fuck Nancy and her mum. Don't piss me off, Jo. You're lucky I'm even speaking to you after what happened last night. Our daughter could have died or ended up with brain damage because of you attracting dickheads with that slaggy-looking blonde hair of yours. How do you think I'm gonna sleep at night back in London, with you lounging around the swimming pool down here, looking like a fucking Barbie doll and attracting cunts, eh?'

Knowing when she was beaten and certainly not wanting to be travelling back to London with Vinny while he was in such a foul mood, Joanna made her decision. 'OK, take me to the hairdresser in Eastbourne.'

Christopher Walker felt as nervous as hell as he drove into Hainault Country Park. He had purposely arrived early in the hope of spotting his tormentor, but when he parked up, he could not see any suspicious-looking vehicles or people.

Picking up his copy of the *Daily Mail*, Christopher tried to concentrate on reading the front-page story, but couldn't.

He felt physically sick, and the only time he could remember feeling so anxious in the past was when he had witnessed Vinny Butler murdering Dave Phillips. He had then been threatened by Vinny before being interviewed and forced to take part in an identification parade by the police. That had been proper scary stuff, but this was his career at stake.

With each new car that drove in and parked up, Christopher felt his stomach churn. So far, each new arrival had been one more dog owner giving their beloved pet their daily exercise. It was gone eleven now, and still there was no sign of the mystery man who had caused him so many sleepless nights.

At 11.15 exactly, Christopher nigh-on jumped out of his skin when he heard a loud tapping on the back window of his car. He leaned over, opened the passenger door and seconds later a tall foreign-looking man jumped in. The man held out his right hand. 'Nice to meet you at last, Christopher. My name is Ahmed. Ahmed Zane.'

Christopher was totally gobsmacked. The caller had spoken with a slight accent, but Chris had never dreamt that it could be Ahmed. So far as anyone knew, Zane and Vinny were joined at the hip. The anxiety that had gripped Christopher was suddenly replaced with a surge of adrenalin as he realized what this meant: if anybody could set Vinny up, it was Ahmed. And DS Christopher Walker would get all the credit.

Trying to regain his composure, he shook Ahmed's hand. 'Look, no disrespect, but do you mind if I frisk you to make sure you're not wired up? It's usual police procedure.'

'Funnily enough, I was going to ask you the same question,' Ahmed replied cheekily.

Christopher patted Ahmed in the places he had been trained to, then allowed the man to do the same to him.

'I hope nobody is watching us, Chris. They will think we are gay lovers having a sly session,' Ahmed joked.

Forcing a polite smile, Christopher got down to business. 'I thought you and Butler were best buddies, what's going on?'

'We were close for a very long time – until Vinny did something despicable to me. It was an unforgivable act of betrayal, which is why I want you to put that man behind bars for many years to come. Obviously, I know what happened in the past between yourself and Vinny. You witnessed the murder of Dave Phillips, then lied to the police and failed to pick Vinny out in the identification parade. I understand why you did that, Christopher. At the time, you were young and scared, but now you are older, I am sure you would like to pay Vinny back for what he put you and your family through, wouldn't you?' Ahmed asked. He would never trust Old Bill as far as he could throw them, which was why he had felt it necessary to bring up the details of Christopher's perjury. For all he knew, the guy might have a tape recorder hidden in the car. Ahmed, who prided himself on being a good judge of character, doubted it, but as a precaution he had recorded his phone conversations with Christopher. It was always wise to have something up your sleeve in the event of a double-cross.

'I would love nothing more than to put Vinny Butler behind bars. Not only would it further my career, it would also give me peace of mind. But can I ask you a question . . .?'

Ahmed nodded.

'What did Vinny do to betray you so badly?'

'Do you remember the accident in which Lenny Harris, Vinny's cousin, died?'

'Yeah, I heard about it. As you're probably well aware, my sister unfortunately married Michael Butler, so I get told a lot of what goes on in that family. You were driving the car that night, weren't you?'

Ahmed shook his head. 'No, I was not. Vinny was driving the car that killed his cousin. Yes, it was my car, but I had wanted to take a cab home because neither of us were fit to drive. Vinny was having none of it. He insisted on driving and he crashed the car. But do you know what the worst part of that was for me, Christopher?'

Amazed that Ahmed was being so open with him, Christopher urged him to continue.

'Not only did that shitcunt leave me in the car to die before he did a runner, he dragged what he thought was my dead body into the driver's seat to make it look as if I was the one who had killed Lenny. I trusted Vinny. I thought he was my friend. What type of man does such a callous thing, eh, Christopher?'

'A bastard like Vinny Butler, that's who. What I can't understand though is why you haven't dealt with the matter yourself, Ahmed? I would have thought a man such as yourself would seek revenge privately rather than involve the police.'

'But I haven't involved the police, Christopher. I have only involved you – a man with a grudge who hates Vinny Butler just as much as I do. I thought long and hard about the best way to deal with Vinny. He thinks he is a hard man, but he isn't. He's a mummy's boy and a very weak person deep down. A long prison stretch would be the ultimate payback for both of us. Being locked up is Vinny's biggest nightmare, and it would kill him to not be able to see his daughter, son and mother on a regular basis. Between you and I, we can make this happen.'

'How exactly?'

'I have everything set up for you to catch Vinny with at least ten kilos of cocaine. How does that rock your boat?'

Christopher Walker grinned. 'That rocks my boat very nicely. Very nicely indeed.'

'Hello, baby girl,' Queenie beamed when Vinny strolled towards the bungalow with Molly in his arms.

'Nanny, say hello to Molly Dolly.'

Vinny gently put his daughter onto his mother's lap. 'Right, I've spoken to Ray King and he's sound. We're all allowed back in the club. You OK looking after Molly until Jo gets back? I need to head off to London to check on Little Vinny. I was meant to ring him at twelve last night, but forgot because we were watching Freddie Starr. Now I can't get hold of him.'

'Yeah, me and Viv will look after Molly. Where is Jo, love?'

'At the hairdressers. She's getting rid of that slutty-looking blonde hair, so she don't pull any more pricks,' Vinny replied bluntly.

About to reply, Queenie saw Brenda marching towards her with a face like thunder. 'I hate this family. I hate you all, especially him,' Brenda said, lunging at Vinny.

Ordering Viv to take Molly inside the bungalow, Queenie tried to calm the situation down. 'Whatever's wrong, Bren? Is it Scott? He's not dead, is he?' she asked, trying to restrain her daughter while glancing anxiously at Vinny.

'She's pissed, Mum. Smells like a brewery,' Vinny said.

'Where's Tommy and Tara?' Queenie asked.

'Scotty's younger sister is looking after them. We brought her with us on holiday so me and Scott could have a bit of us time, but that's all gone tits-up now, thanks to my cunt of a brother, hasn't it? Scotty has told me it's over. He's packing his case as we speak and he doesn't even want to drive me and the kids back to London,' Brenda screamed.

Noticing that the neighbours had ventured outside to be nosy, Queenie chose her words carefully and lowered her usually loud voice. 'Don't you dare call your brother such an awful word. He has always had your best interests at heart, ever since you was born, and if your boyfriend isn't man enough to take a headbutt, then he isn't the man for you.'

'Headbutt! Scott nearly fucking died! He was out cold for ten minutes, so no wonder he wants to bin me. How will I ever hang on to a boyfriend or husband while I'm part of this family, eh? I bet it was you who drove Dean away,' Brenda accused, poking her brother in the chest.

Aware that the notrights were having a field day watching the drama, Queenie nodded for Vinny to go inside then roughly grabbed Brenda's arm and marched her in after him. Much as she loved her only daughter, compared to her sons, Brenda had always been a big disappointment to her. Once she shut the door, Queenie let rip. 'Don't you dare blame your brother for Dean disappearing into thin air. Don't get me wrong, if I ever lay eyes on Dean again, I would knife him myself for the way he left you in the lurch and abandoned his children. But you led that man a dog's life, Bren, with your drinking and your insecurities.'

When Brenda collapsed on the floor sobbing uncontrollably, Vinny knelt down and hugged his little sister to his chest. 'That's enough now, Mum. Soon as Bren's packed up, I'll take her and the kids back to London with me.'

The minute she laid eyes on Johnny, Deborah Preston knew that he was itching to tell her something important. She had sensed the excitement in his voice when she had spoken to him on the phone last night.

'You've got some news for me, haven't you, love?'

Johnny grinned broadly. 'You know I told you my parole hearing had been put back a fortnight?'

Deborah nodded.

'Well, it hadn't. It was yesterday, but I didn't want you worrying and I wanted to surprise you.'

Deborah felt her stomach tie itself in knots. 'Well? What did they say?'

Unable to hide his elation, Johnny leapt out of his seat and did a little celebratory jig. 'I'm finally coming home, babe, and I can't fucking wait.'

Joanna Preston stared at her new image in the mirror and was horrified at what she saw. Her once beautiful blonde hair was now a very dark brown and it did not suit her one bit.

'Is everything OK?' the hairdresser asked.

Biting fiercely on her lip to stop herself from crying, Joanna nodded her head. She felt and looked like a different person. It was as though her whole identity had been stolen.

Joanna paid the bill, then without even waiting for her change, stumbled out of the salon. Seconds later, the tears came.

Scott Mason drove back towards London with a face like thunder and the headache from hell. The hospital had wanted to keep him in for observation for another twenty-four hours, so he had made the decision to discharge himself.

'I can't believe how bad your eyes and nose look, Scott. How long before you'll be back to normal?' Fiona asked. Her usually handsome brother looked terrible.

Scott had suffered a broken nose in the fracas which had given him two black eyes. 'I dunno. The doctor said I might have to have my nose reshaped, but I won't know for sure until the swelling goes down.'

'I think Brenda is going to try and get back with you. Got a feeling she might prove to be a bit of a stalker after the way she was behaving earlier. Don't get back with her, Scotty, will you? You've got enough on your plate with that timeshare malarkey, and you certainly don't need another run-in with the Butlers.'

'I have no intention of getting back with Bren. I wasn't even that into her in the first place, if you want the truth.'

'What about Vinny though? I know what you're like, Scott, and I know you will not rest until you get him back one way or another. Whatever you do, do not involve that lunatic friend of yours from Spain. He's off his rocker, he is.'

Scott smirked. Mad Martin was a psycho who would most certainly give Vinny Butler a run for his money if Scott paid him enough dosh to do so. The man had been known to wipe out family relations for less than fifty thousand pesetas.

'What you smiling at, Scott? This isn't funny. I love you, you know I do, but I am not giving you no more alibis if the police knock on our door – I mean that.'

Scott squeezed his sister's hand. Their mum had died when Fiona was just five years old and Scott had looked after her ever since. They were that close they even shared a flat together these days. 'Stop worrying. I'm not going to do anything, OK? I'm not stupid, Fi.'

Fiona said nothing. She wanted to believe Scott was not going to seek some sort of revenge against Vinny, but in her heart she knew that he probably would.

Ahmed was sitting in a West End restaurant with his friends Hakan and Bora Koç. They had rung him yesterday out of the blue saying they were in town on business.

'How is your dear friend Vinny these days, Ahmed? Are

you still ripping him off or have you now finished him off?' Hakan asked. He and Bora had enjoyed playing the role of big-time drug barons to help their friend fleece Vinny of a fortune.

Without going into too much detail, Ahmed explained that he had Vinny exactly where he wanted him and was hoping that very soon Vinny would be going to prison for a long spell.

'I have to say, Ahmed, and I mean no disrespect, but why fuck about this way? I do not know how you could go on pretending to be Vinny's friend after the way he betrayed you. I would have killed him, if he'd done that to me,' Hakan said.

Ahmed smirked. It seemed none of his friends could understand his desire to play games, putting off the day when he would finish Vinny off. In fact, Ahmed knew without a doubt that the only person who would truly understand would be Vinny himself. Both of them shared the same sadistic nature and thoroughly enjoyed putting their victims through prolonged torture, mentally as well as physically. No wonder they had clicked immediately and been such good pals until Vinny had betrayed him in such a vile way. 'I will try to explain, but you probably won't understand. To kill Vinny would have been far too easy and boring for me. I want and need to watch him suffer. Playing mind games makes me happy.'

'My friend Murat, he fuck many men over for money. Somebody recently kill his daughter. He now broken man. Worst punishment is to kill child,' Bora said.

'How did they kill the child?' Ahmed asked.

Bora put his right hand around his throat and squeezed it. 'They do this.'

Ahmed could not help but chuckle as he imagined Vinny's reaction if Molly were to meet her maker in such a violent manner. Vinny was besotted with his daughter, and would never be able to deal with such a crime. That truly would be game over.

'What is funny?' Hakan asked Ahmed.

'Nothing. I just have a warped sense of humour. Right, let's order some food, shall we? I am starving.'

Little Vinny splashed on some of his father's aftershave, then stared at himself in the mirror. His dad reckoned he was the spitting image of him, but apart from his bright green eyes, Vinny liked to think he looked more like his mum. She had been a pretty lady and he had definitely inherited her small, slightly turned-up nose.

Putting his black braces over his white Fred Perry shirt, Little Vinny grinned as he attached them to his faded Levi jeans. Now he'd had his head shaved and was wearing his good clobber, he looked and felt like a proper skinhead once again. He'd popped round Ben's gaff earlier and brought some of his clothes back home, but he would have to hide them all under his bed once his dad got back from Eastbourne, in case the bastard found them then burned them as he had last time.

About to lace up his DM's, Little Vinny froze as he heard the key go in the lock, then the front door slam. 'You in, boy?' his dad shouted out.

'Yes, Dad. I'll be down in a minute.' Little Vinny was panicking now. He had left his pork-pie hat downstairs, so couldn't even cover up his shaved head.

Vinny poured himself a large Scotch and downed it in one. The journey back from Eastbourne had been a nightmare. Brenda had been crying one minute, then screaming at him the next. Tara had had one of her infamous tantrums because she had wanted to stay at the holiday park, and Tommy had puked up all over the back seat of his motor.

Slamming his glass down on the kitchen top, Vinny marched upstairs to see his son. 'So, how did your party go? Did you have a good time?'

Little Vinny stood transfixed to the spot when his bedroom door was flung open. He knew immediately by the twisted expression on his father's face that he was in deep shit.

Vinny pulled back his right fist and punched his son so hard in the face, he flew across the room and landed on his bed. He then leaned over him and pointed his forefinger in his face. 'How dare you disobey me, you cheeky little bastard. I told you under no circumstances were you to ever get your head shaved again, or wear them stupid cunting clothes. Well, you've well and truly burned your bridges now, boy, because I ain't letting you out of my sight in future. You just can't be trusted, can you?'

Holding his throbbing jaw in his hand, Little Vinny stuck up for himself. 'Why can't you just let me live my own life and make my own decisions, eh? All my mates have got skinheads, their dads don't go into one. Why do you always have to make me the odd one out?'

'Because you're my son! I ain't some two-bob mug like your mates' dads, am I? I am *the* Vinny Butler, and if you think you're going to embarrass me by looking, dressing and acting like some little prick, then you've got another think coming.'

'I hate you. You're a fucking horrible dad, and I hate being your son,' Little Vinny replied defiantly.

Vinny grabbed his son by the throat and gave it a gentle squeeze. 'And I don't like you very much either. Unlike your little sister, you are a total fucking waste of space. Now, get them stupid clothes off and put a suit on. Tonight, you will be working at the club with me.'

# CHAPTER NINETEEN

Over the next week, Little Vinny's life went from bad to worse. When his father had said he wasn't going to let him out of his sight, Little Vinny had thought he was just using scaremonger tactics. The bastard hadn't been, though. Little Vinny wasn't even allowed to stay indoors on his own of a night. He was made to sit upstairs or work as a potboy at the poxy club.

The worst part of being held prisoner was that Little Vinny had been unable to contact Shazza. He had been inebriated and stoned when he had written down her contact details and had taken down her phone number wrong. It was a digit short, and smudged because he had written it with Shazza's lipstick. He could still read the address clearly though and as soon as he got a chance to escape, he was determined to visit her.

Little Vinny had never been a boy to masturbate much in the past, but since he had met Shazza, he had become accustomed to relieving himself on a daily basis. About to do so again, he quickly moved his hand away from his private parts as his dad barged into his bedroom.

'Ain't you fucking dressed yet?'

'I'm getting dressed now.'

'Well, pack some clobber in a sports bag as well,' Vinny ordered.

'Why? Where you sending me?' Little Vinny asked alarmed.

'A children's home.'

'What?'

Vinny chuckled at the look of horror on his son's face. 'We're going to Kings for the weekend.'

'I don't wanna go to Kings, Dad. Can't I stay here? I'll be really good and I'll work at the club all weekend, I promise.'

'Your promises aren't worth a wank, boy. Just pack your bags and do as you're told for once.'

Desperate for some breathing space away from his father and to see Shazza again, Little Vinny argued his point. 'Why have I got to go to Kings? I don't like it there no more and I ain't got no mates now in Eastbourne.'

Vinny glared at his son. 'I could not give a shit what you like and what you don't. You can't be trusted to stay here. As for you having no mates in Eastbourne, you ain't got none in London apart from that doughnut Ben Bloggs. You're coming to Kings with me and that's final, understand?'

About to fly into a rage, Little Vinny had a better idea. He'd had enough of existing rather than living, so forced a smile. 'I understand. I'll pack my stuff now, Dad.'

When his father shut the bedroom door, Little Vinny stuck his middle right-hand finger up. 'Fucking prick! Swivel on that you cunt if you think I am coming to Eastbourne with you.'

Little Vinny grinned as he packed his bag. If running away from home was the only way he was going to see Shazza again, then run away he would.

*

Nancy was giving the bungalow a thorough tidy-up in preparation for Michael and his father's arrival when Joanna poked her head around the door. 'I need some advice. Have you got five minutes?'

Turning off the vacuum cleaner, Nancy checked on the boys who were outside playing football, then made a brew. 'So, what's up? You look like you've got the weight of the world on your shoulders.'

'Nance, if I tell you something, you promise you won't tell anybody?'

'Of course not. You know me better than that.'

'You know I told you I was bored with being blonde which is why I had my hair dyed?'

'Yeah.'

'Well, I lied. Vinny drove me to the hairdressers and forced me to have it done. I wanted to tell you, but I felt so stupid that I allowed him to dictate to me like that. I used to be such a strong-willed person, Nance, and I don't like what I've turned into.'

When her pal began to cry, Nancy held her in her arms. She hated Vinny, but never slagged him off to Joanna. However, she was appalled by Vinny bullying Jo into changing the colour of her hair. 'You need to start sticking up for yourself, Jo, because if you don't, Vinny will lose all respect for you. I know me and Michael have had our ups and downs, but no way would I ever allow him to choose what colour my hair would be. That's really taking the piss.'

'He made me change it because of that Billy. He said being blonde made me look like a slag and that's why I was attracting dickheads.'

Nancy was disgusted. 'Bloody cheek! I'm blonde, so does that make me a slag too? Tell him you don't like it and you're changing it back.'

'It's not just my hair, it's other stuff too. I spoke to my mum yesterday for the first time in ages. My dad got granted parole and is due to be released any day now. Vinny's forbidden me to have any contact with him whatsoever, but I'm desperate to see him, Nance. How can I not see my own dad? I love him.'

'Jo, you cannot go on like this. You must put your foot down and do what you want to do. Even though my dad has always refused to have anything to do with the Butlers, Michael has never stopped me or the boys from seeing him. I wouldn't put up with it if I were you. You should do what I always do when the going gets tough. Threaten to leave, then carry the threat out if you have to. It works every time. My mum gave me that sound advice. She left my dad a couple of times over the years and he soon begged her to go back. Michael hated it when I left him after I came out of hospital that time. Being alone gives men the kick up the arse they need to realize just how lucky they are to have us.'

'But I don't think Vinny loves or wants me. We haven't slept together for Christ knows how long and that makes me feel horrid inside and unattractive. I'm so unhappy, Nance, I really am. Even though I still love Vin, I don't like him much any more. I would leave him if it wasn't for Molly, but I know he would never let me take her with me,' Joanna admitted.

'Jo, you're her mother! Vinny would not have a leg to stand on if you left him. If he tried to get custody of Molly, he would be laughed out of court.'

'But you don't know what he's like, Nance. I bet he would snatch Molly and disappear abroad with her or something if I left him. He's not like your Michael. He always has to get his own way.'

Knowing exactly what Vinny Butler was like, Nancy

decided there was no more she could do or say to help her pal, so she changed the subject. 'Look, today's my mum's last day at Kings and I've promised to take her and the boys to the pier. Dry them eyes, and you and Molly come with us. A change of scenery will do you good.'

Vinny Butler was sitting in the armchair when the phone rang. 'Hello.'

'It's me. I thought you'd be interested to know that your old pal said his goodbyes earlier. Probably as free as a bird as we speak.'

Thanking Scottish Pat for the information, Vinny ended the call and poured a large Scotch to calm himself down. Knowing Johnny Preston was up for parole was bad enough, but the news that the bastard was now breathing the same air as him on the outside was another.

To mellow himself out a bit, Vinny put on a Roxy Music album. Bryan Ferry's voice always soothed him, and as he sang along to 'Dance Away' he stared at the photo of himself, Roy and his mother that occupied pride of place on his lounge wall. It had been taken outside the club on their opening night. He had been nineteen at the time, Roy seventeen and their mother had been so thrilled by what they had achieved.

While Preston had been inside, Vinny had satisfied his lust for revenge by making Joanna fall in love with him, then getting her pregnant. He'd got off on imagining how it must have tortured Preston to be locked up in his cell, knowing that his worst enemy had his big hard cock shoved up his baby girl.

However, now the bastard was free, things were very different. Queenie wasn't the only one who expected Vinny to even up the score for what had happened. The entire London underworld would be waiting for him to get even.

Vinny picked up the phone and rang the bungalow at Kings. 'Is Jo there, Mum?'

'No, love. She dashed in earlier, grabbed Molly and said she was going out for the day.'

'When? What time?'

'I can't remember exactly, about an hour ago. Why? What's the matter?'

'Johnny Preston's been released from prison. She better not be fucking meeting up with him, Mum, because if she is, I won't just kill him, I'll kill her too.'

Hearing his father ranting and raving in the lounge, Little Vinny grinned. Seconds later, with a few of his belongings in a sports bag, he successfully crept out of the house without getting caught.

Johnny Preston took a deep breath of fresh air and sighed blissfully as the sun shone down on him. When he had first got banged up, he had never believed he had the strength to get through such a long sentence. It had been tough at first, really tough, but the worst part had come afterwards.

Finding out that Vinny Butler was involved with his beautiful daughter had been like somebody sticking a knife through his heart. The thought of Butler kissing or touching Joanna had made him want to top himself. And he very nearly had, but as luck would have it the heroin overdose had turned out to be the wake-up call he'd needed. With Deborah's strength and support, he had finally seen a light at the end of the tunnel.

'Johnny,' Deborah shrieked as she ran towards her man and hugged him.

Johnny held her close, savouring the moment. He had been a bastard to her in his younger days, forever having affairs and one-night stands, but she had been his rock during the dark days in prison, and he planned to treat her with nothing but total respect for the rest of her life. Even her weight did not bother him any more. So what if she was a size sixteen? Deborah had a beautiful face and a heart to match.

'You spoken to Jo?' he asked hopefully.

'Yes, the other day. She sounded a bit down, if I'm honest.'

'Did you tell her I'd been granted parole?'

'Yeah, I told her and she seemed dead chuffed. I suggested we all have lunch, but she mumbled something about having to see to Molly and got off the phone. She loves you, Johnny, I know she does, but she's obviously too afraid to meet up with you in case that bastard finds out.'

Johnny could not hide his disappointment. 'No way is Vinny stopping me from seeing my own daughter, Deb. He has no right.'

Deborah sighed anxiously. They'd made it one of Johnny's parole conditions that he had to live in Tiptree for the time being, which had scuppered his dream of moving to London. He was also banned from having any contact whatsoever with the Butler family. 'Please don't do anything rash, Johnny. Joanna will see you, I know she will, but she just needs time to get her head around it all. Now, let's not talk about this subject any more today. I'm so happy that you'll be sleeping next to me tonight, I don't want anything to spoil our reunion.'

Johnny kissed Deborah, then smiled. 'I'll tell you what, let's head home and stop on the way for a nice slap-up bit of grub. Then later, I shall ravish you like you've never been ravished before.'

Vinny Butler was absolutely livid as he pummelled his fist against Ben Bloggs' front door. Little Vinny had left a note on his bed:

Dad,
Can't be held prisoner no more. Need to see my girlfriend.
Will ring you when you get back from Kings. But not coming home if I ain't allowed out again.
Vinny

Hearing Pink Floyd's 'Wish You Were Here' blaring out, Vinny pounded on the lounge window instead. It was opened seconds later by a dirty, bedraggled-looking little girl. 'Is your mother in?' Vinny asked.

'Mum,' the child yelled.

Vinny felt physically sick as Alison Bloggs staggered towards the door in a filthy dressing gown with a joint in her hand. No wonder his son had gone off the rails, mixing with a child of hers. 'I'm looking for my son. Is Ben about?' Vinny did not believe for one second that his son had a girlfriend, so had guessed he would be with Ben.

If there was ever a moment Alison wished she'd had a bath and put on her mini-skirt and make-up, then this was it. Vinny Butler was gorgeous, her dream man, and she would have been only too happy to fuck him and suck his cock for nothing.

'Ben's upstairs, but Little Vinny ain't 'ere. Do you want a drink? I've got some cider.'

'Don't be lying to me,' Vinny hissed, pushing past Alison and running up the stairs.

Ben was asleep, and when Vinny prodded him, he woke up, petrified. 'I ain't done nothing wrong. What do you want?' he babbled, sitting bolt upright.

'I want to know where my son is – and don't fucking lie to me because I will chop your tongue off if you do.'

'I swear, I haven't seen Little Vinny. I'm telling the truth, honest I am.'

'Little Vinny reckons he's got a girlfriend. Do you know if that's true?' Vinny bellowed.

Not wanting to admit that he had been with his pal the night he had met Shazza, but too afraid to blatantly lie, Ben admitted that he knew Little Vinny had met a girl called Shazza and that she came from Dagenham.

'Look, boy, I won't be wild if you have seen Little Vinny, but I need you to tell me his girlfriend's address.'

Ben could feel beads of sweat developing on his forehead. 'I don't know where Shazza lives. Vin met her at a party in Dagenham, that's all I know.'

Vinny glared at the child and then pointed a finger in his face. 'If I find out you're lying, you're gonna regret it big time.'

Alison Bloggs said nothing when her trembling son burst into tears. Nobody messed with Vinny Butler, herself included.

With the late August sun at its peak, Queenie and Vivian were sunning themselves outside the bungalow. 'Gawd, stone the crows! Is that who I think it is, or are my eyes deceiving me?' Vivian exclaimed.

Queenie was furious when she spotted Albie trotting alongside Michael with a suitcase in his hand. Kings was her and Vivian's place of tranquillity, so what was Michael thinking, bringing that old toad down here? 'Ruined our holiday you have, Michael. Thanks very much,' Queenie yelled, the bitterness evident in her voice.

'Yeah, what a bastard liberty,' Vivian added loudly.

Aware that his father was visibly shaking, Michael unlocked the door of his bungalow and urged him to go inside. He then stormed over to where his mother and aunt were sitting. 'That bungalow belongs to me and if I want to bring my father here for the weekend, then I shall. Dad's been through a tough time lately, so if you haven't got anything nice to say, best you say nothing.'

'Who do you think you're speaking to, you cheeky little sod? That drunken, womanizing old goat led me a dog's life for years, or have you forgotten that?' Queenie spat.

'And you led him a dog's life too, Mum. Now let's just leave it at that, shall we?'

When Michael strutted off, Queenie and Vivian were both left dumbstruck. Michael had always been the cheeky, happy-go-lucky type compared to Vinny and Roy. Whatever had happened to him?

Carol Young was a very laid-back type of parent. She had brought her only daughter up singlehanded after her ex had left her when Sharon was a baby, and she liked the fact that her daughter's friends deemed her cool. So when Little Vinny knocked at the door and asked her where Shazza was, Carol invited him in.

'Shaz, you've got a visitor, love,' Carol shouted out.

'Send them up to my room, Mum.'

Little Vinny ran up the stairs. He could hear Althea and Donna singing 'Uptown Top Ranking'; so followed the music. 'All right, Shazza?'

Shazza was surprised to see Vinny. 'What you doing here? You're, like, nearly a week late.'

'I know and I'm sorry. I had some problems at home and I couldn't ring you, your phone number was written down wrong. Look for yourself if you don't believe me,' Little Vinny urged, handing Shazza the piece of paper.

'What's in your sports bag?' Shazza asked.

'Some clothes. I left home today. I bought you a present to say sorry as well.'

Shazza grinned when Little Vinny handed her a box of Milk Tray and a bottle of cider. She wasn't used to lads buying her presents. 'So why have you left home? Have you had a row with your mum?'

'I haven't got a mum. Mine died years ago. I left home because my dad is a bastard. Can you see that bruise on my face?'

Shazza nodded.

'Well, that's where my dad punched me for having my head shaved again.'

'God, that's terrible, Vinny. My mum doesn't really like me being a skinhead, but she would never stop me from being who or what I wanted to be,' Shazza replied, sparking up two cigarettes and handing one to Vinny.

'Won't we get in trouble for smoking? Say your mum smells it?'

Shazza chuckled. 'It's OK. My mum lets me smoke indoors, but says I must never tell my nan and granddad. She knows I sometimes drink cider too. My mum always says she would rather me be truthful with her and do what I want indoors than have me doing it behind her back.'

'Your mum sounds well cool. Wish I could say the same about my old man. It's his fault I wasn't allowed to visit you before. He kept me prisoner.'

'Well, never mind. You're here now. Sit down and share this cider with me.'

Little Vinny grinned as he sat on the bed. Shazza's room was perfect. She had a big Union Jack pinned up on one wall and the other wall was decorated with posters of the Selecter, Madness and the Specials. She also had a massive mobile stereo system and a record player.

'So, where you gonna be living now, Vin?'

'Dunno yet. I'll probably stay at my mate Ben's house.'

'You can stay here for a bit, if you want? My mum won't mind, and if we promise to behave ourselves she might even let you stay in my room.'

'Really?'

'Yeah. My ex-boyfriend used to stay here all the time.'

Little Vinny took a slurp from the bottle of cider, then awkwardly asked Shazza the question he had been gagging to ask her all week. 'Shaz, will you go out with me? You know, like be my bird?'

When Shazza nodded, then leaned towards him and gave him his first ever passionate kiss, Little Vinny wondered if he had actually died and gone to heaven.

Donald Walker was a very inquisitive man, so he'd been none too pleased when his son was rather vague about the details of the meet with his informant.

Today was the first time since the meet that Donald had managed to drag his son out for a pint, so as soon as they sat down at a table, he started his own interrogation.

'What are you keeping from me, Christopher? You've hardly said anything about this chap you met. Surely you trust me, don't you?' Donald asked, putting on his most wounded expression.

'Don't be daft, Dad. Of course I trust you. I've already told you that the meet went well and the informant seemed kosher. There really isn't much more to say at the moment. He's the only one who knows Vinny's movements, so all I can do is play the waiting game until he contacts me again.'

'Have you told anyone at work yet? And how exactly do you plan to arrest Vinny?'

As much as Christopher trusted his father, there was no way he was going to reveal every detail of his meeting with Ahmed. That would be totally inappropriate, and besides, there was far too much at stake, including his own head on the chopping block. 'No, I haven't informed anybody at work yet, Dad. As for your other question, I've told you all I can for now. As soon as I have more news, you'll be the first to know, I promise. Now, can we just drop the subject, please? I want to forget about work on my day off and just have a few pints and relax.'

Donald smiled. He was so proud of Christopher. 'Of course we can, son.'

After leaving Ben Bloggs' house, Vinny Butler shot back to his own, picked up a few bits, made a couple of phone calls, then with a face like thunder, drove towards Eastbourne.

Today had not been a good day, and Vinny's mind was in overdrive. His son was becoming a real thorn in his side, and that disappointed him immensely. When he was Little Vinny's age, he might have been a fucker, but he'd never disobeyed or played up his mother. Did the boy have a screw loose? Because if so, it came from Karen's genes, not his.

Being mugged off by a fourteen-year-old kid was not something Vinny was willing to put up with. Much as he was relieved that his boy was banging some bird instead of knocking about with the likes of Ben Bloggs, there'd be a rude awakening for the little shit when he got back from Kings.

Hooting at the car in front for driving slow in a fast lane, then treating the driver to a wrist sign as he put his foot on the accelerator and zoomed past, Vinny turned his thoughts to Joanna.

Once he'd got the word that Johnny Preston had been granted parole, he'd had a gut feeling the bastard would be out by this weekend, which was why he had planned a trip to Eastbourne. Vinny hated leaving the club unattended by himself or Michael of a weekend, especially since the fire, but he knew his doormen Pete and Paul were more than capable of running the gaff. It wasn't even as if weekends were that busy these days.

Cranking up the volume of his car stereo, Vinny sang along. 'Ashes to Ashes' was David Bowie's latest chart hit and the title gave him a great idea.

If Joanna ever disobeyed his orders by allowing Molly anywhere near that shitbag of a father of hers, she wouldn't just end up dead behind a dustbin like Little Vinny's mother had. He would personally cremate her, while she was still alive, just as he had with Trevor.

# CHAPTER TWENTY

Queenie and Vivian shared a worried glance as Vinny paced up and down the bungalow, letting off steam. Joanna was still nowhere to be seen and Vinny had visions of her, her mother, father and Molly playing happy families somewhere nearby.

'Sit down, love. You're wearing the carpet out. I'm sure Jo has gone out with Nancy, 'cos we haven't seen her and the boys all day either. Nancy's sour-faced mother has been down here for the past week now. Bloody cheek, if you ask me. Didn't have the guts to stay opposite us though. Booked her own chalet, apparently.'

Vinny was too bothered about his own problems to care whether Nancy's mother was still in the vicinity or not. 'Pour us a Scotch, Mum, and make it a large one,' he ordered, collapsing into an armchair.

'Where's Little Vinny? You left him at home?' Vivian enquired.

'Don't talk to me about that little shit. Gonna get the hiding of his life when I get home.'

'Why? What's he done now?' Queenie asked.

When Vinny explained that Little Vinny had run away, then showed them his letter, both women tutted with disapproval. 'Needs a bloody good fawpenny one, if you ask me,' Vivian mumbled.

Queenie sighed. 'You are seriously going to have to take a firmer hand with that boy, Vin. He's spiralling out of control. You, Roy and Michael never gave me grief like that. Brenda was my biggest worry, and that was only because she's a girl. Well, she was a cheeky little mare an' all, but yous boys were angels compared to her and Little Vinny.'

'I bet he's staying with that Ben Bloggs. Disgusting family they are. Vermin of the very worst kind,' Vivian said.

'I went round the Bloggs' place, he wasn't there. Ben reckons Little Vinny has met some bird called Shazza who lives in Dagenham.'

'Oh, my gawd! She sounds choice with a name like Shazza,' Queenie remarked.

'Next thing you know he'll knock her up and you'll be a granddad, Vinny,' Vivian added.

'Don't bleedin' say that. I'm not old enough to be a great-granny yet,' Queenie spat.

'I dunno what I'm gonna do with him. I thought working at the club would help make him grow up, but the boy's got a mind of his own. He's even had his head shaved again. Gave him a clump for that, but nothing I seem to do has the desired effect. He'll know all about it when I get hold of him next week though. I'll knock seven colours of shit out of him if I have to.'

'And so you should!' said Queenie emphatically. 'Better that than he becomes a liability to you. I don't want him spoiling the good name of this family.'

Vinny managed a smile for the first time that day. 'We're hardly that family out of *Little House on the Prairie*, Mum, but I do know where you're coming from.'

'Aw, my Lenny used to love that programme. Cried his

eyes out sometimes while watching it he did. That and *Lassie*,' Vivian reminisced.

'I remember him crying over *Lassie*. I think you stopped him watching it in the end, didn't you, Viv?' Queenie asked.

Whenever he was in the same room as his mother and aunt and they started to discuss Lenny, Vinny always felt terribly awkward. Today was no different, so he quickly changed the subject. 'Aw, bless Champ. Still miss him every day, I do. But going back to Little Vinny: he must take after Dad's side of the family, Mum. He certainly don't take after me and you.'

'Speaking of which, your father is no more than thirty feet away as we speak. You need to have a stern word with that brother of yours, Vinny. Upset your mother terribly, Michael has, bringing him down here. And he was bloody rude to me and your mum earlier.'

Vinny's face was etched with surprise. 'What you going on about, Auntie Viv?'

'Your father. Michael's brought him down here on holiday, the old bastard.'

'You're kidding me! Dad stayed with Michael all last week, I knew that, but I thought Michael would drop him home before he came down here. What did he say to upset you both?'

'Leave it, Viv,' Queenie urged. She hated it when her sons argued.

'No, I'm not leaving it, Queen. Bang out of order what Michael said to you, and Vinny should know the truth.'

Vinny was absolutely livid when he was informed that Michael had accused his beloved mother of leading his tosser of a father a dog's life. 'I ain't fucking putting up with that. Where are they now? In Michael's bungalow?'

When her son stormed out of the front door, Queenie grabbed his arm and begged him not to cause trouble.

'Please, Vinny, I don't want or need you or Michael arguing. What was said was said in the heat of the moment, and I order you to leave it be. Jesus wept, we nearly all got barred from here last bloody weekend and I don't want anything like that ever happening again.'

About to argue his point, Vinny was stopped from doing so by his daughter running up to him. 'Daddy, Daddy,' Molly yelled, her face full of excitement at the sight of him.

Vinny picked Molly up and swung her around in the air. He could see Joanna, Nancy, Daniel, Adam and Lee out of the corner of his eye, but decided to blank them all by taking Molly inside. 'Where you been today then, princess?'

'We been to pier. Mummy won me this,' Molly said, waving a small teddy bear in Vinny's face.

'Was anybody else with you other than Mummy, Auntie Nancy, Daniel, Adam and Lee?'

'Yes, Daddy. Mary was with us too. Where is Molly Dolly, Nanny?'

'In your bedroom, love. Put her down, Vin,' Queenie ordered.

Aware that Joanna was now standing right outside the front door, Vinny leaned towards his mother and hissed in her right ear. 'Who the fuck is Mary?'

'Nancy's mother. I told you she was here. Now will you calm yourself down, because you are making my bastard nerves bad.'

Little Vinny liked Shazza's mum. She hadn't let him stay in Shazza's room the night before, but other than that she had made him ever so welcome and had even cooked him a nice big fry-up this morning. 'So, what are yous two lovebirds up to this evening?' Carol asked.

'I was actually going to ask your permission, Mrs Young, to take Shazza to my friend's birthday party in Whitechapel. We won't stay late, I promise, and I will look after Shaz for you.'

'No need to call me Mrs Young, Vinny. Carol will do just fine. Of course you can go to the party, but do make sure you look after Shaz. And can you bring her home by twelve, please?'

Little Vinny looked at Shazza and grinned. When she had kissed him passionately yesterday, he thought his luck had been in, but when he had grabbed her breasts, his girlfriend had stopped him from going any further. 'My mum trusts me and I would never take liberties by doing anything with a boy while she is in the house. I wouldn't feel right about it and she often walks into my bedroom without knocking. What about your house? Can't we go there if your dad is away for the weekend?'

Today, Little Vinny had rung home. Then, on getting no answer, he had called the club. His father's employee Pete had told him that his father had gone to Eastbourne for the weekend and was not due back until Monday morning.

When her mum left the room, Shazza squeezed her new boyfriend's hand. 'Can't wait to get to yours, can you?'

Even though he was excited, Little Vinny was also quite nervous. He had no sexual experience whatsoever and he guessed, Shazza being older than him, that she probably had plenty. Shazza had no idea he was only fourteen. She had told him when they first met that she was nearly sixteen, so he had told her he was sixteen too. There was no reason for her to doubt him. He was tall for his age and he worked at his father's club.

'Well?' Shazza asked.

'Can't wait.'

*

Back in Eastbourne, Michael and Albie had got to the downstairs club early to grab a decent table. Daniel, Adam and Lee had insisted on accompanying them rather than waiting for their mother, who always took ages to get ready.

For the first time since Dorothy had died, Albie felt his life was worth living once again. Because Queenie and Vivian had pushed him out of the family circle when his own children were growing up, he had missed out on so much. Now it was as if he'd been given a second chance with his grandsons. 'So, are you all going to enter the talent competition for your old granddad, eh?'

Sipping his Coke through a straw, Daniel shook his head repeatedly. No way was he standing on stage, making himself look silly.

'What about you, Lee?' Albie asked.

'No, Granddad. I don't want to go on stage with lots of people watching me.'

'I will, Granddad,' Adam piped up.

Albie ruffled the head of his youngest grandson. Adam was only five. 'What you gonna do then? Dance? Or sing?'

'I'll sing that song you taught me.'

Knowing exactly what song Adam meant, Albie had tears in his eyes as the boy dashed up to the stage to put his name down for the competition.

Christopher Walker nodded politely when Ahmed climbed into the passenger seat. He had given Ahmed his pager number the other day and told him to contact him via that in future and he would call him straight back, so as not to arouse suspicion at work.

'I wasn't expecting to hear from you again quite so soon,' Christopher said.

Ahmed chuckled. 'The early bird catches the worm, and

I'm sure there is no bigger worm we would both like to catch than Vinny Butler, so why waste time?'

Christopher smiled. He knew Ahmed was a villain, but even so, there was something about him that he admired. Perhaps it was the fact Ahmed despised Vinny Butler just as much as he did? Or perhaps it was just his honesty about the whole situation? 'So, what's the plan?'

'I spoke to Vinny yesterday morning and he has a drug deal going down next Thursday afternoon. I have washed my hands with anything illegal I might have been involved with in the past, but I have agreed to accompany Vinny on Thursday just to make sure everything goes smoothly.'

'I understand that, Ahmed, and obviously you will not be implicated in any of this.'

'But this is what we must sort out, Christopher. I *need* to be implicated. A grass is something I am not, and I cannot be tarred with that brush. I got in touch with you for personal reasons only. Had I not known that you and Vinny had crossed paths in the past and you had an axe to grind, I would never have involved the police.'

'What is it you want me to do then?'

'I want you to arrest me along with Vinny, then let me go. On the day in question, I will make sure that we are travelling in Vinny's car, therefore the drugs will be in his boot. I want you to haul me in too, then release me after questioning. Not my car and I had no idea Vinny had drugs in the boot, you get me?'

'Yes, I get you, Ahmed, but without telling my colleagues you are an informer, that's going to be extremely difficult for me to pull off,' Christopher admitted.

'And this is why I do not want you to involve your colleagues. I need you to do this alone, Christopher.'

'But I can't. It would be totally against police policy. Besides, what if Vinny turns violent? I wouldn't stand a chance. I have to have somebody with me as back-up, Ahmed.'

'Well, bring some wet-behind-the-ears PC with you then. I'm warning you, Christopher, if you involve the heavy mob and this goes wrong, I shall have no alternative but to spill the beans about your past, and you really don't want that to happen now, do you?'

Feeling his stomach churn, Christopher clocked the evil expression in Ahmed's eyes, and nodded. Suddenly, he didn't like this man very much at all.

Queenie Butler felt an uneasiness about the evening ahead. Vinny was knocking back the Scotch like there was no tomorrow. She felt sorry for Joanna because her son was virtually blanking her, and to top it all, she had just spotted Albie, Michael, Nancy and the boys sitting on a table opposite theirs across the dancefloor.

'You're ever so quiet, Queen. You all right?' Vivian asked her sister.

The resident band were belting out Neil Diamond's 'Cracklin' Rosie' so Queenie leaned towards her sister and spoke into her ear. 'Got a bad feeling about tonight. Vinny's in a weird mood, I can tell, and I hope he don't start,' she hissed.

'Vinny's all right. He's just put Molly's name down for the talent competition. Can't believe we've got to sit looking at Albie for the evening though. Bloody liberty, Michael bringing him down here, if you ask me.'

The compere's announcement that the talent competition was starting saved Queenie from answering. 'And our first contestant is Adam Butler. A round of applause for Adam, please.'

Queenie and Vivian clapped as hard as anybody when Michael lifted his son onto the stage.

'Hello, Adam. How old are you?' the compere asked, crouching down and holding the microphone near Adam's lips.

'I'm five, Charlie. I come from London and I'm gonna sing a song for my granddad,' Adam replied, remembering the name of the compere who was also the children's entertainer.

Charlie Case and the audience all chuckled at Adam's cute cockney accent and bravado, apart from Queenie and Vivian. 'Singing a song for his granddad! He's only known the old bastard five minutes,' Vivian spat.

When her grandson proceeded to sing Clive Dunn's 'Grandad' an open-mouthed Queenie leapt out of her seat. Albie was grinning like a Cheshire cat and she had seen enough. 'I'm not watching and listening to any more of this old bollocks. Come on, Viv. Let's go to the amusement arcade.'

Little Vinny could feel his heart beating like a drum when Shazza put her hand on his cock. He still had his jeans on, but already his penis felt as if it was about to explode.

'Shall we get undressed and get under the covers?' Shazza asked.

The thought of having sex for the first time was exciting yet scary, and Little Vinny decided to delay the inevitable until he had built up a bit more Dutch courage. 'Let's drink our cider first, eh? There's no rush. We've got the house to ourselves all evening and I ain't got to get you home until twelve.'

'Put some music on then. What records you got?'

Feeling embarrassed, Little Vinny admitted that his father had smashed up his entire record collection.

Shazza was bemused. 'But why would he do that?'

'Because he's a prick and he wants me to be just like him. My dad has a bit of a reputation round here, and he's embarrassed 'cause I'm a skinhead. He wants me to wear smart suits like he does, but I'm my own person.'

'Your dad sounds like a right pig. You're sixteen – he has no right to tell you what to do and how to dress.'

Praying that Shazza would never find out he was only fourteen, Little Vinny glugged down a large amount of cider, then put the empty bottle on his bedside cabinet. 'What's that?' he asked, pointing at the folded up piece of paper Shazza put next to the bottle.

'My phone number. I wrote it in pen this time, so you'll have no excuse not to ring me in future. My mum had a word with me when you was in the bath earlier. She really likes you, but said you can't stay at mine when I go back to school next week. She's worried, what with it being my final year, it will affect my exams.'

'I understand, Shaz. I'll probably need to move back home to go to work anyway. My dad is bound to be pissed off with me for a week or two, so if he makes me work all the time and I can't see you, you won't go off with another boy, will you?'

''Course not. I like you, Vinny. Now let's get under them covers, shall we? It's turned cold tonight.'

When Shazza began to take her clothes off, Little Vinny awkwardly did the same. The only real live naked woman he had ever seen was Joanna, after he accidentally walked into the bathroom as she was stepping out of the shower. Apart from that it was just the ones in the magazines that he and Ben sometimes stole from the local newsagent.

Shazza was rather taken aback when, as soon as she laid down, Little Vinny leapt straight on top of her and, without any foreplay at all, immediately rammed his penis inside her. She was even more taken aback when he came within seconds, rolled off her, then declared his undying love.

Queenie and Vivian arrived back from the amusement arcade just in time to see Molly called onto the stage.

'What's she singing, Jo?' Queenie asked, as Vinny proudly held his daughter's hand and led her towards the stage.

'That song you taught her. I think she's going to do a bit of tap dancing too, but I doubt that will be very good seeing as she's only been to three lessons,' Joanna chuckled. She had felt awkward earlier on when Vinny had been ignoring her, but when his mum and aunt had left the table, he had been quite pleasant towards her, which had cheered Jo up no end.

'Hello, Molly. How old are you?' the compere asked.

'I'm three, and I'm singing a song for my nan,' Molly replied, remembering what her dad had told her to say.

'And is your nan here tonight?'

Molly pointed towards the table where Queenie was sitting. 'Yeah, my nan is here with Auntie Viv, my mum, Dad, and Molly Dolly.'

Aware of the laughs and claps the cute little girl was getting from the audience, the compere asked who Molly Dolly was.

'Dad, show Charlie Molly Dolly,' Molly shouted over the microphone, much to the amusement of the audience.

It was Vivian who grabbed the doll off the chair and waved it in the air.

'My dad named her after me,' Molly explained proudly.

Chuckling, the compere asked Molly what song she would be singing.

Without even answering, a confident Molly grabbed the microphone off Charlie Case and sang the golden oldie 'You Are My Sunshine'. When she did a little shuffle hop and a twirl in the middle of the song, the audience roared with laughter, while clapping frantically at the same time.

As he sat watching the adulation his niece was receiving, Michael Butler was fuming. He had been so chuffed when Adam had got up and sung a song for his granddad. It had been the first time Michael had seen his dad smile properly since Dorothy's death, and he was sure his son would have won the competition had Vinny not pissed on his parade, as usual.

When Molly finished her song and received a standing ovation, Michael saw both Vinny and his mother smirking in his and his father's direction. Absolutely livid, he knocked back his drink in one, then stomped off to the bar to get another.

Christopher Walker had never been a man to frequent pubs, especially of an evening when all the riff-raff were about. His nickname at work had once been 'Boring Chris', such was his dislike for socializing, but tonight he found himself sitting in a boozer alone.

Going out with Olivia and her parents had been a no-go after his meeting with Ahmed. For one thing, he couldn't think straight. And secondly, both Olivia and her father would have known something was very wrong.

To say Christopher's mind was mashed up was putting it mildly. He thought back to his training at Hendon Police College. He had worked so hard there, and had carried on in the same vein ever since to get to where he was today. Now, he was facing the biggest decision of his career. Should he go it alone and try to arrest Vinny Butler himself? Or should he let a superior or Olivia's father in on the plan – and risk Ahmed blowing his dirty secret from the past wide open?

Christopher put his tired head in his hands. He would sleep on it and make his difficult choice in the morning.

Since Molly had been announced the winner of the talent competition, Michael had been knocking back the booze like there was no tomorrow. Sensing he was in a foul mood,

Nancy pleaded, 'Let's go back to the bungalow, eh Michael? The boys are tired.'

Whereas in London he would have had no choice but to escort his family home, Kings was an extremely safe place for women and children to walk about alone at night, so Michael told her to go on without him. 'I want to speak to that cock of a brother of mine, and I'd rather you and the boys not be here when I do so.'

Overhearing the conversation, Albie grabbed his son's arm. 'Leave it, Michael. I know Adam was upset he didn't win, but he'll be fine tomorrow. Don't rise to the bait, your brother isn't worth it.'

Still livid that his brother had also grassed him up to his father for taking cocaine, Michael told his dad to keep out of it, then turned back to his wife. 'Just do as I say, Nance. Take the boys home, now,' he demanded.

Knowing that something was about to kick off, Nancy quickly rounded the boys up and led them out of the club.

Over on the other side of the club, Vinny Butler was bouncing Molly up and down on his knee as yet another couple came across to fawn over his beautiful, talented daughter.

'However did she learn all the words to such an old song at a young age?' the grey-haired lady asked.

Also beaming with pride were Joanna, Queenie and Vivian. 'Me and my sister taught her to sing it, didn't we, Viv?' Queenie said proudly.

'Yep. We've taught her loads of songs. She knows all the words to "Maybe It's Because I'm a Londoner", too – don't you, Molly?' said Vivian.

'Shall I sing it now, Auntie Viv?' Molly asked, thoroughly enjoying being in the limelight.

'No, darling. You can enter the competition another time

and sing that,' Joanna said, stroking her daughter's curly blonde hair.

For the first time in ages, an inebriated Vinny squeezed Joanna's hand and looked at her with genuine affection in his eyes. It might have been a game to him, snaring Jo just to piss off her father, but even so, they had produced the most beautiful child between them. 'Created a future superstar, we have, babe,' Vinny stated proudly.

Thrilled by Vinny's rare display of affection, Joanna was stopped from replying by Michael marching towards them with a face like thunder. 'Happy now, are ya, Vin? Sobbing his little heart out, my boy was. You are one sick cunt at times, do you know that?'

Seeing the elderly couple who had been fawning over Molly flee, Joanna dashed to the toilets with her daughter in her arms before the child could witness yet another scene.

Vinny smirked. 'Dunno what you're talking about. I never picked the winner. Not my fault if the audience found my daughter more entertaining than your son, is it? You pissed, Michael? Or you been on the white stuff again?'

'You fucking arsehole,' Michael yelled, lunging towards his brother.

'Stop it! Everybody's looking. You'll get us barred,' Queenie shrieked.

As frail as he now was compared to his strapping son, Albie somehow managed to hold Michael back. 'Let's go, boy. Come on. He's not worth it.'

Queenie glared at Albie. 'That's rich, coming from you. You're the most worthless excuse for a man God ever put breath in. As for you, Michael, you're drunk – and no wonder, being around him all evening. And what's all this about white stuff, eh? What bloody white stuff?'

'Cocaine, Muvver. Had a problem with it for a while

after Roy and Champ died, but I've knocked it on the head now.'

Unable to control her displeasure, Queenie forgot that all the people on nearby tables had stopped watching the resident band and were now watching the chaos her family were causing. 'You stupid little bastard! How dare you blacken this family's name by taking drugs? As for blaming it on Roy and Champ's deaths, that's the lamest excuse I've ever heard. Bloody ashamed to call you my son, I am. And I bet Vinny is ashamed to call you his brother.'

'Come on, boy. Leave it. You don't need all this,' Albie said, tugging his son's arm to try to lead him out of the club.

Vivian was the next to jump out of her seat. She had always been overprotective of her sister, especially when Albie was involved. 'Like father, like bleedin' son, Queen. You was always going to get one who had that tosser's genes.'

Vinny suddenly sobered up very quickly and realized the error of his ways. He'd had no idea when he had said the words 'white stuff' that Michael would actually blurt out the truth. 'Look, I'm sorry. This is my fault. Let's just all calm down, eh?'

Michael had a dangerous glint in his eye. 'Why? Worried your own sordid secrets are going to come out now, are you, Vin? If only Mum and Auntie Viv knew what a lying piece of shit you really are.'

Queenie pushed Michael in the chest. 'Don't you dare talk to your brother like that. You're the bloody junkie, not him. Vinny is no liar.'

Michael chuckled. A nasty evil chuckle it was too. 'Really, Mum. Well, why don't you ask golden boy who was really driving the car on that night Champ died, eh? Because it wasn't Ahmed, that's for sure.'

# CHAPTER TWENTY-ONE

Holidaymakers screamed and fled in terror as the fight broke out. 'You no good cuntbag. I trusted you,' Vinny yelled. Then he punched Michael so hard, he landed backwards on a nearby table, smashing every glass in the process.

With a deranged expression on his face, Michael charged at Vinny and knocked him flying across the dancefloor.

'Stop it! Stop it! Stop it!' Queenie shouted as she leapt out of her chair and began hitting both of her sons over the head with her handbag.

The bouncers, who had been keeping a watchful eye on the Butler family for the past ten minutes, quickly waded in. But they hadn't bargained on Vinny's strength.

The resident band were playing George Baker's 'Una Paloma Blanca' and quickly stopped mid-tune when they saw Vinny smash a bottle over the head of one of the bouncers.

Anxious to protect Kings' reputation as a fun-loving family holiday park, Charlie Case leapt on stage to assure all guests that this unfortunate situation would soon be under control.

It was too. As soon as more bouncers intervened, Vinny

and Michael were put into headlocks and marched from the premises.

Queenie looked around. She spotted Joanna in tears, hugging Molly, and Albie standing beside her. She ran towards them. 'Where's Vivvy?'

Albie looked at the woman he had once married. His voice thick with hatred, he asked, 'Where do you think she is after finding out news like that, eh? Did you know it was Vinny who was driving that car?'

'Don't be daft! I don't believe it. Michael was drunk, talking bollocks – and it was you who got him in that state.'

Albie shook his head. 'Michael told me, Queen. Just before he marched over to your table. He said that Vinny turned up at his house covered in blood on the night in question, asking him for an alibi. You really need to take your head out from up your arse and see our eldest son for what he really is.'

Queenie's face was ashen. The fight had broken out so quickly that she'd had no time to think about the possibility that Michael was telling the truth, or the consequences for the rest of the family.

'What's Vinny meant to have done?' Joanna asked, both tearful and bemused.

Before anybody had a chance to answer Joanna's question, two bouncers walked over, ordered the family to leave the club and told them they would not be welcome back.

Outside the club entrance, Vivian was in pieces. When she saw Vinny being led to a waiting police car by the bouncers, she flew at him like a mad woman. 'You lying, no good fucker. You killed my Lenny. It was you who murdered my baby,' she screamed, pummelling her nephew with both of her tiny fists.

Vinny knew the game was up. There was no point trying to worm his way out of this one. 'I'm so sorry, Auntie Viv, but it's not what you think. I'll explain everything in full, I promise,' he said in a choked-up voice, as a copper shoved his head into the back of a patrol car.

When the car door slammed, Vivian spat at the window next to where her nephew was sitting. 'Don't you come anywhere near me or try to speak to me ever again. You're dead to me, Vinny. Dead!'

Nancy had just put the boys to bed when her bloodied husband arrived back at the bungalow with Albie in tow. 'Oh my God! Whatever happened? Did Vinny do this to you?'

'Pour me and Dad a brandy, love,' Michael ordered as he took his jacket off and flopped onto the sofa. His head was banging, his face badly bruised, his suit and shirt were ruined, and he was sure he had shards of glass stuck in his back.

'I'm still in shock, son. I always knew Vinny was rotten to the core, but this is still hard to take in. Poor Lenny. Much as I dislike your Auntie Viv, my heart actually went out to her back there.'

Nancy handed Michael and Albie their drinks. 'Can somebody please explain to me what the hell has happened?'

Michael put his battered face in his hands. 'I should never have blurted it out like that. What the hell have I done?' he mumbled.

'Don't you dare blame yourself. The only thing you did wrong was backing that bastard's lies in the first place. But I know how manipulative Vinny can be, so don't you be beating yourself up about it,' Albie told his son.

Becoming more exasperated by the second, Nancy repeated her previous question.

Michael had tears rolling down his cheeks when he lifted his head and looked at his wife. 'It wasn't Ahmed driving the car that killed Champ. It was Vinny.'

Nancy put her hand over her mouth. She hadn't been this shocked since her idol Marc Bolan died.

Vivian felt as though she was in a complete trance as she walked back towards the bungalow. It was like reliving Lenny's death all over again and she felt sick to the stomach.

Joanna and Queenie looked worriedly at one another when Vivian started to mumble expletives.

'What does cunt mean, Mummy?' Molly asked.

'"Hunt", Auntie Viv said. She was talking about the cat that just passed us hunting for food,' Joanna replied.

'Where's Daddy, Mummy?'

'Daddy's had to pop out somewhere, but he'll be back soon, darling.'

'They should lock the bastard up and throw away the key,' Vivian spat.

Joanna still did not have a clue what was going on, but it didn't take a genius to work out that whatever Vinny had supposedly done was very bad. She wanted to ask, but was nervous of Molly picking up on things. In truth, she was even more afraid of hearing the answer to her question.

'Where you going?' Queenie asked, when her sister started to walk in the opposite direction.

'Well, I ain't sleeping in there ever again, that's for sure. Murdering, lying cunt, that son of yours is, and if I set eyes on him again tonight, I swear I will stick a knife straight through him.'

Seeing the horrified realization dawn on Joanna's face, Queenie urged her to take Molly inside, then turned back to her sister. 'Look, Viv, we don't even know if it's true yet.

Michael was pissed and Albie is a born liar, you know that as well as I do.'

'Vinny admitted it to me before they put him in the police car. You was still inside the club, Queen, but his face said it all. There was guilt written all over 'im.'

Queenie was a woman who rarely cried. But her family meant the world to her. Always had and always would, so she couldn't stop the tears now rolling down her cheeks. 'I'm so sorry, Viv, I really am. But I know my Vinny – there must be a reason why he lied. He loved Lenny, you know he did.'

Vivian let out a loud sarcastic chuckle. 'Oh, of course there's a reason, Queen. Probably the same reason he dragged his best pal's dying body into the driver's seat. To save his own fucking skin.'

Vinny Butler laid down on the uncomfortable blue mattress and stared at the ceiling. For all his wrongdoings in the past, it was a rare occurrence for him to spend the night in a police cell and he was discovering that it certainly gave one time to reflect on matters.

The Old Bill had told him he would be interviewed in the morning, but Vinny couldn't have cared less whether the bouncer he had bottled was hurt or not. The only thoughts pulsating through his mind concerned the repercussions of his awful secret being exposed, and what effect that would have on his relationship with those he truly loved.

Real men did not cry, so when Vinny felt the tears forming in his eyes, he sat up and punched the graffitied wall. Now he'd had time to sober up and collect his thoughts, he knew that his brother was not entirely to blame for the unfortunate events of last night. Michael had stuck by him through thick and thin in the past, and Vinny knew if he hadn't goaded him by forcing Molly onto the stage and hinting to their mum about his brother's drug problem, Michael would never have blurted out what he did.

However, Vinny was never one to admit that he was in the wrong. Michael had started it by insulting their beloved mother at a time when he was already riled up because of Johnny Preston's release and Little Vinny running away from home.

Remembering the look of hatred on his aunt's face and the words she had yelled as he sat in the back of the police car, the tears finally rolled down Vinny's cheeks. His mum and Auntie Viv meant the world to him and ever since he was a young lad he'd done his utmost to make them happy. His generosity had given them a life of luxury that most of their neighbours in Whitechapel could only dream of. Surely, once he explained things properly, his mum and aunt would understand why he had lied. Wouldn't they?

Back at Kings Holiday Park, Michael sat with his head in his hands as his mother and aunt fired questions at him.

Nancy was in the bedroom with the boys, so it was Albie who put an arm around his son's shoulders and stuck up for him. For years, Albie had allowed his wife and her witch of a sister to rule the roost, but Dorothy had taught him his worth and he was not about to bow down to that pair ever again.

'Don't you dare be having a dig at Michael, either of you. Between the pair of yous, you created a monster called Vinny. Now you're reaping the consequences of your greed.'

Queenie was dumbstruck by Albie's sudden transformation. What had happened to the weak ferret of a man she once knew? Had he undergone some kind of personality transplant?

It was left to Vivian to give Albie what for. 'Greed! What

the hell you on about? What has greed got to do with Vinny killing my Lenny, and Michael covering the bastard's lies, eh?'

Albie stood up like the proud man he had once been. He pointed a forefinger, firstly at Vivian, but then rested it on his ex-wife. 'Yous pair are the most materialistic women I have ever had the misfortune of meeting in my life. Queenie, you all but forced our sons into a life of crime, such was your love for money and your desire to be better than any of the neighbours. When other mothers were teaching their sons nursery rhymes, you were teaching ours sayings like "Grasses are worse than sewer rats" and "Yous boys always stick by one another, no matter what." Well, Michael obviously took your advice, which is why he has had to carry the burden of what Vinny did on his shoulders for the past four years. I hope you are proud of your wonderful parenting skills. Poor, poor Lenny and poor Roy. God rest their souls.'

Vivian slumped back into her armchair at this, but Queenie got to her feet. 'Don't you dare lecture me on parenting skills, you useless drunken old bastard. Where was you when we needed food on the table? Or when the kids needed new clothes or shoes? Spunking all your money on whores and in the local pub, that's where. Of course I encouraged our kids to make a better life for themselves. What decent mother wouldn't? Anything was better than them ending up like you.'

As she reached out to push his father in the chest, Michael leapt between them. 'Stop arguing! My sons are in the bedroom, trying to sleep.'

'Blame your father. He's the one who started yelling out accusations. Was I a bad mother, Michael? Well, was I?'

'Just calm down and sit down, Mum,' Michael ordered.

Albie was determined to have the last word. 'I warned you

that Vinny was a time bomb waiting to explode. Bet you wish you'd listened to me now. How any of yous ever allowed Lenny to go out gallivanting with Vinny and Ahmed is beyond me. That boy deserved better.'

Joanna Preston stared at her beautiful child. Molly had such long eyelashes and with her pink nightdress on and her mop of blonde curls, she truly resembled an angel in her sleep.

Sighing worriedly, Joanna turned the lamp off and tiptoed out of the bedroom. There was no point in her trying to get any sleep herself. How could she, after what she had learned this evening?

About to put the kettle on, Joanna's heart flipped when she heard a tap on the front door. What if it was the police? She would not have a clue what to say to them.

'Oh, thank God it's you,' Joanna whispered as she ushered Nancy inside.

'Isn't it awful, Jo? They're all arguing over there and I just had to get out. I hope the boys don't wake up, but I told Michael to bring them over here to sleep if they do. Have you heard anything from Vinny?'

Joanna shook her head dismally. 'Poor Vivian. I'm so shocked. I can't quite believe it. Why would Vinny lie about such a thing?'

'To save his own bloody skin, I should imagine. Look, Jo, I know you love Vinny, but for Molly's sake you really need to get away from him.'

'But where would I go? I haven't got any money of my own. And I know he won't allow me to take Molly away from him, Nance. Vinny adores her.'

'But does he adore you, Jo? Last time we had a heart-to-heart you admitted he hadn't been near you for months in the bedroom. That isn't normal. An attractive girl such as yourself deserves so much better.'

'Well, you've said the same about your Michael in the past, Nancy. I remember when he hadn't been near you for ages in the bedroom either.'

Nancy squeezed Joanna's hand. 'Michael and I did go through a rough patch, but we're back on track now and we've been making love regularly. Bloody hell, after trying to keep an awful secret like this all these years, I can understand why Michael had issues. Even though I know he regrets blurting it out like that, I can see the relief in his eyes that it's all out in the open. Look, Jo, I'm only saying this because I think the world of you and Molly, but you need to get away from Vinny. Even his own father despises him – doesn't that tell you something?'

As Nancy's harsh words sank in, a sobbing Joanna clung to her pal for dear life. 'I'll never be rid of him though, Nance. Even if I leave him, he will snatch Molly. I just know he will.'

Vinny Butler walked out of the police station at ten a.m. the following morning facing nothing more than a charge of affray. The bouncer he had bottled had refused to press charges or even give a statement, and Vinny had guessed that Ron, the bouncer he had got quite friendly with, must have warned his colleague not to start a war.

When the cab turned into Kings Holiday Park, Vinny felt his pulse start to race. He'd had little sleep, felt dirty, hungry, and hungover, but he needed to speak to his mother and aunt before he even considered having breakfast or a bath. He was dreading explaining and reliving the night of Lenny's death, but it had to be done and he was determined to be totally truthful from now on. He just hoped they could find it in their hearts to understand why he had done what he had done, then forgive him.

When Vinny unlocked the door of his bungalow, Molly

threw herself at him screaming 'Daddy.' Joanna and Nancy were sitting side by side on the sofa and Vinny had already seen Daniel, Adam and Lee outside playing football. 'Where's Mum and Auntie Viv?' he asked.

'Gone back to London,' Nancy replied in a nonchalant tone.

'How? When?'

'A couple of hours ago. They asked Michael to drive them home,' Nancy informed her brother-in-law.

Aware that Joanna did not seem keen to look him in the eye, Vinny picked Molly up, walked over to the sofa and sat down next to his partner. He then put an arm around her and kissed her fondly on her forehead. 'I'm so sorry, babe, but we will get through this. Michael knows the truth and once I explain everything to my mum and Auntie Viv all will be back to normal, I promise you that.'

When Joanna hugged both Vinny and her daughter, Nancy got to her feet, fighting the urge to vomit. She had tried to help Jo, had even urged her to ring her parents, but if the girl could not see past Vinny's façade, then there was nothing anyone could do for her.

# CHAPTER TWENTY-TWO

Vinny drove back to London with just Joanna and Molly in the car. He had offered Nancy and the boys a lift home, but his stuck up sister-in-law had looked at him as though he was something distasteful on the bottom of her shoe. 'No thanks. I am going to make your dad a nice lunch while I wait for Michael to come back,' Nancy had replied with a sneer.

'Are you going to pop straight round your mum's house? I think you should,' Joanna said, as Vinny opened their front door.

Vinny had a nose like a tracker dog and the distinct smell of stale smoke hit him immediately. 'That little bastard has been back home,' Vinny said, darting up the stairs.

Positive that the smell that hit him when he opened the bedroom door was in fact cannabis, Vinny began searching for evidence. The wastepaper bin was empty so Vinny started going through his son's drawers. When he walked towards the bedside cabinet, he spotted the piece of paper immediately. The name Shaz was written on it and it had a phone number with a loveheart drawn underneath.

Vinny ran down the stairs and flicked through his address book. Most of the names and numbers were written in code as you could never be too careful. He found the number he was looking for and picked up the phone. 'George, so sorry to bother you on a Sunday, but I really need your help to trace an address, mate.'

Queenie Butler handed her sister a glass of sherry, then sat down next to her on the sofa and sipped her own. Viv had been ever so quiet all day and Queenie could do little but hope and pray that this latest bad news did not send her sister back into a depression and the loony bin.

'Please eat a couple of them sandwiches, Viv. You've eaten sod all since yesterday and you're worrying me now.'

'Look, I ain't fucking hungry and, as I told you earlier, I just want to be left alone, Queen. I'm fine, and don't be worrying about me going back into the nuthouse because I have no intention of doing so. I'm more angry and tired, if you want to know the truth. Didn't sleep a bloody wink last night.'

Queenie had never felt more useless in her whole life. Being the older sister, she had always felt it her duty to protect Viv, but how the hell was she meant to deal with this terrible situation? What Vinny had done beggared belief, and even if he did have some kind of a viable excuse, Queenie was not sure if she could ever forgive him herself.

When Queenie said she was going back to her own house for a while but would pop back later, Vivian waited until the front door shut before she trudged up the stairs.

Lenny's bedroom was the shrine to the son that she had loved so very much, and thanks to Queenie rescuing all his belongings before the dustmen had taken them away, it still looked the same as when Lenny was alive. Even his clothes were back in the wardrobe. The only change to the room was the massive framed photo of her son that was hung above his bed.

Taking the sweater Lenny had worn the day before he died out of the drawer, Vivian laid on her son's bed and hugged both the sweater and his favourite toy. It was only then the tears came, and when they did there was no controlling them.

Vinny Butler decided to walk round to his mother's house rather than take the car. A bit of fresh air might help him to prepare for one of the worst conversations he would ever have to face.

Joanna had promised to stay indoors and wait for George to ring back. She had no idea who George was, but assumed he was a friend of Vinny's.

Vinny felt physically sick as he approached his mother's front door. He had his own key, but for once it didn't seem appropriate to let himself in the way he always did, so he knocked instead.

Much to Vinny's dismay, it was his sister who answered the door.

'Is Mum in?' he asked awkwardly.

Brenda glared at her elder brother. Scotty had been the first bloke she had fallen in love with since Dean and thanks to Vinny, she was now single again. Without saying a word, she stomped into the lounge and grabbed Tara and Tommy by the hand. 'I'm sorry, Mum. I know I've only just got here, but no way am I being in his company. I'll pop round tomorrow instead.'

Vinny waited until the front door slammed before he sat on the sofa next to his mother. 'Go and sit over there, Vinny. I don't want you close to me.'

Moving over to the armchair, Vinny knew he was in shit-street when he saw the look of hatred. His mum had never looked at him that way. 'I'm so sorry, Mum. How is Auntie Viv?'

'How do you fucking think she is? I am so disappointed in you. How could you cover up something as awful as that? And why would you? Where had you been? Was you pissed?'

Vinny stared at his hands. No way could he look at his mum. 'Ahmed and I had been drinking at the club. Champ overheard us saying we were heading off to some strip joint and he begged to come too. If you want the complete truth, I had taken Champ there a few times before. Loved it, he did,' Vinny explained, before pausing. He hated talking about the cousin he had loved so much. It upset him greatly.

Usually when she saw her son's eyes fill up with tears, Queenie's heart would melt, but today it did not. 'Carry on then,' she spat.

Vinny took a deep breath to compose himself. 'Well, I felt a bit merry, so Ahmed offered to drive us to the strip joint. We had planned to leave his car there, get a cab home, but by the time we were ready to leave, I had sobered up and felt OK to drive. I would never have driven with Champ in the car had I not thought I was in complete control, you know that, Mum. Anyway, all of a sudden this van appears out of nowhere with its full beam on and I just lost control of the vehicle. I must have knocked myself out, not sure if it was for seconds or minutes, but when I came round, I looked in the back and Champ was dead,' Vinny wept.

Queenie pursed her lips. 'And then what did you do?'

'I panicked, Mum. I opened the back door to see if there was anything I could do to save Champ, but I couldn't. His injuries were far too bad. Ahmed was also in a mess. He had metal sticking out of his head and chest and when I felt for a pulse, I couldn't find one.'

'So, then you thought, if Ahmed is brown bread, you might as well drag his body into the driver's seat and let him take the rap. Am I right?'

Vinny stared at his hands again and nodded dejectedly.

Queenie tutted repeatedly. 'No wonder you nearly fainted when you found out Ahmed was still alive. I never thought the day would come when I saw you as a coward, Vinny, but it has, boy. What you did was disgraceful. How that Ahmed has stayed friends with you, I will never know. He must be a much more forgiving person than me, that's for sure. Running away like some fucking wuss, that's what you did. Why didn't you just call an ambulance, eh? All you had to do was find a phonebox or knock on some bastard's door. You might be a lot of things – liar being one of them – but a doctor you ain't. If you thought Ahmed was dead and it turned out he weren't, how do you know Lenny was gone? Maybe he could have been saved if you'd acted like the man I brought you up to be, eh?'

'Champ's head was hanging off, Mum. No way could he have been saved. As I said, I just panicked. I'm so sorry. If I could change what I did, I would.'

'But why? You already said you was sober enough to drive. What were you so scared of, eh? There must have been something – and don't bastard-well lie to me again, because I will find out the truth if it's the last thing I do.'

Vinny rubbed his eyes with the thumb and forefinger of his right hand. He knew his mum was going to be so disappointed with his reply, but he had to tell the truth in case Michael blurted it out at a later date. 'Even though I felt sober, Mum, I would have still been well over the limit if the Old Bill had breathalysed me. I also had a bit of a drug problem back then. I swear I don't touch drugs now, but I'd had some cocaine that night. I'd never touched the stuff until I became pals with Ahmed, but he was a user, so I'd sometimes take it with him. I wasn't bothered about the Old Bill locking me up, just you and Auntie Viv finding out the truth. I love you both so much and I couldn't have handled it if you both hated me.'

Queenie leapt off the sofa, darted towards her son and slapped him as hard around the face as she could. 'Your crocodile tears don't wash with me, boy. You were bang out of order even taking poor Lenny to strip clubs. No wonder your Auntie Viv caught him with his dingle-dangle in his hand mumbling obscenities. As for driving that beautiful boy about while out of your nut on drink and drugs, that is totally unforgivable. Now, get of my house before I do you some proper damage.'

With tears streaming down his face, Vinny stood up. 'Please, Mum, don't be like this. I loved Champ with all my heart, you know I did. And he wasn't a boy, he was twenty years old. All you and Auntie Viv ever did was treat the poor little sod like an infant. He was a man, not a kid, and he had urges like every other bloke his age. Why do you think he loved to hang out with me all the time, eh? Because I treated him as normal, that's why.'

'And didn't you do a good job of taking him under your wing, eh? You killed the poor little mite while off your fucking face. No wonder that son of yours has turned out to be such a bad apple. You've both got your father's genes, not mine. Albie's a coward who would always do anything to save his own bacon, and you're no different. Now, leave me your key and get out my house. You're officially disowned as my son.'

Joanna Preston opened the front door and was relieved to see Nancy and the boys. 'Thank God it's only you. I thought it might be Queenie or Viv wanting round two. Where's Michael, Nance?'

'He dropped us off home, then shot straight out with his dad somewhere. We've got little food indoors, so I thought it might be nice for us all to go out for something to eat. The boys are bored being back home already, and it's such a nice day.'

'Oh, I better not, Nance. I've just written an important address down for Vinny, and he might ring anytime.'

'So? He's probably only local, surely he can pop home if he gets no answer. Just leave him a note, Jo, and write the address on it.'

'I'm not sure. You know what Vinny's like, especially when he's angry. I can't stand the thought of coming home to another scene. I've had enough the past couple of days to last me a lifetime.'

'All the more reason why you should start being your own person. This is your home; it's not a prison, Jo. Anyway, I was thinking, while we're out you can ring your parents. I bet your dad is dying to hear from you, and you must call him. You only get one dad, babe.'

Having not heard the sound of her father's voice for years, Joanna nodded. 'Yeah, you're right. Give us ten minutes to get ready.'

Nancy grinned. 'That's my girl.'

Albie followed Michael into the Blind Beggar and was horrified to see Vinny sitting at a table alone. 'Your brother's over there. We don't want no more trouble, Michael. Let's just go for a pint at the club, eh?' Albie hissed in his youngest son's ear. It had been Michael's suggestion to stop off for a pint on the way to the club, and Albie had not wanted to go in the Blind Beggar in the first place.

'I ain't walking out, Dad. I'd look a right fucking mug if I did. And what about the regulars, eh? They'd know something was wrong, and you know what the rumour mill is like around here.'

'Please, Michael, you know what an arsehole your brother

can be. He's certain to kick off. Besides, Big Stan is in here. He's bound to be nasty to me after that lie I told him.'

'Big Stan won't say sod all out of line to you. People ain't stupid, Dad. They respect me, so nobody is going to dig you out. As for Vinny, let him kick off if he wants to. I'm not a little boy any more and I am certainly not scared of him.'

Albie sighed. Michael used to be so laid-back, but he wasn't any more. Somewhere along the line Vinny's thuggish behaviour had obviously rubbed off on him, which bothered Albie greatly.

Whenever Michael walked into a local pub, he was always surrounded by well-wishers and hangers-on who wanted to chat to him or buy him drinks. Usually he played along, pretended to be interested in their conversation, but tonight he wasn't in the mood. Everyone else was a blur as he focused on his brother, sitting across the room, drinking by himself. Even though Michael felt bad about blurting out the truth regarding Lenny's death, there was no way he was making the first move to smooth over the situation. Why should he, when it had been Vinny's behaviour and big mouth that had started it all in the first place?

Albie was pleased when Big Stan approached and offered him a drink. Stan did not mention his cancer lie, so Albie decided not to either. Some things were better left unsaid.

'Shall I get us a chaser as well, Albie?'

Albie did not reply. His eyes were on Vinny, who was walking towards Michael.

Vinny tapped his brother on the back. 'Can we talk?'

'Yeah, if you want.'

'Be careful, boy,' Albie warned, as Michael went to follow Vinny outside.

'I'm more than capable of looking after myself, Dad. You stay here with Stan. I won't be long.'

Vinny was standing in a shop doorway, smoking a

cigarette. It was a Sunday and he could not help thinking what a sorry state the Whitechapel Road looked without the hustle and bustle of the market. The properties of hardworking shopkeepers were covered in graffiti, much of it racist – 'NF', 'PAKIS OUT', 'KEEP BRITAIN WHITE' – along with the usual drivel: 'SPURS RULE' 'ARSENAL ARE SHIT' 'ICF' 'TRACEY LOVES GLENN HODDLE' 'SHARON 4 JOHNNY' and 'MANDY NELSON SUCKS COCKS'.

Vinny tutted and shook his head. No wonder he wanted his Molly raised in a better area. It might do Little Vinny the world of good as well. If they moved to a decent part of Essex there'd be better lads for his son to knock about with than Ben Bloggs.

'Shithole round here now, eh? Look at the state of it,' Vinny said bitterly, as he offered Michael a cigarette.

Michael allowed Vinny to give him a light, took a deep drag, then nodded. 'Not like it used to be, is it? Is that what you wanted to talk about? The decline of Whitechapel?'

'Don't get cocky, Michael. It really doesn't suit you.'

'Look, I'm sorry about blurting out the Champ story, OK? But, you fucking started it, Vin. You all but told Mum and Auntie Viv I was on drugs.'

'Yeah, I know I did, and I'm sorry too. Mum threw me out of the house today. I admitted I'd taken coke on the night Champ had died and she said I am no longer her son. I don't want there to be no more secrets, Michael, which is why I came clean with her.'

Michael was not only shocked by his brother's calmness and apology, he was also stunned that Vinny had told the truth. 'Mum will come round. She loves you, Vin, you're her golden boy. Give her a bit of time to get her head around it all, eh?'

Vinny and Michael both had their backs against the wall, staring at the traffic rather than looking one another in the eye. When Vinny finally turned to face him, Michael could see the unshed tears in his brother's eyes. 'What am I gonna do if Mum won't forgive me? I doubt Auntie Viv ever will, do you?'

'I'll speak to Mum and Auntie Viv on your behalf. I'll tell them how cut up you was about everything. It might take time, but things will sort themselves out, Vin, I know they will.'

'Cheers. That's much appreciated. I was livid with you for blurting all that shit out at first, but then I thought, we're brothers and we've got a business to run, so there's no point in us being enemies. Are we cool?'

Michael held out his right hand. 'Yeah, we're cool. We were both in the wrong, so let's just call it quits.'

Vinny pulled Michael's arm towards him, then gave him a brotherly hug. 'You didn't 'arf give me a clump when you knocked me on that dancefloor. Not such a little squirt any more, are ya?'

Michael chuckled. When he was a nipper, both Vinny and Roy used to refer to him as 'Little Squirt'. 'You can talk! Look at the state of my eye, and my back's cut to shreds where I landed on fucking glass.'

'Serves you right!' Vinny joked. 'Now, let's get back inside that boozer, eh?'

When Vinny sauntered into the pub with an arm around his brother's shoulder, he immediately clocked the look of disappointment on his father's face and could not help but smirk. He might be a lot of things, but stupid was not one of them. Vinny knew that the only way back into his mother and aunt's good books was via his brother, forgiveness was a necessary evil.

*

Queenie and Vivian were sitting side by side on Vivian's new floral sofa. The sofa had been a recent present for Vivian's fiftieth birthday and had been bought by Vinny of all people.

Puffing ferociously on a cigarette, Queenie tried to recite word for word what Vinny had told her. The only part she opted to leave out was that her son had admitted to snorting cocaine on the evening in question. Vivian was so anti-drugs and Queenie was worried that that particular snippet of information might just push her sister over the edge.

'Well, I don't believe for one minute Vinny was sober when he got behind that wheel. He must have been well pissed to cover it up like he did, Queen. How could I have ever trusted him to take care of my boy like I did, eh? As for Lenny being dragged off to them sordid places, I'm truly appalled by that. No wonder I caught him doing you-know-what in his bedroom that time. It all makes sense now. If only I'd have acted on the signs and put a fucking stop to it . . . I blame myself, I really do. I was Lenny's mother, therefore it was my duty to protect him – and I failed miserably.'

Queenie felt a mixture of emotions as she held Vivian in her arms. Sadness, anger, but most of all guilt. As much as part of her would always love Vinny, she had no choice but to side with her sister at this moment in time and banish her son from their lives. She not only owed that to Vivian, but also to the memory of her wonderful nephew.

'Please don't be blaming yourself, Viv. Your Lenny adored the ground you walked on. You were the best mother he could have ever wished for, and you know it. As for Vinny, I'm finished with him because of all this. Don't get me wrong, I know he adored Lenny and neither did he mean to crash that car. But it's the cover-up and the lies that has broken my heart. What type of man drags his pal's lifeless body into the front seat of a car while his cousin is lying dead in the back, then legs it without even calling an ambulance, eh? No son of mine, that's for sure.'

Joanna Preston's hands shook as she dialled her parents' phone number. It had been so long since she had heard her dad's gruff voice, she had no idea how she would react when she actually got to speak to him.

After several rings, the phone was finally answered. 'Hello, Mum. It's me. How are you? And how's Dad?'

Deborah did not even reply to the question. 'Johnny, quick – Jo's on the phone,' she screamed.

'Hello, princess. Been sat indoors ever since I got out, waiting for you to ring me. How are you, sweetheart? And how's little Molly?'

Crying, but laughing at the same time, Joanna explained how Molly was not so little any more and was in fact quite a madam. 'She even won the talent competition at the holiday camp on Saturday, Dad. She sang "You Are My Sunshine".'

'Jesus Christ, even I don't know all the words to that. Who taught it to her?' Johnny asked.

'Queenie and Vivian. They're really kind to Molly, Dad, and they've taught her loads of old songs. I started taking her to tap-dancing lessons recently and her teacher reckons she is destined for a career in show business. She said Molly is a natural.'

Johnny Preston felt completely choked up, but did his best to hide it from his voice. He knew if he came across too heavy he would probably put Joanna off ringing again, so tried to keep the conversation as light as possible. ''Ere, you'll never guess who's here having dinner with me and your mum today.'

'Who?'

'Your brother. Travelled down from London and even

cooked for us. You know me, Jo. I wasn't impressed when he got that job as a chef. I thought he was gay when he came to visit me in nick and wore all that bleedin' eyeliner, but I'm pleased to say he isn't. Done well for himself has Johnny Junior. He's brought his girlfriend to meet us as well. And I have to say, he's a bloody good cook.'

Joanna put some more money in the slot to stop the pips from going and giggled. 'I thought he was gay at one point too, Dad. Perhaps it was just the obsession with David Bowie, eh?'

'Yep, must have been, babe.' Johnny took a deep breath. He had to ask the question at some point. 'So, when am I going to see you? Look, before you answer, I know it's awkward after everything that has happened, and I will understand if you can't bring Molly with you in case she puts her foot in it. However, just to see you and lots of photos of Molly would be enough for me, darling. Me and your mum are getting married again at ten o'clock this coming Thursday morning in a local registry office. Your brother will be there and it would mean the absolute world to both me and your mum if you could come too.'

Whether it was the two glasses of wine she'd had with her scampi and chips or just the fact she missed her family so much, Joanna did not know. But she found herself agreeing to the invitation. 'You try to stop me coming to your wedding. Listen, I have to go now, but I'll ring you again tomorrow or Tuesday to get the exact details. Love you, Dad.'

Johnny Preston put his thumb up to Deborah and grinned. 'Love you too, sweetheart.'

Vinny Butler had been furious when he'd read Joanna's note. Who the hell did she think she was, going out galli-vanting with Nancy? She had not even asked his permission, and for all he knew she could be secretly meeting her scumbag of a father.

Being very protective when it came to Molly, Vinny hated Joanna taking his daughter anywhere without him being present. He had old-fashioned values at heart, and in his book a woman's place was at home, looking after her children, unless her man was by her side. Kings was the only place he was happy letting them out of his sight, because he knew Joanna rarely left the holiday park and his mum had always been there to keep a watchful eye on his beloved little girl and her mother.

He bumped his car up a kerb and checked the map once again. Apart from when he had been to Karen's tower block, then tracked down the pub where Yvonne Summers worked, he was no expert on the streets of Dagenham.

Realizing he was only a couple of minutes away from the address that Geary had given to Jo, Vinny put his foot on the accelerator, then turned right into Western Avenue. With a name like Shazza, Vinny had expected the girl to live on a rough council estate, but as he scanned the door numbers, he could tell that this was a much better part of Dagenham compared to the area that Karen had once lived in.

Knowing what a crafty shit his son could be, Vinny drove past the house. He didn't want Little Vinny looking out of the window and spotting his car, because he'd be sure to do a runner out the back if he knew his dad was coming.

When the front door opened, Vinny was stunned to see a rather attractive woman who looked younger than he did. 'Hello, sorry to bother you, but have you got a sister called Shazza? The reason I'm asking, my son has gone missing and I'm desperately worried about him,' Vinny said politely. He had learned from past experiences that wading in like a bull in a china shop was not the way forward. Unless you were dealing with scum like Ben Bloggs' mother, of course.

Carol Young chuckled. She had often been mistaken for Sharon's sister and always enjoyed the compliment. She was also rather taken with how attractive and polite Little Vinny's father was. In his smart suit, he looked more like a rich businessman than the father of the skinhead boy who was currently upstairs in her daughter's bedroom. 'Come in, love. Would you like a cup of tea or coffee? Your son is upstairs with my Shaz. I'm her mum, not her sister. Obsessed with that top forty chart, youngsters are these days, aren't they?'

Vinny smiled falsely. He had just clocked the photo of the skinhead girl on the wall and could immediately tell by her mass of earrings, green eyeshadow and plum lipstick that she was older than his son. Knowing his boy, the deceitful little bastard must have lied about his age. If that was the case, Vinny could not wait to teach the boy a valuable lesson.

'Yes, but I think the music was far better when we were their age, don't you? Is that your daughter in the photo? Pretty girl. How old is she, Carol?'

Carol beamed. She liked this charming man immensely. 'Yes, that's my Shaz. She turns sixteen the week after next. I've arranged a party for her in the hall of the Cross Keys pub. Nothing special, just friends and family, but it would be great if you could come too. Shall I let your son know you're here?'

'No, I'd prefer to surprise him. But do put the kettle on. I'll have a coffee,' Vinny said, grinning broadly to show off his perfect teeth. He could tell Shazza's mother fancied him and was quite enjoying playing on it.

As Vinny ran up the stairs, he could clearly hear the radio presenter announcing that this week's number six was the Piranhas' 'Tom Hark'. He actually quite liked that song, it was very catchy, but as he barged into the girl's bedroom all he could think of was how much he blamed and despised his son for all that had happened this weekend.

If Little Vinny hadn't run away, he would have arrived at Kings in a far better frame of mind and would never have felt the need to wind Michael up the way he had, then his darkest secret would still be safe and his wonderful mother wouldn't have disowned him.

'Fuck off, Dad. Just leave me alone,' Little Vinny yelled as his father smacked him around the head, then marched him down the stairs by his right ear.

'Whatever's going on?' Carol asked, dashing out of the kitchen. She had been so taken with the gorgeous man in the smart suit, she had begun to make a plate of sandwiches.

When Little Vinny kicked him in the ankle and called him a cunt, Vinny punched his son as hard as he could in the side of the head before turning to Carol. 'Look, I'm very sorry about this disruption, but did you know that this little shit who I am embarrassed to call a son of mine only turned fourteen this summer?'

Shazza was standing at the top of the stairs with her mouth wide open. No wonder the sex with Vinny had been so awful, and no wonder when she had told him today that she had to go back to school on Tuesday, so he'd have to find somewhere else to stay, he had responded by asking her to get engaged to him.

Carol Young put her hand over her mouth. 'Oh my God! I am so sorry. I would never have let your son stay here if I had known he was so young. He told you he was sixteen, didn't he, Shaz?'

'Yes, the lying little pervert. Get out of my life, and never come back,' Shazza screamed.

Vinny smirked as he marched his tearful son towards his Jaguar. What goes around comes around had always been his motto.

# CHAPTER TWENTY-THREE

Joanna had just got Molly off to sleep when Vinny arrived home with his red-eyed son in tow. 'Thank God you found him. Is he OK?'

'No, I ain't OK. I hate you and I hate him and I wish you would both die in a car crash,' Little Vinny yelled as he pushed past Joanna and ran up the stairs to the solace of his bedroom.

'Charming,' Joanna mumbled.

Having dealt with his son, Vinny was now ready to deal with his gallivanting girlfriend. 'Me and you need to talk,' he announced coldly.

Joanna knew exactly what Vinny wanted to talk about, but decided to act dumb. 'About what?'

'About you behaving like a single fucking woman. Four times I rang home, trying to get hold of you earlier. You knew I was waiting on that phone number.'

Joanna hated arguing with Vinny, which was why she usually bowed down to him. However, she was desperate to see her parents get married, and knew if she did not fight back, she would never be able to attend their big day. 'And I wrote the phone number down for you. You never said you was going to ring home every five minutes, did you?'

Vinny snarled. 'So, where did you go then?'

'Out for lunch with Nancy and the boys. I put that on the note I left you. We had no fresh food here and Molly and I were hungry.'

'There's food in the freezer and cupboards.'

Remembering how Nancy kept urging her to stick up for herself, Joanna did just that. 'I am not a prisoner, Vinny, and I certainly don't have to tell you my every move. I rarely ever ask where you're going – and if I did, you wouldn't tell me. All you ever do is dictate to me what I can and cannot do, and I've had enough of it. You even made me get my bloody hair dyed and I despise it dark.'

'Who's been putting ideas in that pretty little head of yours, eh? Nosy fucking Nancy, I bet. Wants to concentrate on her own relationship, that one, else Michael might stray again.'

'Stray again! What do you mean, stray again?'

'Never you mind what I mean, but you listen to me carefully, Jo. I own this house and I pay the bills. What I say goes, understand?'

Knowing she had to call Vinny's bluff, Joanna gave a sarcastic chuckle. 'You really think you're the big man, don't you? Our relationship is a farce, Vinny, I know that much. You don't love me, probably never have. When was the last time we made love, eh? It was that long ago even I can't fucking remember.'

'I've barely seen you for weeks! While you was sunning yourself and partying down at Kings, I was here grafting. Somebody has to foot the bill for your luxurious lifestyle, don't they?'

'Well, you won't have to foot the bill any more, Vinny, because first thing tomorrow, I am leaving you, for good.'

Vinny's eyes glinted dangerously. 'Really? And where will you be running off to? Mummy's and Daddy's house? Just leave me a forwarding address, so my solicitor can contact you about visitation rights. I take it you will still be wanting to see your daughter occasionally?'

Crying tears of pure anger, Joanna lunged at Vinny, fists flailing. 'I will never let you take my daughter away from me, you bastard,' she screamed hysterically.

Feeling his penis stiffen, Vinny grabbed Joanna's wrists to stop her from hitting him, then kissed her to shut her up. He then gave her what she had been craving for months. A damn good fucking.

Over in Tottenham, Ahmed and Burak were in a local nightclub. Both high on cocaine and in the party spirit, they were sitting at a table with two English girls who spoke, dressed and acted like slags. Having plied the pair with drinks all evening, both men were certain that their luck would be in later.

Ahmed slid his hand up the mini-skirt of the girl who was sitting next to him. 'Go have a dance with your friend. I need to speak business with my cousin. Come back soon and I will buy champagne,' he said in the heavy Turkish accent that he used for pulling.

When the girls left the table, Ahmed turned to Burak. 'I met Christopher again today. That's why I was late meeting you. It's all systems go for Thursday. He swears he has not mentioned anything to his superiors, and I have promised to remove one of the bulbs on Vinny's brake lights, so he has a legit reason to pull us over.'

'Do you think you can trust him?' Burak asked. He hated the police with a passion, and was worried his cousin was a fool to trust a cop when there was a risk he might be implicated too.

Ahmed chuckled. 'The only time he searched me was the first time we met, so I took a chance today and recorded the whole thing. Gonna transfer the convo onto a second tape and leave that one in your safe. No way he can ever nail me now. I even mentioned how he lied about Vinny murdering Dave Phillips.'

Burak chuckled. 'You are one clever, nasty man, my cousin.'

Ahmed grinned. 'Aren't I just?'

'So, what is the plan? Where is he going to pull you over?'

'Along the A13, I think. I need to speak to him again tomorrow, because we were interrupted. A message came through on his pager about a little girl being missing and a body being found, and he had to shoot off.'

'Shame it wasn't Vinny Butler's daughter,' Burak joked.

High on drugs, Ahmed giggled. 'Bye bye little Molly.'

The following morning, Vinny woke up at the crack of dawn. Joanna was still asleep, so he propped himself up on his elbow and stared at her. The sex between them the previous evening had actually been quite good for once. Because they had been arguing, it had been rough and spontaneous. He had even put his hand around her throat at one point when he was pumping away at her and threatened to kill her if she ever tried to take Molly away from him. Jo had thought he was joking, but he wasn't, which had made his orgasm even more enjoyable.

When Vinny sidled out of bed, Joanna stirred, then sat up. She hugged a pillow to her chest and smiled. 'Did you really mean all that you said last night?'

Vinny sat on the edge of the bed, plastered a fake smile on his face and squeezed Joanna's hand. He was going to contact a top solicitor later today to see where he stood with custodial rights, but he doubted he had a cat in hell's chance of stopping Joanna walking away with his beloved daughter. That was the reason he had given Joanna all the spiel the previous evening. He had told her everything she wanted to hear, even though it had nearly choked him when he told her he really loved her. 'Yeah, course I meant it, babe. I've been too over-protective with you and I shouldn't be, because I know deep down I can trust you. I'll leave some money today and you go to the hairdressers and get your hair done whatever colour you want. You can even have it dyed pink if it makes you happy.'

'And do you still promise to look after Molly on Thursday while I go up the West End with Nancy?'

'Yep. But as I said to you last night, you need to be back here by four at the latest, as I have some important business on that day.'

'I'll be back by four. We're going shopping early and as soon as we've had lunch, I will come straight home,' Joanna lied. Nancy had actually offered to drive and accompany her to her parents' wedding just so she'd have a decent alibi.

'Right, I'm gonna check on the kids. Once I've had a chat with Little Vinny, I'm gonna make my beautiful bird breakfast in bed.'

Grinning broadly, Joanna threw her arms around Vinny's neck and held him tightly. After their amazing love-making session last night, they had sat up and had a few drinks. That's when Vinny had admitted that he had lost his sex drive due to the stress of Lenny dying in his arms and him lying about it. 'I love you,' Joanna said.

Vinny kissed his girlfriend on the forehead. 'Love you too, babe.' He then stood up, turned his back and smirked. Women were so gullible at times, they really were.

'You OK, Mum? I rang the café. Dad said you was ill, then said something about how you deserved to be,' Nancy asked.

'Oh, take no notice of that miserable old sod. I'm in the doghouse, love. We had the Robinses over yesterday and me and Margaret had a bit too much to drink. Been sick as a dog all night, I have, and now I've got one of my migraines. Your father was not amused.'

Nancy giggled. She had only ever seen her mum drunk once in her life. She had been about ten at the time and she remembered her father cursing while desperately trying to take her mother's panty-girdle off, in case it stopped her blood supply while she slept. It had given herself and Christopher something to chuckle about for days afterwards. 'Did they bring Roger with them?'

'Yes, and Roger brought his fiancée. Me and your father have been invited to the wedding next June.'

Roger Robins was the boring lad that her father had been trying to fix her up with before she got together with Michael. Her dad had even forced Roger to buy tickets for *Top of the Pops* once, but even though she'd missed her chance to see Marc Bolan sing live, Nancy didn't regret turning him down. Roger had been far too embarrassing to be seen out in public with. 'Is he still really ugly, Mum? What's his girlfriend like?'

'Roger's that ugly he could haunt houses, Nance. As for the girlfriend – you know that programme *On the Buses*?'

Knowing what her mum was going to say next, Nancy roared with laughter. 'Don't tell me she looks like Olive?'

'Yes, dear. Now, what do you want? I've got to go back to sleep in a minute. I feel terrible.'

'I want you to do me a favour, Mum. Can the boys stay round yours on Wednesday night and you take them to school the next morning? Joanna's parents are getting married, and I'm her cover story for the day. I don't want to involve Michael, so we're pretending to go shopping up the West End. I'll be back in time to pick the boys up from school.'

'Yeah, I'll have the boys. How is that arsehole Vinny treating Jo these days?'

'Awful, Mum. Which is why I want Jo to be back in contact with her parents. I think they might make her see sense. I've got loads to tell you, but you must never repeat it to anybody. Dad and Chris would have a field day.'

'You know you can trust me, love. Look, I've got to go now. I think I'm going to be sick again.'

Queenie Butler was in her conservatory, staring listlessly out of the window, when she heard the post drop through the door.

Shuffling along the hallway in her fluffy slippers, she recognized the writing on the big envelope immediately. It was from Roy's former fiancée.

Apart from when Colleen had turned up at Roy's funeral, Queenie hadn't set eyes on her or Emily-Mae since their move to Ireland. Colleen was married now and last year she'd had a son, but she had never forgotten Queenie. She wrote to her every few months and would still ring her every Christmas and on Roy's birthday.

Staring at the latest photos of her granddaughter, Queenie smiled. Emily-Mae was eight now and a pretty little thing. Blonde, with petite features, she looked just like an older version of Molly.

Suddenly feeling sad again, Queenie put the photos on the table. When she had disowned Vinny, she had not given Molly a thought. She loved that little girl with a passion and could not bear it if she was stopped from having regular contact with her. Surely Vinny would not be that petty, would he?

Vinny sat down on the edge of his son's bed. Had it not been for his mother disowning him, he would have probably given Little Vinny the hiding of his life, but the events of the past twenty-four hours had given him food for thought.

'Can we have a chat, boy? I'm not angry with you for running away. I'm just sick of us arguing, if you want the truth.'

Little Vinny sat up with a sulky expression on his face. 'Why did you have to spoil things with me and Shaz? I really liked her.'

'Vin, you can't go around lying to birds about your age. It's not morally right. Did you have sex with Shaz?'

Little Vinny nodded.

'Well, I hope you had the brains to put something on the end of it.'

'Shaz said she was on the pill.'

Vinny sighed. 'Birds are liars, son. You can never trust what they say. In future, you always use something whether they tell you they're on the pill or not, you get me? Young girls these days just wanna get a council flat or house, and they trap the likes of you to get them up the spout. You don't wanna be a dad yet, do you?'

Furiously biting his nails, Little Vinny shook his head. 'Don't matter now 'cause Shaz hates me anyway.'

'No, she don't. She was probably just taken aback by finding out your real age. I didn't know you'd lied to her, did I? Anyway, there's plenty more fish in the sea.'

'But I don't want another girl, I want Shaz back. Can I go and see her today, Dad, please?'

Vinny ruffled his son's hair. 'I don't think that's a good idea, boy. Never mug yourself off with a bird. I learned that the hard way when I weren't much older than you. Anyway, you're not allowed out for a while. I want you to work hard at the club and prove to me I can trust you again. Once you've done that, I'll put you on a proper weekly wage. I was thinking fifty quid. How does that grab you?'

Little Vinny managed a smile. 'That sounds cool, Dad.'

The boy walked out of the young offender's institution and was led by staff towards the waiting car. 'In you get, love. And don't forget what I told you earlier. You be a good boy from now on, because we don't want to see you back here again, OK?'

The boy nodded, then smiled. Having served three years for stabbing a fellow pupil, he had no intention of returning to this shithole, ever.

As the car pulled away, the boy stared out of the window. If there was one person to blame for everything that had gone wrong in his life, that person was Vinny Butler.

'You OK, son? What you thinking about?' the driver asked.

The boy did not reply. He could hardly say the word payback, could he now?

# CHAPTER TWENTY-FOUR

At five a.m. on the day he was meant to arrest Vinny, Christopher Walker woke up in a sweat. He'd had the most horrendous nightmare about being sacked from the police force, and he knew it must be a sign from God.

Knowing he could not go through with the task of arresting Vinny without proper back-up, Christopher searched through his pockets to find the number Ahmed had given him the previous day in case of an emergency. He stared at it for ages before putting it on his bedside cabinet. It was far too early to ring the Turk, and he needed to think about what he was going to say to him first.

Burak Zane was in a deep sleep when the phone rang. He answered it groggily. 'What's up?'

'Is Ahmed there?'

'No. Who is this?'

Ahmed had told him that the number he had given him belonged to his cousin's restaurant, so Christopher had no option but to leave a message. 'You need to tell Ahmed today is a no go. Tell him to page me.'

When Burak began to abuse him by calling him every

name under the sun, Christopher slammed the phone down.

Ahmed had chosen his wife Anna purposely. She was plain, grateful, let him lead his own life and was a superb mother to his children.

However, this morning Anna had woken with a headache, which had left Ahmed with the unusual task of tending to his children's needs. 'What does your mum usually give you for breakfast? Toast?'

'No, we like Sugar Puffs, Daddy.'

He was about to ask where the Sugar Puffs were kept when the phone rang. Ahmed's heart lurched as he heard what Burak had to say. 'Why the hell did you not tell Christopher I had him on tape, eh? I told you what to say if he rang up and tried to bottle it.'

'Don't be blaming me. As soon as I started to threaten the cunt, he put the phone down. This is all your fault, Ahmed. I told you to forget about the stupid drug bust. There are too many people involved who now know our business. I am not comfortable going ahead with this, not comfortable at all. If you want revenge, just give me the nod. If Vinny loses a child, especially the daughter he adores, this would be far better payback than him going to prison. You have no need to be involved. I can sort it with a click of my fingers.'

Ahmed sighed wearily. 'I need to think about our next move. I will get back to you within the hour.'

Joanna Preston was a bundle of nerves as she tried to decide what to wear for her parents' wedding. Worried about Vinny getting suspicious, she opted for shiny black leggings rather than a pretty dress. She then added a smart apple-green jacket with big shoulder pads and matching high-heeled shoes to tart up her outfit.

Vinny wolf-whistled as his girlfriend came down the stairs. He'd had a meeting with a top solicitor on Tuesday about his affray case at Eastbourne and had asked where he stood regarding Molly. The brief had told him not to worry about the affray case. He said he could get the charge watered down to threatening behaviour as long as Vinny pleaded guilty, and his punishment would be no more than a small fine. The situation regarding Molly was far more complex. His brief reckoned he had no chance of gaining parental custody unless he could prove Joanna was a bad mother, which of course he could not. So for the time being at least he had no option but to go on with the charade.

'Bit done up for shopping, ain't you, babe? Glad I'm not a bird. Sod trotting about in them high heels all day.'

Even though she felt nervous, Joanna knew she daren't let it show else Vinny would cotton on to her deceit. Giggling as if she didn't have a care in the world, she threw her arms around his neck. 'Well, Nancy's getting dolled up too. We're going to Bond Street, so we can't be dressed like tramps. Then we're going to eat at a posh restaurant. I love my hair being blonde again, Vin. Thanks so much for paying for me to go to the hairdressers, and for the money to go out today.'

Grinning, Vinny released Joanna's arms from around his neck and pulled a wad of money out of his pocket. He had met up with Ahmed yesterday and things were looking much brighter now they had changed dealer. He peeled off two hundred quid. ''Ere, take this as well. I can't have you not treating yourself to something nice if you're going up Bond Street, can I?'

Panicking at the thought of explaining why she'd come home with no shopping bags, Joanna pushed her partner's hand away. 'You've given me more than enough already.

Besides, we're only planning on a bit of window shopping. We're mainly going up the West End for lunch.'

Joanna was wearing a tight-fitting black top under her jacket, so Vinny stuffed the money down her cleavage. 'Babe, I insist. Now, sod off, else you'll be late meeting Nancy.'

Vivian Harris loved a good detective series. She liked to guess who the baddies were, and nine times out of ten she'd guess right.

*Shoestring* starring Trevor Eve was Vivian's latest guilty pleasure, and she was thoroughly enjoying the latest episode until her TV screen went blank. The video recorder had been her fiftieth birthday present from Vinny, and as she struggled to eject the cassette, she was fuming to see the useless machine had chewed the tape up. That was the third cassette it had mullered in the past few weeks.

Absolutely livid, she ripped the plug out, lifted the machine up and carried it out to the back garden. She wanted no reminders of her nephew in her house. Why would she, after what he had done. 'Load of old crap,' Vivian yelled, as she smashed the video recorder repeatedly against the concrete.

Queenie happened to be out in her garden hanging her washing out when she heard the commotion. She dropped her washing basket, ran through her house, out the front door and let herself in Viv's with her own key. 'Come on, Viv. Let's go inside,' Queenie urged.

But Vivian was now on a mission and not about to be deterred. 'Rubbish! Rubbish! Fucking useless old tut,' she shrieked, as she continued to smash the life out of the video recorder.

'Everything OK?' Mouthy Maureen asked, leaning over the fence.

'Why don't you fuck off, you interfering fat cow,' Queenie yelled, as she finally managed to wrestle the mangled video recorder out of her sister's grasp.

'Charming, I must say. I was only trying to help,' Mouthy Maureen said as she stormed back indoors.

Vivian chuckled as Queenie dragged her up the garden path. 'I ain't gone off me head again, if that's what you think. That bastard machine ripped my *Shoestring* up.'

Joanna met Nancy at Barking station as previously arranged. 'Oh my God! We look like twins,' Jo exclaimed. They had not discussed what they were going to wear and Nancy was kitted out in an almost identical outfit, except her jacket and shoes were turquoise.

'We are. We're the terrible twins,' Nancy chuckled. 'Well, did Vinny suspect anything?'

'No, I don't think so. Trouble is, he's given me a wad of money to spend in Bond Street, and I have no idea how I'm going to explain coming home with no shopping bags. What about Michael?'

'No bother there. He went out before me this morning. His dad wanted to go back to Ipswich. I think Albie had the hump with him for making up with Vinny.'

Joanna was astounded, but also quite pleased. 'I didn't know they'd made up. Vinny never said. When did this happen?'

'Earlier in the week, apparently. I didn't know either until Albie told me last night that they'd called a truce. Even Queenie has disowned Vinny now, so that says it all really, doesn't it?'

'Has she? Vinny never told me that either.'

With the traffic light red, Nancy put her handbrake on and squeezed her friend's hand. 'You have to leave him, Jo. For Molly's sake if nothing else. He's no good.'

Joanna snatched her hand away. 'Vinny is a great dad to Molly, and we've got our relationship back on track. We had the most amazing sex the other night and Vinny told me how much he loved me. He's been so different since what happened to Lenny came out in the open. I know what he did was wrong, but I think keeping it to himself was a massive weight on his mind. He even told me that he's glad Michael told his mum.'

Knowing if she argued the point it would be like smashing her head against a brick wall, a disappointed Nancy turned the volume of the radio up. George Benson was crooning 'Give Me the Night'. 'I love this song, Jo. Let's forget about our men today, have a singalong and just enjoy ourselves, eh?'

Joanna grinned. 'That sounds like a great idea.'

Vinny Butler was a big believer that it was a mother's duty to look after the kids. However, he and Molly were having some quality time alone together. His daughter took after him for loving Marmite and they were currently huddled up on the sofa scoffing Marmite soldiers and watching *Sesame Street* on the video recorder. 'Daddy, look at Big Bird,' Molly shrieked excitedly.

When the phone rang, Vinny leaned across his daughter to answer it. 'Dad, you need to come to the club quickly. The cellar's flooded. It's in a right old mess. I think it's the washing machine.'

Little Vinny had been good as gold since their father-and-son chat the other morning. The offer of a proper wage seemed to have worked wonders. 'See if you can get hold of Michael, boy. I'm looking after Molly.'

'I've already tried, Dad, but there was no answer.'

Vinny sighed. 'OK. I'll be there in ten.'

Johnny Preston cried as he wrapped his arms around his beautiful daughter.

'Dad, stop it! You're embarrassing me,' Joanna urged, even though she was crying herself.

Johnny chuckled, wiped his eyes with the cuff of his suit, and stood back to look at her properly. He had seen some recent photos of Jo, but nothing beat seeing her in the flesh. 'Wow, look at you. Can't believe my baby girl is all grown up. You look like a model.'

Feeling herself blush as every guest was staring their way, Joanna playfully punched her father's arm. 'Stop it, Dad. No, I don't.'

Deborah and Nancy were standing side by side watching the tear-jerker of a reunion. 'How's that bastard treating her?' Deborah whispered in Nancy's ear.

Joanna had already warned her on the journey not to say anything about Vinny, so rather than betray her friend, Nancy smiled politely. 'She seems happy enough at the moment, Deborah.'

'Really? Well, I bet that won't last long. That bastard is evil, and the quicker my Jo wakes up and smells the coffee, the more sleep I will get at night.'

The boy was lurking in a nearby doorway. He had just seen Vinny Butler pull up in his posh motor and dash inside the club with what he presumed to be his daughter in his arms.

Grinning as he remembered the time he scratched 'cunt' down one side of Vinny's car with a key and 'wanker' down the other, the boy took a swig of his cider. He would up his game now he was older and wiser, that was for sure.

The boy took another swig of cider and scowled at the old man who was looking at him. 'What you staring at, you nosy old fucker? Wanna photo, do ya?'

Mr Arthur tutted, then carried on walking. He wondered what the world was coming to these days. Had he fought in the war and lost so many friends for the likes of that surly teenager?

The boy plastered on a grin as the old man glanced back at him, but the moment the old git looked away his shoulders slumped and he put his head in his hands. It was painful, coming back to this place after everything that had happened. Just the sight of the club brought back Mark's cries of agony as he was being burnt to a cinder that night of the fire. And it hadn't even been Mark's idea to set light to Vinny's gaff, it had been his.

The boy looked up to the sky. 'I will get revenge for you, Mark. Hand on heart, I fucking promise you that.'

Relieved that her sister had not gone off her rocker again, Queenie was stood next to Vivian in the local TV rental shop. Most of their neighbours rented their televisions, and Vivian had decided she wanted to rent a new video recorder.

'This is our latest model and it is very popular,' said the salesman.

Vivian turned to her sister with a look of contempt on her face. 'What'd he say?'

Queenie wanted to laugh, but somehow managed to stop herself. The poor sales assistant not only had a strange face but a bad speech impediment to go with it. 'He said it's their latest model, Viv.'

'Oh right. Can you come and fix it up to my TV?' Vivian asked the man.

'Yes, of course. When would you like me to install it?'

When Vivian turned to her for the second time to ask what the poor man had said, Queenie put her hand over her sister's mouth and dragged her out of the shop.

After half an hour of trying to mop up the worst of the water, a disgruntled Vinny walked back into the club area. Edna his cleaner did any washing that needed doing at the club and this was the second time that poxy machine had caused a flood in the past year. Tomorrow, he would buy a new one and get a decent plumber to fit it this time. 'Vin, Molly, where are you?'

Spotting his son lying flat on his back on one of his leather sofas, Vinny ran towards him and shook him violently. 'Where's Molly?'

Little Vinny rubbed his eyes and sat up. 'She's 'ere somewhere, Dad. Sorry, I must have dozed off.'

Feeling the panic rising, Vinny yelled his daughter's name repeatedly, then told his son to look in the club while he searched upstairs. 'Molly, where are you?' he shrieked, as he took the stairs two by two.

Searching everywhere he could think of and finding no sign of Molly, Vinny ran down the stairs. 'You found her, Vin?' he shouted.

Little Vinny looked ashen-faced. 'No, Dad. I can't see her anywhere. I'm so sorry for falling asleep, but I was knackered. Molly was playing with her doll next to me before I dozed off.'

With a gut-wrenching ache like the one he'd experienced the night Lenny died, Vinny ran towards the entrance of the club. The door that he was positive he'd closed as he rushed in earlier was now wide open. Vinny felt as though his heart was about to pack up as he ran into the street. His daughter was the most important person in his life. She was his little angel whose smile lit up the dullest of days. 'Molly, Molly, Molly!' he screamed.

Receiving no reply, he stopped a passerby. 'Have you seen a little blonde girl? My daughter's gone missing.'

'No, sorry. I haven't.'

Feeling bile rise in his mouth, Vinny vomited into the gutter before setting off at a run down the Whitechapel Road, yelling his daughter's name over and over.

*

Unaware that her daughter was currently on the missing list, Joanna was knocking back the champagne and thoroughly enjoying herself. 'I'm having such a good time, Nance. To watch your parents get married is truly something special. So lovely to see my dad again, and I can't believe how much Johnny Junior has grown up. Me and my brother was never that close when we were young, but I feel we will stay in contact now.'

Nancy sighed. Joanna was not a big drinker as a rule and the champagne seemed to have knocked her sideways. 'We should be going soon, Jo. You know what Vinny is like and if you arrive home drunk, he will go mental.'

'Aww, but I really don't want to go yet. Let's stay for another hour or two, Nance? This might be the last chance I have to spend some quality time with my mum, dad and brother, and there's no other family members here to celebrate with them.'

'Aren't your grandparents here?'

'No. My mum's parents don't like Dad, and my dad hasn't spoken to Grandma Shirley since they fell out over Auntie Judy. Please can we stay?'

Wondering if Joanna had taken leave of her senses, Nancy reminded her friend of the conversation they'd had when they pulled up in the car park earlier. 'Jo, I need to pick the boys up from school, and you said you had to be home early because Vinny has to go out somewhere.'

Joanna giggled. 'Sod Vinny. Can't you ask your mum to pick the boys up, Nance? Please, pretty please?'

Nancy smiled. She would do anything to get her best friend away from that sadistic bastard Vinny, and if that meant bringing her home late, then so be it. 'OK, Jo. I'll ring my mum now.'

Back in Whitechapel, Queenie and Vivian were both on the sherry. Today had been the first day since the truth had come out about Lenny's death that either woman had properly smiled. 'That poor man's face in the shop was a picture, Viv. You are a case.'

Vivian chuckled. 'Not as much of a picture as when you called Mouthy Maureen an interfering fat cow. I was so busy smashing up that video recorder, I never even heard what she said back to you.'

'Can't remember – I was too busy trying to get you back indoors. Why did you smash that up, Viv? Was it really because it had ripped up *Shoestring*? Or was it because Vinny bought it for you?'

Her face turning serious again, Vivian shrugged. 'Bit of both, I suppose. I know we've had a laugh today, Queen, but I need to ask you a favour.'

'What?'

'I want a new headstone for my Lenny. No way can I go to visit him again with Vinny's name plastered across the one we've got.'

Queenie clasped her sister's hand. Vinny was her first born, had always been her number one son, and she would miss him terribly. However, backing Vivian was the correct and morally right thing to do. 'OK, I'll speak to my Michael. He'll sort a new headstone out for you.'

Michael Butler was stunned to see police swarming like flies outside his club. They had even blocked the road off, so Michael parked along the main road and ran round the corner.

When he tried to get near the entrance of the club, an officer blocked his way. 'You can't go in there, sir. The premises are currently being searched.'

Michael's heart skipped a beat. Even though Vinny had always denied it, Michael had known deep down that his brother was involved with drugs, and if anything was found inside the club, Michael would disown the bastard just like his mother had.

'Look, I'm part-owner of this club. Do you mind telling me what the hell is going on? Is my brother Vinny inside?'

Aware that there were more and more gawping onlookers arriving at the scene, the officer led Michael to one side. 'I'm sorry to be the bearer of bad news, but your niece has gone missing. However, I want to reassure you that we are doing everything in our power to find Molly.'

Feeling as though his legs were about to buckle, Michael sank to his haunches. 'Oh no. Not Molly,' he mumbled.

Queenie Butler was thrilled that her sister had her appetite back. Vivian had just scoffed two bowls of her homemade bread-and-butter pudding with clotted cream. 'Bleedin' sirens is all I've heard this past hour. Something bad has happened. Probably another armed robbery,' Queenie remarked.

'Not safe to go out the door these days. Gone downhill terribly has the East End. Not like the old days when we used to leave our front doors open. Some bastard would rob and murder us in our home if we did that now,' Vivian reminisced, her voice heavy with bitterness.

Queenie was prevented from climbing onto her own soapbox by the frantic ringing of the doorbell. 'All right, all right, I'm coming,' she yelled as she marched up the hallway. Why could people not settle for ringing the bell once? Did they think she was deaf?

Nosy Hilda was that out of breath, she could barely get her words out. 'Thank God you're in,' she panted.

'Whatever's the matter?' Queenie asked. Her heart then nearly stopped when a police car pulled up outside her house. The sirens. Surely not another of her sons had been shot?

Nosy Hilda did love to be the first to spread news, whether it be good or bad. 'It's your Molly. She's gone missing.'

# CHAPTER TWENTY-FIVE

Little Vinny sat with his head bowed as he answered the policeman's questions. 'I honestly don't know how long I was asleep for. Not long, I don't think. It could have been five minutes or ten. I swear to you though, before I laid down, Molly was sitting opposite me playing with her doll.'

Unable to control his emotions any longer, a distraught Vinny smashed his fist against the wall. His daughter had been missing for over an hour now, it was lashing it down with rain outside, so why wasn't everybody out on the streets looking for her? The club had been searched thoroughly by the Old Bill and there was no sign of Molly or her doll. 'We ain't gonna find my little girl unless we search for her, are we? Some fucking nonce might have grabbed her, so best you mob get your arses in gear,' Vinny yelled at the copper who was speaking to his son.

Michael laid a hand on his arm. 'Calm down, bruv. The section sergeant has just turned up and he's organizing a search for Molly as we speak. The police are doing all they can, honest they are.'

'Well, I'm gonna search for her too. No way I can sit here any longer, it's doing my fucking nut in. What am I meant to say to Jo, eh? That I let my retard of a son keep an eye on Molly for less than half an hour and she disappeared into thin air? I can't believe this has happened. I keep pinching myself to make sure it isn't a bad dream. I swear, Michael, if one hair on that child's head has been harmed, I will kill whoever is responsible. I don't care if I get fucking life for it. I love that little girl. She is my world.'

Aware of the look of distress in his brother's eyes, Michael gave him a comforting hug. He could imagine the anguish Vinny must be going through. Molly was a little darling and Michael felt sick at the thought of her disappearance. It really was every parent's worst nightmare.

Queenie Butler's hand trembled as she took a sip of brandy. Her house was only a short walk from her sons' club, and the two police officers had just had a quick search to check that Molly had not toddled out of the club to her nan's house or garden without Queenie's knowledge.

Vivian, who was as white as a sheet, knocked back her own brandy in one gulp. Even though she now despised Vinny, she loved that little girl. Molly was a real character and if she would have ever been blessed with a daughter, she'd have wanted one just like her. 'They'll find her, Queen. She can't have gone far,' Viv said, squeezing her sister's hand. The officers had already informed her that it was suspected the front door of the club had accidentally been left open.

The female officer glanced at her male colleague. Like most local coppers, they knew all about the Butler family and what they stood for. Nevertheless, with a three-year-old child missing, finding her was all that mattered.

PC Denning took a notebook out of her pocket. 'I know this is a difficult time for you both, but I need to ask you some questions. Obviously, Molly is our only concern right now, and our aim is to find her as quickly as possible.'

When her sister began to weep, Vivian held Queenie close

to her chest, then gave the policewoman a nod. 'Fire away. We just want Molly back here where she belongs.'

PC Denning sat on the armchair opposite the two distraught women. 'Please don't be alarmed, these are just routine questions, but I have to ask whether there is anybody you can think of who might hold a grudge against Vinny and therefore snatch Molly?'

Queenie dabbed her eyes with a tissue and took a deep breath. Her motto in life had always been to tell the Old Bill as little as possible, but with her beautiful granddaughter missing, she had no alternative other than to spill her guts. 'Johnny Preston. Only just got out of nick and he has every reason to snatch that child. Molly is his grandkid and he isn't allowed to see her. He also has a massive grudge against Vinny. Tried to shoot him once, which is why he got banged up for years. Silly sod was so pissed that he shot my poor Roy instead.'

Hopeful that Molly was with Johnny, in which case she would be found safe and sound, Vivian decided to add her two penn'orth: 'Queenie's right. Seems a bit of a coincidence that Preston comes out of nick then Molly goes missing. Molly's mum, Joanna, is Preston's daughter. But Jo can't be in on it. That poor girl must be beside herself, bless her heart.'

With his colleague furiously writing down notes, the male officer asked Queenie if Joanna and Vinny's relationship was a happy one, and whether Joanna was on good terms with her father.

'My Vinny has his faults, and I doubt he's an easy man to live with. That said, Jo has never seemed unhappy to me. They've had their ups and downs, like any couple, but Vinny is a very generous man, and neither Jo nor Molly go without. He's a brilliant dad to that little girl. As for Johnny Preston, I'm not sure if Joanna is in contact with him or not. I know last weekend my Vinny was proper paranoid that she had met up with her dad, but she hadn't. She was out with my daughter-in-law, Nancy.'

'That's all helpful information, Mrs Butler. Now, is there anybody else you can think of who might hold a grudge against Vinny? Or have reason to snatch Molly?'

'No, not off hand. Can you think of anyone, Viv?' Queenie asked her sister.

Vivian could, but decided to keep schtum in front of the police. If she spouted her mouth off, it would open up a massive can of worms.

When her sister saw the police out, Queenie poured herself another brandy. All she could picture was Molly's angelic little face. 'Please God make that dear child be found safe,' she mumbled.

Vivian walked back into the lounge. 'I didn't want to say anything in front of the Old Bill, but you don't think Molly's disappearance has anything to do with that Ahmed, do you? I've never trusted that shifty-looking bastard, and I find it really strange he has stayed pals with a man who left him to die.'

'I don't know, Viv, but if anything has happened to that child I swear it will be the end of me,' Queenie wept.

Vivian put her arms around Queenie. 'Take no notice of my silly theories. You know I watch too many of those detective programmes. What's the betting Molly's just wandered off somewhere?'

'Well, I can't just sit here doing nothing, Viv. I need to go to the club to find out exactly what's going on. I know I said I wanted no more to do with Vinny, and I meant it. But he must be in pieces, and I can't blank him while Molly is missing. As a family, we need to pull together to find her.'

Vivian nodded understandingly. 'OK. Let's both go to the club.'

*

Since Joanna was a bit tipsy, Nancy decided to drive her all the way home rather than drop her off at Barking station.

'Wake up sleepy-head. We're nearly there,' Nancy said.

Having slept the whole journey on the back seat of her pal's Ford Fiesta, Joanna sat up and opened the window to get some air. 'What's the time?' she asked anxiously.

'Twenty past four, so you're not that late. You'll be home by half past. Have you sobered up now?'

'Yeah, I think so. I feel better than I did. I wish I wasn't late though. Vinny's going to have the right hump.'

Nancy chuckled. 'Well, I did try to tell you that, but you weren't having none of it.'

'You best not drop me right outside my house, Nance. I don't want Vinny getting suspicious. I told him we were going up town by train.'

'OK. I'll drive past yours and drop you on the corner.'

'Turn the radio up, Nance. I love this song,' Joanna urged.

Singing along happily to Shalamar's 'I Owe You One', Joanna ducked her head when Nancy turned into the road where she lived. Vinny was such a bloody control freak, she wouldn't put it past him to be standing at the front door watching out for her.

'Oh my God! Jo, I think the Old Bill are raiding your house.'

'What! Stop winding me up.'

'I'm not, I swear. There's three police cars outside yours, and the front door is wide open. I'm parking up and coming inside with you.'

'But say Vinny realizes we haven't been up town?'

'By the looks of it, Vinny is going to have far more explaining to do than you, Jo.'

Joanna could barely breathe as she ran towards the house. As far as she knew, Vinny did not keep anything incriminating inside. 'What's going on? Where's Vinny and Molly?'

she asked the two policemen who were standing guard outside her front door.

'Are you Joanna Preston?' one of the officers asked.

'Yes. What's going on? I live in this house,' Joanna said, her voice quivering with panic.

'Come inside then, love. Is this your friend?'

'Nancy is sort of my sister-in-law. Please tell me what's happening?'

The police officer led Joanna and Nancy inside. 'The mother's here, boss,' he informed a colleague.

Joanna looked past the policemen and saw Vinny. Registering the pain etched on his face, she cried, 'Where's Molly? What's happened?'

Vinny stood up, walked over to Joanna and wept as he put his arms around her. 'I don't know, Jo. Molly's gone missing.'

Pummelling her fists against her partner's chest, Joanna let out a deafening scream. 'How? When? Not my angel! Not my beautiful angel! I want my baby. I want my Molly,' she cried, sinking to her knees.

Feeling sick to the stomach, Nancy glared at Vinny before kneeling to comfort her pal. 'Molly will be OK, Jo. The police will find her. That's their job. She'll be fine. I know she will.'

Back at the club, Michael hugged his mum and then his aunt. 'Please tell me they've found Molly,' Queenie begged.

'No, they haven't yet. But the dog section are currently out searching for her. She can't have gone far, Mum. Let me get you both a drink. I could do with one myself.'

Queenie and Vivian sat down at a nearby table. Vivian turned her chair so her back was facing the stage. That was where her Lenny had spent so many hours DJ-ing and she could not bear to be reminded of her loss.

Michael poured three brandies, then sat down between his mother and aunt. There was still a police presence inside and outside the club, but most of the officers had departed to join the search to find Molly.

'Where's Vinny?' Queenie asked.

'At his house. The police wanted to search it.'

'Is Jo with him?' Vivian enquired.

'Not as far as I know. I don't even think Jo is aware Molly is missing yet. Her and Nancy went out for the day.'

'Oh that poor girl, what a shock she's in for when she gets home. What exactly happened? The police said something about the main door being left open,' Queenie said.

Michael sighed. 'Vinny was at home with Molly, but there was a flood in the cellar, so he had to bring her to the club with him. He was in the cellar when Molly went missing. Little Vinny was meant to be looking after her, but the fucking idiot fell asleep. The main door was wide open, so Molly either toddled outside or some bastard came in and snatched her.'

'Well, funny you should say that. The police questioned me and your mum. They asked if anybody has a grudge against Vinny, so we gave them Johnny Preston's name. I wouldn't put anything past that bastard after what he did to poor Roy,' Vivian told her nephew.

Michael shrugged. 'I can't see it being Johnny. Not only would his parole be revoked if he got caught, but I can't believe he'd put his daughter through all that trauma.'

Looking around to make sure the Old Bill weren't within earshot, Queenie leaned towards her son. 'What about, Ahmed? He must have an axe to grind after everything that has happened?' she whispered.

'Mum, it has to be some sick bastard to snatch a child. Let's just hope that Molly is playing hide and seek in someone's back garden, eh? Are there still loads of people outside?'

'Looked to be about forty or fifty. The police were telling them to go home. I saw that old bat Mad Freda stood amongst them. I bet she's loving this latest drama,' Queenie spat.

Michael looked at his mother and shook his head. As much as he loved her, she had some strange ways at times. 'I doubt anybody is going to be happy that a beautiful three-year-old girl has gone missing, Mum. Look, I'm sick of sitting here speculating. I'm gonna pop around Vinny's to see if he's OK. I think you should come too, but don't be coming out with any more of your theories, please. Bren needs to be told an' all.'

Unable to stop herself, Queenie broke down in tears once again. The thought of her precious granddaughter alone out there in this vicious world was tearing her heart to shreds. 'I'll ring your sister later. Can't be dealing with her dramatics right now. She'll be more of a hindrance than a help. How could Little Vinny have fallen asleep, eh? Poor Molly could be anywhere. Might even have been picked up by one of them child molesters. There's loads living round here, you know. Big Stan said one flashed his dingle-dangle at his grandson in the public toilets last week.'

Michael put an arm around his mother and kissed her on the forehead. 'Look, I know you're upset, we all are. But as a family, we need to stay positive. Molly's only been missing a couple of hours. I'm going round Vin's. You coming with me?'

Queenie nodded. 'You coming too, Viv?'

Vivian clasped her sister's hand. Whatever she thought of Vinny had to be put to one side for now. Queenie had been her rock ever since Lenny had died and now it was her turn to be there for her sister. 'Of course I'm coming with ya.'

*

Back at Vinny's house, a hysterical Joanna flew at Little Vinny as he sauntered into the lounge. 'How could you not look after Molly properly? How could you fall asleep and leave my baby all alone?' she shrieked, slapping the lad around the head.

Vinny leapt up and grabbed hold of Joanna. He knew she must have been drinking quite heavily earlier as he had smelt it on her breath, and she had since had a couple of large brandies. 'Leave it, babe. I'll deal with him later. Nancy, can you take Jo upstairs and calm her down, please? And do not pour her any more drinks. She obviously had enough when she was out with you.'

Little Vinny put his hands over his face and crouched down. 'I am so sorry. I didn't mean to doze off, but I haven't been sleeping well 'cause I kept thinking of Shazza.'

Vinny looked at the officer who was stood in the hallway. 'You don't need to speak to him any more at the moment, do you?' he asked, pointing at his distressed son.

'No, Mr Butler.'

Vinny took a twenty-pound note out of his pocket and handed it to his offspring. 'Go and visit your mates, or Shazza, or whoever you want. Just make yourself scarce.'

'But I need to know if my little sister's OK. I feel terrible,' Little Vinny wept.

Vinny marched his son into the kitchen. 'Look, I know you never meant to fall asleep, but the fact is you did, boy, and now Molly is missing because of that. Just take the money and get out of the house for a bit, please. I need to calm Jo down and that ain't gonna happen while you're here.'

Snatching the money out of his father's hand, a distraught-looking Little Vinny bolted out of the front door.

Over in Ilford, Christopher Walker was just preparing to leave the station when his pager bleeped. The message read:

WILL CALL YOU TOMORROW TO ARRANGE A MEET. IF YOU MESS ME AROUND AGAIN, YOU WILL REGRET IT.

Pent up with frustration, Christopher slammed the pager against his desk. This shitty situation he found himself in was affecting his whole life, and the quicker he arrested Vinny Butler and got Ahmed off his case, the fucking better.

Ahmed Zane walked into Vinny's lounge and gave the man he had once trusted a brotherly hug. 'I have only just heard. I am so sorry, my friend. Try to think positive, though. Molly is a survivor just like her dad.'

Unable to stop himself, Vinny flew into a rage. 'But she's only fucking three! It petrifies me to think of her out there all alone. Say she wandered outside the club and some fucking paedo grabbed hold of her, eh? I swear to God, I would kill for that child. If I find out one finger has been laid on her, I will find the cunt responsible and rip their fucking heart out with my bare hands.'

Seeing the Old Bill exchanging awkward glances, Ahmed led Vinny out into the kitchen. 'Where is Jo?' he asked.

'Upstairs with Nancy. She's in pieces, we all are. I blame myself, I really do. If only I hadn't left Molly alone with Little Vinny, none of this would have happened.'

Ahmed felt a sudden urge to laugh, but quickly composed himself. 'You cannot blame yourself. Your son is not six, he is fourteen years old and should be more than capable of keeping an eye on his sister. I used to look after my younger siblings back in Turkey while my mamma went out to work, and I was much younger than him. Where is Little Vinny, by the way?'

'I fucked him off out of it. I can't even bear to look at him, truth be known. I will never be able to forgive him if any harm has come to Molly, I know I won't.'

When Vinny suddenly broke down in tears, Ahmed played the good friend and offered him a geezer-type hug. He had a smirk on his face as he did so though. This was after all the cunt who had left him for dead.

# CHAPTER TWENTY-SIX

As darkness beckoned and the rain became even more torrential, Vinny was informed that the CID had been called in to help solve Molly's disappearance. The dog section had found no trace of the child in nearby properties, gardens, garages and sheds, so bringing in CID was the next step, the officer explained.

Vinny sat on the step in the garden and lit up a cigarette. His daughter's toys were scattered across the grass, and the thought of Molly never playing with them again made Vinny want to spew his guts up.

Ahmed had just popped out to a phonebox to cancel tonight's business deal. The ten kilos of cocaine they had been due to pick up off Richie Simpson was the least of Vinny's worries now. Perhaps God was paying him back for dealing in poxy drugs? Vinny stared up at the darkening sky and made a bargain with the big man above. 'Please help me find my daughter. I'm sorry I have done some bad things in my time, but please don't take it out on that little girl. I'll never do another wrong thing in all my living days, if you help me find Molly, I promise.'

The unmistakable sound of his mother's voice snapped Vinny out of his trance. He really needed his mum right now, and he had known deep in his heart that she would be there for him.

Queenie had just put the kettle on to make the police officers a cup of tea when Vinny walked into the kitchen. Clocking the look of despair in her first-born's eyes, Queenie did what any mother would do and hugged him to her chest. 'We've just been talking to all the locals who've turned up at the club. Honest, Vin, you should see the crowd that's congregated outside, there must be well over two hundred of them. And now it's getting dark, they're sorting out torches for everyone so they can join in the search for Molly. You must keep your chin up, because I am sure with so many people looking, she will soon be found, boy.'

'I hope so, Mum, I really do. Thanks for coming round, and you, Auntie Viv.'

When Vivian did not reply, Michael spoke instead. 'Are Jo and Nancy not back yet?' he asked his brother.

'They're both upstairs.'

When Michael dashed up the stairs, Vivian followed him. As much as she adored Molly and prayed that the child would be found safe and sound, no way could she look at or offer comfort to Vinny. After what that heartless bastard had put her through, why the hell should she?

Having an astute eye for a pretty young woman, Ahmed smiled at the blonde who was patiently waiting to use the phone. He had spent the past five minutes discussing recent events and having a good old laugh with his cousin, but now it was time to end the call: 'Look, I have to go. Somebody is waiting to use the phone. I will try to call you again later, but if I can't, it will be tomorrow. We don't want to arouse suspicion, do we?'

Burak chuckled. 'Good luck playing the concerned friend.'

Ahmed smirked. 'I really should have been an actor, you know.'

The blonde smiled as Ahmed told her he had another call to make, but would allow her to use the phone first. 'Would you keep an eye on my pushchair for me, please? I'm taking my daughter in the phonebox with me. Some little girl has gone missing around here today and I'm not letting my Sophie out of my sight.'

Birds loved a sob story, so Ahmed explained how it was his friend's daughter who had gone missing and how upset he was.

'Oh my God! That's awful. My boyfriend comes out of prison next week, and I can't wait. There's so much crime around here lately, I don't feel safe walking the streets with Sophie on my own any more. My John would never allow anything bad to happen to us.'

Realizing the dumb tart was obviously loved up and he had no chance of shagging her, Ahmed urged her to hurry up and make her call.

Five minutes later, he made his second phonecall. 'It's me. Things have not gone to plan, so we have to cancel this evening. My cousin will be with you in the next hour to pick the stuff up.'

'What about my dosh? You are still paying me this weekend, aren't you?'

'No can do, unfortunately. You know the score. The balance of what you are owed will be paid in full once the job is finished,' Ahmed replied.

'But you said that I would be paid in full by Saturday at the latest. You promised. I've already booked my ticket to Spain next week.'

'Well, I'm afraid I can't pay you. Not my fault there has been a hitch,' Ahmed explained.

Carl Thompson aka Richie Simpson slammed down the

phone in disgust. He was not a happy man. In fact, he was fucking livid.

Back at Vinny's house, Vivian and Nancy were doing their best to comfort Joanna. The poor girl could not stop shaking, was crying constantly, and rocking to and fro with a teddy bear that belonged to Molly clutched tightly to her chest.

'Why did I leave her? If I hadn't left Molly today, she'd be here with me now. It's all my fault. I want her back. I want my baby,' Joanna screamed.

Nancy held her best friend and stroked her hair. 'You can't blame yourself. None of this is your fault, Jo.'

'It is. It's all my fault. If Molly doesn't come home, I want to die.'

'I think we should call the doctor. He can give Jo something to calm her down a bit,' Vivian suggested. The pain Joanna was currently going through was bringing back memories of Lenny's death, and although many parts of that dreadful time were still a blank, Vivian did remember the doctor turning up with some pills to help numb the pain.

In the years since she had been part of the Butler family, Nancy had suffered many a bad situation, but nothing compared to this. 'Jo, how about I call your mum and dad, eh? They will need to know Molly is missing and I am sure they would want to be here for you.'

Joanna flung herself face down on her daughter's bed. The bed was quite new, as Molly had been in a cot beforehand, but Joanna could clearly smell the scent of the child who she loved so much on the pillows. 'Noooo. You can't ring my mum and dad. Please don't tell them. Please don't,' she pleaded. 'Just not today.'

Queenie opened the bedroom door. 'Jo, you need to come

downstairs, love. Some officers from the CID have just arrived, and they want to ask you some questions. They also need you to let them have some recent photos of Molly. They're going to start doing house-to-house enquiries soon.'

'I can't talk to the police. I just want them to bring my baby back. Why haven't they found her yet? Why?' Joanna sobbed.

Queenie ordered her sister and Nancy to leave the room. For the past couple of hours, every time a police radio had crackled into life they'd all stopped what they were doing and held their breath, praying it would be a report that Molly had been found or that there'd been a sighting or some new development. The only one who hadn't fallen silent was Joanna, whose sobbing and crying had gone on non-stop as if she was too wrapped up in her own grief to think about anything else. Putting her arm around Jo, Queenie said gently, 'Now, I want you to listen to me, darling. I know what has happened today is awful and you must be going through hell, just like we all are. But you really need to pull yourself together now. Molly is missing, not dead, and we have a houseful of Old Bill who are doing their utmost to find her. It's almost dark outside and your daughter needs you to be strong. So you must stop wallowing in self-pity up here, get your arse downstairs and help the police find her. And you can start by sorting out some recent photos, OK?'

Taking a deep breath, Joanna sat up. 'OK. I'll be down in a minute.'

Little Vinny handed the crisp packet full of glue to Ben Bloggs. 'I'm gonna go and see Shazza in a bit. She won't talk to me on the phone. Every time I ring, her mum answers and says she's out.'

Ben Bloggs glanced at his pal but said nothing. For the

past half hour all Little Vinny had done was describe the sex he'd had with Shazza, and he seemed far more bothered about his bird than what had happened to poor Molly.

Little Vinny opened the third and last bottle of cider. 'Drink that,' he ordered Ben.

'I don't want no more. I don't feel too well.'

'You are coming to Dagenham with me, ain't ya?'

Ben shook his head. 'I feel drunk and out my nut. I need to go home, Vin.'

Hoping his pal wasn't going cold on him, Little Vinny put an arm around Ben's shoulders. 'Friends forever, yeah?'

Ben smiled. 'Yeah, friends forever.'

Vinny Butler squeezed Joanna's hand as she sat down on the sofa next to him. He'd been so out of his mind with worry since Molly went missing, he hadn't given the mother of his child a second thought.

The lounge was becoming fuller by the second, which was why DS Townsend from the CID had asked everybody to leave the room. He wanted to speak to the parents in private. The DS turned to Joanna first. 'Are you in contact with your father, Joanna?'

'What has that got to do with Molly going missing?'

'No, she isn't. Are you, babe?' Vinny said.

Joanna did not reply. She could feel a hot sweat coming on. Should she lie to the police to protect her relationship with the man she loved? Or should she just tell them the truth?

The DS cleared his throat. 'Obviously, when a child goes missing, we have to pursue every avenue of enquiry. Finding Molly is our only aim right now, and a police officer has already been to your parents' address, Joanna, and got no reply. We know that there is bad blood between your family and Vinny's, which is why I need you to be truthful and tell me if you have been in contact with your dad at all?'

'My dad has nothing to do with Molly's disappearance. He can't have,' Joanna assured the police officer.

'How can you be so sure?' Vinny asked.

Joanna knew her reply would probably spell the end of her relationship with Vinny, but for once she didn't care. All that mattered was being reunited with the beautiful little girl she had given birth to.

Snatching her hand away from Vinny's, Joanna stared DS Townsend straight in the eyes. 'My dad married my mum for the second time today, and they're staying in some posh hotel tonight. No way could my dad be involved because I was at the wedding. Ask Nancy if you don't believe me. We didn't leave the reception until gone three, and my dad was still there.'

Vinny would have liked to strangle his lying slut of a girlfriend there and then, but the presence of two CID officers made that impossible. So he stood up and put his foot straight through the glass coffee table instead.

Bobby Jackson was standing at the corner of the bar in the Blind Beggar with a pal and a silly grin on his face. The scar from where Vinny had bottled him was still very visible and a constant reminder of his hatred for the man.

The police had just been in, asking questions about Molly's disappearance and Bobby had spun them a yarn. He told them he'd seen a child matching Molly's description get into a blue car with a black man near the London Hospital earlier.

Micky Dunn shook his head in disbelief. He was well aware of the bad blood between Bobby and Vinny Butler, but he had a daughter the same age as Molly and reckoned that sending the Old Bill on some wild-goose chase was well and truly out of order. 'If you're lying, Bob, you are gonna have to come clean to the pigs. They'll nick you for wasting police time otherwise. Why don't you contact them tomorrow and admit you were pissed, eh? I know you hate Vinny, and you have every reason to, but you shouldn't take your grudge out on a three-year-old nipper. It ain't right, mate.'

Bobby turned to his pal and snarled, 'Yeah? And was it fucking right that that cunt Vinny made my father disappear off the face of the earth? You don't know what it's like to lose someone and never find out what happened to them. Broke my mum's heart and sent her doolally. She still wakes up every morning thinking my dad is gonna walk through the door. Obviously, I know my old man's dead, but no one knows where the body is. That's the worst part, not knowing where his remains are. At least if we knew, we could have a funeral for him. I have so many nightmares about the way he died and I bet he was tortured. Vinny Butler is too evil to have just put a bullet through this head. So, don't be lecturing me, Mick, on rights and wrongs. Vinny is now going through what me and my family has gone through for many years and I hope his cunting kid is never found. It's called payback.'

Micky Dunn shouted up another round. It was a well-known fact that Kenny Jackson had had his fair share of run-ins with Vinny Butler and had then mysteriously gone missing never to be seen again. Micky did feel for his pal, but part of him was beginning to wonder whether Bobby might have had something to do with that poor child's disappearance.

He knew Bobby had had a pop or two at Vinny in the past, like when Champ and Roy were buried and he sent a flower arrangement in the shape of a gun. He'd been on about getting his revenge ever since he came out of nick, but Micky had always thought it was just the drink talking.

Until now. Feeling a sick lurch in his stomach, he wondered if that was why Bobby had blown out work this morning. He'd claimed he had some important business to attend to, but when Micky had knocked at his door to see if he wanted to come down the boozer, Bobby's clothes had been covered in mud.

'What's up with you? Cat got your tongue?' Bobby asked, downing his Jack Daniel's in one greedy gulp.

'It weren't you, was it, Bob?' stammered Micky, his face a deathly shade of white.

Bobby Jackson shrugged. 'Weren't me what?'

'Who took Molly?'

Having been on a drunken high since late afternoon, Bobby Jackson burst out laughing. 'Yeah, I throttled the little brat, then buried her in a shallow grave. Now, what you having? It's my round.'

Queenie Butler marched towards home. As usual when she got the bit between her teeth, there was no stopping her.

'Queen, slow down for Christ's sake. I can't keep up with you in these shoes,' Vivian urged.

Turning to her sister, Queenie's face was a mask of pure hatred. 'I will never forgive Jo for this and I mean that, Viv. What a terrible liar she's turned out to be. No wonder Vinny went into one. She should have been indoors looking after her child, not out fraternizing with the fucking enemy. Molly wouldn't be missing then. Killed my son, that old man of hers did. My Roy's soul was dead for years before he finally shoved a bullet in his own brain.'

Vivian so wanted to remind her sister that Vinny was also a terrible liar and had drunkenly murdered her son, but she somehow managed to hold her tongue. With Molly still missing, this was neither the time nor the place.

*

Vinny Butler was sitting at a table in his club with a face like thunder. He had proper lost the plot with Joanna earlier, calling her every swear word he knew, and if it had not been for Michael and Ahmed dragging him out of the house, he would have probably been arrested for battering the lying whore.

'Shall I get us all another drink?' Nick asked. He part-owned the restaurant in Stratford with Vinny and Ahmed and had come to the club as soon as he heard the awful news.

The only other people present were the two Old Bill who had followed Vinny back to the club, the two constables who had been standing sentry on the door ever since Molly was first reported missing, and Pete and Paul the doormen.

Vinny put his weary head in his hands. He'd thought nothing could be worse than watching his brother blow his brains out in front of him, or looking in the back of the car he'd just wrecked and seeing his cousin's head hanging by a thread. But those traumas paled into insignificance compared with what he was going through now. He loved Molly more than he had ever loved a living soul. Only the love he felt for his mother even came close.

Suddenly he got to his feet. 'I can't sit here drinking no more. Let's go out and search for Molly ourselves. Come on, what are we waiting for?'

Little Vinny staggered up Shazza's path and knocked on the front door. He knew that somebody was in because he could hear ska music playing.

'Open the fucking door, Shaz. It's me, Vinny. We need to talk,' he yelled, kicking the door repeatedly with his right foot.

'Whatever is going on?' a lady asked, appearing from the house next door.

'Shaz is my girlfriend. I need to see her. We need to sort things out,' Little Vinny slurred.

Aware that the music had now been turned off, Little Vinny grinned as the front door was yanked open. He had a grey Nike tracksuit on and hoped that Shazza wouldn't be put off because he wasn't dressed like a skinhead. But when he looked up it was the skinhead he'd befriended on the train, the one who'd invited him to the party where he had first met Shaz.

'All right, Tim? Where's Shaz? I need to speak to her.'

Wearing only a dressing gown, Shazza appeared behind Tim's shoulder. 'Piss off and leave me alone, Vinny. I'm not interested in you any more. Me and Tim are an item now.'

Vinny smirked at Tim. 'You're kidding me, right?'

'No. Shaz ain't kidding you, mate. Now, will you please fuck off before the neighbours call the police? Go home and sober up, you muppet.'

Suddenly realizing that Tim was wearing nothing more than a pair of three-quarter-length jeans, and his button and zip were undone, Little Vinny went ballistic. 'You whore! You fucking slag!' he screamed. He then picked a stone up and lobbed it straight through the downstairs window.

'Leave it, Tim, please, leave it,' Shazza screamed, as her new boyfriend ran barefooted out into the street.

The next-door neighbour appeared again. 'It's OK, Sharon. I've already called the police, love.'

Hearing the word 'police', Little Vinny turned and ran away as fast as his legs would carry him. But as he ran he vowed that he would return and get even another time. No way was Tim or Shazza getting away with mugging him off. No fucking way.

# CHAPTER TWENTY-SEVEN

Vinny Butler tilted his head back and shut his eyes as the hot water rinsed the soap off his tired body. He, his brother, Ahmed, Nick, Peter and Paul had been joined by Big Stan and twenty-odd other local men in their search the previous evening, but had given up at three a.m. Searching for Molly in the dark, even with torches, was like looking for a needle in a haystack.

Hearing his brother calling him, Vinny turned the shower off and shouted, 'I'll be down in a minute.' Both he and Michael had stayed at the club last night. Neither had been impressed to discover that they'd been lied to by Joanna and Nancy. If the girls had said they were spending the day up town when they were actually in Johnny Preston's company, what else had the deceitful pair of bitches lied about in the past?

Vinny got himself dressed and checked out his reflection in the mirror. He had bags under his eyes, which was hardly surprising. How the hell was he meant to sleep when his little princess was missing? Praying that today would be the day when Molly was found alive and well, Vinny ran down the stairs. 'Where is everybody?'

'A police catering van has been set up down the street,

so the Old Bill have gone to get some refreshments. Teapot One they call it – bit different to Fred's café, eh?' Michael remarked, in hope of at least getting a weak smile out of his brother.

Vinny ignored his brother's shit attempt at a joke. 'Where's Ahmed and the others?'

'Ahmed's gone home to get some kip, but said he'll be back this afternoon. Pete and Paul have gone to get changed. They'll be back by ten, and are gonna bring some decent torches with 'em in case we need them later. Nick's still here. He's asleep on our sofa upstairs. So, what's the plan? You can't go out searching in that clobber, Vin. It's absolutely pissing down out there.'

Vinny sighed, then flopped onto a nearby chair. He always wore suits; they matched his status in life. 'Trust it to be pissing down again. Say Molly is lying in some alleyway or ditch, eh? How is she meant to have survived this freak weather? She's only a nipper and didn't even have her coat on.'

Michael did his best to offer words of comfort, but it was a struggle. Vinny wasn't stupid, and both men knew deep in their hearts that the longer Molly was missing, the less chance there was of a joyous reunion.

Old Sid felt as sick as a dog as he was ushered into the interview room. He knew what his beloved wife Sylvie would have said, had she still been alive. Sylvie wasn't a fan of the Butlers or the Jacksons. She reckoned both families were nothing but bloody trouble, and she'd have told him in no uncertain terms to keep his trap shut and not get involved.

'Can you assure me that the information I am about to give you stays anonymous, officer? I am in my seventies, living alone, and I really don't want or need any grief at my time of life.'

'Your name will not go any further than this room. Now, tell us about this conversation you overheard?'

Old Sid had been at his usual table in the Blind Beggar the previous evening, right behind where Bobby Jackson and Micky Dunn had been sitting. He'd not slept a wink for thinking of that poor missing child and knew he would never forgive himself if he didn't share his concerns with the police.

The officer's ears pricked up as Sid began to explain. CID had been planning to pay Bobby Jackson a visit this morning to question him about the girl he claimed to have seen getting into a blue car with a black man. The officer who'd taken Jackson's statement last night had noted that he was obviously inebriated, so they'd been allowing him time to sober up before following up the lead.

'Are you positive that you heard Jackson say that he had throttled Molly Butler and buried her in a shallow grave?' the police officer said.

'Bobby never actually mentioned Molly by name, but Micky did. That was what the whole conversation was about. My eyesight might be going home, but there's sod all wrong with my hearing. Bobby Jackson even laughed as he spoke about that poor child. He said he hoped she was never found, just like his father had not been. He said it was payback.'

The officer asked Sid some more questions, then shook his hand and thanked him for coming forward with such important information.

'If you arrest Bobby, you won't mention me, will you? That pub was packed last night, and Jackson isn't the quietest bloke in the world when sozzled. He has no reason to suspect me unless you drop me in it.'

'I can assure you that your name will not be mentioned.

Now, you go home and get some sleep, Sid. We'll contact you by phone if we need to speak to you again.'

Joanna Preston was in a terrible state. She had not slept or eaten, she couldn't stop shaking, and had vowed to end her own life if Molly was not found alive.

Terribly concerned about her friend, Nancy had remained by her side. Having not been blessed with a daughter herself, she'd taken to Molly as if she were her own, and she adored that dear child as much as she loved her boys.

Lenny's death and funeral had been painful enough, but Molly's disappearance was proving far worse. At least Lenny had been killed outright, so they knew he hadn't suffered. But Molly could be anywhere with anybody, and even now she might be suffering in the most awful way possible. The not knowing was horrendous. Every time she heard a car enter the street, Nancy jumped up to the window hoping it was her husband. She'd heard nothing from Michael since he dragged Vinny out of the house last night. No doubt he still had the hump with her for lying to him.

'Is it the police?' Joanna asked hopefully, hearing a car door slam.

'No. It's your mum!' Nancy exclaimed.

Joanna ran to the front door and flew into her mother's arms. Nancy watched as they clung to one another, sobbing, then excused herself by saying she was going upstairs to freshen up.

'Is there any news? Where are the police?' Deborah asked her daughter.

'The police were here most of the night. They rang this morning to say they would be back soon. Oh, Mum, it's been so awful – and it's all my fault. Why did I leave Molly? I love her so much,' Joanna said, between racking sobs.

'I know you do, darling, but you mustn't blame yourself. You're a fantastic little mum and you left Molly with her father, not some bloody stranger. Where is the arsehole, by the way?'

'I don't know. He went mad when I told the police I'd been to your wedding. I had to tell them because I was frightened they might arrest Dad. How did you know Molly was missing?'

'The police turned up at our hotel room to speak to your father.'

Joanna was immediately alarmed. 'They haven't arrested Dad, have they?'

Deborah stroked her daughter's cheek. She had cried throughout the journey to Whitechapel, but now she was here, she had to be strong for Jo's sake. ''Course they never arrested him. Your dad is at home with your brother. I told him I'd ring as soon as I got here. In bits, he is, love, and he so wanted to be here to support you and wait for news on Molly. He couldn't come though because of his parole conditions. He isn't meant to go anywhere near the Butlers and no way do I want him being carted off back to prison.'

'Mum, what am I gonna do if Molly isn't found? I love her so much, I just can't live without her, I know I can't,' Joanna wept.

Feeling her own eyes well up again, Deborah bit her lip to stop the tears and rested Joanna's head on her shoulder. 'The police are very good at finding children these days. We just need to keep strong and positive for Molly's sake.'

'But do you think they will find her alive?'

Deborah was not a religious woman, but she took her daughter's hand and said, 'Let's both say a prayer together for Molly's safe return, shall we? Your dad sort of found God in prison, and he swears that prayers do work.'

Joanna nodded. She was that desperate to hold her angelic child in her arms once again, she would literally try anything.

Christopher Walker was sitting at his desk, deep in thought. After yet another crap night's sleep, he knew he had to do something, but he had yet to decide what.

Calling Ahmed's bluff was one option. Perhaps he should refuse to arrest Vinny unless Ahmed relented on his insistence that he was not to involve his superiors? Ahmed had little to gain by carrying out his threat to expose Christopher's childhood lies. Somehow he needed to persuade the Turk that all it would take was a word in the right ear and he could guarantee Ahmed would walk free while Vinny was banged up for a long stretch.

His train of thought was interrupted by the arrival of a couple of his colleagues. 'Morning, Chris. You heard what happened to Vinny Butler?' said one.

'I expect Chris knows more than we do, being as his sister is married to Vinny's brother,' said the other.

Having just taken a mouthful of coffee, Christopher spat it all over his desk. He had told his superiors at the beginning of his career that his sister was married to Michael Butler, but the subject hadn't come up since. He never spoke about Nancy or her children at work, because a family association with the notorious Butlers was the last thing he wanted to broadcast.

'You OK, Chris? You don't look well.'

'I'm fine. Coffee just went down the wrong hole and I nearly choked. I haven't heard anything about Vinny Butler. What's happened to him?'

'Looks like somebody's abducted his daughter. There's a massive search going on in the East End. She's only three – but I suppose, being related, you already know that.'

'For your information, I have nothing to do with my sister or that vile family, so I hardly class the Butlers as my relations,' Christopher snapped.

When his colleague apologized then walked away, Christopher picked up his newspaper and pretended to be engrossed. But though his eyes rested on the front page his mind was on Ahmed Zane.

Could it be that the Turk was behind Molly Butler's disappearance?

The Detective Inspector was a different kettle of fish entirely to the CID officers Vinny had dealt with the previous day. Unlike his colleagues, he was in uniform. And his line of questioning made it clear he thought he was dealing with a toerag rather than an anxious father.

Vinny had always had a short fuse and when the DI asked him for the third time whether he had upset anybody lately, Vinny started to lose his rag. 'You got a problem with me, or what? Only you seem far more interested in my life than you do my daughter's. Molly is not a dog that has gone missing in the fucking park, you know. She's a little girl, just three years old.'

The Detective Inspector was no fan of Vinny Butler. As a plod, new to the force, he had worked on the Dave Phillips' murder enquiry, and like the rest of his colleagues he'd been convinced that Vinny was as guilty as hell. But that didn't mean he wasn't concerned about Molly Butler.

'Vinny, I am just as keen to find your daughter as you are, which is why I'm asking you these questions. As we speak, officers are carrying out door-to-door enquiries, and we've flooded East London with leaflets and posters. We're doing everything in our power to find Molly. But with every minute that passes it's looking more and more likely that your daughter did not just wander off. And chances are, if she's been snatched, it's not random. So let's not play games, eh? We both know what you are, and that you've made your share of enemies. So, I will ask you again: have you had any run-ins with anybody recently?'

Vinny shrugged. 'I had a couple of rucks, but they didn't even occur round here, they happened down at Eastbourne. I got nicked for affray, but it was more like handbags at dawn.'

'Who did you fall out with?'

'I had a fall out with some lads from South London. One was hitting on my missus and he picked Molly up and dropped her, so I clumped him. They were only kids though. Apart from one being called Lee, I ain't got a clue what their names were. Oh, and my sister's new bloke stuck his nose in and got it a bit busted. His name was Scott something, but Bren's not with him any more. Then a week later I had a falling out with a bouncer – just a drink-related scuffle, nothing major, but that's when I got nicked for affray. Robert Carson is the bouncer's name, but he isn't from round here. He comes from Hastings.'

The Detective Inspector wrote down some notes and then asked Vinny if there was anybody closer to home that might hold a grudge against him. The DI knew it was a dumb question as he asked it, because there was no way Vinny was going to shed light on any Butler skulduggery, missing kid or not. 'Well?' the DI asked, impatience creeping into his voice.

Vinny shook his head. 'Obviously I've had run-ins with people round here over the years, but I calmed down when my Molly was born. These days I tend to steer clear of trouble and just concentrate on my family and business.'

The DI eyed him suspiciously. He had heard rumours that Vinny and Ahmed were soon to be under surveillance for supplying the bulk of the capital's cocaine these days, and there was no telling whose toes they'd trodden on in the process, but there was no chance of Butler owning up to that.

'OK, if you do think of anybody it'll be in your daughter's best interests if you inform me as soon as possible. In the meantime, I would like you and Joanna to do a TV appeal. The press and the public are a great help in cases such as Molly's and we have found many a missing child alive and well after a tear-jerking TV interview. These appeals tend to bring out the best in people and potential witnesses will then come out of the woodwork.'

Vinny put his head in his hands. He dreaded doing a TV appeal in case his emotions got the better of him and he mugged himself off, but he would do anything to see and hold his beautiful child again. 'OK. What time?'

'I'll speak to the media and get back to you. Are you going to be here? Or at home?'

'Well, my brother and I were planning to head out with some pals and search for Molly ourselves.'

'There really is no point in you searching. My officers have everything under control. It's better you're here if we need you.'

'OK. I'll wait here then. Oh, and did you check out where Jo's father was when Molly disappeared? I know Jo said she was at his wedding, but I wouldn't trust Johnny Preston as far as I could throw him. If anybody holds a grudge against me, it's that bastard.'

'My officers have already spoken to Mr Preston and he has a watertight alibi. At the time Molly went missing, he was at his reception with sixty-odd guests. There aren't many fathers who would put their daughter through the misery Joanna is currently experiencing, Vinny, so I reckon you're barking up the wrong tree there.' He got to his feet and picked up his raincoat. 'Right, I'll get that TV appeal in motion and have a word with the press too while I'm at it. Molly's photo in the local and national newspapers might help jog people's memories. Oh, and while I am gone, try to jog your own memory. Any information you can remember might prove to be vital.'

Staring at the DI's back as he sauntered off, Vinny clenched his fist. 'Sarcastic old cunt,' he mumbled.

Mary Walker got off the train at Whitechapel and walked as fast as she could towards Joanna's house. Nancy had rung her yesterday evening to ask her to keep the boys overnight and take them to school again today, but Mary had no idea that Molly was missing until Nancy had rung up again this morning and explained the terrible situation.

Donald had not been at all happy about her leaving him short-staffed at the café. He had pleaded with her not to go to Vinny's house, but Mary could tell how upset Nancy was and after spending a week down at Eastbourne with Joanna, she'd grown very fond of the girl. As for young Molly, it sickened Mary to the stomach to think what might have happened to the poor little mite. Molly might be a Butler by name, but she was nothing like the majority of that family by nature. She was one of the sweetest little girls that Mary had ever had the pleasure of meeting.

Having never been to Joanna's house before, Mary took the piece of paper with the address Nancy had given her out of her handbag and looked around her. It was almost knocked from her hand by a skinhead barging past. 'Have you never heard of the word sorry?' Mary protested as he strode off.

'Shut up, you old witch,' the boy spat.

Wondering what had happened to her beloved England, Mary hung back to avoid any further contact with him. She hated that skinhead look, found it intimidating, and even though this lad did not have great big bovver boots on, as her and Donald like to call them, he looked a thoroughly nasty piece of work.

As Mary clocked the house numbers, she spotted two policemen knocking on people's front doors and guessed it was to do with young Molly's disappearance. She had seen loads of police officers wandering the streets since she had stepped off the train at Whitechapel.

As she drew level with number twenty-five, Mary was horrified to hear shouting and screaming coming from inside. Worried about her daughter, she banged on the door. 'Nancy, it's me. Are you OK?' she shouted.

When Nancy opened the front door, Mary was shocked to see the skinhead boy who had called her a witch standing in the hallway.

'Get him out of here! Get him out! My Molly wouldn't be missing if it wasn't for him,' Joanna screamed, trying to push the boy out of the house.

'Whatever's going on, love?' Mary asked Nancy.

'It's a long story, Mum. I'll explain later.'

'My daughter is right. This is your fault – and your father's, for allowing you to look after Molly in the first place. Now, please just leave. We don't want you here and you're upsetting Jo,' said a woman with dark hair who Mary had never seen before.

When the skinhead slumped down the wall and started to cry, Mary found herself feeling sorry for him even though he had insulted her not ten minutes ago. Judging by what had been said, this must be Vinny's son. Even though Donald was forever telling her off in the café for getting involved in situations she had no need to, she couldn't help herself. It wasn't in her nature to stand by and see a youngster so upset, no matter who they were or what they'd done.

'Jo, I love Molly so much. She's my little sister and I am so sorry for falling asleep. If anything bad has happened to her, I will never forgive myself,' Little Vinny gasped between sobs.

'Your dad is stopping at the club, Vinny. Go and see him,' Nancy said coldly.

When the distraught teenager dashed past her, Mary was about to chase after him to ensure he was OK until Nancy grabbed her arm and whispered in her ear. 'Leave it, Mum. He's just like his father. The apple never falls far from the tree and in Little Vinny's case it fell closer than most.'

# CHAPTER TWENTY-EIGHT

Fiona Mason was worried when the police knocked on the front door and asked to speak with her brother. 'Scotty's not here at the moment. Can I help you at all? I'm his sister.'

'Would you by any chance know of your brother's whereabouts yesterday afternoon?'

'Yes. Scott was here with me. As you can see, we've been decorating,' Fiona replied, pointing to the dust sheets, tins of paint and wallpaper.

'Did your brother pop out at all?'

'Yes, at teatime, to get us some fish and chips. He was only gone about fifteen minutes though. Why? What's he meant to have done?'

'Nothing. We're investigating the disappearance of a little girl, and just needed to rule your brother out of our enquiries.'

'Why ever would you think Scott would be involved with the disappearance of a child? He loves kids.'

'I'm sure he does, miss . . . Can I take your full name, please?'

'Fiona Jane Mason.' She watched as the officer wrote her name in his notebook, then asked, 'So will you still need to speak to Scott? I have no idea what time he'll be home.'

'The information you have given us should be sufficient. If it turns out that we do need to speak to Scott in person, we'll call back later.'

Fiona waited until the police had driven off before shouting out to Scott that it was safe to come out. Her brother had hidden in her wardrobe when he saw the police car pull up, begging her to tell them he was out and give an alibi if needed. 'What the hell have you done, Scott? Where was you all day yesterday?' Fiona screamed.

'I already told you, I had a bit of business to attend to. What did the Old Bill say?'

'And would your business dealings have anything to do with kidnapping a little girl?'

'What? Don't talk wet! 'Course it had nothing to do with that.'

'Well, that's what the police were asking about. Wanted to know where you were yesterday afternoon because some kid's gone missing.'

'Jesus, Fi. I might be a bit of a wideboy, but I'm no bloody nonce. What did you tell 'em?'

'I said you was here with me and we were decorating. I told them the only time you went out was to get some fish and chips at teatime.'

'What did you say that for? Say they go round the chippy and start asking the staff if they served me?'

Fiona was furious. The least Scott could do was show some gratitude after she'd put her neck on the line for him yet again. 'Well, I had to make it look genuine, didn't I? I did have fish and chips last night and the wrappers are in the bin, had the police asked for evidence. If you've not done anything wrong, why are you so bloody worried, eh? I swear to you, Scott, if you have had anything to do with that kid going missing, me and you are finished – for good.'

*

Queenie Butler had been ranting all morning about what a traitor Joanna Preston had turned out to be, but when she started going on about her poor Vinny, Vivian finally snapped.

'It isn't Jo's fault that Molly is missing, Queen. She left the girl with her father, not a fourteen-year-old babysitter. If anyone is to blame for that child's disappearance, it's your precious golden boy. We all know that Little Vinny isn't capable of looking after a fucking goldfish. As for slating the girl for going to her own parents' wedding, what did you expect? It's her mother and father – and as you're always sayin', blood's thicker than water.'

Stunned by her sister's outburst, Queenie stood up. 'The day my Roy was paralysed was the day his life ended, so excuse me if I'm not happy about that scheming little cow seeing her father behind all of our backs! We welcomed her into this family and treated her like one of our own. Now, I don't know about you, but I'm sick of sitting here twiddling my thumbs. I'm going to the club to find out what the hell is happening. Surely the police must have some leads by now? They told me sod all when I rang them earlier.'

'I'm not going to the club. I'll stay here and wait for news. Oh, and Queen, before you start sucking up to that deceitful son of yours, please never forget that it was he who killed my boy.'

After a heavy night on the tiles, Bobby Jackson was still in bed when he heard someone pounding on his front door. His wife had left him the last time he got sent down, so there was no option but to haul himself out of bed and find out what they wanted. 'All right, all right, I'm coming,' he yelled, stumbling downstairs in just his Y-fronts and a T-shirt.

Yanking open the front door, a bleary-eyed Bobby was rather taken aback to see the Old Bill on his doorstep.

Before he had a chance to ask what was going on, an officer handcuffed him and read him his rights.

Ahmed Zane had thoroughly enjoyed lunch with his cousin. The juicy T-bone steak was delicious and Burak had had him in fits of laughter with his warped one-liners, but now it was time to make a move.

'Right, I must be off. I have arranged to meet Christopher at two, then I shall head back to the club and put on my concerned best friend face. My performance so far has been so convincing, I think I deserve an Academy Award,' Ahmed chuckled.

'And what are you going to say to Christopher when he starts interrogating you about Molly? He is bound to suspect that we have taken her.'

Ahmed chuckled. 'He can suspect what he likes. There is no proof to link us to Molly going missing, is there? And we have the perfect alibi. Besides, I very much doubt Christopher will be accusing us of such a crime. How would he explain his suspicions to his superiors?'

'OK. But I still have a bad feeling about Carl Thompson, Ahmed. I think you should give him some more money. If Carl was as pissed off as you said – and he must have been to slam the phone down on you – then we need to get him back on side.'

Ahmed shrugged. 'Carl knew the score when I set this deal up. I have already paid him a substantial amount up front and I am not parting with any more of my hard-earned cash until the job is finished. If Carl starts to get too cocky, then we shall just have to make him disappear. After all, that is what we specialize in, isn't it?'

Burak roared with laughter. 'You know it, cousin, you know it!'

*

Queenie Butler listened carefully while her son explained that he and Jo were to record a TV appeal which would be shown on the news that evening. 'I dunno how I'm going to get through this, Mum, but I have to do it for Molly's sake. The Old Bill reckon it's the best way of getting people to come forward with information. They've got hold of a replica of Molly's doll and that will be shown during the press conference as well.'

'So, have they got any leads? With her curly blonde hair and big green eyes, Molly's the sort of kid who gets noticed. Some bastard must have seen her. I mean, who wouldn't take a second glance at a pretty little three-year-old toddling down the road without no adult present?'

'That DI said they're following up a couple of leads, but he wouldn't tell me any more than that. They keep their cards so close to their chest these days, the secretive bastards. I rang George Geary earlier, but he wasn't at home. I left a message with his old woman to ring me back. If anyone can find out any inside info, then he can. Especially if I promise him a big wad of cash. The DI seems to think Molly has been snatched by someone out to get revenge on me. I was asked loads of questions and had to admit I'd had a few run-ins with people down at Kings. I told them about the affray charge, but I can't see Brenda's ex geezer, that bouncer, or them young lads from South London snatching Molly, can you?'

'No, I can't. What about your Turkish friend though? You suppose he might be involved? If anybody has an axe to grind with you, it's him.'

Vinny shook his head. 'Ahmed's been brilliant since Molly went missing. He would never harm her – he's a dad himself. What type of company do you think I keep?'

'Dodgy, that's what! Vin, open your eyes, boy. You left that man for dead and then let him take the rap for a crime he didn't commit. Wouldn't you hold a grudge if the boot was on the other foot? I have never trusted that bloke from day one. He's a slimy bastard, and there's something about them cold dark eyes of his that gives me the creeps. I don't think you should rule him out. If you ask me, he forgave you far too easily for what you did. Viv's not going to be quite so forgiving, let me tell ya.'

Not needing or wanting to get involved in another conversation about Lenny, Vinny was relieved when his brother interrupted. 'Little Vinny is sat outside the club crying his eyes out, bruv. He's frightened to come in. Says Jo chucked him out the house and he thinks everybody hates him.'

'And so he should,' Queenie spat. Little Vinny might be her first-born grandchild, but she could honestly say he was her least favourite right now. He had been nothing but trouble for years, and Queenie reckoned it was all down to him being too spoilt as a child. He looked awful with that skinhead haircut, and even if, please God, Molly came home safe, she didn't think she would ever forgive him for falling asleep while he was supposed to be looking after his little sister.

Vinny walked outside the club and immediately spotted his son slumped with his head in his hands in the doorway opposite. It was the same doorway where Christopher Walker had been standing when he'd witnessed the murder of Dave Phillips.

'No point feeling sorry for yourself, boy. I left you in charge of your little sister and you fucked up. So, what did Jo say to you?'

'She chased me out the house and told me not to come back. Dad, I am so sorry. I love Molly and I feel so guilty. I couldn't sleep 'cos of that slag Shazza, which is why I was so tired at work. Please forgive me. I feel so alone. I wish my mum was still alive. She would understand.'

Alerted by the fact that Little Vinny had not mentioned Karen in years, Vinny crouched down and tilted his son's chin towards him. 'You been puffing or something? Your eyes look glassy.'

'No, I swear I haven't touched any puff,' Little Vinny replied honestly. He had however sniffed some glue and downed a bottle of Woodpecker. Realizing he'd have to cop to something, he owned up to the cider.

Vinny shook his head. Perhaps this was all his fault. Would Little Vinny have turned out more of a credit to him had he not had his mother bumped off? 'The state of you, boy. You look and smell like shit, and your clothes are filthy. In fact, lookin' at you, Oliver fucking Twist springs to mind.'

'I had to sleep rough last night. I had nowhere else to go. I was so scared, Dad. It was horrible, and I couldn't stop thinking of Molly.'

Grabbing his son by the arm, Vinny marched him towards the entrance of the club. It chilled him to think of his son out on the streets when someone seemed to be out to get him. 'Right, your nan is inside, so I want you to go straight upstairs, have a bath and get some kip. You do not come down those stairs until I tell you to, else you'll be out on your earhole. Now, do we understand one another?'

'Yes, Dad.'

Christopher Walker was wrestling with a torrent of emotions as he drove to meet Ahmed. Molly Butler's disappearance was the talk of the station and Chris knew it was his duty as a policeman to tell his boss that he had a good idea who was responsible for her abduction. But how could he? He was in far too deep and would most certainly lose his job if he owned up.

When the Radio One DJ played Kelly Marie's 'Feels Like

I'm in Love' Christopher turned the radio off. That was Olivia's current favourite song and a reminder that, not only was he in danger of losing his career, he would most certainly lose her too if the shit hit the fan.

Feeling sick as a dog, he cursed his naivety. With hindsight, it was obvious that he should have told his boss the truth about his past the moment Ahmed made contact. Surely his superiors would have understood that he'd had no option but to lie at Vinny's identification parade? He'd only been a nipper at the time and Vinny had threatened to harm his family.

Punching the steering wheel in pure frustration, Christopher silently blamed his sister for the predicament he found himself in. If it weren't for Nancy being married to Michael Butler, he would have found it much easier to come clean to his boss when Ahmed had first got in touch. How could he though, when he was classed as a relation to that scumbag family?

As he spotted Ahmed's car, Christopher took a series of deep breaths and pulled up alongside. He was as anxious as hell, but no way was he going to show it. Calling his tormentor's bluff was the only way he could play this now. It truly was shit or bust.

Mr Arthur, the old war veteran, was enjoying a mug of tea, a digestive biscuit and the latest episode of *The Sullivans* when one of the policemen who had been assigned to do house-to-house enquiries knocked on his door. 'How can I help you, officer?'

When the policeman showed him a photograph of Molly and explained where she had gone missing from and roughly what time, Mr Arthur felt a chill run down his spine. 'I saw a teenager acting oddly and it would have been about the time that poor child went missing. He was sat staring at the club, drinking cider, and he started muttering abuse at me when I looked at him. I knew he was trouble the moment I set eyes on him.'

'Can you remember what this lad looked like? And what he was wearing?'

'Of course, officer. Had evil eyes, he did, I'll tell you that much. Made my blood run cold, and I fought in and survived two wars. Got a memory like an elephant, I have. My dear Maggie used to say that, God rest her soul. Now, why don't you come in? I'll put the kettle on and tell you every single detail I remember about that lout over a cuppa.'

Mary Walker glanced at the clock. She knew Donald would be in one of his strops when she arrived home, as she'd promised she would only be a couple of hours. 'I'd better be making a move soon. I need to pop to yours, Nance, to pick some more clothes up for the boys before I collect them from school.'

'Thanks, Mum. I'm going to go to the press conference with Jo to give her some moral support, and then I'll stay here again tonight. Are you OK to keep the boys with you?'

'Of course, darling. I haven't told them that Molly is missing yet, but I'm sure Daniel and Lee can sense something is wrong. Adam's fine, bless him Met a girlfriend at school and talks about her constantly.'

Nancy forced a smile. 'Perhaps you and Dad should sit down tonight and explain in a kind way what has happened, Mum? If the appeal is going on the local news, I would rather the boys hear it from you than one of their schoolfriends. They're all very fond of Molly.'

Mary nodded. 'OK, love. I'll speak to them. Your father can be a bit cack-handed with delicate situations, and I don't want him upsetting them.'

Deborah saw Mary out, then went upstairs to see how her daughter was. 'You need to ring your dad, Jo. I rang him earlier and he is so desperate to speak to you, I am afraid that he might come here if you don't call him. You don't want his parole being revoked, do you?'

Joanna shook her head, and picked up the phone next to her bed. Her hands trembled as she dialled the number. 'Dad, it's me. I love you and wish you could be here.'

'And I love you and wish I could be there too, angel. Any news?'

'No, but the police will be here soon to pick me up for the press conference. They seem hopeful that, once the appeal is shown, witnesses will come forward.'

Johnny Preston did his best to control the emotion in his voice. The thought of one day meeting his granddaughter had been one of the things that had got him through the last few years in prison. He'd had photos of Joanna and Molly on the wall next to his bed and he used to talk to them whenever he was in his cell alone. He would always look at them last thing at night before he went to sleep, and had many a dream of a happy family reunion. 'Keep your chin up, babe. And can you promise me one thing . . .?'

'What's that?'

'Even if Molly is found safe, and I pray she will be, I want you to consider coming to live in Tiptree with me and your mum. Before I got out of prison, I wanted to move back to London, but I don't now. We can get you your own place down this way, Jo, via the council, so you won't have to suffer us for long. It's a much safer area for Molly to be brought up in, and it has far better schools. Vinny is a dangerous man, love. I know I've done some stupid, bad things in my time, but he's in a whole different league to me. Molly and you won't ever be safe while you're living with him. Vinny has far too many enemies.'

'Dad, I can't think about this right now. All I want is my baby back. I love and miss her so much.'

When his daughter burst into tears, Johnny did the same. He had never met his beautiful granddaughter, and the way things were going, he was afraid he never would.

Micky Dunn had had many a job. He'd gone from bank robber to bookie's runner to builder to postman to baker – to name just a handful – and his wife often joked that if Eamonn Andrews ever got his big red book out and invited him onto *This Is Your Life* the whole show would be taken up just reading out the list of Micky's jobs.

Micky's latest career move had been to take a job as a milkman. The hours suited him, because he knocked off early and was free to spend his afternoons in the boozer.

Today, however, Micky wished he had gone straight home instead of dropping by the Blind Beggar. The second he set foot in the door, he was approached by two plainclothes CID officers.

'Micky, we'd like a word with you regarding the disappearance of Molly Butler. Car's waiting outside – you're coming back to the station with us.'

Micky was horrified. 'You're not arresting me, are you?'

'No. We just need to ask you some questions.'

'And say I refuse?'

The taller CID officer grinned. 'Then we shall have to arrest you.'

Bobby Jackson was sitting in the interview room, protesting his innocence. He had been nicked enough times in the past to know it was wise to give a 'no comment' reply until his brief arrived, but today he felt compelled to say his piece.

'I was pissed and just talking bollocks, OK? Don't get me wrong – I hate Vinny Butler with a passion. Yous mob know as well as I do that he murdered my father and hid his body somewhere, and yes, I am glad he is now getting a taste of the sort of anguish me and my mum have been through. However, I am a father myself and would never lay a finger on an innocent child. I was just spouting my mouth off in honour of my old man, that's all.'

'You were seen covered in mud on the day of Molly's disappearance, Bobby. We've checked with your employer, and you didn't show up at work. So how did your clothes get so dirty, eh?'

Suddenly realizing he was in serious trouble, Bobby clammed up. He was far more scared of Vinny Butler than he was the Old Bill, and had already said too much without his brief being present.

'Well, can you explain?' the CID officer asked.

Bobby stared at the cocky-looking officer. 'No comment,' he hissed.

Whitechapel was absolutely buzzing with the news of Molly's disappearance, and the boy was earwigging people's conversations, loving all the speculation about what had happened to Molly. He had come to the conclusion that people secretly loved a drama of this kind. It gave them something to talk about and probably brightened up their mundane lives.

He watched as two old dears stopped in front of a poster featuring Molly's pretty face, tut-tutting as they bemoaned the decline of the area and agreed this would never have happened in their day. As soon as they moved on, he glanced around to make sure nobody was watching, then ripped the poster off the lamppost and threw it into the gutter – same as he had with all the other missing posters he'd seen that day.

The boy smirked as he walked away. Life really was all about karma.

# CHAPTER TWENTY-NINE

The Kelly brothers were from Stepney and had been big names in the East End when Vinny was a lad. But a shooting in the Two Puddings pub in Stratford had seen both Billy and Johnny charged with murder in 1963, and when they were eventually released from prison in 1978, they'd moved to Kent to start a new life.

'Christ! This is a surprise. How are you both?' Vinny asked, warmly greeting both men with a handshake and a slap on the back.

'We're good thanks, Vinny. We've got some business up town today, so thought we would pop by and see how you were. We heard about Molly last night. My heart goes out to you, it really does. Is there any more news?' Johnny asked.

'No. But I'm doing a press conference this afternoon that will be shown on the news in hope of jogging people's memories. Hopefully, once that's aired we'll have some witnesses come forward. It's the worst feeling in the world, not knowing where your kid is.'

'You're better off avoiding the press conference, son. Get the female family members to do it instead. You can guarantee that whoever has snatched your daughter will get off on seeing you on TV. That's what happened to Scouse Ray, weren't it, Bill?'

Billy nodded. 'Obviously, you need the filth to search for Molly, but you should make your own enquiries as well, Vin. People in our world don't like kids being brought into any disagreements we might have. Ring around all your contacts. You know enough faces, lad.'

'What happened with this Scouse Ray then? Did his kid get snatched?'

'His grandchild was abducted. Ray had got into a feud with some Irish travellers and he shot and killed one of them. The bastard's brothers took the kid as payback. Ray did a TV appeal, and shortly after it was aired, he got two of the kid's fingers sent through the post.'

'Oh, for fuck's sake. That is proper sick. I will kill anybody who harms my Molly. I will cut their fucking heart out of their chest and stuff it down the back of their throat.'

'Do you want us to make some phone calls for you, Vinny? Someone must know where your Molly is,' Johnny said.

'Yeah, I'd appreciate it if you could do that. I'll have a ring round too, see if I can unearth any info. Can I get yous both a drink?' Vinny asked.

'No thanks. We gotta be somewhere soon, but stay in touch, eh? Johnny, write our number down for Vinny,' Billy ordered his brother.

Vinny swapped numbers, then shook hands with the Kelly brothers again.

'Remember us to your mum and aunt, and if there's anything we can do, anything at all, just ask,' Billy said.

'And we do hope that all ends well with your daughter,' Johnny added.

'Cheers. Thanks for popping in. It means a lot.'

Billy Kelly gave Vinny a manly hug. 'Really proud of you, Johnny and I are, with what you've achieved. We very nearly offered you a job with our firm once, but we were worried you were too young at the time.'

'Really?' Vinny replied.

'Yes, I can vouch for that. We always knew you had great potential, Vinny. Good job you never linked up with us though – we weren't as clever as you and got ourselves nicked! Anyway, keep in touch, son, it's been good to see you again. Only wish the circumstances was different,' Johnny said.

'Likewise, lads. And thanks again.'

Burak Zane had been on tenterhooks all day. He knew how hot-headed his cousin could be and was worried that if Christopher so much as hinted Ahmed was mixed up in Molly's disappearance, then he would lose it big time and get them both into trouble.

When the door finally opened and Ahmed appeared, Burak dragged him into the office. 'Well? What did he say?'

'He tried to give it the big man and I allowed him to get away with it. He told me that there was no way he was going ahead with the drug bust unless he informed his superiors.'

'What did he say about Molly? Do you think he suspects us?'

'Nope. I gushed about what a beautiful child she is and swore that I would never stoop so low as to involve a child in my personal vendetta. I told him about my own children and said even though I hated Vinny, I was sorry for the anguish he was suffering.'

'Do you think he believed you?'

Ahmed chuckled. 'Perhaps. But even if he didn't, I guarantee that he won't say anything. He's just relieved to have been let off the hook – for now, at least. Young Christopher is very afraid of me, you know. I can see it in his eyes.'

*

The press conference was to take place at three p.m. in a room at Arbour Square police station. As soon as Michael arrived with Vinny, the first person he laid eyes on was Nancy.

When the police led Vinny away to brief him, Michael walked over to his wife. 'Is Jo not here yet?'

'Yes. She's speaking to the police. Her mum's with her.'

'You OK? How are the boys?'

'What do you care how me or the boys are, Michael? You haven't even bothered ringing.'

'Of course I care. I was just pissed off with you for lying to me, Nance. Don't get me wrong, I can understand why Jo lied to Vinny, but I thought me and you were better than that. I would have kept my gob shut had you trusted me with the truth. It just makes me wonder what else you've lied about in the past.'

'It's all about you, isn't it, Michael? Seeing as you are now so concerned, the boys are staying with my mum and dad. As for me lying to you in the past, I never have. The only reason I went to Jo's parents' wedding was to give her an alibi. And I would have told you about it, had you not been so up Vinny's arse again, not one week after he tried to smash seven bells out of you for telling the family what he'd done. You knew all along that Vinny had killed Champ, yet you never told me, did you? So don't be giving me a lecture on lying. All I did was go to a wedding, while you covered up your own cousin's death. If anybody deserves an award for lying, it's you not me.'

Michael suddenly felt guilty to his bones. Nancy's words had reminded him of other lies he'd told her, other things he'd kept quiet about – not least his affair with Bella. 'I'm sorry. I know I should have come clean with you about Champ, but I could never have put that burden on your shoulders, Nance. I owed it to Vinny to keep schtum, which is why I suppose you did the same for Jo. Look, I know how close yous two are, so please let's not argue. Molly is missing, and that's all we should be concerned about right now.'

At the mention of her niece, Nancy softened. 'Oh, Michael. What do you think has happened to her? Do you think somebody could be holding her hostage to get back at Vinny? In a way, I hope it is that, because any other scenario would be just too awful to even think about.'

Seeing the tears in his wife's eyes, Michael held her in his arms. 'I have no idea what has happened to Molly, babe, and I know that Vinny hasn't either. He rang around all his contacts earlier, offering a fifty-grand reward for information. I just thank God it isn't one of our kids. Dealing with this is hard enough, but there is no way I could have coped with it being one of ours.'

Nancy clung to her husband. 'Neither could I, Michael. Neither could I.'

Bobby Jackson could tell by the look on his brief's face that he was in big trouble.

'Hugh, I swear on my Jake's life, I had sod all to do with Molly Butler's disappearance.'

'You're going to have to do a bit better than that, Bobby. The police have a witness who heard you confess to throttling, then burying Molly. And on the same day another witness saw your clothes covered in mud. It isn't looking good, so you had better start talking.'

'I was pissed, Hugh, I've already explained that to the police. Do you honestly think, if I'd done a thing like that, I'd be stupid enough to stand at the bar in the Blind Beggar bragging about it? Micky Dunn asked me whether I'd taken the kid, so I cracked a joke, that's all. Me and Micky were both bladdered.'

'Hardly a joking matter though, is it, Bobby?'

'No. I suppose not. But then again, it wasn't your father who Vinny Butler kidnapped, tortured, then made disappear off the face of the earth, was it, eh? I'm telling you, Hugh, it was a drunken joke that backfired. Nothing more and nothing less. I was hardly going to be sympathetic towards Vinny, was I? I have him to thank for this scar on my face. What goes around comes around, I'm afraid.'

'So, where were you on the day Molly disappeared? You're going to need an alibi to get out of this one, Bobby. You also need to explain why a witness saw you in muddy clothes.'

'I did a job for a pal of mine. I was in Dagenham around the time that Molly disappeared.'

'And can your friend vouch for this?'

'I can't bring him into it, Hugh. He's a bit of a villain and he paid me to hide something for him, which is why I was covered in mud.'

'Well, if you want to get out of here you're going to have to give me the name of your friend. Provided he will give you an alibi, we won't need to tell the police what you were up to in Dagenham.'

'I can't do that. My pal is on the run.'

Exasperated, Hugh let out a long sigh. He had represented Bobby Jackson for years and his father before him. Bobby might not be the brightest spark, but he was usually honest. 'Look, let me put this bluntly. You need an alibi more than you ever have before. I know how the police work and chances are, if that child is not found, they will save face by charging you with the murder, then you will go to trial. How did you travel to Dagenham? Did you speak to anybody while you were there? Think hard now, Bobby. We've both been round long enough to know a lot of what you say in here will get straight back to Vinny one way or another.'

'I travelled to Dagenham in my van, but I did see someone I knew. Alison is an old friend of mine, we go way back. I hadn't seen her for years, but I stopped to get some beers and bumped into her outside the offie.'

'And what time would that have been?'

'I'm not sure, I didn't have me watch on. I got home about three though, so I'm guessing it was about two-ish.'

'Do you know Alison's surname? Have you an address for her?'

'I can't remember her surname, but she's in her thirties, has long dark hair and a massive pair of knockers. She used to live in a block of flats called Cadiz Court. Not sure what number, but I think she was on the seventh floor. She has two sons, Kevin and Richard.'

'OK. I'll have another word with the police. In the meantime, see if there's anything else you can remember.'

When Hugh left the cell, Bobby felt sick with anxiety. Vinny Butler would kill him, unless Alison backed him up. He had once broken her heart, but surely he could rely on her to confirm his story – couldn't he?

Vinny Butler felt physically sick when he saw how many reporters were inside the room. He enjoyed being known and feared as a notorious villain, but hated any other kind of limelight. 'I don't think I want to do this. I think it's better if Jo does it with Nancy,' Vinny whispered to DI Smithers.

'It will be fine. You and Joanna will sit at the centre of the table with myself and DS Townsend either side of you. I can answer a lot of the questions on your behalf, but you and Joanna will need to do the actual TV appeal and answer any questions I am unable to. Obviously, anything you are uncomfortable with, you don't have to answer. Here's Joanna now. Would you two like a few minutes alone before we begin?'

Without even looking at or consulting Joanna, Vinny shook his head. 'No. Let's just get it over with.'

The boy stood in a phonebox, took the screwed-up poster out of his pocket, and checked nobody was watching him before dialling the number. He had learned while banged up that if you kept the phonecall short and sweet, the Old Bill wouldn't be able to trace it.

'I'm ringing about Molly Butler. I just want you to know she is still alive, but missing her parents.'

The officer was startled. He could tell the caller sounded young. 'Look, please don't hang up. It's in your best interest to talk to me. Can you tell me where Molly is? If you do, I can assure you that you will not be in trouble. As long as Molly is returned safely, everything will be OK. Would you like to speak to a senior officer? If you hold on a minute, I can arrange that.'

'No, but I'll be in touch again soon,' the boy said, before slamming the phone down. He then left the phonebox, grinning.

Back at Arbour Square police station, Vinny Butler could feel his temper rising. Not only was he having to fend off awkward questions about his own life and business dealings, but Joanna's nosy fucking mother was sitting amongst the reporters, watching him squirm.

'As I said at the beginning of this conference, Mr Butler and Miss Preston are to only be asked questions about the disappearance of their daughter. Anything else is irrelevant at this moment in time.'

Most of the hacks present had done their homework on Vinny Butler, none more so than the *News of the World* reporter. He had spent the previous day visiting pubs and other local amenities in Whitechapel in the hope of digging up some dirt. Most locals knew better than to discuss the Butler family and it seemed he'd wasted a day – until he had the good fortune to come across an elderly lady in the market. She'd given him a wonderful insight into the life of Vinny Butler and a brilliant interview to go in his newspaper on Sunday.

'Next question,' the DI said.

'You mentioned that the door of Mr Butler's club was found open after Molly's disappearance. Is there any chance the club could have been broken into?' asked a reporter from a local rag.

'No, there was no sign of forced entry. We believe the door in question was accidentally left open as Mr Butler rushed into the club to attend to a flooded cellar,' the DI replied.

'I have a question for Miss Preston,' said a female reporter. 'Firstly, I would just like to say that as the mother of a young daughter myself, I truly sympathize with what you must be going through and I do hope Molly is found safe. My question is, had Molly ever run off in the past? Was she a child who liked to explore?'

'No, never. Even in the supermarket, Molly would never leave my side. She's a good girl, and so bright for her age,' Joanna sobbed.

'Who was looking after her at the time?' somebody shouted out.

'Do not mention my son,' Vinny hissed in the DI's ear. Little Vinny might be a pain in the neck, but he was still only fourteen and needed protecting from vultures like the press.

'You can be assured that Molly was being properly supervised on the day in question. As I said earlier, Mr Butler was unaware that the door of the club had been left open,' the DI replied.

At that point, it was all Joanna could do to stop herself blurting out that her beautiful daughter had most certainly not been properly supervised, that she had in fact been left in the care of her partner's rebellious teenage son, but she knew voicing her opinion would only sour things between herself and Vinny even more. The father of her child had made no attempt to speak to her today, let alone comfort her, but even though Joanna despised him at the moment, she could feel the pain he was going through. Only those who had experienced the horror themselves could hope to understand how it felt to be the parent of a missing child.

The *News of the World* reporter put his hand up. 'I've got a question for Mr Butler. Vinny, in light of all the speculation that you are a leading figure in the underworld, do you not think there is a good chance that Molly has been abducted as some kind of retribution—'

'How dare you! How fucking dare you, you unfeeling four-eyed cunt,' Vinny shrieked, as he leapt out of his chair and launched himself at the journalist.

Aware of all the flashbulbs going off and the three policemen wrestling Vinny to the floor in an attempt to stop him from beating up the journalist, an over-emotional Joanna ran from the room.

Having made a pact not to talk about or speculate on Molly's whereabouts any more until they had watched the TV appeal, Queenie and Vivian were currently sipping their third glass of sherry and listening to their second Mrs Mills album. 'Always reminds me of when that bastard Hitler was bombing us, this song does, Queen. Do you remember us singing it when we were holed up in Bethnal Green tube station?'

'On Mother Kelly's Doorstep' was one of her and Vivian's all time favourite songs, and Queenie had to smile. If she had a pound for every time Viv had asked her the same question after a few sherrys, she would be rich. 'The good old days those were, Viv. The camaraderie was special. Not like that these days. Gone to fucking pot, this country has. They've let too many foreigners in, that's what I reckon. I mean every time one of our old neighbours croaks it now, the house is given to Indians. Got nothing against 'em, they seem to work hard, but they're not exactly mixers, are they? Can't see them singing "Knees up Mother Brown" with us at the next Jubilee, can you?'

Vivian was about to get on her soapbox about Enoch Powell's 'Rivers of blood' speech when the doorbell stopped her in her tracks. 'You stay there. I'll get it.'

The last thing Queenie needed right now was the company of Brenda in one of her tantrums, but that's exactly what she got. 'You OK, love? I meant to pop round earlier. Have you heard about poor Molly?'

'Yes, via the Old Bill knocking on my door asking for Scotty's surname and address. How come nobody had the decency to inform me, eh? Do I mean nothing to this family? And why has Scotty been brought into this investigation, eh? Fuck me, does he look like a murderer or nonce? I really hoped that once Scott had calmed down, me and him might have a chance of getting back together, but there's no hope of that now, is there?'

Unable to stop herself, Queenie leapt up and smacked her inebriated, hyperventilating daughter's face. 'How dare you storm in here with not a word of compassion or worry about Molly? You are the most selfish person that I know, which is probably why you were last on my list to tell what had happened. Now, get out of my house and do not come back until you have thought about that poor little ha'porth. You disgust me sometimes, Bren, and I'm embarrassed to call you my daughter.'

'And you disgust me too, Mum. It was you who brought me up to be as hard as nails. Terrible mother you've been, if you want to know the truth. Vinny's evil, Roy's dead, Michael was a druggie and I have mental health and alcohol problems.'

'Get out! Don't you dare speak to your mother like that,' Vivian yelled, grabbing her niece by the elbow.

'It's all true. All she was ever interested in was her beloved boys. Michael's right, you know. My dad is a good man, with a good heart. No wonder he fucking drank and slept around. Any man would have done the same, if they had the misfortune of marrying you.'

Queenie went to clump Brenda again, but somehow stopped herself. 'Viv, she's pissed. Get her out of here before I kill her stone dead.'

Unaware that he had not half an hour ago been the topic of conversation, Albie walked towards his old abode feeling terribly nervous and with a suitcase in his hand.

Michael had rung him the previous evening to inform him of the disappearance of his granddaughter, and unable to think about anything else, Albie had caught a train from Ipswich to London. His first stop had been Barking, but there was nobody at Michael's house, so he had then jumped back on the District Line to Whitechapel, only to get to the club and find it locked up, with a sign on the door saying CLOSED UNTIL FURTHER NOTICE.

Spotting a poster on a nearby fence, Albie stopped and stared sadly at the photo of Molly. He had hardly known the child, but having seen her sing on the stage at Kings in the talent competition, he was proud to call himself her grandfather. She was a little sweetheart, and sod all like Vinny, thankfully.

'Hello, Albie.'

'Hello, Stan. I take it you've heard the awful news?'

'Yes. It's terrible. We've all been out looking for Molly, but the police told us to leave it to them now. I think everywhere local has been searched. They did say that if they get any new leads in other areas and need our help, they'll let us know. There was a good crowd of us out with our torches last night, Alb. Stick together through thick and thin round 'ere, don't we?'

Albie held out his right hand. 'Thanks, Stan, that means a lot.'

'Do you fancy a pint in the Blind Beggar, Albie? Drinks are on me, pal.'

Albie shook his head. He could not face being interrogated about his granddaughter in any local pub, and he knew Whitechapel had a rumour mill of its own. 'No thanks, Stan. But very kind of you to offer. I just need to spend time with the family right now.'

When Big Stan walked back indoors, Albie took a sip of brandy from his hip flask for Dutch courage before he knocked on Queenie's door. He could hear music coming from inside the house, so knew somebody was at home.

When Vivian answered the door, Albie's face fell. 'I'm sorry to trouble you, Viv, but Michael rang me last night and I couldn't not be here. There's nobody in at Michael's and the club is shut. I just want to be here for Molly's sake. Regardless of the way I feel about Vinny, that adorable little girl is still my granddaughter.'

Seeing the tears well up in Albie's eyes, Vivian softened towards him for the first time in years. His place at the top of the list of people she despised had gone to Vinny – and, after today's performance, bloody Brenda. 'Come in, Albie. Queenie's in the sitting room. Put your case over there by the stairs for now. What do you want to drink? Beer or a brandy?'

To say Albie was stunned by Vivian's welcome was an understatement. For a moment he could only stand gawping at her. When he finally spoke, Albie could hear the tremor in his voice: 'Erm, if you don't mind, I'll have a brandy, please, Viv.'

# CHAPTER THIRTY

Vinny stopped in his tracks as he was being led back into the room for the news appeal. He felt emotionally drained and could not stop thinking of the story that the Kelly brothers had told him earlier about Scouse Ray. They had advised him not to appear on TV, and there was no way Vinny wanted to put Molly even more at risk, or be gloated at himself by the shitcunt who had taken his daughter.

DI Smithers was certainly no admirer of Vinny Butler, but the pain the man was going through was clear to see. 'Vinny, I've cleared out most of the media. The only people left in that room now are involved in the TV appeal. You need to do this, and your daughter needs you to do it too.'

Vinny looked around and came face to face with Joanna and her stony-faced mother. 'Look, I'm not Mr Popular. Let those two do the appeal. It will have far more impact.'

'Are you OK, Vinny?' Joanna asked, aware of the anguish on her partner's face.

Unable to control his emotions any longer, Vinny crouched down and put his head in his hands. 'No, I ain't, Jo. I can't stand not knowing where Molly is. It's killing me, slowly but surely. I can't do the appeal, I want you and your mum to do it instead. More people will come forward if yous two do it.'

Deborah snarled as her daughter bent to comfort the man that she and Johnny despised so much. It should be Vinny comforting Jo, if he was any kind of a man, not the other way round. She tugged at her daughter's arm to lead her away. 'Come on, Jo. I'll do the appeal with you.'

Bemused by Vinny's decision, DI Smithers shrugged. 'Let's get a move on then. The TV crew are waiting for us.'

Mary picked the boys up from school and as a treat took them to the Wimpy bar. She had decided to tell them the news about Molly over a burger, chips and a milkshake.

Adam was the last to finish his meal and the minute he had done so, Mary broke the bad news as softly as she could. 'You know you are staying with me and your granddad at the moment, and I told you that was because your mum was busy? Well, there's something else I need to tell you. The reason your mum is busy is because she's looking after Auntie Jo.'

'Is Auntie Jo not well, Nan?' Lee asked. Even though Mary and Donald were not his real grandparents, he always referred to them as if they were now. He didn't call Nancy 'Mum' though, because he still remembered his real mum.

'Auntie Jo is very upset at the moment, and the reason for that is . . . your cousin Molly has got lost.'

'Did she get lost in Sainsbury's like I did that time, Nan?' Adam asked innocently.

'No, love. Molly is very lost at the moment.'

'So who will find her?' Lee asked.

'Well, the police are all searching for her and tonight Auntie Joanna will be on the news asking for people to help look for Molly,' Mary replied. She never mentioned Vinny in front of the boys, not unless they did.

'Do you think Molly is playing hide and seek?' asked Adam, with a quizzical expression on his face.

Daniel gave his five-year-old brother a tap on the head. ''Course she ain't, you div. How long has Molly been missing for, Nan?'

Mary was rather thrown by her grandson's behaviour towards his younger brother and his blunt question. Both she and Donald had noticed a change in Daniel of late. Nothing major, just the odd swear word and the fact he seemed to be growing up a little too fast for their liking. 'Molly's been missing since yesterday afternoon. Now apologize to your brother for hitting him, Daniel. That's naughty.'

'No.'

Mary was not used to being defied. 'You will apologize, because if you do not, I will give you a clump around the head too.'

'Go on then. I don't care. Won't hurt me. I'm a man, just like my dad is.'

Mary looked in horror at her usually polite grandson. From his eyes to his hair to his skin, he had all the features of his father's family. In fact, the way he had just spoken to her and was now glaring at her defiantly, she could see nothing of Nancy in the child whatsoever. And the most worrying thing of all? Daniel was only bloody seven.

Ahmed Zane met Carl Thompson at the yard they had hired for the set-up in River Road. He had taken Burak's words of warning on board and had decided to pay Carl another couple of grand to keep him sweet.

'What's that?' Carl asked, when Ahmed handed him a rather slim envelope.

'Two thousand pounds. I thought it would help tide you over until we have arranged another date.'

With a sneer on his face, Carl slung the envelope back at Ahmed. 'Two thousand! What do you take me for? We had a deal, Ahmed. You knew I was planning to move to Spain and you promised that I would be paid in full this weekend. Only last week I told you I'd put down a deposit on the bar, and the balance is due in the first week of October.'

'Yes, but you know the score, Carl. I made it clear to you at the very beginning that you would not be paid in full until the job was finished. It isn't my fault that Vinny's daughter has gone missing, is it?'

Carl chuckled. 'Isn't it? The way you hate that geezer's guts, it wouldn't surprise me. You can't kid a kidder, Ahmed, so don't ever try to pull the wool over my eyes. What happened? Did you and that cousin of yours suddenly have a change of heart? Did you decide to forget about putting Vinny behind bars and bump off the kid instead, saving yourself the thirty-five grand you owe me in the process?'

Ahmed grabbed Carl by the throat and slammed him against the wall. 'I wouldn't go spouting off accusations like that, if I were you. I am no child snatcher, you hear me?'

'OK, I just thought it was a bit of a coincidence, that was all. Can you let go of my neck now, please?' Carl croaked.

Ahmed released his grip, then pointed a finger of warning in Carl's face. 'I call the shots. You will get the rest of your money when this job is over. Now, do you fucking understand me?'

Carl nodded, waited until Ahmed had left the yard, then smirked. He would give the cocky Turkish bastard one week to come up with the rest of his dosh and if he didn't, Carl would let Vinny Butler know what his faithful mucker was really up to. Carl was always loyal to one thing – the highest bidder.

*

Back in Whitechapel, Queenie, Vivian and Albie were all glued to the local news. 'This is it,' Queenie said, turning the volume up.

'Joanna and Deborah Preston the mother and grandmother of Molly Butler, broke down today during their public appeal for information about the missing three-year-old. Speaking at a news conference in London, alongside DI Smithers, who is leading the case, Joanna Preston pleaded for information and the safe return of her beloved daughter.'

'Where the bleedin' hell is Vinny?' Queenie muttered.

'Shush,' Vivian urged her sister.

'My Molly is the sweetest, most loving, beautiful daughter that a mum could ever wish for, and I just want her back home with me where she belongs. If somebody has her or knows where she is, please ring the police,' Joanna sobbed.

At that point, Albie started to weep too.

'Be quiet. I'm trying to listen,' Queenie hissed.

With Joanna clearly unable to continue, Deborah squeezed her daughter's hand and looked into the camera, fighting back the tears as she asked anyone who had information to come forward. 'What the family is going through is worse than torture and we just need to know where Molly is,' she added.

The appeal was then switched back to the news presenter. 'Molly was last seen at her father's nightclub in Whitechapel at around one thirty yesterday afternoon, but there have been no sightings of her since. Molly was wearing a pink tracksuit and white trainers very similar to the outfit you can now see on your TV screens, and she was carrying a doll identical to this one,' the reporter explained, pausing to allow viewers time to study both images.

A photo of Molly then flashed up and the presenter ended the report by urging the public to call the phone number that was shown below if they had seen Molly or had any information as to her whereabouts. She also said that all phone calls would be dealt with in the strictest confidence.

Queenie switched the TV off and began gathering up her handbag and coat. 'Vinny was meant to be doing that appeal. I'm gonna pop down to the club and find out what's gone on. Deborah bleedin' Preston hardly knew Molly, so Christ knows what she was doing sticking her oar in. It should have been me sat there with Jo, not her.'

Vivian waited until her sister had slammed the front door behind her before turning to Albie. 'I know me and you have never seen eye to eye on most things, but I have to admit you were right about one thing all along. You always said Vinny was no good, didn't you?'

Albie nodded sadly. 'I'm ashamed to call him my son, Viv, and I am so sorry that he was the one what killed Lenny.'

'I'll never forgive Vinny for what he did, not ever. To cover up my boy's death was the lowest of the low. And I bet I know why he didn't do that TV appeal.'

'His arsehole went?'

With a twisted expression on her face, Vivian nodded. 'You got it in one, Albie. Vinny Butler might be a big man around here, but me and you both know he is the most cowardly piece of shit that God ever put breath in.'

The boy switched the television off in favour of listening to Paul Weller. He was a massive fan of The Jam, having got into their music while banged up.

The TV appeal had been quite a disappointment to him. He had been gagging to see Vinny Butler mug himself off on TV, but Vinny was nowhere to be seen.

The boy smirked as he sang along to 'Going Underground'. Every time he heard this song now it would remind him of Molly and the pain Vinny was currently going through. He must be wondering if his daughter was under the ground.

'Boy, your tea's ready. Come and eat it before it gets cold. I've made you your favourite, Shepherd's Pie.'

The boy grinned and lifted the arm off the record. 'Coming, Nan.'

Vinny Butler was back at the club with Michael and Ahmed. He had not been able to face watching the news, but Michael had, and he said it had been a strong appeal and Jo and her mum had done well. 'Is Little Vinny still upstairs?'

Michael nodded. 'He watched the appeal with me and got upset. He blames himself, I think.'

'And so he fucking should,' Vinny said, knocking back his Scotch.

'You shouldn't be too hard on him, Vinny. He's only a kid himself,' Ahmed reminded his pal, even though he had said differently when Molly had first been reported missing.

'Speak of the devil,' Vinny mumbled, as his son walked towards him.

'Is it OK to sit down here with you, Dad? I just want Molly to come home. I feel so guilty. I'm really sorry.'

Aware that his son was crying, Vinny stood up and gave him an unmeaningful hug. 'Sit your arse down next to Michael while I pour you a cider.'

When the phone rang, Vinny dashed to answer it. He had spoken to Geary when he had arrived back from the police station and had been on tenterhooks ever since, waiting for him to call back.

'I've got some news for you. Meet me in our usual spot at eight o'clock, and do not tell a soul. It cost me to get this info for you, Vinny, so you need to bring three grand with you. OK?'

If Vinny had a million pounds in his safe, he would have gladly handed it over to Geary if it meant getting Molly back. 'Fine. I'll be there.'

Back at the police station, DI Smithers and his team were sifting through the various new leads the TV appeal had thrown their way. The phones had not stopped ringing since Joanna and Deborah's heartfelt interview.

''Ere guv, we've got another sighting of that young lad who was watching Vinny's club. A lady has given the same description as that old boy you spoke to. That's the third one now, and the lady said he was acting shifty. He insulted her when she looked at him, same as he did the old fella. She left her name and telephone number.'

'Right, let's get the lady to help us with a photofit and see if it matches the one Mr Arthur came up with. He was a bit unsure and kept changing his mind, so I don't want to put the photofit out unless we're sure we've got it right,' Smithers replied.

'What about Bobby Jackson?' DS Townsend asked.

'We'll let him go as soon as his alibi is confirmed,' Smithers replied. He was now ninety-nine per cent sure that Bobby Jackson had not abducted Molly Butler. Jackson certainly didn't have the demeanour of a guilty man. He had stuck by his story that he was drunk and just joking, and his pal Micky Dunn had also backed that up. Micky admitted that Bobby had made the remark about killing Molly and disposing of her body, but told the police that even though he had been shocked at the time, when he had woken up sober this morning he had known Bobby was only messing about. He'd also said that Bobby was only brazen about Vinny when inebriated; so long as he was sober, he was absolutely petrified of the man.

'We've another new lead, guv. A bloke who was walking

through Victoria Park says he saw a teenage lad with a child in a pushchair and reckons it could have been Molly. He said she had a pink tracksuit on and a doll in her hand. The lad that was with her had a dark woolly hat on and was dressed in dark clothing. The child had some kind of woolly hat on her head too.'

DI Smithers felt the same surge of excitement that he always felt when on the verge of a breakthrough. 'Right, lads, let's follow these new leads up ASAP.'

Vinny Butler swung into the car park and pulled up next to Geary. 'Well?' he asked, as he leapt into the passenger seat. He was dreading what Geary had to say, but any news was better than none.

'You got the money?'

Vinny handed the envelope over. 'Well?' he asked again, but this time with both impatience and anger in his tone.

'I mean it, Vinny, you need to swear to me on both your kids' lives that you won't let on this info has come from me.'

Vinny saw that comment as a good sign. Whatever Geary had to tell him, he knew it involved Molly still being alive. 'I swear, George. You know you can trust me.'

'Bobby Jackson is currently in custody in connection with Molly's disappearance. He hasn't been charged yet, but was apparently heard spouting his mouth off in the Blind Beggar last night. He gave the police a false lead first, and then a witness overheard him say other stuff.'

Vinny's blood ran cold. 'What other stuff?'

Knowing how fiery Vinny could be, George decided to hold back certain parts of the conversation he'd had with his informant. 'Not sure of the exact details, but he hinted that he knew where Molly was. They dragged his pal Micky Dunn in for questioning earlier as well. Micky was with Bobby when the witness overheard the conversation.'

Vinny felt all the colour drain from his face. He had been responsible for the disappearance of Bobby's father Kenny, and had made sure the man died a nasty death. Although Bobby knew Vinny was to blame, he couldn't prove it. The police had tried to make a case but failed because Vinny had a watertight alibi.

'Who's the witness, George?'

'No idea. I asked my source, but he didn't know. Apparently, Jackson is claiming he was drunk and is denying that he had anything to do with Molly's disappearance. Naturally, I'll keep you updated on the situation . . .'

Ahmed Zane smirked as he opened the door of the club and Vinny's mother stormed in like a bull in a china shop. 'Evening, Queenie,' he said, his voice dripping with sarcasm. He knew the truth about Lenny's accident was now out in the open, but since Queenie had always hated him it didn't surprise him that her attitude towards him hadn't changed.

Spotting Michael and Little Vinny chatting away with a pint in front of them as though they didn't have a care in the world, Queenie pursed her lips. 'Well, well, well, isn't this cosy?'

Michael leapt up. 'Hello, Mum. Let me get you a drink.'

Queenie picked up the drink that was sitting in front of her grandson and took a sip. 'Being rewarded for losing his sister, is he?'

'Don't say stuff like that to him, Mum.'

Little Vinny put his head in his hands and wept again. 'Nanny's right. It's all my fault. If I hadn't fallen asleep, Molly would be here with us. I wished I would have played with her more now. She always wanted me to.'

Queenie was not one for crocodile tears and never had been. 'Where's Vinny? And why didn't he do the appeal?' she asked Michael.

'Hey, why don't you talk to your mum in private, Michael? While I have a chat with this young man,' Ahmed said, sitting down next to Little Vinny and putting a supportive arm around his shoulders.

When Michael nodded gratefully, then led his mum upstairs, Little Vinny turned to Ahmed. 'My nan hates me, my dad hates me, Jo hates me. What am I gonna do?'

'You have to do what I did when the same happened to me. I was blamed for Champ's death when it was not even me driving that car, but I just held my head high and took it on the chin. I must admit, I am relieved now your dad has owned up to it though. Your family must have hated me.'

Little Vinny sat with his mouth wide open. 'What! My dad killed Champ?'

'Oh, I am so sorry. I thought you knew. The truth came out recently down at Eastbourne, and because all the rest of your family were there, I just assumed that your dad would have told you, seeing as you're not a kid any more.'

'No, he never said anything.'

'Well, it was an accident. Your dad did not mean to kill Champ, just the same as you never meant to fall asleep while you were looking after Molly. It is probably wisest to keep this conversation to ourselves though, eh? Your dad has enough on his plate at the moment without him finding out I've put my foot in it. Can I trust you not to say anything?'

Little Vinny nodded.

'Well, let me pour us another drink then, and if you ever need anybody to talk to on the quiet, then I'm your man. You can trust me too.'

Little Vinny sighed deeply as he watched Ahmed saunter up to the bar. It was awful his dad had killed Champ, but in a strange way it had lessened his own guilt.

*

Fiona Mason launched herself at her brother the minute he sauntered through the front door. She had been that shocked when she had seen the news bulletin, she had dropped the iron and burnt her hand. 'I want you out of this flat, Scott. I've had enough. You must have had something to do with it, else why would I have to lie to the police for you, eh?'

To stop her from punching him in the chest, Scott grabbed hold of his little sister's wrists. 'What's happened? Have the Old Bill been back?'

'I saw the TV appeal, Scott. The police are bound to come round again because they've appealed for witnesses. If they find out I lied, then I will go to prison as well. How could you put me in that position, eh? And how could you involve that poor child?'

'Have you lost the plot, Fi? I do not have a clue what you're on about. What TV appeal?'

'The one about Vinny Butler's missing daughter.'

'No way! Vinny's kid has gone missing?'

'Oh, don't act shocked, Scott. It's too late for that. You wouldn't have hidden in my wardrobe and made me lie to the police if you had nothing to hide. You think I'm stupid because I've always stood by you, but I'm not. Go and pack your things. I can't take any more.'

'Fi, I swear on my life and yours that I had nothing to do with the disappearance of Vinny's kid. I might be a fucker, but I would never hurt a child. The reason I asked you to give me an alibi is because me and a pal committed a robbery. That's why I thought the Old Bill had turned up here, not because of some kid.'

'I don't believe you.'

'I can get my pal to confirm the story to you, if you like? We did over a jeweller's shop.'

'OK, but ring him now and hand the phone straight to me.'

'I can't. He's gone to Belgium with the jewellery.'

'Oh, how very convenient, Scott – you must think I was born bloody yesterday. Just pack your stuff and get out.'

# CHAPTER THIRTY-ONE

Vinny Butler woke up with a thumping headache. The news from Geary had knocked him for six, and he had sat up until the early hours downing Scotch and bending Michael and Ahmed's ears. The main topic of conversation was how he would dispose of Bobby Jackson, and Vinny had decided to cut the bastard open while he was still alive, rip his heart out with his own bare hands, then feed it to the stray dog that was always hanging around outside the club.

Michael opened the bedroom door. 'Wakey, wakey. I feel like shit, I dunno about you. Ahmed's gone to the café. I ordered you two sandwiches. Egg and bacon, and sausage and onion.'

The thought of either concoction made Vinny want to vomit. He had barely eaten a morsel since Molly had gone missing. 'Answer that, would you, Michael,' Vinny said when the buzzer rang.

He was trying to summon up the strength to have a shave and a shower when Michael yelled out that the police wanted to speak to him. Vinny quickly got dressed and ran down the stairs. Had they charged Bobby Jackson?

'Morning, Vinny. I need to ask you a few more questions

regarding certain information we have received,' DS Townsend said.

Vinny gestured for Townsend and his colleague to follow him into his office. He was fully expecting questions about Bobby Jackson to be fired his way, but to Vinny's amazement, Townsend never mentioned him. Instead, he asked Vinny if he had seen a teenage boy hanging around outside the club recently.

'No. Not that I can remember. Why?'

'We have reason to believe that this lad might prove to be a key witness. We have a description and are planning to release a photofit later today.'

Vinny was gobsmacked. 'What does this lad look like?'

'We're not sure of his height yet, because in all the sightings we have he was sitting down in the doorway opposite your club. But he's described as being between seventeen and twenty, with dark hair and green eyes. On the day Molly went missing, he was wearing a navy tracksuit and white trainers.'

Vinny wanted to ask why they were chasing after some young kid when they had Bobby Jackson in custody, but for obvious reasons he couldn't. 'Are there any other witnesses or suspects?' he asked.

Townsend's answer was noncommittal. 'We're chasing up various leads. The TV appeal resulted in lots of phone calls and we're sifting through them all, but this lad who was seen sitting opposite your club on the day in question might well be able to assist us in our enquiries. The flood you had in your cellar – is there any way it could have been started deliberately?'

Vinny shook his head. 'No chance. I plumbed that machine in myself and it had already flooded the cellar once before. There's a dodgy pipe at the back, and I should have got it properly sorted ages ago.'

'Who loaded the wash and switched it on?'

'My cleaner, Edna. She always sticks the towels, tea-towels and all that stuff in every Thursday. My son noticed the flood when he went down to the cellar to stock up the mixers, then rang me immediately. What are you trying to imply? That some teenage kid came into the club, put a wash on, then flooded my fucking cellar before snatching my daughter?'

'I'm not implying anything, Vinny. We're just exploring all the angles. That's our job.'

'Where's your boss today? I want to know why you've described this teenage lad as a witness when he's obviously a fucking suspect. Why would you release a photofit of him otherwise?'

DS Townsend was none too comfortable around Vinny Butler. The man made him feel edgy. 'The boss is meeting with the media again this morning. He wants to get as much publicity for Molly as possible. As for your question about this lad being a suspect, we can't be sure at this stage. As soon as we receive any more information, you will be the first to know.'

When Townsend and his seemingly mute colleague left the office, Vinny picked up the photo of Molly that sat pride of place on his desk. Tears streaming down his face, he looked at his daughter sitting on her rocking horse. With her mop of curly blonde hair, bright green eyes and dashing smile, she looked so incredibly beautiful. His voice choked with tears, he whispered to her, 'Where are you, my angel? Daddy loves and misses you so very much.'

Christopher Walker was at home with his mother. He had slept better since Molly had been missing. Obviously, he didn't wish the child any harm, but her disappearance could not have come at a better time for him. It gave him the breathing space he so badly needed after the horrendous situation he'd found himself in. It might even mean he would be spared having to arrest Vinny Butler. When a child as young as Molly went missing for this length of time, there was rarely a happy ending. That being the case, participating in drug deals should be the last thing on Vinny Butler's mind for the foreseeable future.

'What you up to on your day off? Doing anything nice?' Mary asked her son.

'I'm meeting Olivia after work and taking her for a meal. Are you not working in the café today?'

'No. I'm planning to pop round to see Joanna and Nancy. The pair of them are in bits, and I can't stop thinking of that poor little girl. I know you hate Vinny, son, but that child is a dear little soul and Jo's a lovely girl too. Do you think Molly will turn up? Has anybody said anything about her disappearance at work?'

'A few of the lads have spoken about it, but I try to distance myself. It's very embarrassing for me in my position to be linked to a family like the Butlers. As for Molly being found safe, I would prepare yourself for the worst.'

The sound of the phone ringing stopped Mary from asking any more questions. Her face fell as she listened to what the caller had to say.

'Are you sure it was Daniel? . . . OK, I'll come and collect him now.'

'What's the matter?' Christopher asked his mother.

'It's Daniel. He's had a fight at school and cut another little boy's head open. He's very distressed apparently, and the school wants me to bring him home.'

Christopher tutted and shook his head in disgust. 'Like father like son.'

*

DI Smithers was flummoxed. Since the TV appeal, four witnesses had come forward to say they had seen the lad opposite the club around the time of Molly's disappearance. Two other witnesses had reported seeing a lad in Victoria Park with a child in a pushchair who could have been Molly.

DI Smithers scratched his head. Even though the lad outside Vinny's club was sitting down, the four witnesses who had so far come forward all reckoned he was tall. One had even said he had long legs. Yet the lad who was seen with the pushchair in the park was described as being short and wearing a woolly hat. Both were described as wearing a navy tracksuit, so surely it had to be the same lad, didn't it?

'Boss, I've spoken to the dog section and they're on their way to Victoria Park as we speak. Robbo and Pat have just headed over to Dagenham again to check out Jackson's alibi. They know where the lady lives now, but she wasn't in last night.'

Smithers nodded at his colleague. His gut instinct told him that the quicker Victoria Park was searched, the better.

Nancy immediately assumed the worst when she opened the front door and saw Michael standing there. 'What is it? Has something happened?'

'No, I just wanted to pop round to see how you and Jo are coping? Can I come in?'

'Yes, of course. Jo isn't here. Her mum has taken her to see her dad. Please don't tell Vinny though. Jo is in a bad enough state as it is, without her getting any more grief from him.'

'I won't say a dickie, I promise. But thanks for telling me the truth. My mum has always said that a liar is worse than a thief and that was why I was so pissed off with you. You could have trusted me you know, about the wedding. I am your husband.'

Unaware that Michael had been anything but honest with her in the past, Nancy put her arms around his neck. 'I know that now, and I am really sorry.'

Vinny Butler put the phone down and digested the news Geary had just given him. Micky Dunn had been released yesterday evening, but they still had Bobby Jackson in custody. Surely they must have some proof that the bastard had something to do with Molly's disappearance? Else they would have let him go by now.

'Ahmed, answer that. It's probably Nick. He rang earlier to say he was popping by.'

Feeling the stress more than ever, Vinny poured himself a Scotch. The longer the search went on for Molly, the more his heart ached and he feared the worst.

'Eddie Mitchell is outside and wishes to speak to you. Do you want me to invite him in?' Ahmed asked.

Vinny was stunned. Since the Krays had been banged up, his family and the Mitchells had been the two main forces in the East End. However, apart from the odd hello and the Mitchells attending Roy and Lenny's funeral, the two families had never really crossed one another's paths. 'Yes, invite him in.'

Ahmed did so, but at the same time told Vinny he had to pop out for a bit. He had heard about the Mitchell brothers and their father and even though he was not scared of any bastard, he would rather steer clear of that family.

'Can I get you a drink, Eddie?' Vinny asked politely.

'I'll have a Scotch on the rocks, but only if you're having one yourself.'

Vinny strolled behind the bar. Did Eddie have some

information about his daughter? If not, what was the purpose of his visit?

Vinny put the drinks on the table, then sat down. 'I take it you've heard about Molly?'

'Yes. I have a daughter myself and I cannot begin to imagine what you must be going through. My Jessica saw the appeal on TV last night, so I thought I'd pop in and see if we can help in any way, just say the word.'

'Cheers, Eddie. That's decent of you, mate. It's been fucking awful not knowing where Molly is . . . it's the worst thing I have ever had to go through.'

Eddie Mitchell took a sip of his drink. 'I can well believe that. I would rip any bastard's limbs off who ever touched my Frankie, that's for sure. Do you have any idea who might have taken Molly?'

'I have my suspicions, but no concrete proof yet. Whoever has taken her will wish they'd never been born by the time I finish with them, trust me on that one.'

'Well, I'll keep my ear to the ground and my father and brothers will do the same, Vinny. Most things are deemed as acceptable in our world, but not when it involves children. I'll be in touch if I get wind of anything.'

'Thanks, mate. Can I get you another drink?'

'No, thanks. My brother Ronny is waiting outside in the car. We have to be somewhere soon. This is my number if you need anything,' Eddie said, handing Vinny a card.

'Well, I really appreciate you taking the time to pop in and see me, Eddie. It means a lot and I won't forget it.'

Eddie Mitchell held out his right hand. 'It's called mutual respect, Vinny, and I hope and pray that Molly is reunited with you soon. I really do.'

DI Smithers was about to leave his office for the press briefing when a colleague came dashing his way. 'We've just had another anonymous phonecall. Same lad as yesterday. He said Molly was being held in a block of flats, but wouldn't say where. I tried to keep him talking. I asked after Molly's welfare and urged him to call back to speak to a senior officer, but he just put the phone down on me.'

'Did you pick up any background noises?'

'Yes, I could hear traffic and I'm sure I heard a trader shout something out. Perhaps he's calling from a phonebox in a market? It could even be Whitechapel.'

'Get on to the TSU in case he calls back again. It could be some crank, but let's not take any chances. We need to trace the next call.'

Joanna Preston could not face going back to her parents' house in Tiptree. For one thing, she wanted to stay near to home in case there was any news of Molly. And secondly, now that her daughter's disappearance was common knowledge, she could not bear the thought of bumping into any of her former neighbours or her old pal Chloe.

Discussing Molly's plight with family was one thing, but she couldn't handle strangers asking about her. That was why her dad had taken a train to Barking and they were currently sitting in the park together.

After the awful rain over the past couple of days, the September weather was now warm and sunny again. Knowing that Johnny wanted to chat to Joanna alone, Deborah said she was off to get some refreshments.

Johnny winked at his wife. 'A nice cold can of beer or two would go down a treat, if you can find an offie, babe.'

When Deborah walked away, Johnny put his arm around his daughter's shoulders. She had looked so happy and vibrant at the wedding, but resembled a different person today. 'The police will find Molly, sweetheart. They know what they're doing.'

'But will she be alive or dead, Dad?' Joanna wept. It had been forty-eight hours now since her daughter had gone missing and Jo knew that the more time ticked on, the less chance there was of Molly being found alive.

'All we can do is pray that Molly is safe, darling. Your mum told me what happened at the press conference yesterday. I would put money on it that Vinny couldn't go through with it because he knows it was down to him that Molly got snatched. He's a wrong 'un, love, and the quicker you realize that, the better.'

Joanna squeezed her father's hand. 'I am starting to realize that, Dad, and I've already decided that if Molly does come home, we cannot live with Vinny any more. No way can I ever go through anything like this again, not ever.'

When Micky Dunn opened his front door, his face fell the moment he saw Vinny Butler. 'What do you want?' he asked, unable to keep the quiver out of his voice.

'A little chat,' Vinny spat.

'My wife and kids are indoors, so we can't chat here,' Micky gabbled. He was petrified of Vinny. His reputation was bad enough, but he also had the most piercing evil green eyes that Micky had ever seen.

Vinny grabbed Micky's arm. 'Best me and you go for a little drive then, eh?'

'I can't, Vinny. My wife has to go out in a minute and I have to take care of my kids.'

Vinny Butler gave Micky Dunn a swift knee in the bollocks, then as the man crashed to his knees, Vinny smashed his head against the pavement. 'If you don't get in my car, I swear on my dear old mum's life I will fucking kill you. And you know how much I love my dear old mum, don't you?'

Absolutely terrified, Micky nodded and got in the car.

*

Donald Walker was utterly horrified on learning of his grandson's violent behaviour and Mary was currently trying to calm the awkward situation down. 'Go to your room, boys, while me and your granddad have a little chat,' Mary ordered.

'I am appalled, Mary. That child needs to be taken in hand. I told you I had noticed a change in him just recently, didn't I?'

Donald was a nightmare once he got a bee in his bonnet, so Mary had no alternative other than to stick up for her grandson. 'You don't even know the full story yet. Billy Jenkins was mocking Daniel over Molly's disappearance, which is why Daniel flipped. He loves his cousin, Donald, and is very upset over what has happened.'

'I don't care how upset Daniel is. That does not excuse the fact he has repeatedly smashed a boy's head against the school railings. As much as I love our grandsons, I have always been worried about how they will one day turn out. Once a Butler, always a bloody Butler, Mary.'

Burak Zane poured himself and his cousin a drink. 'So, how's it going? And how is our dear friend coping with the loss of his daughter?'

Ahmed grinned. 'Not very well. I think he's had some information off that retired crooked Chief Inspector he knows, but he wouldn't say what.'

Burak sighed. 'That is worrying, Ahmed. Vinny used to confide in you with everything. Do you think he has any inkling we are no longer his friends?'

'No. He said Geary had sworn him to secrecy. I presume the police have just tugged somebody in relation to Molly going missing. I will find out later, when Vinny gets pissed again tonight. I am sure he was on the verge of blabbing last night, but changed his mind at the very last moment.

There is good news though: I have now bonded with his son. Little Vinny is my new best friend.'

Burak chuckled. 'So, what are we going to do about this drug set-up?'

'Believe me, the last thing on Vinny's mind at this moment is participating in any drug deal. But I think this can work in our favour. As soon as I find out who the Old Bill have in custody, I will encourage Vinny to kill them, or any of their associates. I will then make sure he gets done for murder. That will carry a much longer sentence than drugs and it will save us paying Carl Thompson. That cunt had the cheek to not only slam the phone down on me, but also throw my money back in my face. I am not happy about that, Burak. Not happy at all.'

'As I said before, I think you should be wary about the Carl situation. We need to keep him sweet, for now at least.'

Ahmed shook his head. 'Carl has already had fifteen grand out of us, and I would rather dispose of him than pay him any more. Nobody disrespects me and gets away with it, Burak. Nobody!'

After his nan headed off for her weekly bingo session the boy settled in front of the big TV in the lounge to watch the local news. The picture was so much clearer here than on the portable set in his bedroom.

When his photofit popped up, the boy chuckled. Not only did it look very little like him, they had even got his age wrong. Between seventeen and twenty? The Old Bill were such mugs. He was only bloody fourteen.

# CHAPTER THIRTY-TWO

DI Smithers was not in the best of moods. Having involved the Technical Support Unit the previous day, he was very disappointed the mystery caller had not rung back.

Bobby Jackson's alibi had now been confirmed, and the dog section had found no trace of Molly in Victoria Park. There had been plenty more phone calls about possible sightings of Molly and a few suggested names for the boy in the photofit, but nothing worth getting excited about.

Smithers scratched his head as he often did when his mind was working overtime. One phonecall or lead could be all it took to crack this case, and he just hoped today would be the day when that happened.

The last person Donald Walker expected to see on his doorstep early on Sunday morning was Freda Smart. 'Hello, Freda. Do come in. How are you?'

'So, so. Got a message for your Nancy from my Dean. He's desperate to speak to her. I also thought I'd better pop round and explain my interview. I purposely never mentioned Nancy or Michael as I would never drag your daughter or young grandchildren into it. I have too much respect for you, Nancy and Mary to do that. Is Mary in?'

'She has just popped to the shop with the boys. What interview is this?'

'The one in today's paper. The rest of Whitechapel might be too frightened to speak out against Vinny Butler, but I bloody well ain't. Don't get me wrong, my heart goes out to that poor child of his, but what hope did she ever have with a father like him, eh? I'll bet you all the tea in China that some rival of Vinny's has snatched that dear little girl, and more than likely done away with her because of his past actions. He has always been fond of doing away with people himself, Donald, and in the end you reap what you sow in life.'

Queenie Butler was a creature of habit and as far back as she could remember, even when times were hard, she'd always cooked some kind of fry-up on a Sunday morning.

'Mmm, that smells nice, love,' Albie politely remarked.

Queenie flipped the eggs over. Albie had been reasonably well behaved since turning up on her doorstep, but the very sight of him and the sound of his voice grated terribly on her. She was also narked that he and Viv were suddenly chatting away like old pals. The two-faced pair of bastards had always despised one another, and she would soon put a stop to that little friendship.

''Ere you go, get that down your neck. Then once you've eaten it, I want you to take a little walk round to the club with your case. Plenty of room there for you to say with the boys.'

'But I don't want to stay where Vinny is, Queen. I would much rather stop here.'

'Well, that won't be possible I'm afraid. This family is already the talk of the neighbourhood, without people gossiping any more. That's all I need, the neighbours thinking I've let you move back in after all your past shenanigans.'

A crestfallen Albie took his breakfast into the lounge. He had thought he had built some bridges at long last, but it was now obvious Queenie still held a grudge against him and probably always would.

'Queen, you ain't gonna be happy,' Vivian said, bursting through the front door waving a copy of the *News of the World* in the air.

'Whatever's the matter?'

Vivian was out of breath from dashing back from the shop so quickly. 'I bumped into Nosy Hilda round the corner. She'd already seen the article. That old cow Mad Freda has given an interview to a reporter. Slagged us all off, she has.'

Queenie's face drained of colour. 'Give us that paper 'ere. She won't get away with this. I'll see to that.'

Nancy Butler was appalled to learn that her son had smashed another boy's head against the railings at school. 'Why didn't you tell me as soon as it happened, Mum?'

'Because I didn't want to worry you. You've got enough on your plate already. You said you'd be popping round to see the boys today, so I thought it would be kinder to tell you in person. Your father is not best pleased, as you can well imagine. Neither is Christopher.'

'And neither am I, Mum. I'm bloody fuming. Is the other little boy OK? Are his parents or the school taking any action?'

'Not as far as I know, although the school did ask me politely to keep Daniel at home next week. The other little boy had to be taken to hospital to be checked over and have stitches, apparently. It's all a bit of a mess, isn't it, love? In his defence, Daniel insists he only attacked the boy because he said something nasty about Molly.'

'That's no excuse, Mum. Whatever the boy said does not

condone violence. I cannot tell you how disappointed in Daniel I am, and will give him what for when Dad brings him back from the park. I'll have to drag Michael up the school with me tomorrow to apologize and sort this out.'

'To be honest, love, it might be best if you take Daniel home or back to Jo's house with you today. I can't look after him all day every day next week. Your dad needs my help in the café.'

Nancy nodded.

'Freda Smart popped around earlier. She gave me a new phone number for Dean. He's heard about Molly, and is desperate to speak with you. I said you would give him a call. I really don't think Freda should have given that story to the newspaper though. As I said to your dad, she certainly knows how to stir up a hornets' nest.'

'What story?'

'The one in today's paper. See for yourself – I thought Michael would have already told you,' Mary said, handing her daughter the *News of the World*.

'I haven't spoken to Michael today. Oh my God!' Nancy exclaimed, putting her hand over her mouth as she spotted the headline on page seven: MISSING GIRL'S FATHER IS NOTORIOUS GANGLAND FIGURE.

Unaware that Nancy was currently reading Freda's interview, Michael was sitting next to his brother doing the same. He was relieved that he, Nancy and the boys were not mentioned. If they had been, he knew his wife would have hit the roof.

The bulk of the interview was Freda slagging off Vinny and insinuating Molly's disappearance was payback for one of his past sins. She described Vinny as a menace and said that most of the locals were terrified of him. She also mentioned that Roy had been shot in a gangland hit, and there had been another fatal shooting at Vinny's nightclub last year.

Freda then took a pop at Queenie and Vivian, before speaking about her own family:

> My son Terry mysteriously disappeared many years ago after an altercation with Vinny Butler, so it does not need a genius to work out what happened there. I knew not long after Terry first went missing that he was no longer with us. A mother just knows these things. I wish the police would re-open the case as a murder investigation and try to find my boy's remains. At least if I could give him some kind of a funeral, it would bring me comfort in the latter years of my life
>
> As for my grandson, Dean, I rue the day he ever got involved with Vinny's sister, Brenda. He was forced into a shotgun wedding, and unable to suffer any more unhappiness, had to leave the area in a hurry. I've had no contact with Dean since, but I am glad he escaped that family. He would have ended up dead like his father had he stayed around Whitechapel.

Vinny threw the newspaper towards his mother. 'Today's news is tomorrow's chip wrapping. Seeing as I have never spent even one poxy day in prison, I really don't see how these papers get away with printing such tripe. Especially as it came from the mouth of that mad old bat.'

'How could she call me and Viv materialistic women who encouraged you to take up a life of crime, eh? I have never been so insulted! Your Auntie Viv isn't best pleased either. Why don't you hire a good lawyer and sue the bastards?' Queenie asked.

'Not worth it, Mum. The press are very careful the way they word such articles and every single insult and insinuation has come from Freda's mouth, not theirs. Fuck her and fuck them. I've got far bigger things to worry about than what that nutty old cow has said.'

'Well, I am bastard-well livid and I'm going round her house in a minute to have it out with her.'

'No, you are not, Mum. Don't rise to the bait. If you march round there kicking off, she'll probably do another interview. I don't believe for one minute that Freda hasn't heard from Dean since he left Bren. One day the truth will come out – and when it does, I'll be waiting in the wings. Dean can pay for his and his grandmother's sins.'

Feeling increasingly uncomfortable around Vinny, Albie stared at his suitcase rather than look at him. It was obvious what he meant by saying Dean would pay and it sent shivers down Albie's spine. He had thankfully not been spoken about in Freda's interview, but he'd had to smile wryly when he heard what she had said about Queenie and Vivian. It was so very apt.

Vinny leapt up and grabbed the phone on the first ring. 'Hello.'

'It's me. Your pal is back on the streets. His alibi stood up.'

Little Vinny was sitting in Ben Bloggs' bedroom drinking cider and chain-smoking. 'Come on, Ben. Let's go out somewhere. It's boring sitting in here. My dad gave me a score, so I've got enough money to get us more booze.'

'I still don't feel too well, Vin. I've had that stomach bug for days now, and I keep spewing up.'

Ben had his own bed, but shared his bedroom with four of his younger siblings who all slept on a big filthy mattress on the floor. The room stank of urine and sick and even though Little Vinny had got used to the smell over the years, he still felt grubby every time he left Ben's house. He put a comforting arm around his pal's shoulders. 'Fresh air will do you the world of good, so will getting bladdered with me. Why don't we jump on a train and travel up and down the District Line, eh? We might even find ourselves some tasty birds?'

'Not today, Vin. I really don't feel up to it.'

'You been watching the news? The police have issued some photofit of a lad that they think snatched Molly.'

'No. I've not seen the news. What does the lad look like?'

'Tall, with dark-hair and green eyes. I think he's a Mod because of his hairstyle, and the Old Bill reckons he's between seventeen and twenty. He was sat opposite the club on the day Molly went missing.'

'Really? I wonder who that is?'

Little Vinny shrugged. 'And I've got some other gossip, but you must promise me you will never tell a soul.'

'What?'

'You know when Lenny died in that car crash?'

Ben nodded.

'Well, it wasn't Ahmed that killed him, it was my dad.'

'No way! How do you know that?'

'Ahmed told me. He thought I already knew. He's OK is Ahmed. Fancy my dad letting him take the blame for something he didn't do. That isn't what pals are all about, is it? I would never do shit like that to you.'

When his spaced-out smackhead of a mother barged into the room demanding some drink and cigarettes, Ben grabbed Little Vinny's arm. 'Come on. I feel better now. Let's go out.'

The boy cut the article out with delicate care and put it inside the LP cover where he had hidden all the others. He had never bought or read so many newspapers in his life as he had over the past few days.

Debating whether to ring the Old Bill again tomorrow,

the boy decided against it. Now that the search for Molly was all over the news and front pages, they might even have a go at tracing his next call. He'd already pushed his luck by tormenting the Old Bill, and the last thing he wanted was to get himself in trouble again. His nan would kill him if he brought the police to her front door.

Thinking of the interview that woman had given about Vinny, the boy put his hands behind his head, laid back on his bed and smirked. Apart from his hair, which he had since had the brains to get cut, that photofit bore no resemblance to him whatsoever. So tomorrow, he would pay another little visit to Whitechapel, just for the fun of it. There was nothing quite like experiencing the excitement of Molly's disappearance in the flesh.

Micky Dunn hobbled towards the front door. He had seen it was Bobby through the curtains. 'Fucking hell! What happened?' Bobby asked. His pal had a black eye and was clutching at his ribs as though he were in terrible pain.

'Your mouth running away with you, then Vinny Butler paying me a visit, that's what happened. You can't come in, Bob. My Paula is furious that the Old Bill hauled me in, then I was the one to get a hiding from Butler. She's only popped round the shops, and will go apeshit if she sees you here.'

'I'm sorry, mate. How about we go for a beer? I'll pay – we don't have to go in the Beggar.'

'No way. I can barely move, thanks to you. Honestly, Bob, if you've got any sense you will make yourself scarce until the police find out who took Molly. Vinny was not a happy man, and I had to tell him the conversation we had because he threatened to slit my throat if I didn't. I told him that you were pissed and that I knew you were innocent, but he is one violent bastard. Look at the back of my head.'

Bobby saw the dried blood and suddenly felt alarmed for his own safety. Perhaps he should shoot over to Dagenham and stay with his pal until the dust settled?

'Look, I'm sorry again, Mick. I'll do as you say and make myself scarce, then bell you in a day or two.'

Michael Butler was none too pleased when Nancy turned up at the club with Daniel in tow and started shouting at him like some nutjob in front of Vinny and Ahmed.

'When I say I need to speak to you urgently, Michael, I do not expect to wait hours – especially not when it involves our son.'

'All right, Nance, calm down. You said Daniel had had a fight, not a bloody heart attack. Let's talk upstairs,' an embarrassed Michael muttered, grabbing his wife by the arm.

Nancy did her best to stay calm as she recounted the incident at the school. She knew that it was a storm in a teacup compared to what had happened to Molly, but that didn't stop her worrying about her son.

Aware that Daniel was staring at him with doleful eyes, Michael ordered his son to sit next to him. 'What did the boy say about Molly, son?'

'Billy said that Molly was dead, and he said his dad said it was because our family were bad people,' Daniel told his father.

'Oh, did he now? Do you know what Billy's dad does for a living, boy?'

'Yeah. He's a policeman like Uncle Christopher.'

'Well, in that case you had every right to clump him, Daniel, and if he ever says anything similar, then you clump him again. Now, dry them eyes. You've done nothing wrong whatsoever.'

'Nothing wrong! Nothing bloody wrong! He smashed a

lad's head against the railings, Michael, and the boy was taken to hospital. I cannot believe this Billy's dad is a policeman. Christopher and my dad will go mad if they find that out. As for you encouraging our son to be violent, I'm disgusted.'

'Son, go in the bedroom while me and your mum have a little chat.'

When Daniel left the room, Michael shut the door then turned to Nancy. 'Our son has done sod all wrong. What that Billy said was fucking despicable, and Daniel had every right to stick up for his cousin and family. I bet that Billy's father is nothing more than some low-ranking PC out of Barking nick. You mark my words, there'll be no comeback. How can there be when a man of the law has said shit like that in front of his young son, eh?'

'I can't believe I am hearing you speak this way, Michael. Have you been drinking?'

'No, I have not been drinking, Nancy. Have you? Only you seem to have forgotten Molly is missing, you're so busy fussing about our son getting into a little scrap at school.'

'How dare you! I've been devastated over Molly – I have spent every single day since comforting Jo.'

'Well, do yourself a favour and go and comfort her again now. Daniel can stay here with me tonight.'

'I don't think so. I'm not going to have you, Vinny and that Turk telling him he's done well for beating up a copper's son.'

'Nance, I really don't need this shit at the moment. I will go to the school tomorrow and speak with Daniel's headmistress, OK? I am sure once she hears what was said, all will be fine. If not I'll tell her where she can shove her fucking school. I would never encourage our sons to be violent without a decent reason. However, in this instance, I think Daniel had every right to stick up for Molly and his family, and I'm proud of him for doing so. Them boys are Butlers at the end of the day, whether you like it or not.'

'Well, that's great parenting, that is. Really can't wait until our sons reach their teenage years now. Probably end up with bullets in their heads like Roy did.'

'You're talking absolute bollocks now, Nance, so please fuck off before I really lose my temper.'

Nancy shook her head in disgust. 'My brother is right, you know. He's always said there's no hope for our sons. Once a Butler, always a Butler.'

Michael's eyes glinted dangerously. 'You knew exactly what I and my family were all about long before we ever got together, Nance. So don't go blaming me if our sons don't turn out to be the church-going namby-pambies you seem to desire. Blame your fucking self, sweetheart. Nobody forced you to marry me and have my kids, did they, Mrs Butler?'

As Michael's hard-hitting but truthful words stung her, Nancy burst into tears and ran from the room.

As darkness fell, a devastated Vinny opened up a bottle of Scotch. He had really thought today would be the day when the police got that all-important breakthrough, but even though Smithers had popped in earlier with an update, the Old Bill still seemed no nearer to finding his daughter.

Having just tucked his son into bed, Michael sat down opposite Vinny. 'What did Smithers have to say, bruv?'

'Smithers said tomorrow they'll widen their search to all areas that surround the park. Not looking promising, is it? I think Molly's dead now, I really do. I was hoping somebody had taken her to blackmail me, but if that were the case they'd have contacted me or the filth by now. I can't bear the thought of never seeing her or holding her in my arms again, Michael. I loved her so fucking much. I just hope she didn't suffer too much.'

Michael held his distraught brother in his arms. He wanted to offer some words of comfort, but this was no time for bullshit. Molly had been missing for over seventy hours and the chances of finding her alive were looking bleaker by the second.

# CHAPTER THIRTY-THREE

Deborah Preston was awoken by her daughter's terrified screams. 'What is it, love? You had another nightmare?'

Joanna sat up, her face deathly white. 'I dreamt the police knocked on the door and told me they had found Molly's body. It was awful and so real. I just want my baby back. I miss her so much.'

Feeling totally helpless, Deborah held her trembling daughter in her arms. She had not left Joanna's side since she had found out Molly was missing, but each day was becoming harder to deal with. Jo would not eat and was wasting away before her very eyes. Stroking her daughter's hair, Deborah kept hearing over and over the words Johnny had said when he phoned last night: 'I truly fear the very worst now, Deb. You need to prepare Jo for that news in the kindest possible way. Breaks my heart to say this, but that beautiful child I never even had the pleasure of meeting is more than likely dead.'

Ahmed picked up the phone. 'It's me, Carl. I've had the guy who I'm buying the bar off in Spain on the phone to me this morning. He wants to complete the deal early, so I need the rest of that dosh you owe me.'

'How many times do I have to tell you, Carl? You will not be getting the rest of your dosh until the job has been completed. That was the deal.'

The patronizing tone of Ahmed's voice was enough to make Carl Thompson see red. He was no fool and would not suffer being treated as if he were. 'See you, you Turkish cunt. You will regret the day you ever met me, trust me on that one. I've got big plans for you, boyo.'

When Carl cut him off, Ahmed rang Burak at the restaurant and related the conversation. 'I told you I did not trust him, didn't I, Ahmed? I said you should be careful. Why not just pay him another ten grand to keep him sweet?'

'Nobody threatens me and gets away with it, Burak. I would not give the cheeky cunt the drippings of my nose now, let alone another ten grand. I have a better idea. I shall call him back, pretend that I am going to pay him off and arrange to meet him at the yard in Barking. Then, when he turns up, we will kill him.'

Old Mr Arthur was on his way to the bookies for his daily bet when he spotted a familiar face. He had found it quite difficult to help the police produce a photofit, but he knew he'd recognize that face again if he were to see it in person.

Mr Arthur looked down as he passed the boy, then quickly turned around. He would lose sight of him if he were to ring the police, so the only alternative was to follow him. People might take him for a daft old bugger, but he'd never forgotten his army training. Mr Arthur was sure he could deliver the goods.

Brenda Butler poured herself another glass of wine. She had been furious over that *News of the World* article, and even more incensed that her mother and Vinny had ordered her not to confront Freda over her comments. Why shouldn't she have it out with the old cow? She had every bloody right to.

'Mum, me and Tommy are bored. Can you take us out somewhere?' Tara asked, with a sulky expression on her face.

Brenda stared at her daughter. She'd kept the kids home from school today, and now wished she hadn't because Tara wouldn't stop whingeing. 'You wanna go out, we'll go out. Go and get your jacket and Tommy's.'

'Where we going? Pictures?' Tara asked hopefully.

'No. We're going to visit that fucking old witch who just happens to be your great grandma.'

When the boy got on the bus, Mr Arthur did the same. They briefly locked eyes as Mr Arthur sat down opposite him, but there was no recognition in the boy's. He'd had his hair cut, but those evil green eyes were unforgettable.

Mr Arthur pretended to be engrossed in picking out his horses as the bus pulled away. It didn't look as though he'd be able to place his bet now though. He had far more important things to do.

As Nancy walked towards the phonebox, she thought back to the past. She had not spoken to Dean Smart for ages and had not been overly keen to reignite their friendship, but yesterday's argument with Michael had changed that.

There was no way Nancy could admit to anybody that Michael had been proud of Daniel for smashing another boy's head against the railings. Her mum would worry, and her father and Christopher would say 'I told you so.' Joanna was the only one Nancy would have confided in, but the current circumstances meant that was out of the question.

Nancy could still remember clearly the conversation she'd had with Dean the last time she had seen him. She had been unwell and in hospital at the time. 'Your Michael is the best of the bunch, but the core of that family is rotten. If I were you, I would run for the hills. You were never cut out to be part of the Butler clan, and neither was I.'

Taking a deep breath, Nancy stepped inside the phonebox. For the first time in a very long while, she was looking forward to speaking to a man who actually understood her.

Freda Smart was no shrinking violet. Like her idol Maggie Thatcher, she considered herself to have more balls than most men. That is why even though she knew it must be a Butler smashing the hell out of her front door, she still chose to open it.

'This is your great granny. You know, that evil old bag that wrote the article in the newspaper yesterday. She is the reason why you could not go to school today. Same morals as your father,' Brenda shrieked.

Freda stared at the mortified look on the faces of the two children. Tara had got so big since the last time she had seen her, and Tommy looked like Dean had when he was about the same age. It was obvious Brenda was inebriated and it was only early afternoon. 'Take Tara and Tommy home now, Brenda. If you have an issue with me, we can talk another time.'

'An issue! A fucking issue! I have a major one with you, Freda. How dare you announce to the nation that you rue the day that wanker of a grandson of yours got involved with me? Seeing as he walked away without a care in the world when I was pregnant with Tommy, I think it is me who had the lucky escape, don't you?'

When Tara started to cry, Freda wanted to hug the child, but chose not to. Her next-door neighbour had come out to see what all the fuss was about and so had Joe across the road. 'Do yourself a favour, Brenda, and take those children home before somebody calls the police. Don't want to get them taken away from you for being an unfit mother, do you now?'

When their drunken mother lunged towards their great-grandma, Tara and Tommy both screamed out in terror.

Having changed buses when the boy did, Mr Arthur was doing his best to keep him in sight as he followed him down the street. His old combat training was coming back to him, and he was pleased to find that he hadn't lost the art of tracking the enemy without giving the game away. With his legs aching far more than usual, Mr Arthur was delighted when the boy took a detour into what he imagined to be a front garden. Obviously, he was too far away to make out the door number, but he could clearly see a green car and a lamppost very close to where the boy had disappeared.

Mr Arthur scuttled towards the green car as fast as he could. He only hoped there was no alleyway between the houses, because if the boy had succeeded in giving him the slip it would be a morning wasted. And if it turned out that horse he'd been on his way to have a flutter on came in a winner, he'd have lost a bloody fortune too.

Queenie Butler opened the front door and was shocked to see a policeman standing there with Tara and Tommy either side of him. 'Have they done something wrong?' Queenie asked, alarmed. Both of her grandchildren were looking sheepish and her first thought was they had been caught stealing, but before the policeman had chance to reply, Tara piped up: 'Me and Tommy never did anything wrong. Mum did though. She got drunk, then hit Nanny Freda.'

*

When he couldn't get hold of Carl Thompson by phone, Ahmed drove to the flat in Emerson Park that he had leased for six months and allowed Carl to live in. The gaff belonged to a Turkish associate of Ahmed's and had been dead cheap to rent compared to other properties in the area.

Feeling slightly edgy because of the conversation they'd had earlier, Ahmed took a deep breath as he pressed the buzzer. When he received no answer, he then pressed the buzzers of the other eight flats in the block.

'Yes, can I help you?' one of the residents asked.

'I have come to visit my pal, Richie. He lives in flat seven,' Ahmed replied. He had instructed Carl never to use his real name.

'Richie moved out earlier today. I saw him leaving with his belongings.'

Instead of thanking the lady who had just given him the vital information, a worried Ahmed ran back towards his car mumbling expletives.

DI Smithers stared at his colleague in amazement. Even though Mr Arthur had not been the greatest at helping put a photofit together, Smithers had never doubted him as a witness. 'What's the address?'

DS Townsend handed him the piece of paper. 'There you go, boss. Mr Arthur is not sure of the exact house number, but insists it is one out of those six. He swears blind it was the same boy who was sitting opposite the club the day Molly went missing – and gut instinct tells mc he might just be right.'

Kimmy and Lindsey Pollard were forbidden by their parents to go anywhere near where they currently were. Their dad said gypsies owned the land and it was a very dangerous place. However, both Kimmy and Lindsey were very fond of the tethered horses, which is why they regularly brought them carrots. The poor creatures looked so sad and always seemed hungry.

'What's that over there?' Kimmy asked her sister.

Lindsey ran over to the object, picked it up and waved it in the air. 'It's a doll!'

'Give it to me. I saw it first,' Kimmy demanded.

Lindsey clutched the doll tightly to her chest. 'No. I picked it up. Finders keepers.'

Ahmed and Burak Zane were worried men as they headed towards Carl Thompson's previous address. The phone number was no longer valid, but Ahmed knew that Carl's ex-girlfriend owned the gaff, and he was hoping Carl had gone back there.

'I do not know why you allowed Carl to live in the flat in Emerson Park, Ahmed. I said at the time, there was no need to lease it.'

'Yes, there was, Burak. Vinny Butler is no man's fool and I was worried, if he had an inkling that something was not right, he would be knocking on the flat door. That is why I told Carl to tell his neighbours his name was Richie Simpson. Butler could have popped around any time and caught us out. And what if his arrest had gone wrong? I did not want Vinny storming round there the following day and finding out that Richie had never existed or lived there in the first place. That would have put us right in the shit.'

'I have a feeling we are going to struggle tracking down this bastard.'

'Burak, I know he is still in contact with his ex, so we will find him. Let's change the subject for a bit, and talk about Vinny's new obsession instead, shall we?'

'Aw, is that poor little Molly?'

'Nope. It's Eddie Mitchell. As much as Vinny is still missing poor little Molly, he has not stopped bragging about Mitchell's visit either. Thinks he is well in with that family now. Keeps saying how charismatic Eddie is. Apparently Mitchell reminds him of himself.'

Burak chuckled. 'He really rates himself, doesn't he?'

'Yep. Turned all religious and serious on me last night after a few Scotches. Reckons Molly's disappearance was God's way of paying him back for flooding the streets with drugs. He said he wants out.'

'Really? Do you think he is onto us?'

'No, Burak, his head is just in a mess. It was the perfect opportunity for me to tell him that I was pulling out too though. I said that we'd had a good enough run and I had been pondering for a while whether to call it a day. I told him that greedy people always get caught in the end and I wanted to build a hotel in Turkey.'

'Was he OK about it?'

'Yes, he was cool. I told him I would reserve the finest room at the hotel and he could use it for a holiday whenever he wished.'

Burak smirked. 'Perhaps you should invite Molly too?'

DI Smithers knocked on the door of number seventy-one. The house was on the street in Poplar that Mr Arthur had followed the boy to, and the bright green Capri that he had described was parked right outside it.

When a pleasant-looking plump lady in her sixties answered, Smithers flashed his badge and asked if he and Townsend could come inside to ask her some questions. 'Of course you can. My name's Janet, by the way. I bet I know what you're here about – it's that menace next-door-but-one, isn't it? Sick of that bloody loud music, we are. He has that racket on full-blast every time his gran goes out and it's so unfair on poor old Jack next door. He's in his eighties and has terminal cancer, you know.'

When Smithers explained that he had not called about the music, but was trying to track down a dark-haired lad who was thought to live close by, Janet was even more helpful. 'Got to be the one I've just told you about. Jamie, his name is. Apart from Margaret at number sixty-seven whose son has Down's Syndrome, he's the only teenage boy living in this row of houses. Between me and you, I don't like his nan much either. Flash old cow, Shirley is. Rumour has it, that grandson of hers has not long been out of a detention centre, so I do hope yous two put him back in there sharpish.'

Smithers pulled the photofit out of his pocket. 'Does this look anything like him, Janet?'

'Yeah, it does look similar. Jamie's nose isn't as pointed as the one in your photo and his face is more round, but I would definitely say it was him. Exactly the same hairstyle – or it was. Saw him yesterday and he's had it cut short. So, what's he supposed to have done wrong?'

'We're not sure yet, Janet. Hopefully we shall find out very soon though. Thank you so much for your information. Do you know Jamie or his grandmother's surname, by any chance?'

'No. Shirley's a funny woman, keeps herself to herself and is very secretive. Wouldn't surprise me if she had a past and was hiding something an' all.'

Smithers and Townsend glanced at one another as they left the house. Both were thinking the exact same thing. Detention centre, new haircut. Surely they had finally struck gold?

Ahmed had a good look around, but could see no sign of Carl Thompson's car.

Donna was the name of Carl's ex-bird and apparently they had only split up because Carl couldn't handle her twin sons from a previous relationship. Carl had once told him that, even though he couldn't see the pair of them getting back together, he still had strong feelings for Donna, which was why she had been staying around his flat a couple of nights a week.

When Ahmed knocked at the door, he recognized Donna immediately. She was half-caste and very beautiful. He had only met her once before, when he had visited Carl at her house to check that he lived where he said he did. 'Hello, Donna. I don't know if you remember me, but I visited you to speak business with Carl just before you split up.'

Donna looked perplexed. 'Carl who?'

'Carl Thompson, your ex. You were here, Donna, when I visited Carl. So were your twin boys.'

'Oh him. Yeah, I remember now. I didn't actually know Carl that well to be honest. I had only met him about a week before you came round here. He seemed keen on me and we went out for a meal. Then he asked me to do him a favour. He said that you were coming round to talk business and he wanted me to pretend that we were a proper couple. He offered me five hundred quid, and bought my boys a load of toys. I was a bit skint at the time, so couldn't really say no.'

'Who is it, Don?' asked a tall black guy who sauntered into the hallway.

'Just some pals of a bloke I barely knew. This is my boyfriend, Steve,' Donna informed the rather shocked-looking men on her doorstep.

'Come on, let's go,' Burak ordered, tugging his cousin's arm.

Ahmed was speechless as he walked back towards the car. Carl had been recommended to him by a very trustworthy contact as one of the best con artists he had ever worked with. It had never occurred to Ahmed the guy would be good enough to con him.

'Told you not to trust an Englishman again, didn't I?' Burak reminded his cousin.

Unable to stop himself, Ahmed grabbed his cousin roughly. 'Vinny would not have trusted another Turk, how many times do I have to tell you that? So, stop fucking blaming me, OK?'

'What do we do now?'

'We find the cunt, cut his lying tongue out of his mouth, then watch him die a slow painful death.'

When Smithers and Townsend introduced themselves, then asked if they could speak to her grandson, Shirley's heart lurched. When her daughter had disowned Jamie and refused to let him come home after his release from the detention centre, she had taken him in out of the goodness of her heart. But she had always warned him that if he brought trouble to her door, he would be straight out on his ear.

'What's Jamie meant to have done?' Shirley asked.

'Nothing, as far as we know. We just need to ask him some questions, that's all,' Smithers replied.

'Follow me. He's in his bedroom. I've only just got back from Chrisp Street, which is why that little sod has his music blaring. Is that why you're here? The neighbours have all complained about him playing loud music when I go out, but he never does it of a night when I'm home. Teenagers will be teenagers, won't they?'

Having been led to believe that his nan would not be back until after teatime as she was meant to go shopping then visit a friend, Jamie was singing along happily to The Jam's 'Eton Rifles' as he carefully cut out all the latest articles about Molly from today's newspapers.

Shirley burst into her grandson's bedroom. 'Turn that racket off. These policemen want to talk to you. What you been up to, eh?'

Jamie went as white as a ghost as one of the policemen walked towards him, then stared at the newspaper cutting in his trembling right hand.

'Well well, this looks interesting. What's your surname, lad?'

'Preston – but this isn't what it looks like. I ain't done nothing wrong, I swear,' Jamie babbled.

The name Preston was the final piece in the jigsaw for Smithers. 'Jamie Preston, I am arresting you on suspicion of the abduction of Molly Butler. You do not have to say anything unless you wish to do so, but anything you do say—'

It was at that point Shirley Preston fainted.

Dickie Murray worked long hours, so as soon as he arrived home the first thing he did was take his beloved Alsatian Rex for a long walk.

Wallis Road and the pockets of land that lay beyond it could be quite an eerie place at the best of times, especially if darkness was falling. The River Lea ran nearby, and if you headed north it was not that far from Hackney Marshes. There was a lot of overgrown wasteland, some of which had been taken over by gypsies and scrap-metal merchants.

'Come on, Rex. This way,' Dickie ordered as his dog began to bark ferociously.

Dickie had never known his dog to totally blank him when he gave a command, so he walked back to where Rex was. Still barking, he was now frantically digging as well. 'What you found, boy?' Dickie asked fondly. His dog was forever burying bones in the garden, then digging them back up again.

As Dickie stared at what Rex had found, his mouth went dry and his heart started to pound.

It looked like the arm of a small child.

Dickie bent down to take a closer look. He could now clearly see four fingers and a thumb attached to the arm. Wondering if it was a doll or some kind of dummy a joker had buried for a laugh, he touched the hand – then let out a scream as he recoiled in horror.

# CHAPTER THIRTY-FOUR

Kimmy and Lindsey Pollard were still squabbling over the doll they had found. 'It's mine because I saw it first,' Kimmy said, trying to snatch it out of her sister's hand.

Lindsey tightened her grip on her find. 'No, it's mine, because I picked it up. You didn't even know what it was.'

Aware of a commotion going on in the lounge, Sarah Pollard stormed in to find out what her daughters were arguing about. 'Where did you get that?' she asked, as soon as she laid eyes on the doll.

'I found it, Mum, but Kimmy reckons she did. I picked it up, so it's mine.'

'But I saw it first. I told you to pick it up,' Lindsey insisted.

Sarah Pollard bent down and took the doll out of Lindsey's hands. She had watched all the news reports about Molly Butler and she knew this was the same type of doll that the police had asked the public to look out for, as she had been planning on purchasing two for her daughters for Christmas. 'Where did you find this, girls?'

Kimmy and Lindsey glanced at one another. Both were scared to tell the truth in case their mum told their dad. 'Just in a street,' Kimmy mumbled.

'What street? This is very important. You know that poor little girl that has gone missing? Well, I think this might be her doll. I won't be angry if you have been visiting those horses again. But you must tell me exactly where you found this, as I need to tell the police and we mustn't lie to them.'

Lindsey started to cry. 'You won't tell Dad if we tell you, will you?'

'No. But you must tell me the truth. That little girl who is missing needs to be found.'

'We found the doll over the fields where the horses are, Mum. We wasn't doing anything wrong. We just bought some carrots because the horses look starving,' Kimmy explained.

Sarah held her daughters in her arms. 'I'm going to phone the police now and you might need to show them the exact spot you found this doll, OK?'

Thankful that their mum was not angry with them, Kimmy and Lindsey both nodded.

Having recovered from her initial shock, Shirley Preston was sitting by her grandson's side at the police station. He was flanked on the other side by a solicitor. Jamie was proclaiming his innocence, swearing that he'd had nothing to do with Molly's disappearance, and for once Shirley actually believed him. Jamie might be a lot of things, and he had got himself put away for stabbing a boy in an argument. But Shirley did not believe he was capable of snatching a young child, even if that kid did belong to Vinny Butler.

About to start the interview, Smithers was called out of the room by a colleague. 'Guv, a woman's just rung up saying she's got Molly's doll. Says her daughters found it over the pockets of land that back onto Wallis Road. It sounds viable – it's just a stone's throw from Victoria

Park. That's the area the dog section were planning to search tomorrow.'

'Send somebody straight round there. If the doll is identical to Molly's, we need her daughters to show us the exact spot they found it.'

When Dickie Murray finally arrived home, both he and Rex were panting. Neither were used to running these days. Rex was ten, which was seventy in canine years and Dickie was fifty-eight himself.

'I'll get you your dinner in a minute, boy,' Dickie said. His hands were still trembling when he picked up the phone. It wasn't every day you went for a walk and found what he was sure was a dead child buried in a very shallow grave.

When the operator answered, Dickie took a deep breath. 'Police, please. It's urgent.'

Back at the police station, Smithers and Townsend were grilling Jamie Preston. 'Look, I admit I was outside the club the day Molly went missing. I even saw her go into the club. But I never took her, I swear.'

'So, why was you there then? And why are you cutting out articles about Molly's disappearance? Come on, Jamie, this isn't looking good for you, is it? Just be honest and tell us where Molly is.'

'I don't know where Molly is. I was at the club to pay my respects to my brother, Mark. He died there, in a fire, and the day I was sat there would have been his eighteenth birthday.'

'He's telling the truth. It would have been Mark's eighteenth birthday,' Shirley chipped in.

'But why cut out articles about Molly? You must have had a reason to do that, Jamie? Very strange thing to do, isn't it?'

Shirley was beside herself with worry. Her house was currently being searched and she prayed the police found no more evidence to link her grandson to Molly. 'Why did you cut the articles out, Jamie? Tell the policeman the truth,' she urged.

Before Jamie had a chance to answer, the door burst open. 'Boss, I need you now. It's important.'

Smithers leapt up and dashed out of the room. The look on his colleague's face was the giveaway.

'Has Molly been found?'

'Looks that way. A dog walker has just reported finding what he thinks is the body of a young child buried in a shallow grave.'

'Whereabouts?'

'The wasteland that backs onto Wallis Road. The search team and dog section are heading over there right now.'

Tarkan Smith was not your average name for a Turkish guy. His mother Aysel had married an Englishman called Reggie, which was why he had been landed with such an unusual mixture of names.

Ahmed had done plenty of business with Tarkan in the past and not once had he had an issue. He did now though. It was Tarkan who had recommended and introduced Carl Thompson to him, which was why Ahmed was now sitting stony-faced opposite Tarkan in a pub in Islington. 'You must have a previous address for Carl? He's done a fucking runner and could cause me major problems if not found.'

'Carl's always been a guy who moves about a lot. He's a bit of a mystery, but he's trustworthy. I know at least four other people he has done business with and nobody has ever had a problem with him. What exactly has happened?'

When Ahmed explained in a roundabout way without mentioning names or a missing child, Tarkan tutted. 'I did warn you before I introduced you to Carl that he was no pushover. You should have just paid him off, Ahmed. It wasn't his fault that the job couldn't be completed.'

'And it wasn't mine either. I gave Carl fifteen grand up front and told him clearly that the balance of his money would be paid on completion of the job. Due to unforeseen circumstances, the job had to be called off. Carl is still fifteen grand better off and has been living rent-free ever since we set this deal up. I also paid the bills at the flat, so Carl hasn't done bad out of this, Tarkan.'

'Yes, but if Carl was relying on that money to buy a bar in Spain, he won't be best pleased.'

'You are speaking about him as if he is some big shot, Tarkan. That obviously cannot be the case as big shots have money. Carl is a fucking pauper; else he wouldn't be relying on my thirty-five grand to buy his poxy bar in Spain.'

'Carl would be worth a fortune if it wasn't for his love of gambling. He used to spend seven nights a week in casinos. He only stopped when he lost everything. That's why this deal he had with you was so important to him. He wanted to buy the bar and move to Spain so he could make a fresh start.'

'The fact he spunked all his money away like some mug is hardly my fault, is it? I want him found, Tarkan, and fast. In fact I will pay five grand to whoever can track him down.'

'And what do you plan on doing with him?'

'Well, I am hardly going to take him for a night out at the casino, am I? The cunt knows too much and needs to be silenced.'

*

Dickie Murray was worried as he led the team of policemen across the cobbled paths which led to the wasteland where he and Rex had walked. It was pitch-dark now and even though the police had torches, Dickie was anxious he would not be able to remember the exact place where he had seen the arm. The police had brought sniffer dogs with them, so Dickie just hoped that, providing he walked in the right direction, the dogs would pick up a scent.

'I so hope I can find the right spot. So bloody awkward in the dark. I think I could find it much easier in the daylight,' he told them.

The search coordinator patted him on the back. 'You're doing just fine.'

'I know I haven't brought you on a wild-goose chase. As soon as I saw that arm and those little fingers, I knew it was real. I touched it lightly and it was definitely human. Made me feel ill. I've never seen anything like it before.'

Tarkan Smith had a difficult decision to make. Being half Turkish and half English, he had no allegiance to either race. He was a massive football fan. His English team was Tottenham Hotspur, his Turkish Galatasaray, and he supported both international teams with a passion. His biggest dread was Turkey and England ever playing one another in a World Cup final, as he would never be able to take sides. However, today he did have to take sides. He knew exactly where Carl Thompson was as he had called him yesterday, and as much as Tarkan liked and admired Ahmed Zane, Carl had been a very good friend to him.

Tarkan sighed, then picked up the phone. He had to go with his heart rather than his head on this particular occasion. 'Carl, you need to come and see me straight away. I have a proposition for you.'

*

The police were still conducting a search of her house when Shirley Preston arrived home. She could see the neighbours' curtains twitching, but was determined to walk up the path with her head held high. She had experienced police raids in the past, thanks to her son Johnny bringing trouble to her door in his teenage years. She had wanted to stay at the police station with Jamie, but he'd refused to speak in front of her, saying he would prefer to have a social worker in the room, which worried Shirley terribly.

Her heart lurched as she spotted a police officer walk down the stairs with what she assumed was two bags of evidence. She could clearly see some of her grandson's clothes in one bag, and the other looked like it was full of old newspapers. 'He didn't do it, you know. My Jamie might not be an angel, but he would never abduct or harm a child.'

'We'll be the judge of that,' the officer replied cockily.

Shirley's hand wouldn't stop shaking as she put the kettle on. She could see two officers in her back garden with a bloody sniffer dog. Deciding she needed something stronger than tea, Shirley poured herself a large brandy.

This situation was a nightmare and she had no family to turn to. She could not ring her daughter as she had already disowned Jamie, and she could not ring her son as it was his granddaughter that Jamie had been arrested on suspicion of abducting.

Specialist police dogs were trained to perfection. When scenting death they would become excitable, their tails would wag, but they were taught not to start digging in case they disturbed vital evidence.

When the dog handler's finest two canines suddenly ran to a spot of land and sat down beside it with their tails wagging, the team of police officers ran towards it. Seconds later, they spotted the arm.

Christopher Walker had been both surprised and horrified to get a message on his pager from Ahmed Zane. It was hard to believe Vinny would go ahead with a big drug deal while his daughter was missing. Then again, with a heartless bastard like that, who knew what he was capable of?

Ahmed was already waiting in the pub car park near to their usual meeting point when Christopher pulled up. The country park was shut this time of night. His heart felt like a lead weight as he got out of his car and into Ahmed's.

'Hello, Christopher. How are you?'

'Fine, thanks. Yourself?'

'Well, I am not so fine. But I do have some good news for you.'

'Go on.'

'The drug bust is off. Vinny had far too much on his plate to want to participate, and I am planning on spending some time in Turkey in the near future.'

Christopher could feel the relief seeping through his pores. It was Olivia's birthday next month and, even though they had not been together for long, their relationship was very intense and he knew she was the one for him. However, he could never have proposed with the Vinny dilemma hanging over his head.

'Thank you for letting me know, Ahmed. I appreciate you driving here tonight to tell me the news.'

'That wasn't the only reason I drove here. I need a favour, and it is definitely in your best interest to help me.'

His elation cut short, Christopher could only mumble, 'What?'

'Well, the other man who was helping us in our campaign to lock Vinny up has done a disappearing act, Christopher.

He knows too much and needs to be found, quickly. His name is Carl Thompson.'

When DS Townsend arrived at the scene of the crime, the area was already cordoned off with tape. Some of the earth had been moved to reveal the identity of the victim, and Townsend bent down to take a closer look.

The skin was discoloured, the insects had most certainly had a nibble, but the body was not that decomposed. The child's mop of curly blonde hair was clear to see, even though it was caked in mud, and as Townsend turned away, he felt sick. There was nothing worse than seeing the dead body of a murdered child. A terrible waste of a young life.

Back at Arbour Square police station, Jamie Preston had now started to talk after his earlier tantrum.

When his grandmother had left, Jamie had started kicking and punching the walls while protesting his innocence, and at the insistence of the on-duty solicitor and social worker, had been put in a cell to calm down.

Smithers had now decided to play Mr Nice Guy instead of Mr Nasty and that seemed to be having the desired effect on Jamie, who was starting to open up a bit.

'As I told you before, I was only sat outside the club that day because it would have been my brother Mark's eighteenth birthday and that's where he died. I miss Mark so much, so I went there to pay my respects. That's why I was drinking cider, to toast my brother's life.'

'So, why did you return to the area again today, Jamie?'

'I wasn't there today,' Jamie lied.

'You're not doing yourself any favours here, lad. If you want me to believe you're innocent, you must be truthful with me. You were seen in the area today.'

When Jamie did not reply, Smithers changed the subject.

'Why did you cut the newspaper articles out, Jamie? The police found lots of newspapers under your bed and all the cuttings of Molly in the sleeve of one of your record covers.'

'Because I hate Vinny Butler. It's his fault that Mark is dead, and I hope he's suffering like my brother suffered when he got burnt. I can still hear his screams now, and there was nothing I could do to help him. Plus he tried to kill me.'

'Who tried to kill you? Vinny?'

Jamie's tears were ones of pure anger. 'Yes – he tried to make my mum abort me. He even paid her to get rid of me and said, if she didn't, he would get rid of me himself. That's why my mum had to move away from the area before I was born. I would have been killed otherwise and so would she. That's why we moved to Suffolk.'

Smithers was becoming more bemused by the second. 'Is Vinny your dad, Jamie?'

'No. Vinny's my half brother. My dad is Albie Butler.'

# CHAPTER THIRTY-FIVE

Smithers crouched down next to the shallow grave. The skin of the child had begun to discolour and there were signs that decomposure had set in, but there was no question that the child was Molly Butler.

A police photographer had just arrived, along with the Scenes of Crime Officers who would conduct the search for evidence.

Spotting DC Clarke, Smithers walked over to him. 'Well?'

'The doll was the same model. It's with forensics now. The two little girls know the exact spot it was found and their mother is allowing them to take the day off school tomorrow, so they can show us in the morning. They found the doll near some horses they were feeding.'

Smithers nodded. There seemed to be no horses nearby, so the girls' information could be vital. It would help them pinpoint the route the murderer had taken, then they could cordon off the whole area. If the doll had been accidentally dropped, there was no telling what other clues might have been left behind. The smallest detail could prove vital in securing a prosecution.

Townsend walked over to Smithers. 'How's it going with the boy? Has he cracked yet?'

'No. Still protesting his innocence. Turns out he's Vinny's half-brother.'

'What?'

'Hates Vinny with a passion. It's a long story, I'll fill you in tomorrow.'

'Have you played him the tape yet?'

Smithers shook his head. The last time their mystery caller had phoned the police station to say he had Molly, the call had been recorded via the intercept equipment borrowed from New Scotland Yard. There was no doubt that it was Jamie Preston. The voice was exactly the same. 'I know we've got our culprit. I'll surprise him with the tape tomorrow. The little shit will crack then.'

Townsend nodded. 'Who's going to deliver the bad news to the parents?'

'You and Clarke do it. Go now. I can handle things here.'

Nancy was sitting in Joanna's lounge. Jo had fainted twice this evening and the GP had not long left. A combination of stress, lack of food and sleep was his diagnosis, and he had given Jo some tablets to help her get some rest.

Deborah had forced Jo to eat a piece of toast, pop a pill, then she'd taken her upstairs to bed, which was why Nancy was currently sitting alone and deep in thought. Dean had not been in the first time she had rung him, but she had finally got hold of him earlier this evening.

It had been strange, hearing his voice again, but at the same time comforting. Dean was living in Glasgow now and had his own painting and decorating company. He was currently single and Nancy had not replied when he told her that he had never forgotten her and urged her to visit him.

Once that awkward moment was over, they had chatted like old friends. Dean had asked lots of questions about Tara and Tommy, and Nancy had told him all about her boys. Molly's disappearance was another topic of conversation, and Dean admitted he was furious his nan had given an interview to the *News of the World* as he was now concerned for her safety.

When Dean asked her if she was happy with Michael, Nancy said she was. But then she found herself blurting out what Daniel had done at school, how Michael had backed their son's violent actions, and how she was worried for the future of her boys.

The conversation had ended with Dean giving her the same advice as he had once before. 'Nance, you have to get away from that family. I miss Tara every day and I'm glad I never saw Tommy as it would have made my leaving twice as difficult. But trouble will always follow the Butlers. Molly hasn't gone missing by accident; she's been taken as some form of revenge. So if I was you, I would get the hell out of there and take those boys of yours with you.'

Knowing Dean was right to some extent, Nancy had ended the conversation by saying she had run out of change. She did however promise to keep in touch and said she would ring him again soon.

Now she was doing her best to forget about their chat and try to relax. She poured herself a glass of wine and turned the radio on. Recognizing the opening bars of Thin Lizzy's 'Killer on the Loose', she quickly turned it off. With Molly still missing, that was the last thing she needed to hear.

When the doorbell rang, Nancy nigh-on jumped out of her skin. A visit at this time of night was an ominous sign.

Deborah ran down the stairs. 'I'll get it.'

Joanna had dozed off, but had woken when she heard the doorbell, and was now standing at the top of the stairs in a pink nightdress. 'Who is it, Mum?'

As soon as Nancy and Deborah saw the sombre look on the policemen's faces, they knew.

'Come in,' Deborah said, in no more than a whisper.

Townsend had had plenty of opportunity to get used to this part of the job over the years. He had told so many people their loved ones were dead, it ought to have been routine by now. But he still found it extremely difficult when a child was involved. Especially one as young as Molly.

Joanna ran down the stairs. 'Have you found Molly? Please tell me she's OK?' she begged.

Guessing what news DS Townsend was about to deliver, Deborah put her arms around her daughter and held her tightly.

'I am so sorry. But we have found the body of a child that we believe to be Molly.'

Joanna broke away from her mother's grasp, picked up Nancy's wine glass and threw it against the wall. She then sank to her knees and sobbed uncontrollably. 'She can't be dead. Not my Molly. It can't be her. It must be somebody else's child. It's not Molly, it's not,' she screamed.

Vinny was sitting at the club knocking back the Scotch with Michael. He knew that the longer the club was shut, the more custom he would lose to Denny McCann, but that was the least of his problems. Right now he couldn't care less if the club never re-opened.

Little Vinny was sitting at the table sipping half a cider. 'Where's Albie gone?' he asked. He never referred to Albie as his grandfather. The reason being, he did not like him very much.

'Yeah, where is the old bastard?' Vinny reiterated.

'Don't call him that, Vin. He's been as good as gold lately. Dad's staying at mine. I asked him to keep an eye on the house for me. I don't like leaving it empty of a night at the moment,' Michael lied. Albie had asked if he could stay at his because he couldn't bear to be in the same room as Vinny.

'Shall I get that, Dad?' Little Vinny asked, when the buzzer rang.

'Yeah, it's probably Ahmed.'

Vinny stood up, his heart beating wildly when he saw DS Townsend and a colleague walk into the club. It was nearly midnight. 'What's happened? Have you found Molly?'

Townsend took a deep breath. Out of all the parents he had delivered such awful news to during his career, he was dreading telling Vinny Butler the most. 'I am really sorry, Vinny, but it's bad news I'm afraid. We have recovered the body of a child that we believe to be Molly.'

Feeling his legs buckle underneath him, Vinny fell backwards onto the leather sofa. Speechless, he put his head in his hands. Images flashed through his mind. Holding Molly the day she was born and vowing to protect her for the rest of his life. His daughter's first smile, steps and words flashed through his mind. The day she had held her chubby arms out and uttered the word 'Dadda' for the first time, he had very nearly burst with pride. Now she was gone. Gone for ever, and part of him had died with her.

Little Vinny was distraught. 'I am so sorry, Dad. This is all my fault. If only I hadn't fallen asleep that day. I loved my little sister and I will never be able to forgive myself, not ever,' he sobbed.

An ashen-faced Michael put an arm around his nephew. 'It isn't your fault. Go upstairs, boy, while me and your dad talk to the police, eh?'

As soon as Little Vinny was out of earshot, Michael asked the obvious. 'Was Molly murdered? Where did you find her?'

'The body was found buried in the wasteland that backs

onto Wallis Road in Hackney. We are treating the death as suspicious, but will not know the exact details until a post-mortem is carried out. Obviously, we will need a family member to identify the body. But we strongly believe that it is Molly.'

Vinny was tapping his fingertips against the table in an odd manner. When he looked up, Townsend noticed a dangerous glint in his eyes. 'Don't give me all that "suspicious" bollocks. You must know if my daughter was fucking murdered or not?'

'We believe that she was murdered, but as I have already said, we won't know the exact details until a post-mortem is conducted. I am so sorry, I truly wish I could have been the bearer of better news.'

'You must have some idea who killed her? We have every fucking right to know the details,' Michael spat. Even though, as time had ticked on, Michael had tried to steel himself for this news, it had still knocked him for six.

'We have made an arrest in connection with Molly's disappearance, but that is all I can say at the moment. However, I assure you, the family will be first to know as soon as there are any more developments,' Townsend replied.

When Vinny leapt up, roaring like a lion, and turned the table over, Townsend and Clarke jumped backwards. 'I have every cunting right to know who killed my little princess, so tell me who you are fucking questioning?' Vinny yelled.

Frightened his brother was going to do something stupid, like clump Townsend, Michael stood up and grabbed hold of him. 'The police will catch whoever did this, bruv. And if they don't, we fucking will. Make no mistake about that.'

Suddenly feeling nauseous, Vinny ran to the toilets. Before he could even reach the cubicle, he spewed his guts up.

*

Donald and Christopher Walker were sitting with serious expressions on their faces. Nancy was on the armchair opposite and a very disturbed and upset Daniel had just been put to bed by Mary.

Unfortunately for Nancy, when the police had left, Daniel had been woken by Joanna's blood-curdling screams. He had padded downstairs in his Batman pyjamas, and Nancy had had no choice but to break the news to her son as gently as she could.

Daniel had not taken it well. He had flown into a tantrum and started headbutting the wall. Worried about his behaviour, Nancy had decided the best thing she could do was take him back to her parents' house and reunite him with his brothers.

'Nancy, I know perhaps you and I have not seen eye to eye over recent years, but you really have to listen to me now. Molly has not ended up dead by accident. The Butlers are hated, especially Vinny. Look at what has already happened to that family. Roy is dead; Lenny is dead, and now Molly. I know you love Michael, but surely you should put the safety of yourself and your children first? You will always be looking over your shoulder otherwise. I know what Daniel did at school. Do you really want your sons to end up dead or as gangsters?'

Having just settled Daniel down, Mary heard the last part of the conversation and rushed down the stairs to her daughter's rescue. 'Christopher, a young child has just died – a child that your sister was very fond of. This is neither the time nor the place for one of your lectures. Nancy is upset enough as it is.'

Donald turned to his wife. 'Christopher was only trying to instil some sense into our daughter. Not everybody can turn a blind eye to danger, like you always seem to.'

Mary glared at her husband and grabbed Nancy's arm.

'Come on, darling. I'll make us a brew and we can talk in the kitchen.'

Back at the club, Vinny was understandably drunk, angry and heartbroken. 'I'm gonna ring Geary. I bet it's that cunt Jackson the Old Bill are questioning again. I need to know.'

When his brother grabbed the phone, Michael yanked it out of his hand. 'You can't be ringing Geary this late. Wait until the morning. It's vital that we tell Mum and Auntie Viv as soon as possible. You know how quickly bad news spreads around here, and I would hate them to hear through the grapevine.'

Vinny threw the phone against the wall. Even though he had feared the worst, the realization that Molly was actually dead had hit him like a ton of bricks.

At the same time that the buzzer rang, a red-eyed Little Vinny trotted down the stairs. 'Dad, I can't sleep. I keep thinking about Molly. Can I sit down here with you and have some cider?'

Unable to control the feelings of hatred he currently felt towards his son, Vinny flew at him like a raging bull. 'Your sister is dead. This is all your fault, you thick little cunt. Your sister would still be alive if it wasn't for you.'

Michael was out in the reception area, explaining to Ahmed what the police had said, but hearing the commotion he ran back inside.

'Stop hitting me, Dad. I'm sorry. I really am. I loved Molly. She can't be dead, she can't,' Little Vinny screamed.

It was Ahmed who dragged Vinny off his son. 'Michael has just told me what has happened and my heart bleeds for you, it really does. The person to blame is the one who committed this terrible crime, not your boy.'

Aware that his nephew had a cut lip and eye, Michael

lifted the distraught child off the floor. 'Go and pack some clothes, boy. I'm taking you to stay at your nan's house.'

'Good. Get him out of my sight,' Vinny shouted. Seconds later, he broke down in tears once again.

Since it was now the early hours of the morning, Michael had thoughtfully stopped at a phone box and rang both his aunt and mum to warn them that he was on his way.

'Do you think my dad will always hate and blame me?' Little Vinny asked, as he and Michael approached Queenie's front door.

'Your dad doesn't hate you or blame you, Vin. He's just upset, angry, tired, and a bit drunk tonight. He'll see things differently once the initial shock has worn off, I promise you that.'

'I bet he wouldn't be so upset if it was me who died.'

'Of course he would. Now, none of that daft talk in front of your nan and Auntie Viv. They're going to be upset enough as it is when I tell them about your sister.'

When Michael let himself into the house with his own key, both his mum and aunt were dressed in everyday clothes and sitting on the sofa drinking brandy. They knew Molly's body must have been found; there was no other explanation for Michael phoning them at such an unearthly hour.

When Queenie saw her grandson follow Michael into the room with a cut lip and swollen eye, her heart lifted momentarily. Perhaps Little Vinny had got himself into trouble again and that was why Michael had phoned?

Queenie's hope was short-lived though. Michael immediately sent Little Vinny out of the room, then sat down between herself and Vivian. She could tell what was coming next.

'Molly's dead isn't she?' she asked bluntly.

Michael wrapped both women in his arms and held them tightly. 'The police came to the club earlier. They've found the body of a child they believe to be Molly. I'm still in shock. I can't take it in.'

'Aw, my gawd! Not another death. That poor little girl,' Vivian wept.

Queenie was in no frame of mind to cry. She had shed many tears over Molly these past few days, had fully prepared herself for this moment, and now just wanted answers. 'So, what did the police actually say? Was Molly murdered? Where did they find her?'

Taken aback by his mother's lack of emotion, Michael told himself she must be in shock. 'The police said they're treating the death as suspicious, which probably means Molly was murdered. Her body was found in Hackney.'

'Hackney! Oh, Queen, there is no way she could have toddled off there all on her own. Breaks my heart to think what that poor child has gone through. She was so special,' Vivian cried.

Michael kissed his distressed aunt on the forehead. She had been through so much already, having lost her only child, and there was nothing he could say or do to make her feel better.

'Whereabouts in Hackney?' Queenie asked coldly.

'In the wasteland that backs onto Wallis Road. Vinny's in bits, as you can well imagine.'

'So why have you brought that little bastard round here with you? And what happened to his face?' Queenie spat.

'Vinny hit him, Mum. Right now he's upset and looking for someone to blame. I didn't know where else to take Little Vinny. He needs somewhere to stay until the dust settles.'

'Well, he isn't staying here, thank you very much.'

Michael looked at his mother in astonishment. He had

assumed she would be inconsolable when he broke the news, the way Viv was, but instead she was sitting there with a face like a slapped arse and an unhelpful attitude. 'Mum, why are you being like this? In the past, it's always been you that has held the family together whenever there's a crisis. Me and Vinny need you more than ever now, so does Little Vinny.'

'Tough. I am fucking sick of death, I've had enough of it. Right now I'm going back to bed, Michael, so see yourself out and take that useless grandson of mine with you. If it wasn't for him, Molly would still be alive.'

With that she ran from the room and up the stairs. It wasn't until Queenie reached the seclusion of her bedroom that she finally allowed the tears to flow. She had loved Molly so very much. A grandmother should never have a favourite grandchild, but from the moment Molly had been born, Queenie had loved that child more than life itself. Now, she was gone for ever, just like Roy and Lenny. Why did life have to be so bloody cruel?

Even though Vinny Butler liked a drink, he rarely allowed himself to get to the stage where he was repeating himself and slurring his words, but that's what he was doing now.

'I mean, if your son left your little girl on her own, then some cunt snuffed her life out, would you be able to forgive your boy?'

Vinny had already asked him the same question at least four times, but Ahmed simply gave the same answer: 'No. I could probably never forgive something like that.'

'So, why did you stick up for the little cunt earlier then?'

'Because he is fourteen years old, Vinny, and you were smashing his face in. I don't know about you, but I could really do with a line right now.' Ahmed opened a bag of cocaine and emptied its contents on the table.

Vinny stared at the white powder. Apart from sampling the produce when he and Ahmed were buying, such was his love for his daughter that he had given up snorting the shit, determined to be the best father to her that he could.

When Ahmed chopped the lump of white up with a credit card, Vinny could smell its strong fumes and was immediately tempted. He then watched Ahmed snort two large lines. When his pal handed him the rolled-up twenty-pound note, Vinny snatched it out of his hands.

Ahmed smirked as he watched Vinny greedily tucking into the cocaine. Finally the so-called friend who had left him for dead was back in his clutches. Payback was such a wonderful feeling, it really was.

# CHAPTER THIRTY-SIX

The following morning, DS Smithers wasted no time in questioning Jamie Preston again. He knew Preston was as guilty as sin; now all he needed was to get the little shit to admit the truth. That was never going to be easy when a brief and social worker were present, especially since both seemed intent on sticking their oar in far too much for Smithers' liking.

'If you had nothing to do with Molly's disappearance, Jamie, why did you go to the barber's and have your hair cut into a different style the day after your photofit appeared on the regional news?'

'Because I knew people would have seen me outside the club. I was there for over an hour, and I guessed when I saw the photofit that it was meant to be me. I'm only a kid and I just panicked.'

'Don't give me all that "kid" bollocks, Jamie. You spent a couple of years banged up for stabbing another boy, so playing the innocent child isn't going to work.'

'Jamie is still a minor,' the social worker reminded Smithers.

Smithers glared at the rather obese do-gooder. 'Yes, I am aware of that, thank you. But let us not forget that a three-year-old child has just been murdered and it is my job to find out who ended that child's life and why.'

With the social worker now put firmly in her place, Smithers turned back to Jamie. 'What did you do with the pushchair, Jamie?'

'What pushchair? I dunno what you're on about.'

'The pushchair you put Molly in to take her through Victoria Park. Did you dump it in the River Lea? My officers are searching the area as we speak – we will find it, you know.'

'I never touched Molly, and I don't know nothing about any pushchair,' Jamie yelled.

'Oh, I think you do, Jamie. We found the woolly hat that you used to disguise yourself in your bedroom, by the way.'

'What woolly hat? I told you, I never fucking touched Molly, you thick cunt!'

Realizing his client was now both upset and tearful, Jamie's solicitor butted in. 'Jamie needs a rest and a glass of water,' he ordered.

When Smithers stormed out of the interview room, he bumped straight into Townsend. 'I was just coming to speak to you, boss. The team have found what they believe to be the remains of a burnt-out pushchair and clothes less than a mile from where Molly was found.'

'Get forensics to check it out immediately.'

'I already have, boss. Have you played Jamie the tape yet?'

Smithers sneered. 'No. The lying little shit is still pleading his innocence. I'm going to play it to him in a minute. Let's see how Jamie fucking Preston is going to wheedle his way out of that one!'

Albie Butler felt awkward as he sat down at the kitchen table opposite his grandson. Little Vinny had despised him even as a five-year-old, and their relationship hadn't improved since.

Nevertheless, when Michael had turned up in the early hours of the morning with the lad in tow, informing him of Molly's death and Vinny beating his own son up, Albie had felt sorry for the child. He knew only too well what it was like to be on the receiving end of violence from Vinny. For all his faults as a father, he had never laid one hand on his children. It was Queenie who used to wallop them when they were naughty as kids, not him.

'Look, boy, I know you've never been very fond of me. But seeing as we are now sharing a house together for the foreseeable future, I feel we should try to get to know one another a little bit better. I am so sorry for the loss of your sister, but I don't blame you. You're only a nipper yourself. Now, be warned, I am not the best cook in the world, but would you like me to rustle you up some breakfast?'

Needing a friend more than ever right now, Little Vinny smiled. 'Yes please, Granddad.'

Having slept at his own house for a few hours after taking Little Vinny back there, Michael was horrified on his return to the club to find that his brother and Ahmed were still drinking and had also been on the gear.

He stared in disgust at the cocaine on the table and the three empty bottles of Scotch. Even though he had been down that road himself and could fully understand why his brother had succumbed to temptation, the last thing he needed was having to contend with Vinny in his current state. It was bad enough trying to comfort his own wife and kids, his mum, aunt, Little Vinny and his dad, without his brother going on a bender.

'Ahmed, I need to speak to my brother alone.'

Vinny chuckled. 'You ain't about to go all Saint Michael on me, bruv, are you?'

Ahmed's relationship with Michael had always been rather strained, and this was the perfect excuse for him to leave the club and phone his cousin to update him on the news. 'Of course, Michael. I think Vinny needs to eat now and so do I. I will pop to the café and bring us back some food.'

Michael waited until the Turk had gone before sitting down opposite his brother. He had never trusted Ahmed, and the way he'd enticed his brother back on to the gear in the hours since he had left the club only strengthened his dislike.

'Look in the mirror, Vin, and have a butcher's at the state of yourself. The Old Bill will be back here soon. They need you to identify Molly's body. You have got to hold it together. The whole family is devastated and I cannot do this on my own.'

Vinny's lip curled into a snarl. 'No way do I want to see my daughter after some cunt has sapped the life out of her. I would rather remember Molly the way she was.'

'Vin, you can't leave it to Jo to identify the body. It's a man's job. I'll come with you.'

'I ain't doing it, Michael. Simple as. Like I said, I would rather remember my little princess the way she was, than see her lying on some fucking slab.'

'But what about, Mum, Auntie Viv, Little Vinny, Jo, Nancy, my boys? You think you can just sit here, getting pissed and snorting gear, and leave me to deal with everything? That Ahmed is a wrong 'un, Vin, I've always said so. I leave you alone with him for a couple of hours and he's got you back on drugs. You ain't no mug, bruv. You are *the* Vinny Butler, so wake up and smell the coffee.'

'Don't talk to me like a fucking child, Michael. I am a grown man who makes my own decisions,' Vinny slurred.

'Well, shame you don't start acting like one then. You can't even talk properly, you're that out of your nut.'

Vinny laughed sarcastically. 'Hark who's talking. The man who went on a cocaine rampage because his fling with some dopey tart didn't work out. You're a fine one to talk, you are. As Mum always says, "People in glasshouses shouldn't throw stones."'

The sound of the buzzer stopped a full-scale argument ensuing. 'Best you disappear upstairs in case it's the Old Bill. And get that crap off the table. I'll identify your daughter's body for you, and take care of our family, you useless piece of shit.'

Back at the police station, Smithers was ready to play his trump card. 'Would you like to tell me about the phonecalls you made to this police station, Jamie?'

'What phonecalls? I dunno what you're talking about.'

'Oh, I think you do. You rang us on more than one occasion. You even told us you had Molly, and that she was well, but was missing her parents.'

Jamie turned to his solicitor. 'He's lying. I never made no phonecalls.'

Smithers smirked as he pressed play on the tape recorder. The expression on Jamie's face well and truly lived up to his expectations.

When Brenda burst into tears yet again, hugging her children to her chest and telling them how much she loved them, Queenie stomped out of the lounge and into the kitchen.

Mother of the year Brenda most certainly was not. Even though her daughter seemed genuinely distraught about

Molly, Queenie was in no mood to watch her doting mother act. The girl should have been a bloody actress.

The police had released Brenda without charge. Freda Smart had insisted that she did not want to pursue the matter, but Queenie was not fooled by Freda's 'kindness'. She had guessed the old bat had decided against pressing charges for fear the social workers would step in and force her useless tosser of a grandson to step up to the mark as a father. The last thing Freda would want was that little shit being forced out of his hiding place.

'You OK, Queen? I was thinking, we should pop round and see Jo. The poor girl must be absolutely devastated,' Vivian suggested.

'Well, think again. If it wasn't for that lying little mare putting her arsehole of a father's wedding before the welfare of her daughter, Molly would still be alive.'

Vinny woke to the sound of the buzzer. After Michael had ordered him to go upstairs earlier saying he was in no fit state to face the Old Bill, Vinny had rung Geary, then crashed out.

With his mouth as dry as sandpaper and his expensive suit creased, Vinny stumbled down the stairs. 'Oh, it's you, Ahmed. How long have I been asleep for?'

Ahmed ignored his pal's question. 'You will never guess who I have just seen? Bobby Jackson! He laughed in my face and asked how Molly was. Told me to give you his regards. That man needs to be dealt with good and proper, mate.'

'Where is he? I'll kill him,' Vinny yelled, running out into the street like a mad man.

Ahmed grabbed his pal by the arm. 'He got into a van with another bloke. I chased after him, but he drove off like a maniac. It's definitely him who took Molly, I could see it in his gloating eyes.'

'Jackson's a dead man once I get my hands on him. If he's still on the manor and giving it Billy Big Balls, he ain't gonna be too hard to find. Knowing what a cowardly piece of shit he is, I honestly thought he would be long gone by now. Big mistake on his part to stick around. I'm gonna get showered, liven myself up a bit, then we'll go and find him. The cunt needs shutting up once and for all.'

Ahmed smirked as Vinny bolted up the stairs. He had indeed bumped into Bobby Jackson. The man had looked petrified, near to tears in fact. He had told Ahmed to tell Vinny how sorry he was, and that he had only said what he had because he was drunk. He also said that he hoped Molly was found alive soon.

Ahmed helped himself to a drink. The plan to get his treacherous 'friend' banged up for drugs might have backfired, but to get him sent down for murder would leave an even sweeter taste in his mouth. It still grated on Ahmed every single day what Vinny had done to him. He even had nightmares about it. The geezer was an absolute wrong 'un.

Michael could sense Nancy's coldness toward him the moment she opened the front door. 'The news is just awful, isn't it, babe? How you bearing up? Where's Jo?'

'She's in bits. She refuses to believe Molly is dead, thinks the police have got it all wrong. Her mum has taken her to be with her dad. We couldn't calm her down here. She screamed and cried all night. As for that brother of yours, I cannot believe he hasn't even contacted her. What a wanker! Talk about showing his true colours.'

'I know. Vinny's in a proper bad way himself, but he still should have got in touch with Jo. The Old Bill came to the club again earlier. They want to do the post-mortem before we identify Molly. They said it has to be that way for evidence purposes, else the body might get contaminated. Anyway, Vinny's in no fit state to do it, and I would hate Joanna to go through such a terrible ordeal, so I said I'd do it.'

'Well, you'd better check with Jo before you make decisions like that. It's her daughter, not yours. And speaking of your children, Daniel took the news of Molly's death extremely badly – so much so, I had to take him back to my mum and dad's house in the early hours of this morning. After what happened at the school, I've decided it's best we all stay with my parents for a while.'

Michael was crestfallen. He tried to hug Nancy, but she pushed him away. 'Look, babe, I'm sorry I've neglected you and the boys since Molly went missing, but please don't move in with your parents. I love you and our sons, and together we can get through this.'

'You certainly have a funny way of showing it. Seems to me that Vinny and your side of the family always get put before me and the boys, Michael. Do you have any idea how tough it's been for me, trying to console Jo? I could have done with you being a bit more supportive. I loved Molly like she was one of my own. That beautiful child was probably the nearest I will ever come to having a daughter, and now she's gone. Breaks my heart to think how scared she must have been and what she went through.'

When his wife began to cry, Michael took her in his arms. This time Nancy did not push him away.

'I know, love. It's awful. I loved Molly too. She was one in a million. I'm so sorry that I haven't been here for you, but you know how dysfunctional my family are. Vinny's blamed Little Vinny and beaten him up, Brenda got nicked for clumping Freda Smart, my mum's acting proper weird . . . Oh, and Vinny is back on the gear, thanks to that bastard Ahmed. To be honest, I've had a gutful of it, Nance. I've done all I can to help them, but all I want now is to concentrate on you and the boys. I know it's going to be difficult after losing Molly, but we need to get back to normal for the sake of our sons.'

'Have you checked on the house? I haven't been back there for days.'

'Yeah. My dad couldn't bear to be around Vinny of an evening after my mum kicked him out of hers, so I thought it made sense for him to stay at ours and keep an eye on the gaff. I had to take Little Vinny back there last night an' all. I couldn't leave him at the club after Vinny had laid into him, and my mum flatly refused to let him stay at hers.'

Nancy pulled away from her husband's grasp. 'Well, you might have asked me! I'm not happy about that, Michael. Your dad being at ours is fine, but I've never been a fan of Little Vinny, as you well know. Have you forgotten that it was him who was meant to be looking after Molly when she went missing?'

'No, of course I haven't forgotten. But the kid's fourteen, Nance. I could hardly let him sleep on the streets, could I? How would you feel if that was one of our boys?'

'Well, hopefully our sons will never turn out to be anything like Little Vinny. But the way Daniel is behaving at the moment, it wouldn't surprise me one iota if they do.'

'Don't talk about our sons like that, Nance. They're good kids. Daniel's had one tiff at school because he was upset over his cousin. Big bloody deal.'

'Our son smashing another boy's head open might not be a big deal to you, Michael, but it is to me. And that's why me and the boys will be staying with my mum and dad for the foreseeable future.'

After enduring the week from hell, Michael finally lost his temper. 'What is it with you, eh? Whenever I try to be reasonable all you ever do is throw it back in my face. Well, let me tell you something, those boys are as much mine as they are yours, and I will never allow you to take them away from me. Not on your fucking nelly, sweetheart.'

If ever there was a client Roger Francis would have preferred not to represent, it was Jamie Preston. At first Roger had been inclined to believe that the boy was innocent, but the moment he heard Preston's voice on the tape-recorded phonecall, he knew he was fighting a losing battle.

'I swear on my nan's life that I never took or killed Molly. She's my Uncle Johnny's grandchild and I love Uncle Johnny.'

Alone with the boy, Roger decided to give him the best advice that he could: 'Jamie, you denied making any phonecalls. Seeing as the police have a tape with your voice on it, clearly saying that you were the one who took Molly, I think you should just tell me what really happened. The police have you bang to rights and I cannot help you unless you start helping yourself by telling the truth.'

Needing to release some pent-up frustration, Jamie leapt up and repeatedly punched the wall. 'I have never even met Molly. I didn't fucking do it!'

Back in Barking, some male bonding was under way. 'Take that, Granddad, and go and have a few pints somewhere. I'm gonna pop back to Whitechapel to see my mate and let him know I'm stopping here. His mum don't have a phone. It got cut off,' Little Vinny explained.

Albie stared at the ten-pound note. He was a bit skint at the moment. 'I feel bad taking money off you, boy. You go and spend it with your pal.'

'No, it's OK. Uncle Michael gave me some money and I still have some my dad gave me. It will do you good to go out for a drink. I'll try not to be back too late.'

'Well, only if you are sure . . .'

'I am, Granddad. I'll see you later.'

When Little Vinny left the house, Albie fingered the stubble on his chin. He had always been positive that the boy was a replica of his arsehole of a father, but perhaps he'd been wrong.

After two fruitless hours of searching for Bobby Jackson, Vinny was now back at the club. 'Let's have a livener, eh?' Ahmed suggested.

Vinny nodded. He'd had little sleep since Molly had first gone missing and needed to keep himself alert. He still couldn't believe he would never see his little princess again. It was the most horrendous feeling he had ever experienced, like a dagger being poked constantly through his heart, and drink and drugs were the only way to lessen that pain. The only other thing that was keeping him sane was the thought of revenge, and he was determined to get his. As Molly's father, that was the least he could do for her. However painfully his daughter had died, he would make sure the bastard who'd murdered her would suffer a hundred times worse. As for Bobby Jackson, even if it turned out that he hadn't killed Molly, Vinny was going to burn him alive. 'Bury treasure and burn rubbish' had been one of his dear old nan's favourite sayings.

'I'll get that. Hide the gear. It's probably the Old Bill,' Vinny told Ahmed.

When Vinny opened the door and laid eyes on his mum, his lip wobbled as it had done when he was a small child.

'I've been so worried about you, boy. I came here early this morning and Michael said you had popped out. Twice, I've been back since and I've rung the club three times. Why haven't you got back to me?'

'Because even though you popped round the other day,

things haven't been the same between us since you found out about the Lenny business. You said you wanted no more to do with me, Mum, and I was so hurt over that. Thanks for coming to see me today though. It means a lot. I loved Molly so much, she was so special to me.'

Queenie held her strapping handsome son in her arms. 'Molly was very special to me too – and so are you, boy. What I said was in the heat of the moment, Vinny. I was just sticking up for your Auntie Viv. Us Butlers are made of strong stuff, and together we will get through this. You were my first-born, and whatever you do, I could never disown you, never.'

Ahmed Zane was standing in a phone box in Whitechapel market. He had excused himself as soon as that old witch Queenie turned up and was updating his cousin on the latest. 'How should we play this, Burak? Now that I've told Vinny what Bobby Jackson supposedly said, I can guarantee he won't rest until he's killed the guy. But he expects me to help hunt him down, and obviously I cannot afford to take the risk of being implicated.'

'Why don't you suggest using my friends? He's trusted them with similar matters in the past, so it shouldn't be too hard to persuade him. Only this time they will leave Jackson's body where it can be found, along with all the evidence to tie it to Vinny.'

'And then I will see to it that Christopher will be the one to find the body. He can be relied upon to keep me out of it.'

'I agree. You don't want any suspicion pointed your way. Have you spoken to Tarkan lately? We still need to find Carl.'

'No. I rang Tarkan earlier, but couldn't get hold of him. It's of no importance though. Once Vinny's banged up, our worries are over, Burak. Carl Thompson won't be able to inform him of our deceit once he's in prison. He's hardly going to write Vinny a letter, is he?'

'No. The quicker we get Vinny banged up the better. I have a bad feeling about Carl Thompson and will rest easier when this is dealt with. I will phone my friends immediately. Just stall Vinny for the time being.'

Smithers put the phone down and turned to Townsend. 'Strangulation. No sign of any other physical injuries, apart from some bruising to the wrists and arms, and no sign of any sexual interference.'

'Well, that's some consolation for the family, I suppose. At least the poor child didn't suffer the sort of agony some of these poor little mites get put through before we find their bodies.'

'Joanna and her parents want to identify the remains, so I think it's best you accompany them. I'm going to have one last crack at getting a confession out of Jamie Preston. And if that lying little toerag carries on protesting his innocence, I'll charge him regardless. We have more than enough evidence for this to stand up in court.'

Alison Bloggs was thankful when she opened the front door and laid eyes on Little Vinny. 'Yous two fallen out or something?'

'No, course not. Me and Ben are best pals.'

'Well, he's been a miserable little bastard lately. Not even been helping me properly with the kids. Why ain't you been round here as much? You're the only friend he has.'

Little Vinny looked at the toothless smackhead in disgust. He might not have known his mum for long, but from what he remembered, she was kind, very beautiful and treated him well. 'I haven't bloody been round here because my little sister is missing. Have you not seen the news?'

'Oh, I'm sorry, Vin. I'm a bit out of it today and forgot about that. I hope your little sister is found alive. You're a handsome young man and if you ever want a bit of comfort, you know where I am.'

Remembering how Alison Bloggs had tried to molest him not so long ago, Little Vinny darted past her and ran up the stairs. No wonder poor Ben was unhappy. So would he be, living with a mother like that.

Ben Bloggs was sitting forlornly on his bed when Vinny burst into the room. 'Come on, pal. I've got plenty of dosh, so let's go out and get smashed.'

'I really don't feel like going out, Vin.'

Little Vinny sat down on his pal's stinking bed, and put an arm around Ben's shoulders. From the moment they had met, these two lonely souls from very different backgrounds had clicked. 'Look, mate, I know how hard it must be for you living here, and I'm sorry I ain't been round much. But my dad beat me up – look at my face, if you don't believe. So I'm staying at Michael's house in Barking.'

'Has Molly been found yet? Is there any more news?'

Being the kind and considerate person that he could be at times, Little Vinny shook his head. His pal seemed depressed enough without him making it worse by informing him that the police had found his sister's body. 'Please let's go out, Ben? Getting pissed and forgetting our troubles will do us both the world of good. I've already bought some puff and glue and I can easily afford a few bottles of cider. Let's ride up and down on the District Line, eh?'

Ben Bloggs forced a smile. 'OK, why not?'

*

The moment the Prestons followed DS Townsend into Poplar Mortuary, both wanted to vomit. It had the most horrendous stench. It stank of what they could only imagine was the smell of death. 'Just wait here while I check the body is ready for viewing. I'll be as quick as I can,' Townsend told the family.

Seemingly oblivious to the awful smell, Joanna turned to her parents. 'It's not Molly, I just know it isn't. I know this is not a nice thing to say, but I will be so glad when I look at the body and see it's somebody else's child and not mine.'

Johnny cast a worried glance at Deborah. Ever since Deborah had brought her home in the early hours of the morning, Joanna had been adamant that the police had made a mistake. 'Jo, why don't you let me identify the body? It's no job for a female. You stay out here with your mum.'

'No. You've only seen photographs of Molly, Dad, and you might get it wrong,' Joanna replied indignantly.

'Well, let me do it then, Jo. You can wait out here with your dad,' Deborah bravely offered.

'Mum, Molly is my daughter and I will never believe she has left me until I see it with my own eyes. I keep telling you: the police have got it wrong, I just know they have. It isn't my Molly.'

DS Townsend looked extremely solemn when he re appeared. Molly had had what the police referred to as a special post-mortem. That involved skin being peeled off the face, the organs weighed, and other procedures necessary to establish the cause of death beyond a doubt. Even though she was currently lying wrapped in a shroud with only her head visible, it was not a pretty sight. 'I really do feel that somebody other than Joanna should identify the body.'

'Noooo! You only said you believed it was Molly – I know it is not her,' Joanna yelled.

'We will all identify the body together,' Deborah told Townsend. It was obvious that Joanna was never going to believe the worst until she saw it with her own eyes.

Townsend nodded. He knew exactly what Joanna's reaction was going to be once she saw the state of her daughter's once perfect face, and even though he had been in the force for many years, it was never easy to witness.

Johnny Preston took a deep breath as he followed Townsend into the room. He had thought about his granddaughter so often while he was in prison and was distraught that, having longed all this time to see her in the flesh, he was about to be confronted with her dead body.

The room was very small, the smell even more awful than the one outside. When Deborah Preston laid eyes on Molly, she started to gag. 'Oh my God! Johnny, let's go. Please, let's go now,' she wept.

Joanna was momentarily stunned into silence. She then let out the most blood-curdling scream that Townsend had ever heard.

'Come on, sweetheart. You're going to come and stay in Tiptree with me and your mum,' Johnny said. Even though he was heartbroken over the death of his grandchild, the one good thing to come out of this was that Joanna no longer had any ties with Vinny Butler.

'Molly, wake up. Mummy's here now. Please wake up,' Joanna sobbed. Seconds later, she lunged towards her dead child.

# CHAPTER THIRTY-SEVEN

The following morning, Christopher Walker had a bad feeling as he drove towards Hainault. When he had last seen Ahmed, the Turk had ordered him to discover the whereabouts of Carl Thompson and leave a message with Burak at the restaurant. His efforts to locate Thompson had been half-hearted at best and there was no progress to report. So he'd been filled with apprehension when Ahmed contacted him earlier that morning and said he needed to see him urgently.

Christopher got out of his car and with a heavy heart climbed into the passenger seat of Ahmed's. 'What's so urgent?' he asked bluntly.

'How would you like to lock Vinny Butler up for murder?'

Christopher sighed. 'Ahmed, I've already told you how difficult it will be to arrest Vinny without involving my bosses. The guy's far too dangerous for me to tackle him alone, especially now his kid's dead and he's got nothing to lose.'

Ahmed smiled. He could smell the fear coming off Christopher and it made him feel powerful. There was no doubt who was in control here. 'You can involve whoever you want in this arrest. All you have to do is pretend you received an anonymous phonecall about a van with a dead body in the back. Vinny will not be at the scene of the crime, but I can guarantee you he will be responsible for the murder and his prints will be all over the body and the murder weapon.'

'And where will Vinny be when I find this body?'

'Back at the club with me, getting pissed. I have barely left his side since Carl Thompson disappeared – I daren't, obviously. Have you any news of Carl's whereabouts for me?'

'No. I checked him out, but I can't find a police record that matches the guy you're searching for. I came up with half a dozen Carl Thompsons, but two are sex offenders, and the others live up north. I will keep my eyes and ears open, but for obvious reasons I can't bombard my colleagues with questions.'

'Well, getting Vinny put behind bars seems to be our only option then, Christopher. Once he is banged up, we can both relax and get on with our lives, can't we?'

Knowing the threat that lurked behind Ahmed's words, Christopher nodded. This was a much better proposition than trying to arrest Vinny alone with a boot full of drugs, and getting a notorious villain put away for murder wouldn't do his career prospects any harm. Quite the opposite. It would probably make him a legend overnight.

'Obviously, we'll need to meet again to discuss the plan in finer detail, but I'm willing to go ahead with it on one condition . . .'

'What?'

'That you never come back to me and ask for any more favours. This has to be the end of our association, and we take this conversation and any others we've had to our graves with us without telling another living soul.'

Ahmed held out his right hand. 'You've got yourself a deal.'

*

Feeling like death warmed up, Vinny Butler unbolted the front door to find DS Townsend on the doorstep.

'I have some news for you, Vinny. May I come in? I tried to get hold of you yesterday evening, but there was nobody here.'

'I popped out for a few hours last night. Needed a change of scenery,' Vinny said, as he flipped dejectedly onto one of his leather sofas. He could hardly tell Townsend that he had got so out of his nut, he'd ended up in a whorehouse in Leyton and got himself and Ahmed slung out for behaving too brutally towards one of the girls. 'So, what news you got for me? Finally charged some scumbag with the murder of my daughter, have you?'

'Not yet. But we're hoping to have some news on that front very soon. The reason I'm here, and I'm sorry to have to be the bearer of bad news once again, is that the body we found has now formally been identified as Molly. The post-mortem was completed yesterday, and the cause of death was strangulation. Apart from bruising to the neck and wrists, there was no sign of any other injuries of a physical or sexual nature. I am truly sorry for your loss, but I can assure you we are doing everything in our power to catch the bastard responsible.'

Aware that he was trembling, Vinny walked up to the bar. 'I need a drink. Do you want one?'

'No, thank you. I need to get back to the station. If you would like to say your goodbyes to Molly, just call me and I'll arrange it.'

When Townsend had gone, Vinny sat in a trance, drowning his sorrows. A small part of him did feel relief that Molly had not been interfered with sexually. He would never have coped with that. What father could? But it still didn't alter the fact that some evil cuntbag had put their hands around his daughter's throat and throttled the living daylights out of her, and for that they would pay dearly.

Imagining how scared Molly must have been, Vinny put his head in his hands and sobbed his heart out. Though he carried on breathing, it felt as if a part of him had died with her.

Smithers couldn't help feeling deflated. He had been certain the SOCOs would have found something to link Jamie to the crime scene, or that his fingerprints would be found on Molly's body, but they'd drawn a blank.

'You OK, boss? I finally caught up with Vinny and delivered the news.'

Smithers brought Townsend up to date on the latest development. 'Jamie must have worn gloves throughout. He probably burned them with the clothes he was wearing and the pushchair. No gloves were found in his bedroom. We had a phonecall this morning about the pushchair. A woman says her son's was stolen not five minutes' walk from Vinny's club on the day that Molly went missing. Said it was taken from her front garden. We also had another call not ten minutes ago. A bloke insists that he saw a lad matching our photofit of Jamie ripping down the posters we put up in our search for Molly.'

'I take it Preston is still denying everything?'

'Yep. Oh well, let's see how he gets on denying it to a jury, the lying little shit. We have a motive for the murder, the newspaper cuttings we found in his bedroom, witnesses who are willing to stand up in court and say they saw him opposite the club at the time of Molly's disappearance. And most importantly, we have his phonecall on tape.'

'I take it you haven't charged him yet?' Townsend asked.

'No. I'm going to do that very shortly. If you want, you can sit in with me and watch him fly into another frenzy while protesting his innocence. Good little actor the kid is, I'll give him that much. Wonder if he'll be able to convince his fellow inmates in Feltham that he isn't a child killer? He'll get what's coming to him in there, that's for sure.'

Nancy Butler and Deborah Preston were both in tears as they put all Molly's belongings into black dustbin sacks. They had packed Joanna's things earlier and loaded them into Deborah's car. 'I am so going to miss seeing Jo all the time, Deborah – and Molly, of course. My life is going to feel so empty now, I know it is.'

Deborah gave Nancy a hug. Joanna had been in such a state after viewing Molly's body, she and Johnny had literally had to drag her kicking and screaming from the mortuary. It had been a horrid experience for all the family, and Deborah would never forget that stench of death as long as she lived.

Johnny had been the one who suggested that they drive Joanna straight back to Tiptree. The realization that Molly really was dead had knocked her for six, and she was in no fit state to return to the house in Whitechapel and see all her daughter's toys, clothes and other belongings.

'You're welcome to come and stay with us whenever you like, Nancy, you know that. Joanna is going to need you more than ever now.'

'I know, and when I visit I won't bring the boys with me. It will be too raw for Jo if I do. Too much of a reminder of what she's lost herself, bless her.'

'You're such a kind and thoughtful girl, Nancy. I'm glad you're going to stay with your parents for a while. You need looking after, and I'm sure your lovely mum will take good care of you. As Johnny said to me last night, sad as this terrible situation has been for all of us, the one good thing to come out of it is that Joanna will no longer be in Vinny's clutches. Poor Molly was the only thing holding that relationship together. Vinny has made it perfectly clear that he wants no more to do with Jo, and there is no way she would ever get back together with him. I only hope that she can get through this, meet a nice lad and have more children. They will never replace Molly, I know that, but I just pray that at some point she will be strong enough to move on with her life.'

Feeling a bit teary, Nancy nodded. 'I'm sure she will in time. Jo is made of strong stuff. Let's pack the rest of this stuff up and get out of here, Deborah. This house gives me the bloody creeps.'

Jamie Preston sat opposite DI Smithers with his mouth wide open. He had just been charged with Molly's murder and was absolutely furious. Apart from the obvious, the Old Bill had nothing on him and he knew it. 'I didn't fucking do it! I never even knew Molly,' he screamed, trying to lunge at Smithers.

Jamie's social worker and solicitor stayed frozen in their seats as Townsend leapt up and restrained their awkward client.

Smithers smirked at the furious child as he continued: 'You are not obliged to say anything unless you wish to do so, but anything you do say will be taken down in writing and may be given in evidence.'

'I'm innocent! It wasn't me! Tell them, Nan, tell them,' Jamie cried.

Shirley Preston was dumbstruck. She had been ringing the police countless times a day since Jamie had told her he didn't want her in the interview room, and the longer the police had held her grandson without charging him, the more confident she had become that he was innocent.

'I need you to sign the charge sheet, Jamie,' Smithers said.

'I ain't signing nothing. I'm telling the fucking truth,' Jamie spat.

'Just do as the policeman has asked you to, Jamie. You're in enough bloody trouble as it is,' Shirley ordered her grandson. How was she meant to break this news to Judy and Johnny? It was going to cause ructions.

Jamie wept when he signed his name. 'Nan, you must believe me. Ring Uncle Johnny, he will know what to do. I never touched Molly, I swear on your life I didn't.'

'Don't be swearing on my life, boy. I've had bad enough chest pains these past few days as it is.'

Vinny cursed and thumped the cigarette machine. He, Ahmed and Michael had been chain-smoking this past week, and he must have taken the last packet out of the vending machine in the early hours of this morning when he returned from his disastrous trip to Leyton. The last thing he wanted to do was go to the shop and have to face people, but he desperately needed some fags. He had no idea what time Ahmed would be back as he couldn't even remember him leaving. As for Michael, he'd gone all saintly on him again last night and stormed out in a huff. He couldn't recall his brother's exact words, but he knew Michael had given him a right earful of abuse.

Vinny opened the bag of cocaine that Ahmed had given him, racked up a huge line and immediately felt slightly less pissed as it hit the back of his throat. He had already done over half a bottle of Scotch since Townsend had left.

Praying that he wouldn't bump into anybody he knew during the short walk to the newsagent's, Vinny picked up his keys. He then remembered he had heard no more from Geary, so decided to call him first. Finding out who was responsible for murdering his beautiful child was a billion times more important than his craving for nicotine.

Eight miles away in Barking, Albie and Michael were having a heart to heart. 'Honestly, Dad, if I hadn't left the club when I did, I'm sure I would have been tempted myself. I don't even think of the shit any more, provided it's not laid out on a table in front of me. But I could smell it and I really wanted some. Makes me feel so fucking weak, admitting that.'

'Don't beat yourself up, Michael. I'm really proud of you for walking away. We all have our demons in life – look at me with the booze. Whenever you feel tempted again, just think of your lovely Nancy and those wonderful boys of yours. What happened to Molly is incredibly sad, but now she has been found you should really concentrate on your own family. Your brother will only drag you down otherwise.'

Michael sighed. 'I know you ain't no fan of Vinny's, and neither am I at times, believe me. But he is still my brother and I can't just leave him in the lurch. What about the club, eh? Our takings were going downhill before all this happened, and there's no way we can open up again until after Molly's funeral. That would be far too disrespectful. As for my wonderful wife, she isn't as fucking wonderful as you think, Dad. Every time the chips are down, she pisses off back to her parents and takes my sons with her. I stood by her when she went into nut-nut mode, but she never bastard-well sticks by me in a crisis. Selfish cow, she is at times.'

Albie was about to try to make his son see sense when Little Vinny wandered into the lounge in nothing but a pair of grey Nike tracksuit bottoms. He had been studying himself in the mirror upstairs. His hair had now grown from a skinhead into more of a crop, and after everything that had happened, being a skinhead would forever remind him of his disastrous relationship with Shazza and Molly's death. So he had decided to become a Casual now instead. He and Ben had seen a few Casuals when they were riding up and down on the District Line last night, and they seemed to have far more success with birds than skinheads did.

'My turn to make breakfast today, Granddad. What do you and Uncle Michael want to eat?'

'I'll have a bacon sandwich, boy,' Albie said.

'And I'll have the same. You sure you can cook, Vin?' Michael added.

'Yeah. Nan taught me when I lived with her. I won't poison yous, I promise.'

When his grandson wandered off to the kitchen, Albie turned to Michael. 'Pleasantly surprised me, that boy has. I thought I was gonna have murders with him, but he's been as good as gold.'

'Unfortunately, Little Vinny is a replica of his father. When he's good he's very good – but when he's bad, he's pure evil.'

Vinny Butler marched towards the newsagent with a face like thunder. Geary's main source of information at Arbour Square was apparently on holiday and wasn't due back until next week. The only thing Geary had been able to confirm was the police had somebody in custody, but for the first time ever the useless old bastard could not find out who.

'Hello, Vinny. I am so sorry to hear of your loss. Me and the missus have shed a fair few tears, let me tell you. Such a lovely kid, Molly was.'

'Not now. I'm not in the mood,' Vinny said, glaring at Big Stan before barging past him.

'I want two hundred Marlboro. My vending machine has run out of fags,' Vinny announced, as he entered the shop.

Derek put the cigarettes into a bag and handed them to Vinny. 'No need to pay me, just replace them when you can. So sorry to hear about your Molly. Such a lovely kid and I will miss seeing her little face in here.'

Vinny snatched the bag and stomped out of the shop without replying. He knew people were only trying to be kind, but he did not want their fucking sympathy. Nothing was going to bring his daughter back, was it?

'Hello, love. So sorry to hear the bad news. I saw your mum and aunt earlier and passed on my condolences. Do the police know how Molly died yet?' Nosy Hilda asked.

Vinny felt his hackles rise. Less than fifty yards away Bobby Jackson was strolling along without a care in the world. 'Hold that,' Vinny ordered, shoving the bag into Hilda's hands. He then darted behind the market stalls so Jackson wouldn't spot him.

Peeping around the side of a fruit-and-veg stall, Vinny's face reddened with fury. Bobby was standing outside the bookies, laughing and joking with One-Eyed Harry.

Unable to stop himself, Vinny ran at Bobby like a raging bull. 'Thought my daughter going missing was funny, did you? Not laughing now, are you, cunt!' Vinny yelled, as he repeatedly smashed Jackson's head against the bookies' window.

The sound of shattering glass had women and children screaming as they fled the violent scene in terror.

'Stop it, Vinny. You're gonna kill him, and they'll put you in prison,' Nosy Hilda shouted. She could barely wait to go to bingo tonight to tell her friends what had happened. For once she wouldn't need to exaggerate the drama.

'You're a sicko, you scum of the earth. You joked in the pub that you'd throttled my daughter and that's how she died. It was you who killed her, wasn't it? Well, now it is your turn to die,' Vinny screamed, as he repeatedly kicked Bobby in the head and face.

The petrified young woman who had only been working at the bookies for six weeks ended her call to the police and ran from the shop in tears. Bobby was a regular, one of her favourite punters, and she could not stand by and just watch him die. 'Do something! Bobby's dying, I know he is,' she shouted at the gawpers.

It finally took three stallholders, two brave passers-by, and twenty-stone Helen who worked in the baker's to drag Vinny away from his victim.

Nosy Hilda put her hand over her mouth. Bobby Jackson had a huge shard of glass jutting out of his head, and it reminded her of a horror movie she had recently seen.

One-Eyed Harry, who had been frozen to the spot in fear of losing the sight in his other eye, crouched down next to Bobby Jackson. His bloodied and battered body lay motionless. 'Call an ambulance, quick! I don't think he's breathing.'

Queenie and Vivian had spent the morning visiting and tidying up the graves of their loved ones. Neither woman had fancied going to the cemetery, but the job had to be done.

'Once Molly's funeral is out of the way, I'll have a word with Michael about getting Lenny a new headstone,' Queenie said, giving her sister's hand a squeeze.

'Thanks, Queen. There's no rush though.'

'Speaking of no rush, I reckon we might as well jump off this bus. The poxy thing ain't moved for five minutes, and all I can hear is sirens. I reckon there's been a bad accident up ahead.'

When Queenie and Vivian leapt off the bus and crossed the road, they guessed by the crowds of people congregated near the market that some drama had occurred.

'It looks near to the bookies. I bet it's another armed robbery,' Queenie said, craning her neck.

Because of their bleach-blonde identical shoulder-length hairstyles and the fact they were always dolled up to the nines, Queenie and Vivian were easy to spot from a distance.

'Oh, here we go. Nosy Hilda has just broken into a run – desperate to be the first to tell us what's happened,' Queenie said.

'Be funny if she fell arse over tit, wouldn't it?' Vivian replied, chuckling at the very thought.

By the time Hilda reached Queenie and Vivian she was completely out of breath. 'You heard the news?' she panted.

'No, but I'm sure you're about to tell us,' Vivian mumbled.

'It's Vinny. He threw Bobby Jackson through the bookies' window, then did him over real bad. I even saw him stamp on Jackson's head a couple of times.'

'Oh dear God no. Where is Vinny now?' Queenie asked.

'Dunno. He ran off before the ambulance and police showed up. It looks as though Jackson's brown bread. Got a big lump of glass poking out of his head – definitely looked a goner to me. No sign of life whatsoever.'

Queenie had tears in her eyes as she turned to Vivian. 'We must have been wicked bastards us in our past life, you know. Talk about it never rains but it pours . . .'

As soon as Vinny heard the buzzer go, followed by the pummelling on the club's front door, he knew it was the Old Bill. He walked into the reception area and shouted out. 'Who is it?'

'Vinny, it's DS Townsend here. You need to open the door, mate. Don't make things any worse for yourself.'

'OK. Just give me half an hour to have a shave, shower and change of clothes.'

'You need to open up now, Vinny. We have officers around

the back of the club, so there is no way you will be able to do a runner.'

'If I planned to do a runner, I would have hardly come back here in the first place, would I? As I said, just give me half an hour to freshen up, then I'll open the door to you.'

'Don't mess me about, Vinny.'

'I won't, Townsend. You have my word on that.'

Townsend's colleagues looked at him. 'Why don't we just kick the back door in?' one asked.

'Because it is made of thick metal, same as this one.'

'OK, so we get the cutting equipment out and let ourselves in.'

'No point. By the time the cutting equipment arrives, Vinny will have opened the front door,' said Townsend.

'You actually trust him, boss?'

'Yes, I do.'

Shirley Preston picked up the phone. She had once been so close to both of her children, but arguments and events over the years had taken their toll and the family had drifted apart. Johnny had not invited her or Judy to his recent wedding, and Judy had not invited her or Johnny to her forthcoming one.

Shirley sighed. She was dreading these calls. Deciding to ring Judy first, she put the phone down without speaking when her daughter's answerphone machine urged her to leave a message.

Hands trembling, Shirley then dialled Johnny's number. 'Hello, Deborah, it's Shirley. Can I speak to Johnny, please?'

'He's upstairs at the moment with Joanna. I take it you've heard about Molly? Been in a terrible state we all have, especially Jo. She's moved back in with us now.'

'I am very sorry for your loss, Deborah, but it's Molly I'm calling about. It's very urgent that I speak to Johnny.'

There was a rustling as Deborah covered the receiver before shouting out, 'Johnny, your mum is on the phone. She says it's urgent.'

Johnny ran down the stairs and grabbed the phone. 'What's up?'

It was at that point Shirley burst into tears. 'It's Jamie. They've arrested him for Molly's murder.'

'What! No, not Jamie. It can't be!' Johnny whispered, as his legs went from beneath him and he collapsed onto the armchair.

'Jamie swears he didn't do it, son, and part of me believes him.'

'I feel sick. I'll have to call you back.'

DS Townsend pressed the buzzer, then began pounding his fist against the door again. 'Your time's up, Vinny. Either you open this door, or we cut through it. Your choice.'

Vinny smirked. He'd had a nice shower, shave, brylcreemed and combed back his thick dark hair, put one of his finest suits on and was almost ready to be arrested.

He walked into the reception area and tapped on the inside of the metal door. 'Give me two minutes and I'll be all yours.'

'Two minutes is all you've got Vinny, and I mean that,' was Townsend's reply.

Vinny walked behind the bar, poured himself a large Scotch, then sat down on a sofa. He knocked back half of his drink then lifted the glass in a toast and stared at the ceiling. 'What I did today was for you, Molly. Rest in peace, my little princess.'

*

Deborah and Johnny Preston were sitting opposite one another in the lounge. Half an hour after Johnny had spoken to his mother, the police had arrived to confirm the horrendous truth. Both were stunned by the news and currently debating whether the time was right to tell their daughter.

'Johnny, we have to tell her. Jo has been having nightmares that Molly was sexually abused. I know being strangled isn't much of a consolation, but at least we can now convince her that Molly's death was quick and she never suffered. The policeman said that the post-mortem indicated that Molly died on the day she was snatched. I know my own daughter, and even though she obviously won't be jumping for joy, the truth will be a comfort to her.'

'And do we tell Jo her own fucking cousin strangled Molly? I cannot believe Jamie could do something like that. I honestly thought Vinny had upset some bastard and it was that which led to Molly's death. It beggars belief, it really does. I am so fucking shocked,' Johnny said, putting his head in his hands.

'Well, if your mum reckons he's innocent, maybe he is? We have to tell Joanna though. It'll be on the news and all over the place before long, and we can't have her hearing that from somebody else.'

'I know. I suppose it must be him, Deb. CID aren't mugs. Jamie was loitering outside the club that day, they found newspaper cuttings in his bedroom, and the sick little cunt even rang the fucking police and said he had Molly. I'll kill him for this when he gets out, you mark my words.'

'Shush. Joanna's coming.'

'What did the police want?' Joanna asked. She had not come downstairs herself as she had been busy making her brother's old bedroom into a shrine for her daughter. Molly's clothes were now hung in Johnny Junior's wardrobe, her quilt was on his bed and all her toys were scattered about the room, just as they had been in her old bedroom when she was alive.

'Sit down next to me, darling,' Johnny urged.

'Please tell me Molly wasn't raped or sexually abused, please, Dad,' Joanna wept.

Johnny held his daughter close to his chest. 'Thankfully, she wasn't. The police are certain that Molly didn't suffer too much, Jo. She was strangled not long after she first went missing.'

Joanna burst into tears and clung to her father. 'My poor baby. This must sound weird, but I'm relieved she was just strangled. Are the police sure that nobody messed with her?'

'Positive, Jo. There were no signs of any sexual interference whatsoever.'

'Well, thank God for that one small mercy. Have they arrested anybody yet?'

Johnny glanced at Deborah. She came over to the sofa to sit the other side of their daughter and took her hand.

'The police have arrested your cousin Jamie.'

Joanna looked at her father in astonishment. She barely knew her cousin Jamie, hadn't seen him in years. 'What do you mean? That can't be right. They must have arrested the wrong person.'

With his daughter's mind in such a fragile state, Johnny didn't want to go into too much detail. 'The police have lots of evidence against Jamie. They aren't usually wrong, darling.'

'But why? Why would Jamie do that? He hardly knew me, and he'd never even met Molly. It just doesn't make sense.'

Deborah stroked her hair and said, 'There are some things you don't know about, love. Family secrets, that myself and your dad never spoke to you or Johnny Junior about. You know when your dad got locked up?'

Joanna nodded.

'Well, that all started because of Auntie Judy. She got pregnant by Albie Butler. Jamie is his son,' Deborah explained.

'What? Are you winding me up?'

'No. Your mum is not winding you up, Jo. Judy getting up the duff by Albie was why we had to move to Tiptree in the first place. When Vinny found out about Judy's pregnancy he went round her flat and threatened her. I had to step in, Judy had nobody else to turn to. I took my pal Dave Phillips with me to Vinny's club and politely asked him to leave my sister alone. Vinny then stabbed Dave to death, and he'd have done for me too if I hadn't ended up behind bars. I have very little to do with Judy now, but she must have told Jamie who his father is and that Vinny threatened her. That's probably why Mark set fire to Vinny's club – I suspect Jamie was with him that day, only he got away and Mark died in the fire.'

'This is unreal. It sounds like something out of bloody *Dallas*. I still can't understand why Jamie would kill my Molly though.'

'He must have held a bad grudge against Vinny, Jo. That's the only reason I can think of. Jamie was no angel, he got put away for stabbing a lad after Mark died. But I am truly shocked he would take his anger out on Molly and us. I always got on OK with him.'

Joanna leapt up, her eyes blazing with anger. 'Yous two are as much to blame for keeping all these secrets from me. Perhaps I could have protected my daughter more, had you been honest with me.'

'Jo, it isn't our fault. We didn't even know that Jamie was living in London with your gran until today. We don't have much to do with your dad's side of the family,' Deborah said.

'Well, I tell you something now, we better start packing and move a bit further away than Tiptree. Because when Vinny finds out that it was Jamie who killed Molly, he will come after all of us. I just know he will.'

Back in Whitechapel, Queenie and Vivian were sitting opposite one another at a table inside the club. Michael was in the office speaking with DS Townsend. 'I really hate this club now, Queen. Everytime I look at that stage, I can see my Lenny stood there playing his records. Brings it all back to me, it does.'

Queenie leaned across the table and squeezed her sister's hand. 'We'll go home as soon as we've spoken to Michael. He's been in the office for ages with the Old Bill. I wonder whether they're talking about Molly or Vinny? Knowing the luck this family has, Bobby Jackson has croaked it.'

'Whether Jackson's kicked the bucket or not, Vinny is bound to do bird, Queen, so you need to prepare yourself for that.'

Queenie nodded. She had been amazed when her son had walked out of the club reeking of expensive aftershave, then calmly kissed her on the cheek before getting inside the police car.

'I'm gonna encourage my Michael to sell this bastard place. I'm sure it's cursed. So many bad things have happened here.' She looked up as Michael emerged from the office. 'Oh dear, he doesn't look happy. More bad news heading our way, no doubt,' Queenie muttered. She waited until her son had shown the two policemen out before asking what they had said.

Michael ignored the question, poured two large brandies, then handed them to his mother and aunt. 'Drink that. You're gonna need it.'

Queenie knocked hers back in one gulp. 'Bobby Jackson's dead, isn't he?'

Michael sat down on the chair next to his mother. 'Not yet. But the police don't know if he'll last the night. The results of the post-mortem are in. Molly was strangled on the day she went missing. Joanna's identified her body, so hopefully we can arrange a lovely send-off for her before long. They're holding the body at Poplar mortuary and the police said they will take us there if we want to say our goodbyes. Vinny was given the details of Molly's death this morning, which is obviously why he flipped when he saw that shitbag Jackson.'

Vivian took her handkerchief out of her handbag and dabbed her eyes. 'Poor Molly. I don't think I can face seeing her in that mortuary. She isn't going to look too clever, is she? Not after being strangled. Such a beautiful child. It's a wicked bastard world we live in now, it really is.'

'What type of person could put their hands around that little girl's neck and strangle her? There are some fucking sickos in this world,' Queenie spat.

Michael took a deep breath. He was dreading delivering his next sentence. 'The police have charged somebody with Molly's murder, Mum.'

'Who?'

'Jamie Preston – Judy Preston's boy. Turns out that slag did keep her baby after all. Jamie is Dad's son.'

Carl stared out the window of the aeroplane. Tarkan Smith had come up trumps for him in more ways than one. Not only had Tarkan lent him the money to finalize the deal on his bar in Spain, his pal had also warned him to leave England as quickly as possible because Ahmed was searching for him with a view to kill.

Ahmed Zane had turned out to be a true snake in the

grass. Carl had toyed with sending Vinny Butler a letter before he left England, to let him know what a shitcunt his best pal really was, but had then decided against the idea. With Vinny's daughter still missing and presumed dead, chances were Ahmed would be stuck to Vinny like glue in case he turned up, and would probably be checking the post every day too. Knowing what Ahmed was like, it wouldn't have surprised Carl if he was the one behind Molly's disappearance in the first place.

Carl lit up a cigar. No way would Ahmed ever find him in Spain. For a start, the bar he was purchasing was not in Lloret de Mar as he had led Ahmed to believe, it was actually in Benidorm. Neither was his surname Thompson, it was Tanner.

'Would you like any drink or snacks, sir?' the pretty blonde stewardess asked.

Carl smiled, then shook his head. He had no desire for lager or peanuts at the moment. Payback was the only thing on his mind, and he would make sure Ahmed the snake Zane received his one day, preferably via Vinny Butler.

# CHAPTER THIRTY-EIGHT

At five a.m. on the morning of her granddaughter's funeral, Queenie Butler was sitting in her conservatory drinking tea and cursing the rotten November weather. She had prayed for it not to rain today, but as per usual, him up above had ignored her wishes and it was currently lashing it down.

It was over a month now since Molly's body had been found. The police pathologist had conducted the first post-mortem, but had not been able to release the body because Jamie's defence had ordered a second. Vinny in the meantime had been granted bail, thanks to a good brief and a caring judge, even though the Old Bill had opposed it. Their argument was that Bobby Jackson's head injuries were so severe, he could die at any time, and they were afraid Vinny might do a vanishing act if his GBH with intent charge was increased to murder.

Thankfully, Bobby had not died. He was still in hospital though. By all accounts he'd suffered brain damage and was unable to communicate with family or friends. Vinny's brief had told him that it could take anything up to eighteen months or perhaps even longer before the case made it to court. He had also told Vinny to expect a lengthy custodial sentence whether Jackson's health improved or not.

The thought of her eldest son getting banged up worried Queenie greatly. With his temper, Vinny was not cut out for prison life. She worried that he would get himself into more trouble on the inside than he had on the outside. Her only hope was that, once the judge and jury heard the full story, they would be lenient towards her boy.

Dreading the funeral, Queenie decided to have a long soak in the bath to try to relax herself a bit. Seeing that tiny coffin and knowing her precious grandchild was lying inside was going to break her heart. But Queenie would not show that outwardly. Putting on a brave face for the sake of her family was what she did best.

Joanna Preston put on her dressing gown, picked up her handbag and tip-toed towards the bathroom so she would not wake her parents.

Taking the box out of her handbag, Joanna read the instructions, and carried them out. She then put the white stick on the window sill so she could not see the result until she was ready.

Exhausted, she sat on the toilet seat and held her head in her hands. She was dreading Molly's funeral, did not have a clue how she was going to get through the day. She was also dreading seeing Vinny again. The rose-tinted glasses she had once worn when looking at him were now well and truly off, and the way he had behaved this past month had taught her to see him for what he really was: a callous, arrogant self-centred bastard. Molly had been the only chink of goodness in his heart.

The letter Jo had received via Nancy had been the final straw. Vinny had informed her when and where Molly's funeral service was to be held and then told her that Molly would be buried next to his brother and Lenny in Plaistow cemetery. He had also made it clear that, seeing as he was paying for everything, she had no say in the matter.

Joanna guessed that the reason Vinny had not given her or her family any real grief over Jamie being arrested was because he was now under strict bail conditions. Nancy had found out from Queenie that the judge had warned Vinny he'd go straight to jail if he got himself in any more trouble between now and his trial. And he wouldn't risk missing Molly's funeral, not even for revenge.

Taking a deep breath, an incredibly nervous Joanna turned around and stared at the pregnancy test. Thankfully, the result was exactly what she had hoped it would be.

Jamie Preston's eyes widened with fear as the five lads backed him into the corner of the washroom. 'What you doing? Have I done something wrong?'

Glen Pritchard, who was not only the leader of his own little gang but also saw himself as one of the top boys in Feltham, grabbed Jamie by the neck. 'Rumour has it, Preston, that you throttled your own little niece. Like it done to you, would ya?'

As his face reddened through lack of breath, Jamie slipped down the wall and onto his backside. 'I never touched my little niece. I've never even met her.'

Pritchard snorted. His dad used to go to school with Michael Butler and had asked him to give Jamie a tough time on Michael's behalf. Apparently, Michael had got in touch with his dad and promised to see them OK if Glen obeyed his orders and kept his mouth shut. 'Yeah, that's what all the nonces say. Bet you fiddled with her before you killed her though, eh?'

'I swear to you, I ain't no nonce and I didn't kill Molly.'

Glen Pritchard turned to his gang and grinned. He was

desperate to impress Michael Butler. What lad wouldn't be? 'Do the cunt, and do him good and proper.'

Queenie and Vivian were already dressed in their finest black clothing even though Molly's funeral was not due to take place for another four hours.

Because of the awful circumstances, Vinny had insisted the club play no part in Molly's send-off. Instead, the funeral was to leave from his house and the wake afterwards was to be held in the restaurant Vinny part-owned with Nick and Ahmed in Stratford.

'There is no way I am going back to that restaurant, Queen. I'm coming straight home after the funeral. If Vinny is laying on free booze, it's bound to end up in fisticuffs. Not like the old days any more, when people had respect for the dead. We should come back here and crack open a bottle of sherry to toast Molly. What do you reckon?'

The phone bursting into life stopped Queenie from replying. At the sound of Albie's voice, her lip immediately curled up. 'You've got some fucking nerve, ringing here. What do you want?' she spat.

Albie had been as shocked and devastated as anybody to learn he had another son and it was Jamie who was responsible for Molly's death. Vinny had banned him from attending the funeral, so Albie was now back in Ipswich, living with Bert. 'I just wanted you to know that I am so sorry for everything that has happened, and I will be thinking of you all today.'

'Thinking of us! I bet you are, you dirty old bastard. If it wasn't for you having wandering-cock disease and creating a monster with that slag you shagged, my beautiful granddaughter would still be alive. Now fuck off. And if you ever ring here again, I'll send Vinny down there to finish you off.'

*

Little Vinny was all suited and booted as he strolled towards Ben Bloggs' house. Uncle Michael had taken him out yesterday to buy him his new clobber, as his old suit and black shoes were now far too small for him.

'You look smart, boy. All the neighbours will be at the funeral to support your family today, including myself of course. How you bearing up? Is your dad OK?' Nosy Hilda asked.

Little Vinny's eyes welled up. 'None of us are bearing up very well. My dad blames me and I blame myself.'

'It's not your fault, boy. You mustn't blame yourself.'

Knowing he was about to burst into tears at Hilda's kind words, Little Vinny ran to his pal's house as fast as he could. His dad had looked at him with hatred earlier, and he needed Ben's support today more than ever. 'Ben, open up, it's me,' Little Vinny yelled, banging on the front door for the second time. He knew the doorbell didn't work and Ben's mother never surfaced before noon.

'What the fuck! I thought you were the Old Bill. Whaddya want?' a dishevelled-looking Alison yelled as she hung out of her bedroom window.

'I'm looking for Ben. It's my sister's funeral today and he promised he'd come with me.'

'Aw yeah, sorry about your sister. I forgot. Hang on, I'll wake Ben up for you.'

Little Vinny shook his head in disgust. How could that poor excuse for a woman forget that his sister had died? The whole of Whitechapel was talking about Molly's death and funeral.

When the front door was flung open, it was not Ben standing there, but Alison. 'The little cunt ain't here. Been acting really strange since you moved to Barking. Best you pop round and see him more often, Vin, because I need help with these kids. They're his brothers and sisters and it's his duty to help me bring them up. I'm a single mother.'

Unable to stop himself, Little Vinny hissed at Alison. 'You, a mother? Don't make me laugh. You are the scum of the fucking earth. Ben's a good lad and I feel so sorry for him living here with you, I really do.'

About to tear Little Vinny off a strip, Alison Bloggs suddenly remembered whose son he was and thought better of it. Big Vinny was her dream man, but he also scared the life out of her. 'Yeah, perhaps you're right. I ain't been the best mum in the world, I admit that. But I do try my best and I love my kids. I was still up at five this morning and Ben was definitely here then. I heard him get up to see to little Kylie. Perhaps he's gone to school, eh, Vin?'

Collecting some phlegm from the back of his throat, Vinny spat in Alison's face, then ran from the house. No way would Ben have gone to school today. But he was sure he knew where to find his pal.

Over in Tiptree, Johnny and Deborah Preston were both relieved that their daughter's appetite had miraculously returned. Jo had lost so much weight lately, she was beginning to look anorexic.

Deborah waited until Joanna had swallowed the last piece of her egg on toast before giving her a big hug. 'Well done, darling. It's so good to see you eating again. Me and your dad are both proud of you, aren't we, Johnny?'

'I have no choice but to eat now, Mum. I'm eating for two again.'

Johnny spat his mouthful of tea back into his mug. 'What?'

For the first time in weeks, Joanna managed a smile. 'Yes, I'm pregnant. I only did the test this morning. It's like a gift from God, isn't it? No child will ever replace my Molly, but this baby will help me deal with her loss.'

Deborah and Johnny looked at one another in a mixture of astonishment and horror. Both were thinking the same thing, but it was Johnny who found his voice first. 'You can't keep the baby, love. You will never be rid of Vinny if you do. One day you will meet a man worthy of you, and you can have his children.'

'Your dad is right, Jo. No way can you keep Vinny's baby.'

With a look of determination in her eyes, Joanna leapt out of her chair and smashed her fist on the table. 'This is my baby, not Vinny's, and no way will he ever find out about it. I have already lost one child, and I am not losing another. It's up to yous two if you choose to support me, but whether you do or not, I am keeping this child and that's final.'

When Little Vinny arrived at his dad's house he was taken aback by the display of flowers. There were literally hundreds of wreaths, arrangements and bouquets, and he found it hard to look at them as it made him feel terribly guilty.

Sick of being in Ahmed's company, Michael was standing outside the house, smoking a cigarette. 'You OK, boy?' he asked, putting an arm around his nephew's shoulders.

Little Vinny nodded, then stared at his muddy shoes. He was anything but OK. He was worried. Before he and Ben had taken to riding up and down the District Line, they used to hang out in what they called their special place. Little Vinny had thought he'd find Ben there, but there had been no sign of him, and he did not know how he was going to get through Molly's funeral without Ben by his side.

'Look at the state of your new shoes, Vin. Where you been?' Michael asked.

'Looking for Ben. His mother is such a cunt to him. I hate her.'

'Let's go inside and get you cleaned up before your dad sees you. You want to look smart for your sister's funeral, don't you?'

Little Vinny wiped the tears from his eyes. 'Yes, Uncle Michael. I loved Molly and I miss her so much. I will never forget her, not ever.'

In the depths of Hainault forest, Ben Bloggs sat alone, chain-smoking and drinking his second bottle of cider. He had never known this forest had existed until earlier this summer. Little Vinny had brought him here when they got off the District Line at Hainault station one day.

Needing to relax some more, Ben rolled himself a joint. His mother had been out whoring last night and he had raided the tin where she kept her money and drugs stash. He'd left the heroin there, but taken the puff and twenty-five quid. His mum would go apeshit when she found out, but Ben didn't care. It served her right for being such a shit mother. He hated her, and was glad he would never have to clap eyes on her again. He did love and worry about his siblings though. Their future was bleak, just like his had been, and he would miss them terribly.

When the cannabis took effect, a light-headed Ben lay down on the leaves and stared at the sky. It had stopped raining now and the sun was peeping through the trees.

Ben had planned his death a few weeks ago, but had not had the guts to go through with it up until today. No way could he live with himself after what had happened. It had haunted his mind every minute of every day since.

Taking a deep drag on his joint, Ben closed his eyes and thought back to that fateful day. He could remember every detail clearly.

When Vinny had popped round that morning and asked him for a special favour, saying he'd pay him fifty quid. Ben had jumped at the chance. Fifty quid was a fortune to him, more money than he had ever had in his pocket in his lifetime.

He had only started to worry when his pal made him steal a pushchair and told him to hide in the garage next to the club.

'What do we need a pushchair for?' he'd asked.

'You'll find out soon enough. Wait here, I won't be long,' Little Vinny replied.

Ben didn't own a watch, but at a guess he would say it was about an hour later when his pal returned with Molly in his arms, and a carrier bag containing two hats and a pair of gloves. 'Make sure Molly doesn't pull her hat off, and if anybody passes you, look down, don't let them see your face, OK?' were Vinny's exact orders.

'What's going on, Vin? Where am I taking Molly?'

'To our special place. I'll meet you there as soon as I can. Now, put that hat on and if you have to touch Molly, make sure you wear the gloves.'

'But why am I taking Molly there? This don't seem right to me, Vin.'

That was the moment his pal had grabbed him and pushed him up against the garage wall. 'Do you remember when Black Joe was picking on you? Or that gang of girls that bullied you when you were in the first year? And have you forgotten how I stuck up for you against Stephen Daniels and his wanky gang?'

'No, 'course I ain't forgotten, Vin.'

'And what about all the fags, booze, puff, and glue I've bought you? Who pays for that shit every time we go out, Ben?'

'You do, Vin.'

'Well, isn't it about time you did me a favour back then?'

Ben Bloggs had always had a weak nature. Vinny was the only friend he had and the thought of losing him was unbearable. 'OK. But you ain't gonna do nothing bad to her, are you?' Ben asked, nodding towards the child who was now asleep in the pushchair he had thieved.

'Course not. I just wanna teach my old man a lesson,' Vinny assured him.

The walk across Victoria Park was nerve-racking to say the least, but the torrential rain meant the park was quite desolate. Two young women dashing past him sharing an umbrella, one old tramp, and a couple of dog walkers was all Ben could recall seeing, and he had kept his head down and run all the way to make it look like he was escaping the weather.

Molly had cried throughout the journey through the park, but by the time he reached his and Vinny's special place, the child was hysterical. 'I want my mummy and daddy. Where is my mummy and daddy?' she'd sobbed.

Ben's and Vinny's special place was on some land that ran not far from the River Lea in Hackney. It was a secluded spot amongst trees and bushes, and once you stepped inside it was like a little den. 'Stop crying, Molly. It's OK, darling. I'll look after you until your mum or dad comes to get you,' Ben had whispered, cradling the child in his arms. He was good with kids, had virtually brought his own siblings up single-handed.

'Where's Molly Dolly? I want my doll,' Molly wept.

Ben had cursed at that moment. The doll had been in the pushchair with Molly and must have been dropped on the journey. 'We'll find Molly Dolly when the rain stops. Your brother will be here soon, then he'll take you home to your mum and dad.'

When his little sister Kylie was upset, or could not sleep,

Ben had often sung nursery rhymes while cradling her. This seemed to have a calming effect on Molly as she dozed off in his arms during 'Little Miss Muffet' and was still asleep when Little Vinny finally arrived. 'Thank God, you're here, Vin. I don't wanna do anything like this ever again. Molly's wet, tired and upset 'cause she lost her doll. We need to take her home now.'

Vinny bent down, unzipped the sports bag he had brought with him and put on a pair of yellow Marigold gloves.

'What you doing? What else is in that bag?' Ben asked, unable to keep the panic out of his voice.

His pal never answered his question. Instead, he grabbed Molly out of his arms, laid the petrified child on the ground, and cold-bloodedly throttled the life out of her.

The look of bewilderment and horror in Molly's eyes had been the most sickening sight Ben had ever witnessed. Unable to move, he had stood open-mouthed and rooted to the spot.

Vinny had then crouched down; put his head in his hands and started rocking to and fro next to his sister's lifeless body. 'I'm so sorry, Molly. I really am.'

With tears streaming down his face, Ben knelt down the other side of Molly. He prayed that a miracle might have occurred and the child would still be breathing. But unfortunately there were no signs of life. 'What have you done, Vin? Why did you kill your little sister?'

When his pal stared at him with a glazed expression in his eyes, Ben knew Vinny had already been puffing, drinking, sniffing glue, or all three.

'Because my dad loved me until she was born. Molly stole my dad from me. Now, let's bury her. I've got a shovel and it will be easy to dig a hole because the ground is so wet. I've also brought some petrol and matches with me so we can burn all the evidence.'

Feeling sick to the stomach, Ben shook his head. 'I'm going home, Vin. I can't deal with this. It's fucking madness.'

'No, you are not. I need your help.'

As Ben's trembling legs tried to make a run from the den, Vinny had grabbed hold of him. 'Ben, please don't do this to me. Remember when we cut ourselves with my penknife that time? Then rubbed our cuts together? Well, that made us blood brothers. We are in this together, and unless you help me, we'll both get nicked.'

'I never killed Molly. It's not my fault,' Ben reminded his pal.

'No, but you brought her here, and you'll be in just as much trouble as I will. You'll get done for child abduction.'

A dog barking in the distance in Hainault forest snapped Ben out of remembering any more of that awful day. He had thought of nothing else since and he knew the only way to rid himself of those terrible memories was to end his own sorry life.

He drank the last of his cider, sparked up another joint, took the rope out of his bag and then calmly started to climb the big tree.

As he did so, Ben thought of the only friend he had ever had. Vinny had been good to him over the years, which was why he had decided to kill himself in Hainault forest rather than their special place. Ben was not the brightest boy in the world, but he knew if he ended his life near to where Molly's body had been found on the day of her funeral, it might point the finger of suspicion towards his one-time pal and himself.

After the murder, Vinny had refused to discuss his sister. Apart from admitting that he'd started the flood in the cellar on purpose, he hadn't wanted to talk about what had happened or why he'd strangled Molly. Ben could not believe that his pal was happy to get pissed, stoned and ride up and down the District Line like sod all had happened. The whole experience had haunted him and he was not even responsible for poor Molly's death.

Ben knotted the rope around a thick branch of the tree. He was not afraid of dying now, in fact he was quite looking forward to it. Surely the afterlife had to be better than the shitty cards he had been dealt in this one? No way did he want to be around his junkie whore of a mother any more; neither did he want to be around his evil child-killer of a friend.

He smoked the last of his joint and flicked the tiny remainder onto the leaves below. Then he bravely looped the rope around his neck. Smiling his first proper smile in weeks, Ben prepared to take the plunge.

Seconds later, he was dead.